OCHRE DRAGON

Ochre Dragon

The Opal Dreaming Chronicles
Book 1

V. E. Patton

First published 2019 by Veronica Eileen Strachan as V. E. Patton

Cover by Creative Girl Tuesday 2019

Paperback ISBN: 978-1-62747-393-4

Ebook ISBN-13: 978-1-62747-342-2

A catalogue record for this book is available from the National Library of Australia

For Strack
who's been there from the beginning,
and kept my dream alive.

Praise for Ochre Dragon

'Noooooo!!!! That can't be the end! I need more! What happens next?!?! Right are you finished writing book two yet? It is so freaking good!!! I literally got only a few hours sleep because I couldn't stop reading and couldn't wait to wake up and keep reading. Holy shit – you have written something truly fantastic! (In both senses of the word!)' – *Cassi Strachan, Creative Girl Tuesday*

'When drawing from the deepest of creative wells there comes the chance of newfound inspiration and literary magic. V. E. Patton has not only traversed these depths but has reached territories unknown, and returns from her journey with words and tales ready to ignite the imagination like never before.

…"Ochre Dragon – The Opal Dreaming Chronicles", is book one of a new fantasy series ready to sweep the reader away to a world of science, magic, mystery… and dragons. Written with breathless excitement, Veronica has beautifully structured a dream like narrative that introduces us to three women ultimately bound by a spiritual quest to protect the greatest of creations – life itself.

With effortless world building, characters to capture your heart and a style that blends elements of fantasy, science fiction and mystery against a backdrop dripping with spiritual secrets, "Ochre Dragon – The Opal Dreaming Chronicles" will capture the minds and imaginations of fantasy literature lovers everywhere.

I have no doubt that Australia has a new author to be proud of. It is an intricately woven tale with imagery that stays with you long after the pages

have been closed, and a vision of the power of the spirit that can be found deep in us all. It is both dystopian and uplifting, scientific yet magical, but most important of all it is a world you may never want to leave. If you haven't read Veronica's work before, welcome to something truly special…'
- Darren Kasenkow, author of The Hallucigenia Project, See the City Red, Dust and Devils, and The Apocalypse Show

'…the author strikes a deep down forgotten cord that connects us to our cosmic origins, our dreams, our soulmates, our yearning of coming home one day.' – *Dominique Severina, author of The Hidden Faces of the Grand Canyon ~ A Galactic Ascent*

What a great read. V. E. Patton takes readers on a dark and twisted journey into the futuristic world of the Ochre Dragon. – *Kristin Yodock*

'This intriguing fantasy keeps you on your toes! As you enter into a world where the old ways intertwine with a dystopian world, the lives of three very unique women whose essence is connected at its very core unfolds. Magic blends with science as they fight for what they believe in, merging together in a way that could save or destroy the world. The story takes you on an exciting adventure that challenges and uplifts you in ways you wouldn't expect. The author's creative talent threads a web of enchantment throughout the story to keep you guessing at every turn, a great read.' - *Suzanne de Malplaquet - Author of bestseller 'Eddie Motion and the Tangible Magik'*

Acknowledgements

Though writing is essentially a solitary practice, most books owe their birth to more than just the author. This book is no exception. It's my first work of published fiction, and its long gestation has been guided by an abundance of midwives. Below are just a few.

My gratitude and love go to Lesley Thornton, my first reader and great friend. She nursed a good idea and a novice author through countless drafts and plot changes, life crises and work deadlines. Without her unflinching generosity and honest advice this would have been a very different book; and would likely be still stuck in Scrivener and not in your hands.

Thanks also to Ronnie Zeinstra, friend, fellow author and patient reader for always asking how the book is going, and trying to devise ways to keep us both on the writing and editing track.

It's rarer for children to spout about their parent's achievements than the reverse. My daughter Cassi made my day by telling me how proud she was of me for writing my first fantasy novel. She admitted that though she'd begun to read the manuscript as a favour one weekend (aka she ran out of downloaded shows and internet), she ended up reading into the wee small hours, and then waking up early the next day because she couldn't wait to finish it. That's priceless. And of course, I thank her for all those times she helped me with plot and character revisions, grammar, and formatting, as well as designing a brilliant cover and chapter art.

My heartfelt appreciation goes to Tom Bird for his belief in me, and my writing. I attended one of Tom's writing workshops, full of ideas and hopes of being an author. With decades of non-fiction writing and personal angst holding me back, Tom helped me drive a truck through the blockade to unleash my creativity. Then as the deluge of words threatened to drown everyone in sight, Tom patiently coached me through countless re-writes till I slowed the torrent and found my flow, and my fiction voice.

Then, just when I thought I almost had it done; I sent the manuscript to Tanja Gardner of Crystal Clarity Copywriting for what I naively suggested would be a *light* edit. Tanja went above and beyond my expectations with her expert, challenging, and insightful feedback. She diagnosed my inclination to sesquipedalian loquaciousness (the overuse of big or long words), treated my comma splice infestation, and resolutely weeded out many other plot and grammatical horrors – the book is so much better for it.

And to Strack, my best friend and the love of my life. I couldn't have done it without you. Sorry about all the 5:30am starts, midnight finishes, and weekends on your own in the garden – just to name a few of the things you've put up with. Perhaps our vows should have read "for better, for worse, and through the writing of novels". It's been a long time coming, thanks for waiting, and for always believing.

Finally, to you the reader. Thank you for your time. I hope you lose yourself in the fantasy for a little while.

The Dogs of Doom come way too soon
When Fate's Foe emerges
She will be chosen for her Grace
Though driven by her Urges
Unless controlled against her Whims
Life's Destiny unfurls
The Chosen Ones when they Become
Will save or damn our worlds...

A fragment of the Chosen Ones Prophecy

Contents

Sibling Rivalry

The future has an ancient heart
We wonder how they came apart
Through loss and love
And loss again
When will this soul's journey ken
The hand of woe
Misery's foe
Down
And
Down
And
Down
They go

Excerpt from The Lament of the Cosmic Mother

Falling, tumbling through an endless dark ocean of stars. So cold.

So alone.

The tiny humanoid newborn, bloody placenta still attached via a thick blue cord, cried out and her form changed – she *shimmered*. Her dark curls and smooth, shadow-blue skin roughened to a scaly red. Her eyes blackened, and her arms and legs became four stout limbs tipped with sharp talons. Tiny wings emerged from her spine, and a furiously lashing spiked tail beat against the void. She shrieked her anger, and blasts of sulphurous fire erupted into the implacable Cosmos.

She *shimmered*, keening her loss, and her scales became thick, grey skin – smooth, sleek, dorsal and tailfins. She swam the currents of the frigid timestream, shedding salty tears, her eyes now blue.

The Cosmos remained obdurate.

She *shimmered* again, her eyes turning livid in a face now of dark granite, mottled skin. Rough, spatulate hands whirled fiercely, battering at a rainbow of seven aetheric threads that chased and tried to ensnare her. She *shimmered* yet again, now a mass of willowy vines, eyes verdant green. Branches twisted frantically to escape the confining threads.

She *shimmered* once more; then dissolved into air, blown this way and that, frightened now. The seven energies strove to contain and comfort. As their agitated forms ringed her, she howled, and slipped away.

So cold.

So alone.

In time, her wails subsided to hiccups and puffs of mist. As the aetheric threads anticipated her pause to *shimmer* again, they linked and wove a net. A small puff of her mist-being observed and separated, hurtling away from the main. It sped off faster than light, frightened, but determined to stay free.

What remained of her exhausted soul *shimmered* back into her human form, gasping, dying. Her dark hair had blanched to a shock of white. She let the seven dancing colours approach. They vibrated, soothing and crooning. With eyes now reflecting the ocean of stars, the newborn reached puny hands for the undulating threads. Sensing her surrender, the threads enlarged and merged, forming a soft rainbow shell around her: at her feet red, then orange, yellow, green, blue, indigo, violet. At the top of the cocoon, bright, white light – a link from her own soul – darted out. It wove into the threads and capped the covering, enclosing her. Each colour of the rainbow anchored a tendril into the withering placenta, feeding and re-energising it.

She breathed, she warmed, her hands and feet shadow-blue again. The rainbow sang to her, her hiccups ceased, and her eyes – one green, one blue – closed. The cocoon hardened and began to spin, rotating alone in the starry sea. There was no sign of her missing wisp.

– – –

The cosmic timestream is fickle. Moments or aeons later, a fine gold brume circled the rainbow casing. A tendril of gold touched the cocoon and shared its thoughts with the occupant.

Hello, little one.
Such a violent beginning.
Such a lonely life ahead, so many sorrows and so much loss.
Yet you are destined to bring so much joy and power for those that matter.
I've waited for so long.
Will you be my way Home?
I must return to where I belong.
You are my key.

The gold mist spun the cocoon, tumbling end over end until it changed direction and shot towards a pulsing yellow star. It became an arc of bright, white light; a blazing trail across the velvet night sky of a blue-green planet. On into daylight, it slowed near a massive stone monolith that was shaped like the cast of a deity's footfall erupting from the ochre soil. Near a simmering oasis, the cocoon slowed. It settled on the damp leaf litter beside a small billabong. A harsh, hot morning dawned, drawing the thick eucalyptus fragrance from the drooping leaves of a handful of tattered timber sentinels guarding the precious pool of moisture.

The gold mist withdrew, *shimmering* into a flaxen-haired female, accoutred in sparkling gold armour, her hip-length braid tied off with a silken band. Removing her dragon-horned helm, she pivoted. One hand opened wide, and golden light misted into the still air. Animals and insects of all sizes and shapes were drawn toward the glow. Meana, older sister to the Elemental Four, and the most powerful energy elemental, lowered her hands to her hips. She contemplated the gathered menagerie, her lips pressed together with a hint of anxiety even as her tawny eyes catalogued the growing crowd.

From the red earth, another female form arose, green and verdant – her long, khaki hair fluttering leaves, her thin hands reminiscent of twigs. This was Garule, earth elemental and First of the Elemental Four. The atmosphere churned with the smell of humus and life.

A fiery dragon screeched above them, diving towards the gathering. His wings folded, and as he plummeted, his red, orange, yellow and white scales smoothed, until a broad-shouldered, red-skinned male stood before them on two legs: Wyak, fire elemental, the youngest of the Four. Sparks crackled from the tips of his wild, white hair as he settled.

From the nearby billabong, another male – Sleene, water elemental – stepped out, leaving wet footprints as his pale blue form approached his siblings. He shook his copper-brown hair, spraying water on his fiery brother, who hissed at him. Sleene was the Third of the Four.

The leaves on the nearby trees stirred to attention, and a willy-willy – a small whirlwind – swirled dry, red dust: Jindi, air elemental and Second of the Four. Her translucent white female form emerged from the whirlwind, her hair continuing to twist in an aetheric breeze. Deep blue eyes watched her siblings follow her hands, as she trailed them down her shapely figure. A self-satisfied smile quirked her thin lips. Her sisters tossed their heads at her vanity. Her brothers turned to each other, ignoring her.

'And we're waiting for big brother Time, again,' Sleene complained as water continued to drip from his shoulder-length curls and down his body, disappearing into the red sand.

'Does anyone see the irony in that?' Wyak planted his hands on his hips, matching his eldest sister's stance. Fire smouldered in his black eyes.

Garule huffed, tossing her long tresses over her shoulder, and combing them back with spindly fingers. She stroked the tree beside her, and it quivered towards her touch.

Meana's eyes tightened. Garule, of all her younger siblings, annoyed her most. She couldn't resist touching this or that creature or plant, nurturing them, patiently urging them to grow. Sleene was the opposite. A being as slippery as his water element, he was hard to hold and the most impatient of her siblings. She could see he itched to begin.

'Let's get this done,' Sleene urged. 'With this soul, we finally have a tool powerful enough to bring these humans to their knees. This will show Mother that her little human pets are no more than that. Their spirits are weak and selfish. They cannot rule, they cannot create, and they cannot care for the land, sea, sky and air.'

'Always you forget Energy,' Meana accused her younger brother, though she was pleased with his rebellious rhetoric. He had agreed to her plan swiftly and entirely.

'And Time.' A male humanoid, purple-black skin, slipped through from the Shayde between worlds and snapped into the moment with a hint of cosmic frost.

'Late as ever, Brother,' Wyak grouched.

Aeon, the god of Time performed a mocking bow to Meana and the others, his long, unbound black hair sliding around his shoulders like silk.

'I arrive exactly on time, as always,' he said, his usual condescending smirk in evidence.

'Let's get it done,' Wyak glowered at his oldest brother, before turning to Meana for instructions.

With the Cosmic Mother's six outcast offspring gathered, Meana began. She took a deep breath. This event advanced so many of her plans. Vengeance would be hers. She composed herself, flicking off the remnants of her earlier anxiety. She'd waited this long: a few more years would pass in a blink. And she had plenty of strings to pull and weave while she waited. Her single-minded gaze met each of her siblings.

'As agreed, each of us places a gift of magic into this abandoned soul. The gift should lay quiescent until a particular event or emotion activates it. I'll leave it to you to choose your gift's threshold, but make sure it's low enough to trigger when the creature is young. With each gift building on the others, the chance of this soul becoming the catalyst who causes all out Armageddon expands exponentially.

'Once all the gifts are triggered, chaos will spread like a contagion. Each use of the gift will further fray the planet's aetheric network. Other humans will find their magic unravelling and uncontrollable. There'll be nothing they can do to stop it. Humans are greedy and ambitious. They'll tear themselves and this world apart.' Meana paused, soothing her ire.

'Naturally, we'll be asked to step in and save them from themselves. The only solution being to wipe them from existence before they infect the other worlds and the Seven Realms of Heaven. Mother will realise we're wise, selfless and compassionate, and we'll be welcomed Home.'

— — —

Aeon watched as Meana forced each of her younger siblings to meet her eyes. Her intense focus demanded a nod from each of The First Four. But pride at her own cleverness clouded Meana's vision: she failed to see the uncertainty that Aeon noted lurking in the gaze of all bar one of the four. Aeon avoided her gaze and crouched next to the cocoon, his hands stroking its rainbow shell.

'Brother?' Meana moved to stand next to him. 'You have doubts? Wasn't this your idea in the first place?' Meana's brow creased with annoyance as Aeon stood and gestured at the cocoon.

'What about this soul? It's not receiving our compassion — quite the opposite. It isn't fully human by the way, so it may not respond to your prodding in quite the way you expect,' he informed her.

'What do you mean not fully human? What do you know about its heritage? I found it cast out through one of your precious gates from a human world. Barely born, obviously unloved.'

Aeon declined to remind her that they weren't his gates. Nor was he intending to tell her that he'd found a way to use them, and that he'd been using them – a lot. The less she knew about the gates the better.

'How do you know it's unloved? Someone wove this cocoon for it after all,' he said. Aeon leant and stroked the warm surface again, absorbing the soft healing energy, and sensing a familiar feminine scent.

Meana's gaze narrowed as he straightened. 'We agreed on this plan. The sacrifice of one for the good of the many was accepted by all. Don't you want to return to Mother? To return Home?'

Aeon paused for a heartbeat. His gaze took in the rainbow cocoon and then each of his siblings, finishing with Meana.

The siblings stilled.

He'd spent such a long time alone with Mother. Meana was the playmate he'd begged Mother to make. Meana had always been able to persuade him to get into mischief, to scheme and play tricks. And he loved her for it. Though every now and again, his conscience pricked.

After Meana, the Mother had created his siblings to guide and guard the four elements of earth, air, water, and fire. They followed his lead. It was really his fault they'd all been cast out. Guilt momentarily clouded his thoughts. He could choose differently. But they all looked up to him, and thought him infallible. It had been such a small lie, and he did so enjoy being the object of their adoration.

I can always intervene later, or earlier. He had all the time in the Cosmos now that they'd been banished to this universe. Mother had no right to restrict his creativity. As her firstborn, he should be able to shape and give life to creatures as he pleased – or to take it from them. Surely, she made mistakes too. What did it matter if his mistakes were crowding the Seven Realms of Hell? If Mother wasn't absent so often, he would have learnt better control. It was all her fault. She gave birth to him. He withdrew his hand and straightened.

'You're right. It's of no consequence. Let's get done and get out of here. Being on this physical plane irritates me. I dislike corporeal existence.'

A collective sigh of relief rippled through the siblings. Aeon was the most unpredictable of them, his magic strong and his anger legendary. Each of the youngest four had spent millennia in isolation at some point for a perceived slight against their oldest brother. Only Meana had escaped his wrath.

'What is it? What's changed?' Meana asked.

Aeon looked at Meana's face, and her eyes searched his. He considered confiding his doubts to her. She had always been his favourite sister, and she so wanted to go Home. She must miss Mother as he did. He loved Meana dearly. But what of the other? Had it really been a dream? Or one of his Mother's erstwhile lessons? His sister put both hands on his arm, gifting him a burst of lifting energy.

She smiled. He contrasted her golden touch and pale hair with the memory of auburn curls and fine copper fingers stroking his skin to fire. He hoped he didn't regret his choice. He returned Meana's smile and answered, 'Nothing has changed. The plan goes ahead. We'll find our way Home. It's our birthright.'

Meana half-smothered a triumphant smile, and turned calmly to the mob of assembled animals. Her glance settled on a female feline, a hellcat.

'Hello, little mother.' She beckoned, and the hellcat inched forward on her belly, head lowered. The golden elemental stroked her, tickling behind her black tufted ears, and the animal rolled over and bared her belly in submission. Meana laughed and rubbed her tummy as the feline purred. Garule stepped over and stroked the hellcat's head. She gazed into the cat's eyes, noted her sagging belly and engorged nipples.

'Mmm, just right. Take me to your cubs my love. We have a task for you.' The hellcat leapt up and padded off through the bush, tail twitching. Garule addressed the gathered wildlife. 'Follow.'

Meana lifted the cocoon on an energy thread as she followed the hellcat and her sister.

The strange procession of animals and siblings flowed – walking, flying or crawling according to their species, following a worn track through the dusty bush away from the billabong. There was no need for the hellcat to hide her lair in this desert. The feline's confident walk showed she was top of the predator chain.

They climbed for a few minutes and arrived at a minka; a shallow cave created by a fall of tumbled rocks at the foot of a small ragged cliff. The mob dispersed around the front of the minka according to species. Wyak *shimmered*, his dragon form flapping up to the clifftop as lookout, though there was no one likely to challenge this gathering. Aeon let his own awareness slip unbidden into his brother's. From here, Wyak – and Aeon – could see the stone monolith and the surrounding desert valleys as slashes of green against the ochre dust.

Aeon withdrew from Wyak to watch the scene in front of him as Wyak returned to the ground. The mother cat slipped inside and brought out a mewling cub, only days old. She went in again and again until eight small, furry bodies blinked in the bright light, tumbling over each other at the feet of the Elementals.

Garule smiled and crouched down to touch each one on the head, giving each a protection blessing. She was the earth elemental, so all these creatures were close to her heart. A heart that she so often wore on her face. Aeon could see her doubt resurfacing. She held her charges close. Their trust in her protection was absolute.

Meana must have felt Garule's energy waver too, and she placed a heavy hand on her shoulder.

Garule stood to face her sister, and the determination in Meana's eyes frightened her into stepping aside.

Meana looked at the cat. 'A sacrifice for you, little mother. A small burden. Will you care for this precious soul?'

The feline sitting placidly beside her offspring dipped her head once.

You do not refuse a goddess, especially one who controls the energetic fabric of the Cosmos, Aeon thought wryly.

Meana smiled, flicked a hand, and the rainbow cocoon began to dissolve. The seven colours unravelled into single threads. Each thread circled the head of a different cub and entered through their eyes, leaving the smallest untouched.

Meana shrugged as seven of the cubs stilled, absorbing the energy. Aeon suspected she had not anticipated the threads having a mind of their own. The cocoon's human passenger remained sleeping, the cord and placenta still attached. At a gesture from Meana, the hellcat padded forward and chewed through the umbilical cord. The babe cried out at the withdrawal of nourishment; its face scrunched with anger as it breathed in a lungful of warm air. The mother cat's rough tongue licked it all over, the rhythmic strokes encouraging its breathing, and comforting the baby's cries. That complete, the hellcat grabbed the placenta and devoured it in two swallows.

Meana touched the child's forehead with one hand, and the remaining cub with the other. With complex energy threads she began to bind their forms together, though the effort it took showed in the sheen of sweat on her face. She leant forward, willing them to join. Eventually they *shimmered* and became one. The cub's eyes flashed black, grey, red, blue, green, then settled to tawny, matching the rest of her litter mates.

'It's done.' With a smug look at her handiwork, Meana stood, tossing her braid over her shoulder. 'At last, we've taken a real step on our way Home.' She inspected her siblings and impatiently motioned them forward.

'Come, come. Bestow your gifts – your darkest gifts, remember. We don't want any new rivals for Mother's attention.'

Wyak and Sleene jostled to be first. As the youngest, they competed at everything, always trying to outdo each other. Many lands bore the scars of their battles to prove their dominance.

Jindi slipped in ahead of them, dissolving and reappearing next to the cub. Meana stopped her sister. Jindi was always the most disengaged member of their group. She was content to spend her time drifting over the world, in her element, untouched by the inhabitants on the surface.

'Concentrate, Jindi. This is important: your darkest gift,' Meana said. Jindi shrugged off her sister and touched the cub with one slender hand. 'It's done.'

The remaining siblings bestowed their bound gift of magic on the tiny cub. Then Aeon crouched finally to touch the cub's downy white head.

The cub opened her eyes, and one green, one blue stared back at him. He paused with delighted recognition. *Maybe more than a dream then.*

His fingers tingled when he examined a small red star peeping out from the soft white fur of her chest, feeling the faint trace of the motherline thread there. He sobered and whispered, 'Ah, little one. Even as we try to control you, you have a choice to change the outcome. In the end, the decision will be yours. I have no doubt she'll be looking to find you. Enjoy life, little flower.' He touched her forehead and her eyes flashed to amethyst as a black thread joined the others. A ring of fur around her eyes darkened.

Garule addressed the circle of birds and animals. She gestured to the stone monolith in the distance and the trees whose branches waved closer to hear her.

'You've seen this spirit child. She has an important role in the world, and not only this world. You must all play a part in protecting and caring for her. For some, this will be hard, and for some, a joy. I charge you to do what you can and spread the word. The little one will need your help, your friendship, and your love. She will walk a lonely road until the day of Armageddon dawns. And then…' she paused and gazed down at the eight cubs snuggled up against their mother's belly, suckling and massaging with their tiny claws.

Meana stepped in to stop her sister undermining the plan by becoming maudlin, and spoke to those gathered, 'And then… we will see. Care for her well. All life depends on her. She is the key.'

With a haughty nod to the other elementals, she donned her helm, *shimmered* into gold mist, and disappeared. One by one, each of the siblings departed until only Aeon remained. He stepped closer to the cubs and stroked the smallest one. From his heart, a silver thread appeared – a fatherline thread. It slipped into her soul to join the others. He stood back, feeling the thread explore its new home.

'Well, that was unexpected.' He contemplated snipping the thread, as the youngest cub paused in her drinking and gazed trustingly at him. He sighed. 'What will be, will be. The future is mine to see. Or so I thought.' With one final wry glance, he left.

– – –

A divine being emerged from a tree where she'd observed the event unfold. In this physical plane, the Cosmic Mother was all colours and none, constantly shifting. Her form was voluptuous, sensual, and nurturing. Her hair finally settled to long and black with sparkles of white, reminiscent of the ocean of stars. Her dark, full-lipped face was breathtaking with large almond-shaped eyes of amethyst, like her eldest son's.

'Ah, my foolish children, can you not see that I have room in my heart for everyone and everything?' She observed the gathered fauna and the surrounding flora, who were drawn towards her beautiful energy.

'Dearest Aeon, my first, my treasure. Even now, your heart doubts. Forcing the future is not the answer. Your need to strive and to win is not a gift of mine. You chose this life, these lessons; and many will suffer as you learn. We could have remained two, just you and I. Alas my heart is too soft.'

She touched the tree that had sheltered her in its trunk, its bark creamy smooth. She stroked the soft feathers of a tiny brown bird perched on the tree's lowest branch. She glided towards the cubs who had settled in for a drink and plucked the smallest from its mother's teat. She held it up by the scruff.

'And now you've chosen this tiny soul, already a part of you, and burdened it with a heavy responsibility and such a dark future.' The cub struggled in her grasp, black-rimmed eyes closed, mewling for its mother, milk dribbling from its pink mouth.

'Perhaps it can all be laid at my door. Perhaps I should meddle – a little.' She drew a circle on the cub's belly with her finger, and a tiny rainbow serpent appeared in her hand and slid through the cub's skin to settle deep in its pelvis. She hugged the cub close, kissing her furry head.

'For every dark shadow they've given you, there is an opposite of light, though neither one is good or bad. They're merely what each of us makes of them. In every gift, I've placed a gate. Open and close the gates with darkness or light – the choice is yours. Choose well, little one. On you, the future of this Cosmos depends.'

The cub squirmed, indignant. Its claws scratched at her hands, drawing a tiny red bead. 'So, you're not going to be a compliant tool then.'

Her captive eventually settled in her arms, absorbing the Mother's gentle energy, and sniffing to capture her scent. It licked at her cradling fingers, its rough tongue lapping up a droplet of blood unseen by the Mother, its contented purr building.

The Mother hugged the cub close once more, then placed her back on the ground. Determined, the cub climbed over her siblings to the last vacant teat.

'You are the key – for this world, at least.' She smiled to herself, 'Let the fun begin.'

She opened her arms and twirled around, laughing out loud with joy, head thrown back, black tresses spinning. The animals capered about; enemies forgotten in the moment. Flocks of birds wheeled overhead, and trees and grasses swayed to the silent music streaming from her form. Rainbow lights sparkled from her fingertips, darting about and touching everything. The stars in her hair shone and twinkled. She danced in circles, stamping her feet, voicing an ancient wordless chant. When she stopped, the air pulsed – and each animal and insect was a little stronger, each plant a little greener, while earth and rocks vibrated with stored energy.

The Mother lowered her arms and did an abrupt about face, beckoning to two birds that perched on the edge of the entertainment, watching, and waiting. They couldn't refuse her summons.

'The Trickster and the Sage.' She nodded regally to Magpie and Owl as they settled on the nearest branch, keeping a little distance from each other. One warbled, turning his fiery amber eye on her. The other ruffled her spotted feathers, blinking and sitting in stiff disapproval of such frivolity.

'And who has sent you? Who watches this little soul and dares to spy on these world-changing events? Who has strings tied to those children of mine?' She stepped between them, stroking the plumage of both birds, delving into their minds. Both allowed her hands to smooth their backs. She withdrew, her smile turned shrewd.

'Mm, so that's the way of things. Well, watch you shall. And…' She touched each bird on the throat. A thread of rainbow light trickled from her fingers into the birds and a delighted laugh burst forth. 'Now you will have to share the information both ways, and you will be unable to speak of anything that would bring her harm.' She nodded to the two birds. 'You can keep this child company on her long journey, tell her stories, comfort her, and give her advice. If she'll listen.' She turned to the circle of creatures behind her.

'You are all guardians in one way or another. These next few months will be her most cherished time. Let them be beautiful, carefree memories. Ward her as you would your own; we are all one – always. And thank you for the dance.'

Her appreciative bow took them all in, and she vanished, leaving a hint of lavender and a soft, enchanting memory.

Daydreams

Excerpt from Melba Dome: The Ten Tenets Year 1 PC.

The dual computer screens blurred, and Alinta Morrow sandpapered her lids, rubbing out the grittiness of exhaustion for the tenth time in as many minutes.

Jeez, I'll need an optical regen if I keep this up. I shouldn't let these things slide so far.

She knew how hard it was to get permission for tank time if a critical body part deteriorated, even at her job rank. Yet the Federation castigated anyone who couldn't complete their allocated work on schedule and on budget: a budget that did not include sick leave or tank time.

Who wants to spend days in the sensory tank anyway? She grimaced at her own sarcasm. *Imagine, days of doing nothing; time to think, reflect, relax – just floating in a sea of protein. Heaven on a bloody stick.*

Weariness dropped her head to the back of the chair, and she inhaled a lungful of the musty recycled air. Her dark lashes fluttered down, shutting out both the dreary office and the ubiquitous, Federation-mandated *"WATCH OUT FOR YOUR NEIGHBOUR"* sign plastered above her screens.

She drifted.

Ali had a gift for memory and order, perceiving the world in patterns and seeing sequence and symmetry in her mind in glorious three-dimensional detail. She could keep track of and connect millions of people, items, events, and dates in her head. And she could access this secret third eye tapestry with her physical eyes open if she chose.

As a child, she'd thought her gift magical, and imbued it with a character of its own. It was a laughing ochre red dragon who flew through her mind and her world, weaving rainbow threads from the tips of her shiny black talons and blasting fiery holes in imaginary monsters to make Ali laugh.

When she'd first realised that other people didn't see their world with a textured rainbow overlay, she'd been afraid. Her gift made her different, and different was *not* what you wanted to be in the Dome – especially when you were already a Federation ward living on borrowed everything.

The child centre supervisors had called her a liar and a cheat for her aberrant wisdom and frequently threatened her with realignment from the Grey Shirts – the Federation Committee's cultural enforcers. Her mostly older dorm-mates labelled her a weirdo. They beat and bullied her into a ghostly, silent existence until an education lottery plucked her from obscurity at ten and transferred her to a school in the North Quad.

So for decades, Ali had kept her wealth of knowledge to herself, learning to only display her skill with a middle-of-the-road anonymity. Not too smart, not too stupid – something average and boring. Average and boring kept you under the Grey Shirts' radar, which *is* where you needed to be in the Dome. Despite every cultural decree ever issued by the Federation Committee, interactions with the Grey Shirts were *not* good for your health.

There's gotta be something better than this. Year after dismal year of the same grey, dull, monotony. If only I had some real bloody magic. Then I could zap myself away to somewhere better.

Magic – that was Ali's not-so-secret obsession. Scant though fiction was in the Dome, she nurtured her childhood illusions by reading anything and everything she could about magic and fantasy.

She was lucky – most Domers didn't get to handle real books anymore. Post-Crack, hard copies were only for libraries, the Museum, and rich collectors from the Dome's East Quad. But her project work involved cataloguing those East Quadder's collections while everyone else had to rely on their Fed Comm issued and very temperamental personal communication device – their comli.

Ali especially loved stories with feisty heroines and fire-breathing dragons. It was harmless escapism that helped her navigate the endless drudgery of life in the Dome with wishful thinking. Imagining herself as a dragon with mysterious talents was one of her favourite entertainments in long, boring meetings. She'd picture herself using various special powers to escape from the room in unusual ways, or plan what mythical or lowly creature she'd turn each of her colleagues into if she could. Her sometimes untimely smiles at her own antics drew a few odd glances.

A few odd glances were fine; they kept people from getting too close.

As if anyone would want to get close to little old me anyway.

Most of Ali's colleagues were younger and spent their time and energy wheedling and jostling for the attention of Ali's boss – climbing the job ranks as fast as they could. At fifty-two, Ali had no ambition for rank or privilege, she'd made peace with her ordinary life – mostly. Her plans for conquest lived only in her dreams, along with her dragons.

Yearning tickled the edge of her awareness, tugging at her gift, frustratingly close. It was always this way when she thought about dragons and magic. She felt something swim nearer, brightening as it eased through the murkiness in her mind, a familiar sense of – something.

No. Someone.

Impatient, she stretched towards that someone. The shadow behind her lids whirled from dark nothing into a shade of deep dark red. Then the someone loomed, an enormous shadow crowding the space.

'Ping. Ping.'

Ali's comli sounded a task reminder, its palm-sized plas screen flashing, and whoever it was slithered away leaving her bereft. A dismal black fog followed in its wake.

Drats.

Ali's gift, what had been her practically perfect picture of her own life, was now full of gaping holes – holes about which she had no clue. Starting about twelve months ago, missing hours, days, and sometimes weeks had begun to disfigure her previously unblemished memory. The absent sections made her edgy, and she sometimes felt as if her life was an unravelling tapestry whose threads she couldn't grasp to stop it disintegrating.

Feck, I know it's there somewhere, this, this… whatever. I've forgotten something basic, somewhere. I know I have. If I can find that one event, the rest will fall back into place and everything will go back to where it belongs, including me.

Another deep breath, eyes firmly shut, and she drifted deeper.

The lean face of a birri – a young girl – glimmered into being behind her lids. Snow-white hair, shadow-blue skin, and a glimpse of eyes coloured like her own swung away to negotiate the steep bank of a verdant, overgrown creek.

It's her.

She'd dreamt of this birri before.

Running water danced noisily over sharp black rocks then divided into several streams, each easing their way through scattered stone and deep red earth. A riotous tangle of green plants, bushes, trees – the kind of things she'd only ever seen in history vids – worked together to deny the birri access.

Ali's skin pricked with breathless heat. She smelled fecund dampness, and heard the crack of dry twigs crushed underfoot. Vibrant colours assaulted her wretched Domer senses. She squinted, her eyes burning in the bright sunshine. The Dome skin always filtered light to a muted, dismal beige; and its ever-present dust-grey coat dimmed the light even further. Robotic cleaners failed to keep more than a few square klicks clean at any one time.

Ali shook her head, but the dream remained.

Why am I always dreaming about her?

The flint knife slipped in the birri's sweaty grip as thirst kept her edging towards the water. Her swollen tongue tried to dampen cracked lips, and her stomach growled in chronic hunger. Ali felt herself slipping. She merged into the birri and knew in her bones the weeks of struggle: hunting for diminishing game and scrounging for wild berries as summer's warm bounty faded to autumn in the mountains.

Unreal. Ali tried to pull out of the dream. Domers lived in steamy, humid, controlled sameness all year round, and ate processed rations from the Quad Store.

She slid back into the birri, at the mercy of the dream's strange virtual reality. Ali felt the birri's flutter of hopelessness, and her hands trembled in sympathy. She paused, one palm steadying her descent on a branch, the bark rough and dry beneath her fingertips.

Ali glanced towards her hand, feeling the unusual texture, and blinked at a younger hand than hers with shadow-blue skin grasping the tree limb.

What the…?

– – –

Insects hummed, birds screeched, and a tickling breeze sighed, playing with her fine white hair, snagging, and loosening her long braid.

Someone was watching.

Dee waited.

Slowing her breathing, she wished herself invisible, wished her magic was more reliable, and that she could access her Grace – her storehouse of magic – at will.

Dee had felt this watcher before. The Brown Lady. A second heartbeat. Surprise. A Red Lady too. She'd never had two at the same time. Unlike most of the beings that haunted her existence, the intention of the two women felt distant, harmless. Yet they were closer than ever before – the Brown Lady almost as though she moved under her skin.

'No, I am not she. I am Dee,' she croaked.

– – –

'And I'm freaking Ali,' Ali declared, though the birri Dee didn't appear to hear her response. Ali tried again to disengage without success, though she could sense her own hands now, glowing a soft but insubstantial red. She became aware of another woman watching and turned to see her coming closer. When she looked directly at her she could see the trees through the woman's body.

Dammit, what the bloody hell is happening? Who are these people? Ali tried to wake herself, but the dream refused to let go.

– – –

Dee wiped her sweaty palms on her coarse brown trousers, moving the knife to her left hand. Tucking in a stained grey shirt with her right hand, she stepped to the edge of the creek. Taking a last scan of her surrounds, she squatted and leant over to scoop a handful of precious liquid into her mouth.

The reflection in the water showed three surprised faces, all with one green eye, one blue. Dee pivoted to confront the others, her knife slashing at their bellies.

– – –

Ali leapt back, her eyes snapped open, the chair thudded against the wall. She was back in her office, heart pounding, a fine sheen of sweat dampening her skin. Her mind refused to process what her eyes saw – the faint rosy glow of her fingers fading to brown. She blinked to clear her vision.

Feck, what was that? Who was that? Where was that?

She ferreted a crumpled hanky from her skirt pocket and wiped her clammy face and hands.

That was so real. This bloody dreaming's getting worse. It's taking over my days now, not just my nights. I've so gotta get some sleep or the Grey Shirts'll realign me for sure. Unless they already know what's happening and they're waiting for me to break down.

Her paranoid tech-head neighbour Andie had a theory that the Fed Comm were experimenting with thought control through the monthly inoculations every Domer received. The Fed Comm assured everyone that the vaccines kept them safe from the plethora of Outside diseases that snuck in through the thousands of disintegrating filters.

Bloody Feds trying to influence my thoughts with some new spy tech. Make me do something I don't want to? Bloody hell, I'm already as obliging as I can possibly be. What else do they want from me? Surely at least my thoughts and dreams are my own?

Annoyed, she moved her chair to the side and looked under the desk, feeling along the edge for any kind of electronic bug. Then she opened the desk drawers and shuffled half-heartedly through them.

Don't be ridiculous. No one's gunna bug you or bother trying to influence your thoughts. You're not the bloody Fed Chair for Fed's sake. A drab little drone, that's you. You do exactly what you're told and very little else.

Something about that thought made her squirm. *There's more to me than that.* She ceased her search. Ali rubbed her eyes again, smudging what little makeup remained. With a sigh, she walked over to inspect the damage in the small wall mirror by the door.

Her black curls, cut unfashionably short, ended with fuchsia pink tips; her own tiny rebellion against the drear FEN, the Federation Expected Norm.

I am such a rebel.

Skin she liked to call "coffee froth brown" was now a shade paler after her heart-jumping daydream. Her nose was a little too pronounced, and she had what, decades ago, had been well-defined lips. Now her generous mouth carried deep corner lines, matched with a spray around her eyes. Lives were long in the Dome, so she could look forward to another half a century working without a blink. And though the Fed Comm may have eradicated a bunch of diseases, the years still marked their passing for citizens who couldn't afford cosmetic regen.

Ali's eyes were dark-ringed with fatigue and bright with adrenaline from the dream. Most Domers had eyes some shade of brown between amber and chocolate, with a sprinkle having hazel and green. Ali had one sapphire-blue and one emerald-green eye. Even though they were wildly non-FEN, no one ever mentioned them – at least not in her hearing. She'd decided years ago that other people didn't want to admit to seeing them. The cataclysmic melting pot of the last three centuries had blurred ethnic groups into a single race: survivor. She didn't need to check her facts with her gift. Ali had never seen anyone else with eyes like hers – not in real life.

Echoes of the young birri flickered in her gift. Ali's nose remembered the myriad of smells, the warmth, water, and moist decay. Her hands feeling the texture of the rough bark.

The light, bloody hell, the light was so bright. Everything was so clear and colourful. So... new.

Her fuchsia tips felt anaemic in comparison.

Why would it feel so real? Why did they both have my odd eyes? But that young birri's skin was kinda blue. No one blue-skinned under the Dome, possibly copper like the auburn-haired one though. Maybe it's my past lives leaking through like that crazy lady said?

A random woman, ragged and malnourished, had grabbed her three nights ago as she'd been leaving the North Quad Store. Her bony fingers had latched onto Ali's wrist, and she couldn't shake her off without dropping her rations. So instead she'd smiled politely and waited for her chance to break away.

Then she'd stopped and looked into the woman's dusty face, and felt a staggering surge of compassion as she'd glimpsed what the woman's existence must be. Her long hair had been matted with filth; her skin caked in years of grime. The nails that had clutched her were broken and dirty. The pungent perfume of poverty had wafted from her stained clothes and unwashed skeletal body. Yet bizarrely, those ancient copper eyes had held nothing but gratitude and adoration.

Ali's gift had vibrated, the tapestry undulating with blue and green waves.

'I've stayed true my Lady, I've lived as ya asked, even though *They* think I'm crazy. It's kept me magic hidden, same as yours. My drift time's comin' soon though. I can't watch any more. I know They're comin' for me. Grey Shirts are comin' for me.'

She'd drawn Ali closer, checking both ways like a conspirator, her foul breath making Ali's eyes water as she'd whispered into her ear.

'I know ya dreams are growin'. They're ya other lives leakin' through. I've felt the energy, the magic, seen the memories tryin' ta merge. Ya gotta remember 'em all. The world needs ya ta remember. Remember Jiemba, ta open the Gate.'

Her face had crumpled then, tears tracking muddy squiggles down her grubby cheeks.

'I need ya ta remember, ta tell me it'll be all right. That ya'll be there to open the Gate when I come Home. It's time to come Home, Alinta. We need ya.'

The woman had let go, sobbed uncontrollably for a moment, and then hobbled away, muttering to herself. A few other citizens shopping late had looked askance at Ali, no doubt wondering why she'd attracted a weirdo, and wondering if it was contagious.

Probably wondering whether to report me to the Grey Shirts. Watch Out for Your Freaking Neighbours!

Nothing the woman had said made any sense. It was straight out of a fantasy novel. As a teenager, Ali had harboured a secret idea that being born with different coloured eyes made it certain she'd be a heroine in a fantasy. But now that people were sprouting this stuff aloud, it was way too freaky. Energy, magic, memories, gates. She was just a crazy old woman, and she'd obviously mistaken Ali for someone else.

And yet, when she'd spoken her name – Alinta – it had fallen into her mind like a warm caress. Her gift had gone a little berserk, coloured threads racing around her mind like wildfire. Nothing came of it though, and her gift settled back to wary somnolence.

The Federation's ubiquitous cams – their so-called *safety* cameras – would no doubt catch the woman illegally sleeping rough in the North Quad, and then the Grey Shirts would pick her up for realignment. Still, Ali had wasted a few hours the next morning researching past life memories and magic. Trying to avoid being nabbed defying the Feds' Sixth Tenet, *"Mind Your Own Business"*, she'd logged onto a public computer, so her search couldn't be traced back to her private comli. Nothing helpful popped up apart from finding out that Jiemba meant "laughing star" in a defunct pre-Crack language. And strangely that same language had included Alinta which meant "fire or flame". After work, she'd even done an unsuccessful drive by of a few poorer suburbs along the West Quad border to search for the old woman. Eventually, she'd called herself an idiot and gone home, admonishing herself for *not* keeping to Tenet Six.

Anyway, if what she said is true, I've surely got more crazy memories than any one person could have lives. Her gift's unnatural tics were shuffling peculiar memories through her life tapestry into places they could not possibly belong, including this young, blue-skinned Dee. She'd showed up in mysterious dreams and flashes on more than one occasion and at all sorts of ages. Ali plonked herself back in her chair, running a hand through her hair, then tucked a wayward curl behind her ear.

They can't all be mine. Can they? Can I have lived so many lives? Am I going crazy? This is so not FEN.

Her heart slowed, and her mood plummeted as she stared past the mandatory Federation Community Guidelines that monopolised one wall of her tiny office. In the unlikely case that any Domer citizen forgot what was expected of them, the Federation Expected Norm, the FEN, was plastered in every living, working and community space. Her gaze slid over the faded Ten Tenets that were scarred into her DNA. The tenth admonishing *"WATCH OUT FOR YOUR NEIGHBOUR"* glared back.

She followed a scummy water stain that meandered down the peeling partition into the faded carpet. She rarely noticed the slightly funky stink of her workspace anymore, though now it pinged olfactory senses that were still in shock from the aromatic bouquet of her daydream. Her gift was fruitfully occupied in the background cataloguing the odours, sounds and colours. Not that she'd ever need to use the information here. She wrinkled her nose and focused on the outline of the stain.

Looks like an island map. Kind of familiar. I wonder where it is? Wonder if there are any other people there. Her gift sifted through the history of her planet, analysing the evidence.

A little over three hundred years ago, the Crack had severed global communication on Torpid. The planet had been called Earth for thousands of years before the Crack – officially it still was – but for regular citizens like Ali, the nickname Torpid, with its stagnant and sluggish overtones was the name they used. Despite more than two millennia of global development, planetary disintegration had only taken a few months. Surviving the initial upheaval of the geostorms and earthquakes had been the prime task on people's minds – then surviving the devastation of the aftermath, infrastructure destroyed, and anarchy threatening.

The Domes had been the best option with the air full of poisonous, radioactive dust. Hundreds had been rapidly cobbled together with technology hastily shared and adapted to solar power. Sun, they had plenty of, despite the dust. Once sealed inside, the survivors of Melba Dome soon lost track of any other Domes or continents. Each Dome became self-sufficient and isolated. For all they knew, Melba Dome held the only living people left on Torpid. It was a sobering and uninspiring thought.

The office lights and com screens flickered. The power brownouts had become an almost predictable part of Domer life in the past few years. The Fed Comm assured everyone that all was well, but it didn't feel or smell that way. More and more machines went unrepaired, and the stink outside air-filtered buildings had become so thick you could almost cut it with a knife.

Restless, Ali gave up looking for answers and drifted to her window. She flicked her only family heirloom, a twisted gold ring on her left middle finger with her thumb, feeling the embedded rough-cut ruby with every third flick.

She didn't remember any relatives who might have given her the ring. She'd always considered that incongruous, given her gift. Her citizen files claimed she'd been abandoned not long after birth, left in a West Quad hospital nursery with no record of her parents. She'd longed to believe that she'd been kidnapped, and dreamt of her mum and dad arriving out of the blue one day to rescue her from her lonely childhood and take her home to their fabulous East Quad estate, or to slip her through a magic portal into the real world, any other world but this one.

Her hopes had faded with each birthday.

She'd been fostered for a short time when she was nine with a woman she'd called Nanna, but the woman had been Nanna to a platoon of kids — a veritable army of apprentice delinquents. It could've been worse. As a Federation ward, she could've spent her entire youth in the detention centres, pimped out to whoever had the grift for their supervisors. Winning the education lottery and attending a school in the North Quad had made a world of difference. With her skill for memorising and knowing how things fit together, she'd readily made a niche for herself. Not too big, not too small, middle-of-the-road anonymity again.

Four decades later, she now had her own office in the City Grid: the central business district of Melba Dome. Admittedly, it was a tiny cubbyhole off the conference room and main reception area for her floor, but she *was* the sole occupier. Very few Federation workers could boast their own workspace, scummy stain or not, let alone a window on the world.

She had no idea why her job as a mid-level project manager had suddenly warranted an office twelve months ago. Besides, it wasn't exactly salubrious — her window mostly looked out on the building next door. To see the ragged city skyline properly, she had to get up and stand close to the window as she did now.

They only give offices to smart, reliable workers who deliver without complaint.

Compliant, butt-kissers you mean. Your dreams and those weird episodes began not long before you got the office, you know.

She stomped on that thought.

Don't look a gift horse in the mouth, birri.

In the Domer Federation the popular adage *"Don't ask questions you don't want to know the answers to"*, was more like a dictum for life, and was a common response to the Sixth Tenet's *"Mind Your Own Business"*. Better than good advice in this post-Crack world, it was a survival strategy for continued existence. There were some uncomfortable truths out there.

It was easier to fly under the radar, stay quiet and play dumb. To do what you were told and conform to FEN. You were less likely to be accused of sedition and realigned or disappeared that way. Dissent against the Domer Federation was stomped on swiftly and brutally. Grey Shirts and Feddies – the local law enforcement – saw to that.

Naturally, that bred a defiant underground in Melba Dome. With generations of self-righteous survivors in the West and North Quads refusing to buckle under the yoke of highbrow East Quad politicians before the Crack, insurgents abounded in this isolated southern dystopia. But factions fought the Feds and each other with equal vigour, so nothing really changed.

Nothing changed… except that conscientious citizens like Ali often ended up as collateral mortality statistics. Truth be told, Ali often wondered if the Fed Comm cared as much about the losses as they espoused. Deaths meant fewer mouths to feed and house, and more places in the lucrative Mumma Lottery. Domers were just numbers to the Federation – too many numbers.

Despite their contrariness, the majority of Domers were chronically risk averse. There was a lot of underground talk, but most would do – or not do – anything to keep the status quo.

Stick with What You Know, Ali admonished herself. Tenet number nine.

She unconsciously smoothed her right thumb over the bump of the citzcode implanted on the underside of her left wrist. Citizen 75.313.492.105.

Ali's workspace dimmed as she mused, lit only by the blue light of the com screens and a soft yellow autoglobe that switched on because she'd worked past dusk, again. She stirred for the glimpse of sunset – the horizon a smear of orange and pink through the pollution haze inside the Dome. Wisps of greasy smog flirted with the tattered, grey skyscraper forest. If you ignored the funk of about half a million people living under one roof and didn't know that the concrete towers were full of unhappy, unhealthy workers grinding away for the Federation, the scene held a surreal beauty.

At least the air inside her workspace was triple-filtered. Her nose wrinkled again at the thought of heading out into the foetid stench of the city. Though the Dome pumps worked night and day, the smell of this pocket of humanity living cheek by jowl was pervasive.

Ali shuddered and rubbed her arms, unaccountably chilled.

Damn goose running over my grave. Thanks, Nanna, for that superstitious nonsense.

Though Melba was possibly the only surviving Dome on Torpid, for Ali it was a box with too many sharp edges and too much conformity. She preferred soft, flowing lines and reconnecting circles. She doodled curves and curlicues on everything, and her favourite drawing of three intertwined rings peppered her notepads and comli – no doubt there was a Fed Com file on her somewhere that stored all the images for later. Sometimes, the overlapping area became a flattened eye with a vertical pupil. Often, her three rings became fierce dragons, each biting their own tails. Habitually she drew them surrounded by twisted flames, and old-fashioned keys all adorning the branches and roots of a single enormous tree. Hours spent poring over old books at work helped her imagination supply images aplenty, but these themes came back over and over.

What if they ARE my memories?

Don't be ridiculous. This is your life. It's small, but you chose it. Get over it. Wishing won't change it. Besides, what more could you ask for? You've got a job, a place to sleep and people who need you.

She squirmed at that. *Okay, well two out of three ain't bad.*

Night leached away what little colour the drab Dome held. With the descent of darkness, the yearning jerked back – a physical ache in her chest. Ali moved closer to her grimy window.

It's more than the unfulfilled chasm of uselessness that haunts every human on this dying rock of a planet. What am I missing? Is there something I should be looking for? Something worth living for? Something bigger than me, worth taking a risk at sticking my head up out of the crowd?

Ali's mind skipped to her dream of visiting Outside. She'd be able to smell non-recycled air, feel real earth, touch real trees. She'd tried keeping plants in pots at her apartment, but with her long work hours, it had felt cruel taking them to die a lonely death by dehydration.

All she'd done about her dream was glance at a few brochures, watch a few vids and imagine doing it. She hadn't applied for permission to leave, hadn't begun the fitness program she needed for the trek. She tightened her belly but let go with a sigh. Outside was a long way off in more ways than one.

The Dome had finally been opened almost ten years ago. Embarrassingly for the Feds, rumours abounded that they could've opened it a half century earlier. It'd taken rebel factions busting holes in the Dome edge and repeatedly breaking the filters to get the population's attention that the Feds were basically holding them prisoners for no reason. But it was hard to imagine a place where there was no magnetic field to run the flocar system. A place where you had to ride non-AI machines or walk. She'd been to the edge of the Dome and seen the dustbowl outside the walls. For generations, they'd been taught that the devastation continued for thousands of kilometres. But now reports were trickling in that the countryside was recovering much quicker than the Fed Comm had led the population to believe.

Yet most Domers stayed in their polluted, crowded tenements and bent their backs to the Federation grindstone. The aversion to change was hard to break. Centuries of Tenet Nine dictating *"Stick with What You Know"* would take time to temper.

Besides, there were untamed flora and fauna out there. Ali shuddered at the stories of insects in their millions that could infect or kill you with one bite. The Fed Comm *loved* spreading those warnings. *Three hundred plus years without bugs is one bloody good reason to stay Inside.* It'd take generations to ease people away from the vapid security of the Dome – much longer than it had taken to cram them in when the Crack happened.

A few brave souls had ventured Outside, without any precious resources from the Feds of course. Some even stayed Out, making small self-sufficient communities. Occasional trinkets and fresh foodstuffs had hit the black market, but they were way out of Ali's price range. Then a few citizens had contracted a kind of madness at the whole open air thing, and had to be medicated and returned to the Dome. There was lots of well publicised we-told-you-so and head shaking when this happened. In the last few years the surge of early pioneers had slowed to a trickle.

Enough, Ali. You know you're too chicken-shit to go Outside. Even a daydream of being in the open gave you the heebie jeebies.

She laughed and stretched her arms over her head to ease the long day's aches. It was then she noticed the short slash in her shirt.

Exactly where the birri tried to gut me. She looked closely, realising that the edges were jagged and the tear only a few centimetres long.

Jeez, I have holes in my gift and an old woman mistaking me for some saviour. To top off this craziness, my night dreams are becoming daydreams and one of the characters has sliced my shirt for real.

Ali burst out laughing, and shook her head at her wild imagination.

Get a grip. Daydreams are just that. You probably jagged it on one of the desks in the gopher pen. All their furniture is old and splintery. It's definitely time to go home.

Still smiling, Ali stuffed her comli and a stack of work folders into her dillybag – a handbag that was so much more – and flung the overloaded carryall over her shoulder.

She thumbed off her computer screens, and headed for the door.

Ambition

The Dogs of Doom come way too soon
When Fate's Foe emerges
She will be chosen for her Grace
Though driven by her Urges
Unless controlled against her Whims
Life's Destiny unfurls
The Chosen Ones when they Become
Will save or damn our worlds

Excerpt from the Yarran Journal, translated Nina Nightshayde,
Chief Occultist, Order of Occultology, Geboor Librarium,
Mirrabooka 3314

My foetal scan could *be wrong. Adventurer and analyst both start with A. Maybe I'm the victim of some freaky typo?*

Merindah's vision blurred over the squiggly black glyphs. She kneaded her temples, smearing a little magic into her copper skin, knowing she'd pay for disrupting the negentropy – the order and structure of the cosmic aether – later. Magic wasn't free. Manipulating it messed with the natural aetheric patterns, created the chaos of entropy in the fabric of the universe, and there were always consequences for that.

Entropy's such a bitch. Deep breath, blow it out. I am destined for great things. I'm sure I've got the genes for cosmic adventures. I just need someone or something to give me a break. All I'd need is a little extra training in aether. Mmm, which also starts with A.

Even wishing for that felt too fanciful to be true. She harrumphed at herself. No amount of training was going to promote her out of this wretched job. And who would waste their time training her puny talent anyway? She'd already tried experimenting on her own, and still bore the scars of a botched shortcut. Her belly itched in sympathy and she tightened her fingers on the book to stop herself scratching at the healing skin.

Nope, only a major new aetheric discovery will do it.

Merindah needed something that could save the entirety of Heavens Gate – her world – and zoom her to the top of everyone's favourite researcher list at the same time. Then she could adventure wherever she wished. She touched her thumb to her smallest finger and tapped her forehead three times with the remaining three – entreating Sága, her personal goddess, to grant her "wonder, wisdom and wit". She tapped the same three fingers three times on her heart, appealing to Sister Diligence, one of her world's fourteen virtuous goddesses, to grace her with "effort, expertise and excellence".

Easy.

Eyes clear, she twitched her yerlendj – the innate magical sense and intelligence that denizens of Heavens Gate carried in their genes – then ignited her magic and scoured the page for clues. Her enhanced vision slipped between the faded ink of the symbols to the frayed fibres of the yellowed parchment, and then deeper to the infinitesimal rainbow energy surrounding individual molecules.

Merindah's esoteric research involved hunting for obscure aetheric links between the spiritual, the scientific and the magical. She spent her days mentally and magically sifting through dusty parchments and crumbling tomes for hints of the Portals. Like every other student of the arcane on Heavens Gate, she yearned to be the one who found the key to opening a Portal. She belonged to an unpopular minority, an Order of esoteric cosmologists who believed the Portals were gates for traversing the Astral Spheres of divine existence between this world and Heaven.

Why else would our planet be called Heavens Gate if we weren't meant to open the way to Heaven for Hecate's sake? If only my yerlendj was stronger. It's so unfair. What I wouldn't give to find that key.

With the Portals at her fingertips she'd have access to the Aether Tree, the Tree of Life, the source of the Cosmos and every existence under Heaven. And then she'd have the answers — to everything and everyone. Her sometimes irritating ambition and always unquenchable curiosity would be sated – at least she hoped it would. As would her unvoiced wish for a little payback. Perhaps she would deny Portal access to every single person who'd ever snubbed or wronged her over the thirty-three years of her life.

Merindah had done her share of "wronging" others on her way to this moment – there were few in this fading world who hadn't. She hated to admit that her conscience did give her the odd sleepless night.

She could be nicer once she had the power. That was her plan. She'd nudged a few ethical boundaries, obtained some of her artefacts from irregular sources, plagiarised a few obscure papers. So far, she'd seen little benefit – or detriment, for that matter. She was still in this poky lab, unknown and unpublished after more than a decade of work. She had to be more ruthless to get what she wanted, to get *where* she wanted to go – and that was through a Portal.

Librarium analyst roles didn't rely solely on foetal scans to identify a person's appropriate profession. While perspicacity was mandatory, a position on the District's Portal Collaborative staff depended more on yerlendj than intellect and discernment. Yerlendj was more than just magical acumen, it gave its bearers the potential to detect and control the energetic threads that bound the order of all things – to manipulate aether.

Merindah's elusive and inconsistent yerlendj barely scraped her across the competent line as an aetheric mage, however. While she had shown promise as a child, her magic had stopped developing almost overnight after her mother died, just after Merindah turned thirteen. Luckily her family's genetic pedigree bumped her onto the Librarium's recruitment short list.

Thank Holy Hecate for famous ancestors. Wish I was more like Auntie Jean. That woman was a force of nature. All lightning, thunder and big fat drops of rain on a parched desert. People ignored her at their peril.

The Nightshayde family's political connections then bought off the competition to squeeze her into a junior job on the staff. And of course, it helped that she was female.

Thank the Cosmic Mother for that! I wouldn't wish to be a bloke for all the tea in the North. Mmm, but what if someone offered me enough magic to unlock the Portal in exchange? Would I change gender for that?

With few exceptions, males didn't possess the temperament for investigative research. They were best supervised as field grunts and manual workers, leaving the leadership of vital intellectual work and running the planet to women. Men weren't exactly viewed as less than women: all beings were equal under Heaven. Or at least that's what they were taught in school. It was just that women were *naturally* better at most things than men. After all, men's contribution to world leadership had almost destroyed the planet half a millennium ago – again. They were kept in check now for their own sake, and for the sake of the rest of humanity – namely, women.

Merindah's Librarium position required her to use her yerlendj to examine the miscellaneous artefacts that appeared on her desk with monotonous punctuality every month. According to her annual review she was "working steadily"; though her decade of plodding progress garnered scant interest from anyone outside her own Order, let alone further afield.

Each of the seven Librariums on Heavens Gate had their own Portal Collaborative of dedicated researchers. Each hoarded their scant learning, unwilling to divide potential fame and fortune. Merindah wanted a piece of that fame and fortune. She wanted a seat on the Portal Collaborative. With that kind of influence, she could research whatever she wanted. And get a bigger lab.

I'm so far away from fame and fortune that it's not funny.

Merindah sighed, unclenched her hands, and eased the fragile volume flat. She closed the cracked leather jacket before she did any damage. She glanced at the five stubby texts squatting like poisonous toads on her right. None of them offered a glimmer of promise for her aspirations. She could just make out the slight almond and vanilla whiff of deterioration in the stack, and hoped it didn't mirror her career prospects. A slim, deep red journal was all that remained. And, unlike the rest of the books, it seemed oddly well preserved.

Maybe it'll hold some salacious gossip that I can blackmail their descendants with.

A recent excavation somewhere far out west had uncovered a cache of old books in a thousand-year-old temple ruin.

Merindah lifted her chin and smirked. 'Ha! Take that Nina Nightshayde.'

For the first time ever, Librarium authorities had expedited the handful of books directly to Merindah for an opinion. Her young stepmother Nina, the Librarium's Chief Occultist, never failed to wrinkle her sharp nose dismissively at Merindah's endeavours, academic or otherwise.

Family rivalries aside, competition between Orders within each Librarium was as fierce as that between the facilities. Her acquisitive stepmother stalked any and every opportunity for reputation and influence, championing herself and her aetheric craft above all. Merindah's Esoteric Cosmology Order held a dismal last place in the pecking order at Geboor's Librarium, while Nina's Occultology occupied the pinnacle. That position was aided in no small way by Nina's impressive yerlendj, and her discovery and translation of a new fragment of the Portal Prophecies five years ago.

Like everyone else on Heavens Gate, Merindah could recite the new fragment word for word. Of course, saying it was one thing, but grasping the meaning and implications for the continuation of her planet's human race was an entirely different story.

And it was a story that no one had yet been able to interpret convincingly.

The Dogs of Doom come way too soon
When Fate's Foe emerges
She will be chosen for her Grace
Though driven by her Urges
Unless controlled against her Whims
Life's Destiny unfurls
The Chosen Ones when they Become
Will save or damn our worlds

Sadly, the antique philosophical treatise on the Music of the Spheres and Fibonacci sequences she'd just examined had no story to tell. It offered no useful secrets, not even a hint. She plonked it on top of the other five.

Another useless toad. A bedtime read, bound to put you to sleep in less than a minute. And not the link I'm looking for.

Disappointment, like an odious relative at a Librarium dinner, guffawed loudly in her mind and wrapped her in its loathsome embrace. She shuddered.

With only the personal journal left to examine, a quantum leap in circumstances remained a distant tease. Merindah drew the journal closer and ran her fingers over the two binding-bumps on its spine. She lay the journal flat and traced the three conjoined glyphs on the cover with her index finger. The overlap of the three circles was filled in, but had a thick vertical line traversing its midpoint.

Looks a bit like a flattened eye.

She'd seen this before, somewhere in Geboor. Her fingers twitched, sensing stone.

Ha. It's like the eyes on the old pictographs of dragons in the Librarium. Carved on the stairwell into the deepest archives. Is it connected? Or only a coincidence?

'There are no meaningless coincidences. Coincidence is a clue,' the Head of her Esoteric Cosmology Order, Yaxa Cody, had often propounded to her students. 'Our lives are ruled by synchronicity – meaningful coincidences. Your job as an aetheric researcher is to find that meaning.'

A sniff of familiarity pinged a distant chord in her mind. She brought up the memory of tracing her fingers across the eye on the wall of the Librarium basement, and marvelling at the sharpness of the outline, knowing that the carving had been there for hundreds of years, even though no one had seen a dragon in the flesh for hundreds of years before that.

Focusing again on the journal, she wondered how many others had touched the embossed symbols before her.

What kind of people were they? What lives did they lead?

She centred herself, activated her yerlendj, threaded a trickle of magic into her touch, and re-traced the mark.

Nothing. The familiarity evaporated. She persisted, took another deep breath and with eyes firmly shut, drifted deeper.

Merindah floated above a scene. She glimpsed the lean face of a young girl with snow-white hair and shadow-blue skin. The girl swung away to negotiate the steep bank of a verdant, overgrown creek.

An older woman stood behind the girl. Unlike the girl – who matched this bright place – this woman was indistinct, as though she was not quite there. And the woman's attire: a loose purple blouse and tight dark skirt, didn't match the stained grey shirt and coarse brown trousers of the girl.

Merindah's analyst mind began to take notes. Though she was disconnected from her body back in the Tower lab she felt no fear – she was here to See. Her heart beat a little faster.

The young girl eased her way down the sharp bank towards the water, the older woman following mistily behind.

Merindah's eyes ached in the burning sunshine and bright colour, this planet was young. This was not Heavens Gate. Her own sun was much older and the light softer. She wondered if this was a past Seeing or a future Seeing. Perhaps her dedication to Sága had finally born fruit and her magic was manifesting as visions. She calmed herself to focus on the scene.

Merindah could see the girl hesitate at the water's edge and took herself closer. The girl's hands trembled as she reached to steady herself. Merindah sensed her fear, her aloneness, her hunger. She observed as the older woman gravitated closer to the girl, peering over her shoulder. Merindah hovered close behind, watching. Watching the older woman watching the girl, the two of them drifted closer till their forms began to merge.

'No, I am not she. I am Dee,' the young girl croaked suddenly.

'And I'm freaking Ali,' the older woman said, though Dee didn't register that she'd heard Ali's response. The older woman's form tried to disengage, and her hazy hands glowed a soft red as her body separated slightly from the girl's.

For a moment Merindah thought she saw another shape – this one enormous – begin to coalesce around the pair. She floated closer, but the massive form dissipated. She watched and waited.

Dee squatted and leant over to scoop a handful of water into her mouth. Ali leant forward and Merindah found herself leaning too.

The reflection in the water showed three surprised faces, all with one green eye, one blue. The girl pivoted to confront her watchers, her knife slashing at their bellies.

Merindah leaped back. Her eyes snapped open, and her chair rolled away from the desk. She was back in her tower room, heart pounding, feeling the fine sheen of sweat that dampened her copper skin.

Sága's stockings, what was that? Who was that? Where was that? I'm almost certain I just had my first Seeing. But that girl had my eyes, and the older woman did too. What does that mean? Merindah's heart began to slow its gallop.

How do Seers have these all the time? How do they know what it means?

Her analyst inclinations kicked in. She rescued her chair, sat down, and grabbed a notebook. In measured words, she recorded everything she'd seen, felt, and thought during the experience. She considered any triggers and finished the entry by posing a series of possible explanations. Whatever had initiated it, she wanted to do it again. She was *not* going to let that red journal out of her sight. It had to be connected to that.

Exploring the archives for images of that flattened dragon eye symbol was now high on her list of actions. Merindah paused as the large shape that had begun to manifest over the other two women tickled at the edge of her mind, its definition just out of reach.

She shrugged. At the moment, she couldn't make a link to her current research – but it didn't matter. It had been so *real*. She was desperate to tell someone, someone who could help her work out what she'd done and what it meant. Still, she knew to be wary around who she shared it with.

This was *hers*.

Merindah scooted her chair back and stood, stretching her hands over her head, and wriggling her fingers towards the flaky painted ceiling until her spine popped.

Yaxa Cody, that's who I need to share it with.

The head of her Order would know if it was a true Seeing – and was the least likely to steal her glory. Yaxa was already influential. Merindah tried calming herself, but excitement bubbled over, and she flung open the door to her lab. Her exuberant exit from the room frightened a mage student hurrying past. The young woman squeaked and dropped several heavy books. Merindah noted the dark blue stripe on the hem of the student's pale blue Esoteric Cosmology robes as she gathered her volumes.

A first year then. Easily frightened. Not my fault.

Merindah beckoned her closer. The young woman's flushed face reflected her scare though she bobbed her head. *As she ought.* A qualified mage, even a junior one with minor talent, did not apologise to students. Right now, Merindah was too busy trying to look nonchalant about her Seeing experience to worry about anyone else's feelings anyway.

'Go to Mistress Cody's Rooms, and tell her assistant to give me the next available appointment to see the Head,' she instructed. Her excitement sharpened her voice. 'Go now, no delays. I expect to see you back here within the quarter hour.'

The young mage knew better than to make excuses, but Merindah saw her surreptitious glance at her belly.

Before she could give the student an earful about respect, the young woman nodded and hastened away, hugging her unwieldy armload.

Merindah closed the door and pressed her head against it, breathing slowly. She peered at her belly to see what had drawn the student's gaze. Rather than a food or ink stain, there was a slash in her shirt, right where the young girl in the Seeing had lunged at her with a knife.

Seven Sisters save me. It was real. I was there. She fingered the jagged edge of the small tear.

It was time to gather her thoughts. She'd discarded her shoes hours ago, and the cool wooden floor soaked into her aching soles. She loved the feel of the natural surface, and her yerlendj slithered into the aetheric signature of the timber. She felt the resilience of deep roots anchored in the soil. Smooth branches that reached for the sun, surviving floods, fires and famines buoyed her spirit and strengthened her resolve. Somewhere in their distant past, these floorboards had been part of the Aether Tree.

If only I had more magic for my yerlendj to work with. Then I know I could delve deep enough to experience another Seeing or to find the link. If only.

Well, wishing doesn't make it so. Get on woman. You're thirty-three. Soon you'll be too old for fame. You're halfway to the dreaded sixty-six already. Time's running out, and not just for you.

Still though, a thrill of excitement shivered through her body as she remembered the brightness of the light. She wondered if other Seers had this type of immersive experience, then sternly instructed herself to be calm. One event did *not* make her a Seer. She scanned the leather-bound volumes and paper folios lining three walls of her tiny lab, every author a legend in Portal research. One day, her work would line someone's walls too.

The square racks and straight corners nagged her. By the end of each day, the lab always shrank to coffin size.

At least one wall's curved.

She perused the smooth, white stone of the outside wall. It currently sported a plethora of her research images, stuck on in apparent spontaneous disorder. Ancient paintings, colourful mandalas, antiquated alphabets, each item numbered with her own peculiar code and all connected with multi-coloured threads tracing the aether links she'd explored. It looked more like the efforts of a drunken spider than of a respectable academic. First things first. She copied some basic facts from her recent experience onto clean sheets of paper and tacked them to the wall.

No threads to connect to yet. Wait for more information.

For Merindah, numbers and letters told a story – a colourful tale of time and adventure. Her gift for dramatising alphanumeric symbols and assigning them with colour and sound caused her no end of teasing as a child. She perceived mental images in her own unique way. Numbers were music, hence the labyrinthine representation of her research and the symphony it performed in her mind.

Once her birth mother had explained that not everyone understood letters and numbers in that way, she'd learned to keep her perceptions to herself. Then, when her mother died, her gift had grown quiescent. Lately though, those unique perceptions had leaked more and more into her scientific brain, skewing her objective findings, and granting her flashes of intuition, all linked to the streaming patterns of numbers and letters in the Cosmos.

Yawning brought in a lungful of Portal history; her nose tickled by the accompanying dust. Her brow furrowed and lips pressed tight. She wanted other people to speak *her* name with awe and respect. Maybe this Seeing would be the key. Perhaps her yerlendj was finally developing after lying dormant for so long. This research would be her breakthrough, the one that got her noticed by the right people and out of this boxy cell.

And through the Portal to another world. The link is there – it has to be. What am I missing? I know magic and spirit are connected. I know I can explain them with science. So what does my Seeing have to do with it all?

She shook off her vehemence with a flick of her long fingers, dispelling the negative energy. She made a diamond over her lower belly with her hands, shuffled her feet to widen her stance and closed her eyes, focusing her yerlendj. She breathed in the smell of old paper and history mingled with a hint of sour coffee and stagnant flower water from a vase on a nearby shelf. She wrinkled her nose.

Ugh, totally ruining my Zen. Note to self: must replace flowers and throw out coffee dregs. Scratch that. Note to self: reconsider habit of picking flowers on random cliff walks and leaving them to rot.

She focused on her belly again and tried to capture the stillness.

Nope, not happening. The excitement of her Seeing refused to subside.

Her hands dropped and her eyes – one green, one blue – opened. She'd always thought being born with odd-coloured eyes meant she'd have anything but the ordinary life that she had. Her mother had always told her she was special. And she had believed it – right up until her mother died and left her father and a new stepmother in charge of her life. But now she'd had some sort of dream event about two other women with those same eyes.

Why?

Tucking errant curls behind her ears, Merindah ambled to the single window of her lab and shoved the bottom half up, wincing at its habitual reluctant squeal. She wondered for the millionth time why her Order had abandoned technology for magic with such zeal. Surely technology wasn't all bad. She envied other Orders who'd found a compromise and allowed existing technology to support ongoing development of their magical specialty. *I'm sure their windows and doors open and close smoothly.*

She levered in her battered copy of Jensen's Orbital Senses to keep the pane propped open. The sharp sea breeze readily dispelled the stale odours in her fifth-floor tower lab. Leaning her elbows on the cool stone of the sill, she cupped her chin in her hands. Merindah's mind drifted across to the crowded city opposite, where a plethora of faint life threads swirled, tickling her yerlendj.

The Librarium and its cramped enclave clung to the rocky cliffs at the edge of the Anthozoan Sea like a crusty limpet at low tide. Towers and blocks connected in a haphazard network strung between the Ivory and the

Obsidian Towers on opposite sides of the campus. Buildings were added on as each new theory and sponsor surged to prominence, and renovated with each swing of the influence pendulum among the Librarium's Orders.

By contrast, Geboor – the capital of the island nation of Mirrabooka – perched at the other side of the tiny half-moon bay like a celestial goddess brought to earth. Elegant ivory spires were surrounded by petticoats of pearly dwellings, edged with a frothy lace of bleached marketplaces that flowed with surreal majesty to connect the turquoise ocean and cerulean skies.

Merindah frowned. The idyllic illusion preserved a thin facade for a people under the shadow of extinction under their dying sun. The end of the patriarchy's destructive rule saw technological advancement stagnate and prowess in non-mechanical fields rise to prominence. But mental enlightenment failed to provide the much-sought freedom from corporeal existence that most of humanity aspired to.

Lives were easier and healthier now, but thirty odd centuries of sameness had sucked humanity's innovative spirit dry. The unearthing of the Yarran Journal and the first Portal five hundred years ago had changed all that. One of the early partial translations from the journal hinted that a capacity to work magic could be significantly increased with selective breeding. Anyone with even a suspicion of any magical ability had shot to the dizzy heights of global celebrity overnight. So-called experts had emerged from the woodwork.

But after the initial wave of enthusiastic, and ultimately fake entrepreneurs had a sceptical populace baying for blood, the governing World Council reverted to science for an answer. Their first crucial step saw genetic engineering to strengthen the power to manipulate aether become mandatory. Initially there were naysayers, those who decreed messing with genetics and manipulating aether would bring down the wrath of Heaven. *From all seven of Heaven's realms no doubt.* Nowadays, most people had at least a little skill at magic – enough to help with their everyday chores anyway. And of course, some had much, much more.

So many people scurrying about their little lives. All ignoring their fading sun and dying world. So few know of the life-changing work that goes on behind our famous white walls.

Infamous white walls more likely, taxes and more taxes to fund the Librarium's work. But all for their – our – own good.

Heavens Gate was old, and its raw resources grew scarcer every day, despite the "re-use, re-cycle, re-purpose" mantra that was drummed into every citizen from birth. Even with severely regulated birth control and voluntary euthanasia at sixty-six, the planet's dissolution continued. It was all too little, too late. Humanity had plundered too deep for too long. Global temperatures and oceans rose, food bowls withered, and natural disasters peppered the news with uncomfortable regularity as their sun continued its death throes. The remaining tribes of humanity clung to existence on coastlines that had been a long trek from the sea hundreds of years ago. Still, the oceans both fed them and kept the rising humidity bearable. Merindah suspected they'd be aching for the humidity once their star stopped warming the planet and they began the long decline into the cold dark of eternal night.

With their own world disintegrating around them, the World Council focused on finding the key to expand and mine the many other worlds hinted at in the Yarran Journal. The translations were frustratingly fragmented and obscure. Speculation by the best minds on the globe had determined that the journal was – amongst other things – some kind of manual for the Portals.

Merindah also foraged for details of the Yarran Prophecy's Chosen Ones, their origin, their arrival, and their legacy. An existing legend fragment forewarned that the Chosen Ones would emerge to save or damn her world. It was widely believed they'd miraculously appear to unlock the Portals and lead Heavens Gaters to salvation and glory. As long as their "Whims" were controlled, whatever *they* were. And with the year augured for Armageddon looming in the not too distant future, the demand for answers was developing a frenetic urgency.

The sea breeze lifted wisps of hair from Merindah's face and brought her the tang of ocean saltiness along with the mouth-watering aromas of a shoreline barbecue.

I could do with a snag – both the sausage and the Sensitive New Aged Girl.

She chuckled to herself.

You are a sad excuse for a woman. You need some downtime.

Another waft of delicious food floated up. Families often pooled their food reserves to relax together at the end of the working week.

Mmm, barbies. Must be Friday again. Where did that week go?

The weekend's eve drifted snippets of a family relaxing to her window.

Friday night. Was I supposed to be somewhere?

Feminine voices laughed.

She frowned at two carefree children, a girl and a boy, playing tag along the sand with their mothers. The cherished under-fives were free from the burden of their gender and foetal scans until their fifth birthday.

Most magical abilities didn't manifest until then. After that you were either training for a job, doing the job, or training the next person for the job until you died or took the Green Dream at sixty-six. If you did work of value and couldn't be replaced, you were allotted another five years. At least, you were if you were female.

Don't they know it could all be over before their children have children of their own? Ugh, what a grouch. I definitely need to get out of this lab. And I need some better company, someone who knows nothing about what I do or who my family is. Maybe someone I could get to know intimately? A little physical release could relax my mind.

The busy streets quietened abruptly into a twinkling swirl of lights as the sun set in tangerine and copper flares over the mountains. The laughing families had gone home, and only the soft, rhythmic sweep of the waves remained. Even the ubiquitous gulls were silent tonight. Merindah eased back from the window and rubbed her elbows. She checked her watch.

Damn, I've been daydreaming for an hour. Where is that dratted student?

She stomped to the door and dragged it open again. A note fluttered at her feet, and she bent to retrieve it. Her appointment with Yaxa Cody was tomorrow at midday. With a grimace, she realised that an apology to the student for her fright might have encouraged the dratted woman to knock on the door and let her know earlier.

She straightened and re-entered the office, slamming the door for good measure.

Assassin

From Federation Expected Norm:
The Ten Tenets, Melba Dome,
gazetted 14 March 35 PC.

Ali sighed and pressed her forehead against the cool glass of her window. It was late. Her mind was fuzzy, gorged on work and worry, and now too full to function after another long day at the com screens. Below, the twinkling twin lights of flocars – the Dome's magnetic powered vehicles – snaked their way through the crowded streets, white in one direction, red in another.

All going home to their pointless little regimented Federation lives. Putting one foot in front of the other, going nowhere, with a capital N. All wishing they were somewhere else. And Somewhere Else sounds like a better place than this.

Ali dreamed of living in the East Quad, but suspected the closest she'd ever get was a share-house in the South. Every aspect of Domer life, including permission for where you lived, was overseen by the Fed Comm and their interminable guidelines.

Theoretically, the Fed Comm included representatives from each Quad to ensure citizens had an equal voice under the Dome, and that the more vulnerable citizens were cared for. After three hundred and eleven years living under Fed Comm rule, however, not a single Domer was surprised when all decrees ultimately benefited the East Quad more – the most spacious, well-resourced Quad under the Dome. East Quadders, Easy Easties, already had more than anyone else, and the Fed Comm's definition of "vulnerable" was notoriously flexible. Corruption was as much a part of Dome life as the humid stench and capricious power grid.

Fed Comm members wrangled endlessly for influence, but everyone knew that The Chair made all the key decisions and had done for decades. The enigmatic force that was The Chair courted obscurity and never spent time in public, which left the separation of fact and fabrication surrounding her difficult to navigate.

The Chair's anonymity is protected by law. Wonder why she worries about people knowing who she really is when she has so much power? Other Fed Comm members trying to kill her and become The Chair? At least I don't need to worry about people trying to assassinate me. I'm already invisible. One day I'll just turn beige and merge into the carpet. No one'll ever see me go. They'll vacuum me up as dust.

She smiled at her fanciful image.

The window glass warmed suddenly, burning against her forehead. Ali leant back and reached up to steady herself on the pane with both hands. The glass under her palms heated. A mottled rainbow texture appeared, spreading beneath them. The window seemed warped, not quite right.

Jeez, what the hell?

She blinked a few times, took her hands from the glass, and shook them. Her fingers were glowing with a ruddy phosphorescence.

This is not happening, not again.

Wait, again? Ali's gift flickered with hazy images. *Where did "again" come from? When has this happened before? That last crazy daydream that's when.*

She shook off the random thoughts to concentrate on her hands. With the glow, she could see right through the machinery of her right middle finger, the one replaced with a cyber unit after her accident at school. The ring on her left hand glowed too, the ruby pulsing like an emergency beacon.

She jerked back. Behind her reflection, the conference room door eased open, outlining a hand and shoulder. Ali turned, stumbled in her high heels, and fell awkwardly to her hands and knees. Her clumsiness saved her life. A flash of silver flew above her head and pinged on the metal window frame behind her.

'What the…' Heart in her mouth, she crawled under her slimline desk.

Damn, I should've kept the ugly, big-arsed metal desk that was here.

Ali peeked up at the image outlined on the window by the soft glow of the com screens. A slight figure dressed in black stepped into the room.

I really wish I had some bloody magic. Then I'd be invisible.

She tried focusing her mind on her belly, the apparent centre of magical energy, according to all her reading and research.

My magic power is invisibility. No one can see me if I don't want them to.

Her belly churned, and her hands began to shake. Her mind registered something familiar about the reflection.

A she?

A memory tugged at her, something about the stance.

Shit, shit, shit! What the Fed's going on?

Ali realised the intruder would soon work out there was only one place she could be.

Why isn't Sophie bloody interrupting now? Ali's personal administration assistant – her addi – had an annoying habit of disturbing Ali at exactly the wrong moment – a lot.

This woman will be on me in a moment to do… whatever she bloody well wants. I'm invisible. I'm invisible. I'm invisible. Her gut flipped, heat churning. Rainbow auras framed her vision and a monster headache loomed.

What in Fed's furry fanny is she doing here? I'm nobody. I'm invisible. None of my work is classified, I'm a glorified project manager – a proji for Fed's sake. Where's my bloody comli? On the desk. Where on the desk? Right-hand side, on the edge.

Ali crept back a little way and raised her hand to sneak her fingers onto the surface.

Bloody hell!

She withdrew her hand as it started to glow again. She took a breath, rested back on her haunches, and shoved her hands into her armpits to hide their light.

I'm invisible. They are not *glowing – that shit is just a dream. There's no such thing as magic. I'm asleep. And if I'm not, I'd like to be invisible.*

Get a grip, birri. Breathe.

She checked her hands. Normal, no glowing, and her ring was just a beautiful, twisted band of gold holding a deep red stone.

See! You did *make the whole thing up. But… just in case.*

She used her tech-ed finger to feel along the desk surface.

If she smashes that, at least it won't hurt. And I've got a spare at home.

The assailant crept further into the room. Ali could see her bottom half from under the desk: soft soled boots, fitted pants, and knees bent, ready to spring. She saw a flash of silver in the woman's gloved hand and her heart lurched.

Ali's finger touched her comli. She eased the slim unit towards the edge until it slid into her sweaty grasp.

Now what? I can't com the Feddies. I'll be dead before they answer. Think, think. You've gotta save yourself, birri.

She clutched the comli to her belly to hide its tell-tale green screen glow. Then she slipped one shoe off, and gathered her limbs into a crouch. Holding her comli close to her chest with her right hand, she poised her thumb to swipe and press. With her left hand, she gripped the shoe and got ready to launch.

You can do this. Come on, you can do it. You can do it. You've got surprise on your side. She surged to her feet behind the desk, throwing her shoe in the opposite direction as a distraction, and swiping the comli's torch on at the same time.

As the assailant shielded her eyes in the spotlight, Ali stepped back further, preparing to make a run for the foyer door. She miscalculated, bumping into the arm of her chair, which unbalanced and fell crashing into the back wall. Another silver flash spun by her head as she staggered. Mouth dry, pulse pounding, gut heaving, she floundered towards the door, expecting pain or worse at any moment.

The door opened before she reached it, a pale hand slipped in and swiped the main light on. Ali wrenched the door wider, and staggered into Sophie's stylish embrace. Ali slammed the door shut behind her with one hand and they fell in a tangle of limbs.

Sophie was too svelte to cushion their fall however, and Ali's breath whooshed out as she banged her right elbow and knee on the hard tiles of the foyer.

'Quick. We've gotta run. Code Black, intruder.'

Sophie rubbed her own elbow where it had hit the floor.

'What? Wait. Are you all right? I heard a crash.'

'Ninja attack, silver thingy.' Ali's words felt all wrong. As if someone else had control of her mouth. Her mind struggled to make sense. Her gift scrambled to catalogue the last few moments, and connecting threads raced across her internal memory display.

Sophie wriggled out from underneath her and stood. She straightened her grey pencil skirt over her slim hips, and raised a delicately drawn eyebrow at the ladder in her stockings – a victim of the fall.

'Come on, we've gotta run!' Adrenaline surged in Ali's system as she staggered upright on shaky legs, still wearing one heel. She couldn't understand why the assassin hadn't already come after her. There was no time to lose. She tried to grab Sophie's arm and drag her towards the stairs.

'Ali Morrow.' Sophie channelled her best teacher's voice and loosened Ali's manic grip. 'No one has been in the office for the last two hours. You must've dozed off again and had a nightmare. It's been a long day, the latest of many. You know you haven't been sleeping well. And you have been having those vivid dreams.' She slipped past Ali, reached for the office door, and disappeared inside.

I should save her. I'm her boss. She's my responsibility. "Watch Out for Your Neighbour" and all.

But all Ali could do was shake and clench her teeth, jamming her knuckles into her mouth, feeling her teeth sharp on her sweaty skin, and tasting her fear. She wanted to run in the other direction, flee for her life, and leave Sophie to her fate.

If the assassin stops to kill her, then I can escape. Ali felt sick at being so gutless. Indecision kept her frozen to the spot, expecting a scream at any moment. With her eyes glued to the door, rainbow sparkles began to crowd her vision.

A trilling female voice hooted with laughter in Ali's head. She clutched her temples. ***You should SO run.*** Impossibly, the voice sliced through her brain like a hot knife.

She's not who you think she is. She'd definitely run if the shoe was on the other foot.

'Who's there?' Ali rasped, fear drying her mouth.

Come on. Did you see what I did there? Shoe on the other foot. You're only wearing one shoe. SHOE-ON-THE-OTHER-FOOT. Surely that's worth a groan at least.

'Who is it? Come out now. This is *not* funny. We're in a Code Black,' Ali couldn't imagine how the voice was in her head.

You know who I am Ali Morrow. That is who you're calling yourself in this incarnation, isn't it Alinta? Invisible, anonymous Proji and Cataloguer Extraordinaire.

The voice continued in a huffy tone. *And that was very funny by the way. I've been practising my comedy routines while I waited for you to come to your senses.*

Ali swivelled, searching the foyer for the owner of the voice.

We don't have time for theatrics. We're close to the century congruence. It's me. Jiemba. I'm through. I'm back. We needed a life-threatening event so I could break through this ridiculous nightmare you call existence.

Ali's gift flashed a picture of a cranky red dragon in her mind. Dragon. Mammoth body, sinuous neck, enormous frilled head, covered in scales, dragon. Dark red threads charged around her gift like lit fuses, blasting holes and breaking connections in her mind's tapestry.

The dragon sat on its massive haunches in the chaos and bared a set of sharp, glistening fangs. It tilted and lowered its head so that Ali got a glimpse of one enormous eye peering at her – from inside her head. Apart from the vertical obsidian pupil, the dragon's eye was like a gigantic opal. The eye drank in light, leaving the smattering of sparkling rainbow flecks a brilliant counterpoint.

Hello breakfast.

Ali shook her head, her heart hammering a ragged tattoo. She must be going mad. The old woman had told her to remember Jiemba. Something about her shadow seemed out of sync and Ali glanced down to see that it had transformed into the shape of an enormous dragon, its head crowned with curled horns.

She dragged her gaze past outstretched wings, taloned forelimbs, and a lashing spiked tail. Its hind legs and enormous feet joined at her very real single shod pair. Her mind threatened to explode.

'No. Absolutely not. There are no such things as dragons.' She barely realised she'd spoken aloud and closed her eyes as an offended huff sounded in her head.

There certainly are such things. And you and I are one. So let's get outta here. The voice turned a little plaintive. *I wanna go Home.*

Ali squeezed her eyes tighter.

Aren't you even a little bit glad to see me? I was only kidding about the breakfast thing. I haven't eaten a human in ages. At least a couple of hours. Kidding. I'm just kidding. I only eat the bad ones. Kidding again. Well, no actually. That bit is true.

Ali put her hands over her ears. 'Not real. Not real. Not real,' she chanted.

Jiemba sulked in the background, mumbling about humour and bad gigs. All of which only upped Ali's panic level. A noise had her whirling as her office door opened and Sophie strolled out, the epitome of composure.

She looks more like a bloody manager than me, all cool and graceful. Ali did not qualify for cool or graceful just now.

'Nothing there but shadows and an over-active imagination. Come on, come and see.' Sophie beckoned her closer.

How can she be braver than me? I've got at least a quarter-century on her, and she's just an addi.

I could've helped you with that. I have enough courage for both of us. And then some.

Sophie's not hearing the voice.

Well, she wouldn't, would she. I'm only in your head.

Ali gulped, swallowing the bile that fear had driven to her throat.

Ugh, that burns. I am so heading to that stress session tonight.

Sophie beckoned again, her lifted eyebrow questioning Ali's hesitation.

Ali approached, limping in her single high heel, and peeked past Sophie's smile. Nothing. No one. She stepped into the small room, getting a whiff of Sophie's citrus perfume and nothing else. She edged past the upended chair, bent and looked under the desk and then over to the floor beside the window.

Nope, no ninja assassin. No silver thingies.

Her body sagged. She ran her fingers through her hair, gathering the soft escapees and tucking them behind her ears.

'What about the conference room? Did you check in there?' Ali asked.

Sophie nodded. 'Nothing.'

'Jeez, I must look like an idiot.'

Sophie patted her shoulder sympathetically.

Can't disagree with you there, Jiemba chuckled.

'Ali, you've been working like a fiend to get this report out. You're exhausted. And you don't eat well. Is it any wonder you're jumping at shadows? Go and save your work and I'll make you a cuppa for the trip home. Time we both left anyway. Federation won't love us if we file for burn out.'

Sophie marched off and Ali listened to her confident clip, clip, clip across the tiles to the kitchen. The sound of the boiling kettle seemed so prosaic to her overwrought senses.

She realised she was standing forlornly in the middle of her office, adrenaline still churning her gut. She took a long, slow, deep breath, remembering her stress relief classes and glanced around.

'Right, nothing to see. You're ridiculously busy, so stressed that even in the daytime you're imagining wandering wild women and nefarious ninja assassins.'

Seriously, why the hell would ninja assassins want to kill me? It's not like I'm anyone important. I'm nothing. I know I'm good at my job, but jeez.

You forgot a dragon talking in your head. Jiemba sounded snarky. Ali ignored her.

'One step at a time,' Ali told herself. *And that one step is to take a bloody holiday. Three weeks at least, disconnected, no tech. A wilderness adventure. That'll de-stress you, old birri. It'd make you feel human, getting back to nature.*

She ignored the flashing warnings in her head about insects and animals, weather, and wilderness. She would prepare as she always did, and nothing would surprise her. She hated surprises. It did feel good to create a time and event, though she had yet to slot it into her schedule anywhere. Her mind filed it under "soon".

I can be myself on a wilderness adventure. She told herself there'd be no need to hold onto her posh City Grid work language. No need to check that every word was polite and FEN-compliant. Now all she had to do was convince her boss that he could spare her, and that the entire project wouldn't collapse without her there to hold it all together.

Who am I kidding? The only thing he'd miss is getting his coffee on time and his ego stroked. He's got plenty of willing minions for that.

Ali retrieved her other shoe – heel still intact – from near the printer in the corner. She swiped off the data systems, and headed for the door with a pile of files. Stuffing the work and her comli into her dillybag, which was already full of the usual personal paraphernalia every Domer needed, she grabbed her coat, and caught a glimpse of her face in the wall mirror.

It's gonna take more than a wilderness adventure to make that *face look relaxed.*

You're telling me, sister.

Black rings darkened her adrenaline-bright eyes. *Maybe I'd prefer normal brown eyes, even though nobody mentions that they're odd.*

It's because you've shielded them. People already think your eyes are brown, the same as almost everyone else in this hellhole.

Ali refused to acknowledge Jiemba's grumbling. She grimaced at her reflection and attempted to smooth her intractable curls into place, making her large, triangular earrings jiggle. Her small personal rebellion to battle the mountains of Federation conformity included non-FEN bling.

Yep, I am such *a rebel. Just an out-of-shape one.* She smoothed her purple shirt over the navy skirt that covered her full hips, sucking in her belly and wishing she were fitter and thinner.

'Holiday. Adventure. Away from work. Outside.'

Thank the Mother, Jiemba snorted.

As she let her belly relax and turned to swipe off the light, a twinkle from the window caught her eye. Her heart gave a double thump. Still she stepped towards the glint. When she moved her head to peer closer, an oily rainbow appeared and disappeared on the surface of the glass.

Magic residue. Yours. The smugness pushed her buttons. Ali couldn't help the sputtered response.

'I don't have magic.'

Ha. Gotcha. Knew you were listening. Though you're right. You don't have magic.

Ali relaxed her tight shoulders.

You are magic.

Ali's shoulders crawled back up to her ears.

'Tea traveller's ready Ali,' Sophie called from the kitchen.

Don't be a stupid proji. No such thing as magic. It's an imperfection in the glass that you haven't noticed before. Nothing in this whole Dome is perfect and new.

Except if you're on the Fed Comm or live in the East Quad.

Ali kept a firm hold of her coat and dillybag and resisted touching the window with her fingers, or acknowledging the snarky voice in her head.

Well, I wouldn't be so snarky if you'd listen to me and get us out of this stifling Dome. Its filters kill magic, Jiemba protested.

Straightening her spine, Ali rested one hand on her belly and tried to practise the grounding stillness thing from stress class. Dadirri the teacher called the technique or going Home.

That's what I need right now, to be going home.

Yeeha Home!

The fragrance of high, cold spaces tickled Ali's nose – along with images of soaring mountains, ragged tors, smooth bluestone walls and the comfortable companionship of peace. She sneezed. Her raging mind refused to contemplate any kind of stillness. She gave up and headed out of the office, thumbing off the light and firmly closing the door.

As Sophie handed her the lidded teacup, she reached to touch Ali's forehead, her silver bracelet flashing in Ali's eyes. Ali flinched away from the contact and Sophie moved closer, her bracelet tinkling.

Don't trust her. Don't let her touch you.

'Let me feel your forehead to make sure you don't have a fever.'

Ali stepped back again, out of reach. A vision of Sophie's hands as claws flashed a warning in her mind.

'Don't baby me, Sophie. I'm fine. I've managed to take care of myself for this long,' Ali grumbled.

Sophie looked miffed.

'Really, Soph. I'm just knackered and a little wrung out. I'll be better after a good sleep.'

Sophie reluctantly dropped her hand, unusually nervous as she fiddled with her bracelet.

Ali forced a smile and softened her voice, 'Come on. We're outta here.' Their building wasn't tall or important enough to warrant a solar-powered lift for all the floors, only the top ten. Climbing the seven flights each morning and descending at night was Ali's only exercise. She waved Sophie to precede her down the stairs, insisting to herself that she would have done that anyway.

Yeah, right.

The malodorous street scents infiltrated the dim stairwell the closer they got to street level. They stopped to insert their nose plugs at the second floor.

As they walked away from the building, the back of Ali's neck prickled, urging her gaze up. She counted the seven rows of windows to find her office, two windows from the front corner. A tightness grabbed her chest. With the level lights off, she couldn't see inside. No smart comments from her dragon friend.

A twitch from Sophie indicated that perfectly raised eyebrow again. Ali shook her head, too tired to make any sense of what had or hadn't happened. Sophie touched her arm, and Ali felt a rush of gratitude for her. She may be just an addi, but she watched out for Ali more than she needed to.

More than I deserve. What would I do without her?

Jiemba's tone was scornful. ***You wouldn't believe me if I told you. Don't trust anyone, especially her.***

Ali gestured Sophie to take the first flocar. Her old lungs could take a few more seconds of rancid air. She swiped her wristcode across the scanner of the next vehicle in line and eased back in the seat. As she reached to take off her nose plugs, Jiemba shouted in her mind.

Leave them in! The chems will shut me out again. And your building is too heavily warded.

Ali removed her nose plugs and took a deep breath as a hiss of anti-odour zeolites freshened the air. Fed Comm insisted that's all they were: air fresheners. Then the flocar joined the serpent of red lights and headed to the outer North Quad suburbs and home.

— — —

The evening settled deep shadows into Ali's office. One shadow detached itself and stepped towards the window, watching the scene below, and watching the women leave. The small, dark figure slipped a black glove from her hand and slid two connected rings onto her fingers from a pocket in her cuff. She attached the silver-and-crystal ensemble to a terminal at her waist and gestured over the rainbow stain. With a rosy glow, the glass was perfect again.

She unfastened her device, replaced her glove, and stepped back into the shadow.

Gatekeeper

When a century is combined
Soul bound seeks the mind
Cross cold and space
And time and place
No barrier to her Grace

Beware the Shayde
The lies that made
The treacherous orphans flee
The Mother's wrath
Armageddon lies in their path

From the oracular records of the Sága Sisterhood –
Mirrabooka, Autumn 3033

Merindah stomped back to her desk and folded her arms. She wanted to share her experience now while it was fresh, not tomorrow. Too much could happen overnight. The breeze from the shore had picked up and begun to blow papers around her desk. Grouching, she went to the window and forced it down, resting her forehead against the cloudy glass.

How will the world ever see me as a world saver if I spend all my time in this musty old lab, dressed like something the cat dragged in?

She tried to straighten her crumpled cream blouse, tsking at the tear and scrubbing at a coffee stain on her green trousers. Perhaps she should switch to wearing the pale blue Order robes like most of her colleagues? But she'd barely passed her exams, and being such a lowly magical practitioner made wearing a mage's uniform feel a little fraudulent. She examined her still-rumpled state.

Ah well, lucky I'm not meeting anyone influential tonight.

Succumbing to her one personal vanity, she pulled her hair clip out to comb her waist-length curls into order, letting the silky auburn strands flow through her fingers. Two pencils rattled onto the wooden floor.

Huh, that's where they got to.

The headache that signalled the payback for using her magic earlier throbbed into existence, with rainbows sparkling at the edge of her vision.

Damn. Why do I get such huge headaches when I have such pathetic magic? It's not fair.

Merindah reached into the pocket of her trousers for her blue pills. She popped one under her tongue and closed her eyes, waiting for the amelioration, and trying to dismiss her childish crankiness.

I'm a different person now. Yeah, that sad, skinny kid became a morose, chubby teenager. But now I'm a joyful, curvy thirty-three year old. Her birthday had come and gone a week ago with no fanfare and zero acknowledgement from her father. She didn't know why she'd imagined he would remember. Her only other immediate family was Nina, and it was unlikely that the anniversary of her birth featured high on her stepmother's list of things to do to achieve world domination.

She eased the tight band of her trousers and sucked in her belly, her mouth twisting wryly.

Who the hell am I kidding? I'm turning into a melancholy, overweight moaner. Maybe the Librarium will turn my body into parchment when I die, and they'll roll it up and catalogue it under U for unknown and useless. If I'd learnt to keep my opinions to myself while some of those blatherskite Major Mages told me their theories, it could've been a whole different story.

Merindah's oft-aired opinions and her willingness to argue for them had put her into more hot water than any other analyst in the history of the Esoteric Cosmology Order. A fact that Yaxa Cody, the Head of the Order, had informed her of last week during one of her semi-regular "chats".

Merindah would have preferred to make her own way through the Librarium hierarchy, but was shackled by her dismal yerlendj. The security of her position hung by a thread. There were only so many times the Head could look the other way – citing her family's generous funding – when irate Mages lined up at Cody's office demanding that Merindah be punished for her insolence, impertinence, presumption, rudeness, or any other flavour of insubordination they could think of.

Despite her run-ins with the academic establishment however, Merindah's expertise was growing. Yet very few people acknowledged her research endeavours.

Even a modicum of personal attention would be nice.

'I can promise you more than a *modicum* if you're willing to take a risk.' Merindah whipped around, almost tripping into a stack of books. A sublime being floated in a rainbow swirl in the centre of the room. As Merindah righted herself, the exquisite creature stepped closer and the mist dissipated.

Her skin was all colours and none. Merindah's brain refused to process the flickering tones until her eyes registered that whoever it was shared the same dark copper shade as her own. Long, black hair dropped in shining waves to the being's waist and sparkled with silver lights. Large, amethyst eyes vibrated with a divine spirituality. Caught in her radiant gaze, Merindah felt as though her every fault was spot lit by brilliant white light.

Surely something so magnificent is more than human. Her mouth hung open. She'd heard of heavenly manifestations, but never spoken to anyone who'd experienced one.

Into the pregnant silence, the goddess – for that *must* be what she was – suddenly laughed, leant forward, and placed a finger under Merindah's chin, gently closing her mouth.

With her laugh, the goddess's other-worldly persona abruptly faded, leaving only her earthy grin, and Merindah's body sagged with relief and a face-cracking smile. The dregs of her headache disappeared with an audible pop. She felt buoyant. She could take on the world and win.

'Why stop at the world? Take on the *Cosmos*. You've got it in you.' The goddess captured her hands and twirled her round in the cramped room. Tingles of energy shot up Merindah's arms from her touch. She watched as a rainbow of aetheric threads danced into her own being, and felt them tickle a knotted nodule near the base of her spine.

Her heart swelled, her aura exploded, and ecstasy beckoned. The music that she usually heard in her head sounded as if it were coming from the Voice. The twirling stopped and Merindah gasped, chest heaving, heart hammering. The goddess was unaffected and stopped dead, her hands on her hips and her huge smile in evidence.

Merindah managed to gasp out, 'Who in the Seven Realms of Heaven are you? Wait, did you read my mind then?'

Two dark eyebrows jiggled suggestively.

'Of course, dear. And your heart and soul. And so can you. You have a veritable throng of talents and enough intelligence and Grace to mistress them all,' the goddess announced.

Completely ignoring Merindah's first question, the goddess's eyes narrowed as she peered at Merindah's belly. Merindah sucked her gut in self-consciously and straightened, nervously tucking her hair behind her ears, and flicking the loose curls back over her shoulders. She wished she'd kept a change of clothes here. What with the tear in her shirt and the stain on her trousers, she wasn't exactly dressed for a spiritual encounter. Her robes would have been more appropriate.

A frown creased the beautiful visage facing her, and Merindah glanced away, her eyes tracing the figure's generous proportions, and her sensual warm energy.

'Mmm. Someone's been messing with your Grace. There's a holding ward. Who thinks they have the right and the power to constrain my Gatekeeper, I wonder?'

At Merindah's puzzled look the goddess's face cleared. 'Never mind that now, dearest. We'll deal with it later. Or it won't matter. Let's focus on one thing at a time.'

Merindah's mind was awash with questions, desperately trying to get a handle on the strange meeting and conversation. Merindah's questions began to tumble out. 'One thing? What One Thing? Who are you? What are you? Am I dreaming? Is this another Seeing? Is it the pills? The headache? How did you get in here anyway? How did you breach my door wards?'

An elegant hand waved her queries away. 'What you should be asking is what can I do for you. I *am* a goddess after all, and I'm in a generous frame of mind,' the goddess said, with a little quiver of excitement.

Merindah took a mental gulp. A feather of fear tickled her yerlendj, but a deeper knowing recognised something familiar about this being. The bubble of laughter, the zing of spirit tickling joy clicked into place.

'I know you.' Merindah narrowed her eyes and let her yerlendj send out a questing thread. The goddess laughed and batted the thread back to its owner.

Merindah's face paled as realisation surfaced. 'I've been hearing you in my head my whole life. You've been on my shoulder, and in my heart.'

The goddess stilled, her smile beneficent.

The presence Merindah spoke of had often been her only playmate in a world of few children, and she'd simply called it the "Voice".

Her mother had indulged this imaginary friend, but worried when the Voice was still keeping her company at twelve. After multiple visits to medicos, mages, and shamans, Merindah had simply stopped speaking about the Voice, and so her mother's worries had moved on to her own health.

But the Voice hadn't gone away. It had been there during her mother's illness and death. There on the lonely nights when Merindah had cried herself to sleep, her father far away. Over the past two decades though, the Voice had become an inconsistent friend, its visits briefer and further apart. She'd thought perhaps she was finally growing up.

'You're the Voice. You're real. Are you? It's not the pills?' The Voice was real. The Voice had always believed in her. The Voice had said she had a throng of talents.

A goddess has been keeping me company. Merindah fell to her knees and lowered her head to the floor, humbled by the goddess's generosity. The Voice assisted her back to her feet and gently kissed her, first on one cheek, then the other.

'You are one of my Chosen. Always have been, always will be. Never forget that. Whenever you doubt yourself, I am only ever a prayer away.'

Merindah's eyes misted, and her face ached with joy. 'Then why have you been so distant these past few years? I've missed you.' At the pained look on the goddess's face Merindah's cheeks flamed, and she covered her mouth with a hand.

'Oh. I am so sorry. I didn't mean to accuse you of anything. I'm sure you're busy with divine duties and didn't have time for all my little tears.' Her eyes widened as she realised she was making it worse. She clapped both hands over her mouth.

'It's become harder to visit as you've grown. Children are more open to Seeing than adults: scepticism erects barriers in minds and hearts. And I suspect whoever's been messing with your Grace has also been messing with your faith,' the goddess explained. 'Let's see what we can do about both.'

She rescued Merindah's hands from her mouth, and Merindah shook her head and stepped back.

'Wait. What do you mean my Grace? And did I hear you say Chosen as in the Chosen in the Yarran Prophecy? Which goddess are you?'

'Now dearest, I have a bit of catching up to do, so I'll keep it brief. On this world I believe you call your Grace "yerlendj". Your Grace exists at the pleasure of the Cosmic Mother. Yerlendj, meaning innate wisdom, is accurate; but Grace is closer to what the Mother intended, and I should know,' she smirked.

When Merindah's perplexed look continued, the goddess went on. 'As for Chosen, here's your opportunity. Are you ready to hear what I can do for you?'

Ignoring the unearthly nature of the moment, Merindah felt ambition win out over caution. She nodded, and her mind raced to catch up to her emotions. 'This is so freaky. I have a bucket load of questions, but fine. Let's start with what can you do for me.'

The Voice clapped her hands. Aetheric threads burst into a delightful tinkling melody, and danced around her head like a cloud of angels.

'Good woman.' Then her face stilled. 'How much would you risk to save your world and the Cosmos? I've grown fond of it, and I'd rather not have to start again so soon. It messes with my Grand Plan.'

Merindah's mouth dropped open and her gut plummeted. With shaking legs she dropped to her knees again, her hands slapped onto the timber, drawing on their strength. The Voice knelt beside her on the floor, swathes of soft violet material settled in waves around her. She rested a hand on Merindah's head, and Merindah slowly raised her eyes to meet the goddess's depthless gaze.

'You know I'd give anything. Everything. It's what I dream of doing every moment of the day,' Merindah whispered. But with her dream suddenly in reach, her courage deserted her, fear taking its place. She broke into a sweat and began to shake.

This can't be real. My magic barely lights a candle. All I have is ambition and opinion. How can I save the Cosmos with that?'

'Do I have it in me to save the Cosmos?' She searched the wise eyes before her.

'Yes, you do.' The goddess held a finger to Merindah's trembling lips to hold in her next question. 'Because you and I are one and the same. You are a Divine being, a child born from the womb of the Cosmic Mother. You are special. You are Chosen. You are Armageddon's Gatekeeper. And it's time to come Home.'

Merindah's dry mouth failed to form any of the protests that whirled around her brain.

Home. With that word, Merindah was swept up into a fragrance that smelt like a thousand flowers blooming.

How? How is this happening? How can I save the Cosmos?

The Voice responded to her thoughts. 'The question isn't how, it's *why*. You have a brilliant analytical mind. Begin by asking *why* this is happening now. *Why* do you have what it takes to save the Cosmos? *Why* are you the Gatekeeper? *Why* do you exist? *Why* do you think, feel, do, and believe?

'I wish I could give you time to go deep, way past the ambition and the vengeance, but my plan is a little awry, and the century's convergence approaches. Just keep asking why. Your curiosity will lead you to clarity. Your reflection will take you to the right action.'

The goddess's exuberance muted with sorrow, the aetheric threads around her dropped to a subdued murmur.

'Your road Home will be fraught, child. Your choices will not be simple. The quest will ask more of you, and of any who aid you, than any one soul should be asked to bear.'

She leant forward and wrapped her arms around Merindah. The hug felt like heaven ought to be, warm, generous, and loving. Every cell in Merindah's body hummed in incandescent joy, all except a blob of clanging grey shackled deep in her belly that rebuffed the love. The discord slipped into the background as her beloved Voice eased back, running a soft hand down Merindah's tear-streaked cheek.

'You won't be alone. Armageddon needs a Key and Fire too. I believe you met them both just a little while ago.'

Merindah's eyes widened and the goddess nodded.

'You'll find unexpected friends and allies to help you battle the villains and ogres along the way. Trust in yourself to know the difference. I believe in you.' The Voice stood and tugged Merindah to her feet.

'Are you ready? Will you do whatever it takes?' she asked, compassion and a universe of hope in her amethyst eyes.

Merindah stood at the precipice, a chasm of possibility and pain opening before her. She scrubbed the tears from her face, and inhaled a deep breath, absorbing the glorious scent of the goddess.

'I'm ready.'

Tears glistened in the Voice's eyes. Relief flashed before her smile broke out again. 'Thank you, my darling woman. We are all in your debt.' She slipped a silver chain from around her neck, then opened her hand to show Merindah an amulet of black opal wrapped in twisted silver. It looked like a world held in the branches of the Aether Tree. Rainbows sparkled at the inclusions and reflected in the goddess's eyes as she tilted it to catch the light.

'It's beautiful. It's like an ocean of rainbow stars.'

The Voice placed the amulet around Merindah's neck, and Merindah lifted the stone, feeling it warm her hand. As she gazed into the gem, she felt herself falling.

The Voice covered the amulet and drew Merindah's gaze to hers. 'Don't stare into it until you're stronger. You'll understand it more soon. Now I need to remove that gate on your power. Let Sister Shayde beware.' The Voice touched one finger to Merindah's forehead over her third eye and Merindah felt her eyelids drift closed.

'Because of that constraint on your Grace, it will be better for this memory and your power to trickle out slowly over a few days. This will keep those who would hinder you unaware of your quest until you're ready to step into your destiny. When the time is right, you'll remember. Trust yourself. You are magnificent.'

One rainbow thread slipped into Merindah's mind, coiling around her memory; and a second slipped into her belly to encapsulate the grey sludge.

The Voice peered at the sludge and murmured, 'Quite expertly done, dear Sister. Had I not come myself, this might not have been detected until it was too late. But alas for you, she is no longer bound. This will be an unveiling to rock the halls of the Seven Realms to their very foundation.'

The Voice kissed Merindah's closed eyes and vanished.

Plans

Ali switched her dillybag to the other shoulder so she could jiggle the key in the front door. The thumb scanner had stopped working a couple of months ago, and the building manager hadn't seen fit to prioritise her safety and privacy with a repair.

So much for Watching Out for Your Neighbours.

Luckily, it was an old building and still had actual keys. Once inside, she threw her dillybag under the small side-table and picked up an Outside Trek brochure from the floor. Ali slammed the door, locked it, dropped her keys and the brochure on the entry table. She rested her head back against the hard surface. Shoes kicked off, nose plugs out, she breathed deeply, picking up a faint whiff of lavender – her go-to fragrance for keeping Dome odours at a bearable level. Even though it was also manufactured, it was better than sewerage and sweat.

She could've taken her plugs out in the building's enclosed foyer, but her hands were full of files and the warning of that ridiculous voice in her head poked her stubbornness button. She would *not* be dictated to by an imaginary dragon. Enough people told her what to do already. Like taking work home to finish.

Just a few files to get a head start on tomorrow. She shook herself and took another deep breath, massaging the back of her neck with one hand and flicking out her earrings with the other. Travelling the streets this late was risky, especially to her suburb of Vale, and her neck was tighter than a drum. Her flat in the North Quad bordered with the West; and the Nutbag North and the Wild West were a deadly combination for nocturnal violence and crime.

Maybe it's time to apply for a new place further east. Who am I kidding? A single woman my age with no children is never gunna get into the East Quad.

The Easy East, gated, secure and exclusively for people with a higher tally than Ali and her whole building put together. South Quad held most of the Dome's essential services and small living enclaves for professionals: health centres, schools, industry, defence, water, science, technology, and the flocar network grid control. Flocars weren't immune to carjackers though, despite what the Fed Comm decreed.

So for Ali, the last few klicks were always a hairy ride of watching for danger, her finger on her comli's emergency code. Everybody knew dissidents met at night when the street cams were less able to make out faces – or were even turned off in certain suburbs to save power, assuming they'd been working in the first place.

So many things were in a state of disrepair that it was a wonder they had lights at all. Brownouts were way too regular, and last month a blackout had grounded the entire flocar system for twenty-four hours. Underground news hinted at a complete breakdown of the Dome in the near future, which was vehemently denied by the Fed Comm.

Of course few of her precautions would be necessary if she'd just left the City Grid at a reasonable hour. Too much work made that deadline fly by. Or she could use the Fed-funded flobus which came with armed Feddies. It was the plain-clothed Grey Shirts who rode the bus, always on the lookout for anti-Fed activity, that made her avoid those.

Ali sighed, untucked her pale pink shirt and undid the band on her skirt. Hands on hips she surveyed her domain: a single living room and bedroom combined – a studio if you believed the building brochure.

Any excuse to squeeze another person into an itsy-bitsy space. At least the air filter works... mostly. She flapped her hands in front of her face to move the sticky air. Summer in the Dome hovered between uncomfortable mugginess and sweltering heat. Though her building at work was comfortably cooled, Ali's room lacked a cooling unit, even if she'd had the tally to keep it running. Autumn couldn't come soon enough.

Despite Ali having moved in eight years ago, the room held an impermanent feel. One of the faded beige walls held three small prints of Domer life – nailed on to make sure renters didn't *accidentally* pack them when they were reallocated. *You'd have to be pretty desperate to take them.* Her glance took in her three-seater couch that transformed into a sofa bed, a linen cupboard and a desk that accounted for the living room. A tiny, round table and two ladder-back chairs with the fridge, sink, ration re-cycler and bench pretended to be a kitchenette. She never cooked. In the lives of most Domers, cooking was an anachronism. Ali didn't possess the black-market connections for the scant fresh produce anyway, so re-heated rations were her staple. Her miniscule bathroom closet was at least behind a closing door. There were no personal photos, no personal effects. She'd just never got around to it

Who would I have a photo of anyway?

Ali was close to very few people. She never seemed able to hang on to a friend for long, let alone an intimate partner. Emotion detracted people from *Minding Their Own Business* or from *Watching Out for Their Neighbours*. Grey Shirts jumped on anger and rage in particular, but tended to view even joy and affection askance. Basically, the Federation frowned on strong emotions.

Hundreds of years ago in a bizarre attempt to reduce street violence, they'd outlawed PDAs – public displays of affection. The logic was laid out in the Fifth Tenet, which blathered on about the dangers of uncontrolled emotion, but was most often shortened to *"Control Yourself"*. Consequently, Domers tended to play their emotional cards close to their chests. They weren't encouraged to be demonstrative or creative. And so everything in her flat was basic, functional, and practical.

Just like me.

Jeez, stop being so maudlin, birri. It's just a place to lay your head and feed your belly so you can get up and do it all again tomorrow.

Maybe after this project is finished, I'll have time to find a nice picture for the wall, or even draw one myself.

After downing a heated ration with a cup of tea, Ali unfolded her sofa bed and dragged the blankets from the linen cupboard. As she reached to turn off the lights by the front door, the brochure caught her eye. She shook her head, smiling, and picked it up. Andie must have slipped it under her door – she'd been encouraging Ali to take a real break for months.

With a sigh, Ali settled into her lumpy bed. The strange events, or non-events, from earlier in the day replayed themselves in her head. While she contemplated, her right hand performed its habitual flick, flick, flick of her ruby ring. She stopped flicking when the ruby was uppermost, and polished the gem on her camisole. She examined her hands, remembering their strange reddish glow. All perfectly normal now.

Glowing fingers seems to be a recurring theme in my dreams. Why? And why do those dreams feel more and more real? That white-haired birri, Dee, I could see the dust on her shadow-blue face.

She sighed again and smoothed the crumpled brochure on her knee. It outlined an Outside Trek to a temple ruin a few weeks' walk from the Dome. The cost was reasonable – she could afford the deduction from her tally. Surely work could manage without her for a few weeks at least. Her boss Geoff had been nagging her to take a break. Her mind skittered away from the reason he'd begun to insist.

Well he shouldn't give me so much work if he wants me to take a break. He can't have it both ways.

Ali went back to reading the brochure. The isolation it promised sounded fantastic. Even now, in the quiet of the late hour, she could hear the buzz of the Dome: people, machines, filters, and the usual white noise of thousands of people living in each other's pockets.

What would it really be like Outside? Would it smell and feel and look like my dream?

The dragon voice had urged her to go out. Maybe listening to that voice *was* a good idea. She might find some answers to the gaps in her memories. It might also prove whether or not the Dome and the Federation were messing with her gift.

It couldn't hurt to go on this guided trek could it? Surely all the warnings about people-eating fauna and poisonous flora were over-dramatised. Ali resolved to do some investigating of the trek and the ruins tomorrow.

As she hovered on the border of sleep, it occurred to her that the buzzing she'd heard in her daydream could've been the drone of hundreds of dangerous insects.

She slept and dreamed.

Plots

From Devotees of Sister Diligence –
the Acolyte Journals, Geboor Temple

The Voice, in the form of the goddess Hecate, reappeared on the roof of Geboor's Ivory Tower. She drew a thread of darkness around herself, muting her divine luminescence. A subdued glimmer of her light illuminated the open circular space. A large ginger cat stalked from the shadows to her dimly glowing feet, then circumnavigated her ankles twice, sniffing at the hem of her gown.

Satisfied, it leaped onto a crumbling crenellation that bordered the parapet wall. The feline also circled the crumbling stone twice, ignoring the dizzying drop to the jagged rocks below, and finally settled on her haunches facing Hecate. She wrapped her tail neatly around her front paws and yawned, displaying a set of sharp, white teeth and a pale pink tongue. The goddess gave an exasperated sigh, hands on hips.

'Are you done playing cat, Justice? Armageddon is coming after all.' A twitch of the banded tail was the only response. That's if she didn't count a topaz-eyed stare that could flay skin from bone.

'Time to reset. My absence these past decades has put our plans for this world out of sync. My sister has had the temerity to put a block on my Chosen's magic. That is *not* watching out for her as I requested. My

Grand Plan is in shambles. I'd hoped this Chosen would have a decade of magical experience under her belt, and significant influence with the Portal Collaboratives and the World Council. Instead, she's a frustrated novice mage full of unproven theories and dreams. She's not ready for what lies ahead. It's too much to ask of her.'

The goddess began to pace, the diameter of the small tower allowing half a dozen steps before each turn. The cat observed the threads of energy swirl in agitation around Hecate's head. As the sky darkened, the threads brightened, dancing like fireflies.

The cat had to bridle her feline twitch, which longed to chase and catch the lights.

The goddess ceased her pacing, gazing into the velvet night. She didn't see the smattering of stars emerge above her or the tide smoothing the silver sands below. She sighed, resting her hands on the dusty wall, still warm from the day's heat.

'I suspect that my years of distraction may have been a little too convenient for my sister – and possibly a few other more nefariously inclined Seven Realms denizens.'

'And what a lovely distraction he was, Dark Lady.' Justice purred. Her tone was droll with a just a hint of sarcasm. 'I didn't see you in any great hurry to get back here. You took your finger off the pulse. I did warn you it was not the time for self-indulgence.'

Justice began a calm wash of a paw with her pink tongue. Hecate remained silent, contemplating the subject of the distraction. Her cheeks heated, and a tingle began in her lower belly. She had lingered long past when she should have left. Justice stopped licking her fur and glared her annoyance.

Hecate shook off her memories and stepped back. Her flowing gown transformed into slick black armour, leather straps crossing her chest, and silver-embossed vambraces and greaves appeared on her arms and legs. She held out her left hand and gestured to retrieve her staff from the pocket of Shayde where she'd concealed it.

It was smooth, round, and solid to shoulder height, and then – like an arthritic hand – it twisted to form an empty, five-fingered cage. The wood was yellowed with age, the iron-shod heel dark and pocked. Her other hand gestured, and her bow and quiver appeared. She attached the quiver and slung the bow over her shoulder. With her weapons in place she took a deep breath and turned to Justice, her voice deeper, firmer. 'Well old friend, what did you learn?'

'I wondered when you were going to remember my incomparable information gathering skills. Humans are such imbeciles when it comes to cute kitties.'

'No one who knows your reputation would dare call you a cute kitty to your face. I'm surprised you tolerated it even in *that* form,' Hecate laughed.

'Needs must,' Justice completed her grooming and stepped off her platform. Before she reached the ground, a massive, silver-ruffed wolf *shimmered* in her place. She padded to stand before Hecate, her eyes level with the goddess.

'There are more players in this game than you could possibly imagine. It's a veritable smorgasbord out there. Seems someone's sister has been busy blabbing about the impending prophecy. Rather than Heavens Gate being a little backwater planet dying its due death and hiding your Chosen, it's become supernatural central. Factions and forces are gathering from every corner of the Cosmos, their hands ready to roll the dice – and the fate of the Comos is the winner's prize.'

Hecate's face paled. 'Tell me.'

'Let's retire to somewhere with a little more privacy and a few less ears,' the wolf suggested.

Hecate's nod was grim. She drew a doorway with her staff, and a lantern-lit room appeared. She gestured the wolf through, but before she moved, the wolf asked, 'And what of the dragon? I sensed only a single heartbeat.'

Hecate's eyes slid to the empty cage of her staff. 'There was no dragon.'

The wolf shook itself and trotted through the opening. Hecate stepped over the threshold and the door closed to a vertical black line behind her, the line narrowed to a single bright point before it disappeared.

– – –

A greater sooty owl ruffled its grey-spotted feathers and shifted on its perch in the shadows. Its four raptor talons clicking softly on the stair rail leading from the Tower roof to the floors below.

A brown mouse, halfway across the rooftop, froze at the sound, its nocturnal quest for insects forgotten.

The owl's head swivelled. Dark-ringed black eyes in its silver, heart-shaped face considered the petrified rodent for a heartbeat before launching into the night. Its powerful wings silently caught a thread of air and it soared towards the mountain fortress and its divine mistress.

Currency

Influence = the ability to change the way people think, feel, and behave for the benefit of both parties.
Manipulation = the ability to change the way people think, feel, and behave for the benefit of yourself.
The methodology is the same – the intent is what counts.

From the Journals of Yaxa Cody,
Former Mistress Esoteric Cosmology, Geboor, Thoughts on
Librarium Leadership – the Early Years

Merindah's awareness bubbled to the surface. She was standing amongst her scattered books and papers, staring at the crowded evidence of her research endeavours on the curved white wall. The Librarium's Ivory Tower possessed an elementary sentience, and the walls glowed faintly when living beings were close. Tonight, the walls had chosen murky, rather than illuminating light. A faint floral fragrance clung to the air, like warm sunshine on spring blooms.

Damn I must be more tired than I thought. Now I'm dead asleep on my feet. What was I doing? What was I thinking? Something about those useless fat toads on the desk.

Merindah ran her hands through her curls, drawing them back from her face into a loose braid.

At least these latest analyses gave her doctorate grist for the mill. Though her postgraduate paper was advancing at a snail's pace, her optimistic ambition let her visualise her future clearly. She'd present her research to the full faculty first, taking in their amazed and deserved congratulations in the exclusive Chancellor's Gallery. Then she'd deliver an inspirational speech as the saviour of the world to adoring thousands at a global conference in the city's famous Apex Amphitheatre. People would flock to Geboor from all over Heavens Gate to hear her orate.

She raised her arms above her head – grinning at the thunderous applause, inhaling the heady perfume of the bouquets flung onto the stage, basking in the sunshine of their adoration – and practised her humble bow. And then, best of all, she had a solo meeting with the esteemed World Council Portal Authority, leaving a glowering Nina outside the renowned red doors of the Council Chamber.

Note to self: Prepare dot points for Portal Authority funding request.

Greatly heartened, she rubbed her fingers on her temples again, but resisted using magic as a shadow of an ache whispered into being. A sparkle caught her eye, and she inspected the ring on her left hand. Besides her memories, it was the only thing of her birth mother's that she could call her own. Not particularly precious, it was just an old-fashioned twisted gold setting that clasped a heptagonal cut aquamarine.

Just precious to me.

Even eighteen years after her birth mother's death, thoughts of the woman tightened her throat and made her blink away tears. She'd been so young when her mother had first become ill. Her father replaced her mother as a global transport mogul and Merchant Councillor with unexpected alacrity. The role kept him away travelling and politicking for most of the year. He was one of only a handful of men in a senior leadership role, so couldn't take his attention away from the business for long. People just didn't trust that he could do the job as well as a woman could, and he was rapaciously determined to prove them wrong. At least, that's what he told his daughter on his infrequent visits home.

It fell to twelve-year-old Merindah to put her aetheric studies on hold and nurse her mother through three years of a wasting disease until the final tragic release.

She'd had help in the beginning: the medicos, mages and healers were so optimistic, especially with her family's money smoothing the path. But with no improvement in sight, all bar Mietta – a spiritual healer – had drifted away, leaving her to wash and feed and care for her mother until the bitter end. And even Mietta had disappeared after that.

Just the memory brought an olfactory overload of her mother's rotting flesh flooding to her senses. She slammed the door on her recollections. Those days had changed her, aged her. They'd taught her lessons about life that children weren't meant to learn. She'd reflected more and more of late on how that tragedy had shaped the woman she was now. She was tougher, more ambitious, and more fiercely determined to make the world better for all (and to do what *she* wanted to do), no matter what.

Huh, how's that working out for you? Tiny lab, lowest role in the Librarium, wicked stepmother, no life partner, no prospects, zilch.

At the word prospects, her head throbbed, as though ambition pounded against her brain seeking escape. An image flashed into her mind – a pair of amethyst eyes, a warm hug, and a floral perfume. Her headache hammered again, and the sensations faded.

I don't need another payback headache today. What I need is to find a key to the Portal.

She sighed, and her eyes randomly tracked one coloured strand after another across the cobweb of research, catching on the new sheets from her Seeing. Her vision unfocused; and in the blur, she glimpsed a face in the threads with amethyst eyes that stared at her. Lost in her daydreams, she dismissed the sharp knocks on her door. And when a petite, red-haired woman stepped into her line of sight, Merindah jumped.

'Holy Hecate, Bridget, you scared the life out of me! Sheesh, I need to ramp up those wards. You're the second person that's beaten them today.' Her best friend laughed, grey eyes crinkling in her red-skinned face.

'Ha, you were daydreaming again, Merindah Nightshayde. You'll never save the world if you spend all day dreaming. And you'll ruin your eyes, working in this light.' Bridget flicked on the overhead lights and turned to examine her friend. Her scrutiny took in Merindah's rumpled clothes, dusty, ink-stained fingers, and bare feet.

She shook her head, her short red curls bouncing.

'Merindah you are a rare gem, an extraordinary package of beauty, brains, and – when you remember the rest of the world – compassion.' Bridget continued to expound Merinda's virtues. 'Some might say a goddess accidentally fallen to an earthly existence amongst us mere mortals.'

Merindah, who had begun to protest at the compliment, twitched at the word goddess. Before she could follow the thought, Bridget chuckled. 'And like any goddess, you have your shortcomings. We'll begin with impatient, stubborn and oddly forgetful to name a few.'

The two women had been friends since childhood, and despite their vastly different gene scans, the friendship survived. It was unusual but not unheard of for people from different social scales on Heavens Gate to mix. Merindah occasionally felt Bridget was offering more than friendship these past few years, but her future did not include life-partnering a lowly midwife. Especially one as nosy and nagging as Bridget. Ambition and knowledge were Merindah's lovers; and though they'd disappointed her time and again, Bridget's affection remained nothing more than a bastion of comfortable, uncomplicated friendship.

'Who was the other?' Bridget asked.

'The other?' Merindah's thoughts were still jumbled around the word "goddess" and whether she should scold Bridget for her teasing.

'The other person that wandered through your door wards today,' Bridget prompted.

Even Merindah's basic mage skills allowed her to form door protection wards. No one should get through them without her express permission.

Merindah hesitated. *Who* was *the other?*

A warning sounded in her mind, and she reached for the memory.

Weird. I remember they surprised me. But was it a good surprise?

A flare of rainbow gleamed in her mind. A spark of warm joy and excitement.

'Well? Who was it?' Bridget asked as Merindah's smile broadened. 'Come on. Share! You don't get so many visitors that you'd forget one of them.'

Bridget was right. These days, Merindah rarely thought about anything beyond her research and she should have remembered a visitor. Then again, maybe not so surprising that she'd forgotten a person. She was great at artefacts but terrible with people. They always wanted something from her and were always way more complex than they had a need to be. Artefacts were much simpler to deal with; they didn't have messy feelings. Like Bridget.

Who knows if her sunny disposition hides a slew of dark secrets. Why does she put up with me anyway? I'm such a poor friend. I'd have ditched me long ago.

Merindah's memory of the pleasurable feeling faded, leaving an undercurrent of anxiety, a yearning. Her yerlendj stirred.

'They've slipped my mind, that's all. Anyway, I wasn't daydreaming, I was thinking about my Mum.'

It was close to the truth. She *had* been thinking about her mother earlier.

But was it before the last visitor, whoever they were?

Merindah's eyes glistened. She rubbed her thumb over the aquamarine. When her mother's beautiful hands had shrunk with disease, she'd insisted Merindah wear the ring for her.

Bridget's expression softened and she wrapped her arms around her friend. Her shorter stature meant her head rested on Merindah's breasts. She bounced her head up and down. 'Ah, so much lovely bosom. You could feed a hundred children.'

She threw back her head, giggling at Merindah's exasperated snort as she pushed her away.

'Where did you get that?' Bridget asked, plonking herself on Merindah's chair and scooting in to rustle among the disorganised chaos on the desk.

'Get what?' Merindah straightened her shirt.

'The amulet. I haven't seen it before. Did your visitor give it to you? Was it your mother's? Is it a family heirloom?' Bridget's queries sounded more like an interrogation.

'Talk about twenty questions. You are always *such* a sticky beak.' Merindah was used to Bridget wanting to know everything about her life, and often accommodated her. Tonight, however, she didn't. She had no idea where the amulet had come from. It felt familiar when she held it in her hand. She was about to examine it more closely, when Bridget picked up the tattered tome Merindah had been reading earlier and flicked through its crackling pages.

'Come on, cheer up. You might meet your perfect match tonight. You know there'll be a queue of suitors who want to make babies with you.'

Merindah plucked the book away, shifting papers and priceless artefacts to somewhere beyond Bridget's restless hands. The perfect match and parade implication went straight through her radar without a blip. Her workspace may have seemed messy, but she knew where every single item was, including the vase of flowers with the stinky water.

Ugh! I need to chuck that out.

'There are no sweets hidden on my desk, and you've got to have another topic of conversation besides babies. Some women have better things to do than to reproduce mewling offspring. Anyway, what Council in their right mind would want me conceiving?'

As Bridget began to splutter a response, Merindah planted her hands on her ample hips. 'I'm way past prime impregnating age, with a minuscule yerlendj, and I've got a family history of wasting disease. Highly unlikely to qualify for reproductive coupling.'

Bridget jumped up to match Merindah's stance. 'Babies are the most important thing in the world. They're our future, after all.'

'It's not much of a future. A worn out world, sixty-six years of indentured posturing, and then death.' Merindah's smirk was like a red rag to a bull.

Bridget grabbed onto the rag – as Merindah had known she would – and continued, 'You could still be eligible! You don't know what's in your genes until they're scanned for the parenting contract. And there's plenty of life in this old dust ball yet.'

Merindah could see Bridget gearing up to pontificate on the joys of babies and biology, and held up her hands in mock surrender. 'Fine. Fine. I give in.'

Her friend settled back smugly on the chair, planted her clog-shod feet on the desk, and grabbed the slim, red journal. Merindah shifted Bridget's clogs back to the floor, rescued the journal and brushed imaginary dust from her worktop.

Bridget playfully snatched the book back from her hand as a knock at the door interrupted their exchange. 'A veritable parade of visitors today,' she said.

Merindah rolled her eyes, stalked over, and jerked open the door. The most unctuous occultist in the Librarium, nicknamed Boris the Bore, took a step back from the opening. She had to stop herself from closing the door without speaking to him. She was within her rights. It was her lab after all, and he couldn't enter without her permission.

She took a calming breath. Boris's verbal repertoire bordered on the inane, and his social skills were worse than hers. He was the perfect stereotype for why men should be kept in the fields. She had no idea why her stepmother kept him around. And it was his association with Nina that stayed her hand from closing the door again.

He must have redemptive political connections or money. It couldn't possibly be sexual prowess. Merindah shuddered at the thought of his greasy hair in an intimate embrace. She generally gave most men the benefit of the doubt, but she'd yet to find anything redeeming about Boris.

Men in the Librarium are such a waste of time and space.

A strained silence grew. As a woman and the lab occupant, it was her right to wait for him to declare what he wanted. And as a male, courtesy dictated he declare his purpose first. If he did not, she was within her rights to report his breach to the Librarium's Etiquette Governance Committee. She held her hand on the door, prepared to slam it in his reptilian face at the first breach of propriety. His eyes, which should have reflected obsequiousness, leered instead, his tongue darting out to run over a thin lower lip.

'Mistress Nightshayde. Greetings from your most esteemed Mother.' He gave a short nod, just inside the boundaries of deferential.

'Stepmother,' Merindah corrected.

'Greetings from Chief Occultist Nightshayde,' Boris glanced directly into her eyes with a flash of anger. She nodded, satisfied that he'd noted the reprimand. If he looked at her directly again, she would report him. Men needed to know their place. It was for their own good.

'A delivery of artefacts from the West was erroneously addressed and delivered to you by mistake. You are hereby ordered to immediately surrender said artefacts to the Occultology Order for authentic and proper examination.'

Merindah felt the smirk in his lowered gaze.

Damn, they didn't mean to send them to me at all. Another freaky typo? Her sharp demand echoed with disappointment.

'Paperwork!'

Boris handed her the requisite forms, in triplicate. She speed read the formal wordage.

Double damn.

'I'll have them sent over tomorrow.' The little man wrung his hands anxiously, his gaze twitching between her face and the floor.

'Your pardon, Mage Nightshayde, but I'm instructed by Chief Occultist Nightshayde to retrieve them now, and to wait as long as necessary until you transfer them.' Merindah's heart sank. *So much for a last-ditch all-nighter.* If Nina wanted these, then Merindah had considered it worth racing through the artefacts one more time.

'Wait here,' she instructed.

Merindah closed the door firmly, returned to her desk and gathered the volumes from under the scattered papers. Her lips were a thin line as she slipped the books into the padded delivery satchel they'd come in and marched back to the door. Bridget wisely remained silent. When Merindah opened the door again, her disapproving glare was enough to make Boris squirm, his lank brown hair jiggling over his narrow face as he returned his eyes to the floor.

'Here, take them. I warn you to be careful. They're priceless. If they arrive damaged, more than your career will be forfeit.' Merindah thrust the parcel into Boris's hands. She shut the door firmly in his horrified face before he could say another word.

'Dammit, just when I thought I'd caught a break, Miss Magic Pants shows up and steals my chance,' Merindah groaned.

Bridget knew exactly who she was speaking about. 'Why do you let Nina get to you? You're just as good as she is. Better. You could've said no. We are all equal under Heavens Gate,' Bridget recited the common codex at her.

'Ha. All equal, except those that are more equal than the rest of us,' Merindah fumed.

Bridget laughed, watching as Merindah grumbled and flounced up and down the small space.

'And I shouldn't let her get to me, I know. I just need one little break,' Merindah's last comment was a whisper, filled with longing. She stared at her curved wall, following the coloured threads from image to page to chart and back.

'What about this?' Bridget asked, waving the slim journal at her.

Merindah's eyes followed the journal and ignored the swirl of guilt at keeping the book.

It was an honest omission, really. I'll send it over tomorrow or the next day.

'Looks more like a diary than an ancient artefact.' Merindah took the book and flicked off the band holding it closed. She'd found it tucked in the bottom of the delivery satchel, although it hadn't been listed on the consignment sheet. This fact alone argued that she didn't need to send it to the Chief Occultist anyway.

She'd initially presumed the journal belonged to a dig worker from the temple and had been included accidentally. She retraced the three conjoined glyphs on the dark red cover with her index finger. Nothing.

She flipped it open. Almost every page was covered in precise cursive script. The layout of the pages with numeric type headings suggested it was probably a diary, but the language was like nothing she'd ever read before. Some sort of secret shorthand language with neat pictographs randomly interspersed. She ran her finger across the horizontal lines trying to pick out the meaning. An occasional word was familiar, but the rest was gobbledygook.

'Ahem,' Bridget reminded her, not so subtly.

Merindah turned, smiling an apology. 'Oh Bridge, I'm sorry. You know how much I want to crack this. I'd do anything. It's all I can think about at the moment.'

'Merindah, you and ninety percent of the world are obsessed with opening the Portals. The other ten percent is making sure there's food on the table and power in the grids, so the Ivory Tower Brigade doesn't waste away in the dark, still planning to save the Cosmos.'

'Save the Cosmos.' The words brought a copper-skinned face to mind, adding to the mesmerising pair of amethyst eyes she kept seeing. Dark hair. Powerful.

'Ahem,' Bridget coughed again, bringing Merindah's focus back.

'Sorry, sorry. Now what brings you to my Ivory Tower at this time of night?' She tucked the slim volume onto a shelf between Hogan's Historic Horoscopes and a tattered edition of Advanced Quantum Mechanics by Bridie Bird. 'Shouldn't you be preparing for a celebratory weekend eve assignation tonight?' She smiled at Bridget.

Her friend's dark grey eyes were solemn, and she shook her head, both eyebrows raised in exasperation at Merindah's puzzled look. She stood before Merindah, hands on hips, radiating bossiness.

'I knew you'd forget. Merindah, you've got to get some political savvy, or you'll spend the rest of your days in this room, or worse. You'll be put out into the fields with the men. Contrary to what you think, wisdom is *not* the real currency in this world. Influence trumps knowledge every time.

'You know Nina's trying to find ways to get you out of the Librarium. In ways I can't fathom given your incy-wincy power, you threaten her. She wants you out of sight, out of mind, and out of inheritance.'

Realisation hit Merindah like a tonne of bricks. 'Oh Holy Hecate! The soirée! I'm going to be so late. You've got to help me,' she squeaked.

Her family and her place in the Librarium, low though it was, meant she registered on the political radar as an asset. So she was frequently courted by social climbing matriarchs who wanted her genes in their family tree. Merindah didn't want to settle for a strategic partnership, however. She wasn't interested in parenting, only portals, though she was not averse to enjoying the occasional consensual coupling.

She flicked off the lights and re-activated the door ward, her research and her earlier visitor forgotten. On her way out the door, Merindah reflexly touched the symbol of Sága on the lintel of the doorframe with two fingers, then tapped her forehead, mumbling her "wonder, wisdom, wit" mantra. So far, the Seeress hadn't shown her anything miraculous, but she lived in hope.

She raced from the lab, a protesting Bridget staggering after her. Few people scared Merindah, but an annoyed and angry stepmother required allies and armour: the kind of glamorous armour that Bridget *excelled* at creating.

Desire

There is a goddess for every purpose under Heaven – and then some.

Mirrabookan Proverb

'It wasn't my fault. It wasn't my fault.' Merindah chanted the refrain as her heeled black sandals tapped a rapid rhythm on the cool white tiles. A light zephyr wafted in through the open arches, drawing in the ocean's damp to cool the stone from the day's heat.

Damn it, it was my fault, and I'm going to be late, again. If I say it wasn't often enough, maybe I'll believe it. Why can't I be punctual for once? Just once.

Note to self: check diary more often. No, that's not it. Note to self: put all events on the Hell's damned diary so you can check them.

Her brow furrowed as she contemplated the impending reception from Nina when she finally arrived. Her stomach curdled and she quickened her pace to a whisker short of a panicked run, clasping the top of her single strapped dress.

Thank Heaven's Seven Realms for a sea breeze, or I'd be a sweaty mess when I arrive. A curl escaped her complicated coiffure and flopped onto her face. She brushed it aside. *I'll fix it when I get there. There. To Nina's dinner party. Another pointless and painful affair in aid of advancing Nina's rising star.*

It was an affair Merindah dared not miss unless she wanted to work in an academic desert. Food sharing had become an almost sacred ritual on Heavens Gate, and wastage was most definitely frowned on.

Security guards in their summer uniforms of Geboor silver and sea green were stationed at regular intervals along the long corridor. She barely noticed the men. They were where they were supposed to be, and doing what they were supposed to be doing. She didn't notice their heads turn to follow her as she raced past, leaving the scent of her perfume tickling their nose.

What does Dad see in her? How can he not see how she manipulates everyone around her? Especially me. She doesn't give a fig for him or anyone else.

A disloyal thought bounded in. *And he doesn't give a rat's arse about you, except for what you can do for his reputation.*

Her mood vacillated between resentment and dread. *I'm just an asset to be leveraged so people don't focus on the fact that he's a man. I really need to get better at looking out for myself.*

Merindah slowed as more of her silky hair escaped its confinement and tumbled around her shoulders.

Drats, Bridget was right. Not enough pins. Fine. I'll fix it now.

She remembered the mirrors surrounding Sister Lust's sculpture in the Librarium's Atrium and did an about face. The goddess's zealous adherents insisted that full-length mirrors line her alcove. In her flustered state Merindah couldn't remember their reasoning, but tonight they had her gratitude. She hiked her long skirts up, slipped her sandals off and jogged down the darkened cross corridor, the building's automated lighting struggling to illuminate her speeding path.

Heavens Gate overflowed with deities. If there wasn't an existing goddess or god you fancied devoting your allegiance to, you could make one up. All it took was faith. And faith was a tradable commodity. The discovery of the Portals had brought more than science to its knees: religious leaders had also seen the writing on the wall. A hastily convened clerical convocation drawn from the seven continents had created a utilitarian armistice between factions and loosened all theological guidelines. Armageddon was approaching, and it was a godly free for all.

The Librarium city of Geboor was no different. Deities abounded, both old and new. Tall, white marble effigies of fourteen different goddesses lined the illustrious Atrium. These seven pairs of Sisters represented the seven seeker and seven contrary virtues, all older, pre-Yarran deities. Most citizens of Geboor publicly followed at least one of the Seven Contrary Virtues: humility, kindness, temperance, chastity, patience, charity, and diligence. Meanwhile, substantially more were secret practitioners of the Seven Seeker Virtues: pride, envy, gluttony, lust, anger, greed, and sloth.

Geboor's young women all dedicated three years of volunteer service to one of the virtue temples between the ages of fifteen and eighteen. Males were apprenticed as assistants to take care of the more mundane tasks. Each virtue's temple dominated a separate district of the capital. Temple law decreed that living true to each virtue carried bounteous divinely granted boons, so families lined up to offer their daughters into what was little more than compulsory indenture. Businesses where children resisted their conscription tended to fall on "difficult" times.

If you call boycotting, arson, and beatings difficult.

Merindah had completed her tenure at the temple of Sister Diligence with little incident, and gained a whole lot of organisation skills. She gave a short respectful nod to the three-metre statue of Diligence grasping her book and broom as she rushed by.

Mildly useful but bland, just like my life. No offence, Sister Dili.

These fourteen deities were believed to exist in the closest astral sphere to Heavens Gate: the first of Heaven's Seven Realms. According to spiritualists, this first realm, The Field – as it was known – housed a veritable multitude of divine beings whose whims decided the fate of every individual on the planet. It was difficult to keep track of the deluge of ideologies that had sprung up over the centuries since the Portals discovery, and hard to take some of them too seriously.

Most of Geboor's inhabitants followed the Sisters' tenets in a fairly lackadaisical manner, while paying homage to a plethora of more commonplace deities that were tied to hearth and home. Records of apparent direct interventions from all these celestial beings existed, but proven occurrences were rare. The Sister Temples preached that the strength of each goddess's intervention increased with sheer numbers and with followers' manic dedication to all aspects of the relevant virtue.

Sister Lust's adherents were particularly favoured for their willingness to explore and exploit their sexual proclivities. All temples competed amongst themselves: collecting acolytes like bees, especially acolytes with strong magic; enticing them with bright flowers full of the promise of power, and then working them like drones to extract every morsel. And like beehives, each temple preferred their devotees to service a single queen. Attempts at cross-pollination evoked harsh penalties.

Merindah's hurried footsteps echoed in the cavernous space. Her pace and racing heart slowed as the sacrosanct surroundings of the temple steadied her frazzled nerves. She loved this place, and bringing her angst to its stately quiet felt sacrilegious. She paused, took a deep, calming breath, and tilted her head to the soaring dome of the ceiling and its magic sky. The huge columns that supported the roof were painted as trees whose branches held up the roof of the world. The ceiling had originally been a soft white, but one day – the day of Merindah's birth – it had turned sky blue. And now the ceiling changed faces like a real sky – just not with the weather outside the Librarium, or anywhere else known on Heavens Gate. The silent magic included scuttling clouds, sunshine, and storms, though no rain fell.

No one had been able to explain the phenomenon, and when researchers had attempted to take a sample scraping, lightning strikes had zapped the technicians. After that, the Atrium had been declared a national treasure and off limits to any further *hands-on* research.

Merindah had often felt that the sky ceiling had an uncanny knack of mirroring her moods. When she was sad and frustrated, the sky seemed to glower at everyone who came in, and when she was excited and happy, it always seemed to be some version of sunny. She'd hinted at a possible emotional connection to a couple of colleagues, but they'd laughed at her self-centred theory.

As her composure settled, the stormy clouds thinned, and the ceiling reflected a clear starry sky. Huge alabaster urns of flowers perfumed the air and subtle lights illuminated the sacred Sister spaces.

Merindah's eyes swivelled to the lodestone of the Portal. The ancient edifice crouched on one side of the Atrium, portentous and impenetrable. Its abstruseness evoked a reverent hush, and she held her breath as she tiptoed across the marble mosaic of the atrium in her evening finery.

The Portal began with seven steps, a rainbow of colours akin to the seven spiritual chakras, all topped by a white hexagonal platform. On the platform were seven arches framed by seven intricately carved ebony pillars that supported a domed obsidian roof some five metres high. The sultry darkness of the Portal's stonework breathed with a life of its own, akin to the texture of the Librarium's Ivory Tower.

Threads of sparkling rainbow mottled the inky surface of this construction. But the warm pillars supplied only part of the Portal enigma. Though the entire edifice was named "the Portal", it was the seven archways that formed the actual ingress to the unknown. A lapis-blue haze drifted within each doorway, alternately revealing and obscuring a tantalising view of a trillion glittering stars.

To this distant ocean of stars, scholars, sages, and shopkeepers had dedicated countless hours of pondering. What did the Portals do? Where did they lead? Why were they here? Could they hold the answer to Heavens Gate's slow demise? The Yarran Journal, discovered with the first Portal at Bedangi, offered tantalising hints of other worlds.

Portals had eventually been unearthed on all seven continents on Heavens Gate. At each of the seven sites, a Librarium had been constructed to aggregate research, and to house and protect the Portal from the people – and vice versa.

For decades after the Portals had first been uncovered, the world had lost countless skilled mages and researchers to the mesmerising blue haze. No matter how determined or how skilfully researchers had tried to anchor or track people, no one who went through an archway ever returned.

Finally, the World Portal Council had been formed to halt the loss of intellectual and magical expertise. Heavens Gate needed saving and the people gambled on the Portals to be that saviour. So the Council had created an annual lottery that was open to all people, magical or menial. They asked for forty-nine volunteers to decipher the Portal puzzle.

Every year, thousands lined up to win the chance to step through the arches: one through each of the seven archways on the seven portals around the world. And even though no one who'd stepped through came back, people still tried for a place. *Perhaps because their families were so well compensated for losing a loved one?*

Despite half a millennium of study, researchers were yet to unravel the Portal's operational secrets.

Surrounded by the cloying fragrance of the Atrium's floral gratuities, Merindah couldn't smell the distinctive brumal scent of the Portal. Even though it was the tail end of summer, she shivered at the thought of the way a colleague had described it: "Mountaintop, mid-winter, fresh falling snow, with an underlying whiff of desolation". More than just an evocative perfume, the scent provoked a sense of lurking potentiality that grew more redolent with power the closer you approached.

Though Merindah was tempted to dash up the stairs and trace the glyphs carved into the pillars, the threat of her stepmother's wrath discouraged her. Time evaporated when she studied the Portal. When she closed her eyes and let her fingers do the reading, tantalising views of distant galaxies twinkled into her mind like gentle melodies.

She replaced her sandals and stood in front of the nearest of Sister Lust's full-length mirrors. She re-twisted her curls; clipping them at her crown with as many pins as she could find in the mess. Bridget would be horrified at the end result, but it would have to do.

With her arms raised for one final pin, her single shouldered gown slipped and fully exposed one breast. She hitched the bodice back up, mortified. After she'd hastily showered and thrown on the dress her stepmother had sent, she'd been dismayed at how much of her décolletage it bared.

Then she'd lost a battle with Bridget about wearing her amulet – her friend had insisted she leave it off to display an uninterrupted expanse of skin. She'd again demanded to know where Merindah had got the amulet from and who had given it to her. Merindah still couldn't remember, though she felt unusually anxious about leaving it behind. She settled on weaving a small concealing spell and hiding it in her room. Bridget had gone off in a huff, disbelieving Merindah about her memory lapse.

The garment left little to the imagination. At the time she'd thought *Holy Hecate! One deep breath and they'll mistake me for Sister Lust.* Iconography inevitably depicted that goddess's sensual figure with one breast uncovered. Lust's credo urged people to pursue their desire – primarily their sexual desire – above all else. And here she was in front of a three-metre likeness, mimicking her display. Synchronicity indeed.

Why would Nina leave something this provocative for me?

Usually her stepmother sent some frumpy, frilly thing, insisting her father would be mortally offended if Merindah didn't wear it. Though that was unlikely, Merindah knew her father suffered most when Nina didn't get what she wanted or when one of her little schemes went awry. But these sapphire swathes clung and shaped Merindah's plentiful curves into something magnificent.

She critically appraised her reflection. Bridget had insisted she outline her eyes in grey kohl and shade her eyelids a dusky granite as well, so her eyes dominated her face. Her cheeks were flushed from running, adding colour to her copper skin. And with the deep fuchsia gloss on her lips, she looked completely unlike her usual messy and homely self.

I actually look beautiful.

Her heart beat faster as she thought of the furore she'd cause showing up with one breast exposed.

That would get me more than a modicum of attention. Her cheeks flushed even more at her temerity and her yerlendj sparked. She imagined Sister

Diligence would be horrified to see her mimicking Sister Lust. Reflexively she tapped three fingers over her heart three times, accompanied by her oft repeated lessons in diligence. *Effort. Expertise. Excellence.* And three taps to her forehead for Sága. *Wonder. Wisdom. Wit.*

While many citizens professed their devotion to Sister Lust, most simply sought an excuse for unadulterated sexual pleasure. Few considered the consequences of fulfilling their desire. Lust could be an insatiable goddess, and many believed "lecherous" a more apt description of her acolytes than "devoted". Their canons were a corrupting influence on hundreds of thousands of people. Lust's priestesses defended any blame laid at her graceful feet by espousing their favourite maxim.

Be careful what you wish for. The price of desire is yours to bear alone.

Passionate desire could soar you to lofty heights to achieve wondrous things. But it also left you open to manipulation by deities and daemons, as well as earthly villains.

'The price of desire is mine to bear alone,' Merindah repeated aloud as she smoothed the satiny material over her hips, watching wide-eyed as her breast threatened to escape again.

'And the power to grant your desire is *mine* alone,' a sultry voice responded.

Merindah's head jerked towards the sound, grasping her bodice, every nerve taut. She wasn't supposed to visit the Atrium after hours.

A glorious creature emerged from the carved likeness of Sister Lust and stepped down from the marble plinth. She swayed over to Merindah, sending a waft of heady fragrance before her, her form visibly shrinking to just over Merindah's height. Her dark gaze roamed over every detail of Merindah's body. Finally, she leant down; her breath warm on Merindah's neck, inhaling the expensive scent Bridget had sprayed.

'Mmm, delicious. Close your mouth dear or you'll catch flies.'

Merindah's mouth snapped shut as the apparition gave a throaty chuckle.

'Sister Lust? You… you're real?' Merindah squeezed her eyes shut then opened them again. Her mind lurched with déjà vu.

Sister Lust oozed sensuality. Her silky black hair coiled intricately on top of her head, exposing exquisite cheekbones and the curve of her graceful neck. Her sapphire-blue eyes contrasted with cherry-red lips. Lust's skin was pearlescent, almost luminous in the subdued light of the Atrium. Her sheath of matching cherry-red silk accentuated her feminine contours, and exposed one generous breast. When Merindah continued to stare, Lust tapped her foot and raised a perfectly arched eyebrow.

'The night is young, dear. But it's getting older by the moment. What do you desire? It's in my power to grant you anything. Think carefully – I'm in a generous mood.' She stole a glance behind her. 'And don't tell Sister Charity, or I'll never hear the end of it.'

Merindah wet her lips and finally found her voice, addressing the paragon of luscious beauty and desire incarnate.

'Am I dreaming? Surely you're not real.'

Lust's mouth twisted in distaste. 'Don't start with the disbelief. I hate it when they do that. Come on, woman. Surely your studies have shown you we *do* exist. Tap into that prodigious mind of yours.'

At Merindah's bemused nod, Lust continued impatiently. 'Though we can step onto the earthly plane, not everyone can see us. Our forms vibrate at a different frequency, and most humans struggle to process it. You'd have to ask Diligence about it, but it's something to do with neurological discharges and the temporal lobe of the brain. Boring. Regardless, your genes pre-dispose you to Seeing truly; and now through your studies your mind is open to the possibility, so voilà! Here I am. Besides, we get a little bored in the First Realm, and occasionally slip down to Heavens Gate for a little entertainment. Or in my case, a little debauchery.' The wicked gleam in her eye was disarming, and the shimmy of hips that accompanied it alarming.

Realisation hit Merindah like a tidal wave and she gasped. 'So I'm right, there *is* a link! Spiritual beings exist. Magic exists. Genetics holds the key.' Merindah reeled, her senses clashing with her rational mind.

'Oh Hoary Heavens girl, yes there's magic, but not *in* the world. Magic *is* the world,' Lust drew herself up and began impatiently ticking items off on her elegant fingers.

'The Fields, the Threads, the Elements, the Molecules, the Atoms – all magic. Spirituality is still energy; it's just directed towards the incorporeal rather than the practical.'

The goddess's lips thinned. 'It's high time the beings on this plane got on with using magic for its proper purpose – to move up and traverse the Realms. You've almost trashed this existence with your focus on scientific facts and evidence. Now enough theory. What's your desire?' Her smile became predatory, her presence rapacious as she leant forward. 'And be careful what you wish for.'

Merindah's mind teemed with questions. Lust sashayed closer and touched the centre of Merindah's forehead with one cherry-tipped finger. The world wobbled.

Colours she'd never seen leapt into being, sounds, smells and tastes pounded her into sensory overload. Every molecule within her thrummed with energy. A kaleidoscope of aetheric threads swirled and danced, combined, and separated in a divine display. Heavenly music played in her mind.

Sister Lust was a ball of deep crimson, pulsing with power. Merindah watched mesmerised as numbers and symbols cascaded through the timestream – histories, futures, connections to the present – all with herself at the centre of a vast web of existence. She knew all things, she was connected to all things, she *was* all things.

Home. She was Home.

A deep golden swell began in a distant corner of Merindah's mind as though suddenly aware of her. A fierce presence hunted for her, and it was angry. Merindah observed it crash through the web like a tsunami, obliterating all before it.

Lust tapped Merindah's forehead again and the sensations faded, leaving her blinking and rocking back on her feet over a chasm of fearful yearning.

'What did you do to me?' She dropped to her knees, her hands searching for the stone to ground herself. The feeling of déjà vu surged again.

'Fully opened your third eye dear. The first time can be a little overwhelming. Sorry about that. I thought your Sága would have helped you out there. She *is* the all-seeing Seeress after all,' Lust smirked, unbridled desire in her dark gaze. 'You're destined for greatness anyway. I'm just speeding things up a little. As a favour for a friend.'

Her brow furrowed. 'But she *didn't* mention the binding. Someone has been holding you back, though it looks like the shield has cracked recently. Your magical well is huge. You could have raised your vibrations yourself years ago without that binding.'

Lust's face smoothed as she shrugged, dismissing her misgivings, and continuing in a more subdued tone, 'You won't be holding back for very much longer. I don't think I want to be on this plane when you open the floodgates.'

Merindah's heart still pounded in her ears. She shakily stood and wiped damp hands on her dress. The odd synchronicity swirled in her mind.

'Now that you've seen what's possible, what do you desire?' Lust asked.

Merindah's thoughts see sawed. *This is it. This is my break. It's what I wished for. I can be an adventurer. I can save the world and I can have what I want, do what I want.*

But what if it's a trap and I can't pay the price? Deities always demand a price. What if I'm not good enough anyway? What was that golden thing? Who was it?

No, I'm not holding back, not this time. I'm doing it, grabbing it with both hands. I'm doing it for humanity.

No, be honest at least. You're doing it for yourself, so you can show all those naysayers that they were wrong. You are magnificent.

Merindah straightened, tilted her chin, and gathered her thoughts.

'I'd like my doctorate paper to be accepted by the Council Portal Collaborative so that I can plan a mission through the Portal.'

Lust exploded with laughter, holding her sides as she rocked. When she stopped, she brushed the tears from her eyes and glared at Merindah. 'You are too funny. That's way too prosaic. Stop wasting my time. Think bigger. Try harder. I am the Goddess Lust, for Heaven's sake.'

At Merindah's worried frown, she groaned theatrically. 'Mother's milk. Let's hunt down that base desire. This night is wasting. Much as it bores me, we'll start where you are.'

Her eyes sharpened and she pointed an interrogatory finger at Merindah. 'Why do you want your paper to be accepted?'

Merindah paused to state her reason: 'Because I want the World Council to give me unfettered access to the Portal?'

'Why?'

'So I can study the Portal and understand what it does.' That response Merindah was certain of.

Sister Lust tucked it away for later use, and continued her questioning. 'Why do you want to understand what the Portal does?'

'Because I want to know?'

'Why?'

'Because I do.'

Lust's eyes held a mischievous gleam as she trotted out the now familiar why. 'Why do you want to know?'

Merindah hesitated. This was not a child's game of tit for tat. This was a life-changing moment.

Why do I want to know?

'I just need to know. I've always needed to know.'

Lust planted her hands on her hips, raised one eyebrow and delivered the final, 'Why?'

Merindah took a breath. Honesty would serve her best here. 'I want to be the first to know. I want to be the one they remember as the person who saves the world.'

Lust nodded with a satisfied smirk, and crossed her arms. 'There, that wasn't so hard was it? Your deepest desire is to save the world. Very meritorious of you. Meritorious and ambitious.'

Merindah felt a shiver shimmy through her at Lust's words, leaving a sour churn in her gut. She straightened. *What's wrong with being ambitious?* Merindah squashed down her doubts, though she hesitated as Sister Lust narrowed her eyes and queried.

'How far would you go? How much would you sacrifice to save the world? To be the first?'

A heaviness ballooned in Merindah's belly, a cloak of dread settling across her shoulders. *How far would I go?* Thrusting the panic aside, she lifted her chin. She heard the Voice whisper in her mind. *Feel the fear and do it anyway. I'm with you.*

'I'll do whatever it takes.'

'Be careful what you wish for,' Lust smiled to soften the warning, but a sparkle of triumph flickered across her porcelain features, and Merindah's unease returned.

'What will I owe you?'

Lust laughed again. 'Oh, you won't owe *me* dear. I have it on good authority that we will all owe you. Still, since you remembered to check, the rules about bargaining with deities are all true. Always ask the price first.' Merindah had been taught that deities always demanded payment for their gifts. She gulped, realising she'd foolishly promised to do anything. Yet now Sister Lust was refusing to name her payment.

When will I learn to look before I leap?

Lust patted her shoulder. 'No need to worry about that now. It's aeons away. Now is the time to voice your desire. And don't forget to invest every word with powerful intent, opening your magic as you do. The stronger the intent, the stronger the fulfilment.'

Merindah closed her eyes. Her hands created a diamond on her belly as she centred herself and called on her magic. She took a deep breath.

Lust's eyes widened at both the magical and the physical display. A smile twitched her lips and she nodded to herself.

'My desire is to save the world and the Cosmos, and I'll do whatever it takes to be the first.' Merindah felt her magic burgeoning, slipping threads through her belly, then falling back into nothing. She opened her eyes to

Lust's disconcerting smirk, which held a hint of some mischief she couldn't quite grasp. Seconds ticked by.

'Is that it? I don't feel any different.' Sister Lust bent down, slipped a hand under her hair at the back of her neck, drew her close and kissed her lips. It was not a chaste kiss. Merindah's body erupted in a thrill of pleasure. Her hands came up to Lust's arms to drag her closer but Lust broke contact before Merindah could grasp her.

'Sealed.'

Merindah staggered back, gasping.

Sister Lust's eyes were bright, and her tongue moistened her parted lips. 'I knew you'd be delicious. Such a shame to waste those curves on science and saving the world. I'm sure *She* won't mind if I borrow you for a while.' She shivered in anticipatory delight. 'And you have so much power. With destiny about to take a hand, you won't miss this little snip of time.' Lust shrugged off her promise as her base nature took over.

'But I don't have power. My yerlendj is puny.'

Sister Lust ignored her, reached for Merindah, and *shimmered* into her body. 'Time for Lust to go to the party. Sleepy time for you Merindah. I've got lechery to engage in. I promise I'll have you back in time to save the world.'

Merindah's vision swam as Sister Lust took control of her body. Her mind screamed as she slipped into cool, unconscious darkness.

Destiny

Sister Lust twirled, admiring her borrowed form in the mirrors. She was oblivious to the ominous storm clouds covering the Atrium's ceiling.

Mm, mm, this body is built for indulgence. Sooo many curves. Lust smoothed back an auburn curl, enjoying the new colour. Her sultry smile darkened Merindah's eyes, which had switched to Lust's own sapphire blue with her possession.

Who knew that hanging with the good girls could be so much fun? As Lust prepared to depart for the entertainment, her attention caught on an azure flare from the Portal. She spun towards it as one of the blue-hazed archways cleared. Thick rainbow threads surged out with a fierce swirl.

Lust shuddered as the aetheric threads swept over her, leaving a wash of outrage in their wake. A gush of sharp ozone accompanied the appearance of a being thrust from the portal. Purple-black skin and amethyst eyes signalled an alien heritage, while his nakedness left no doubt of his maleness.

Staggering out, he stretched a hand to the nearest pillar for support. Lust drew nearer, her avarice stirring as he shook his head and ran a hand to gather black glossy strands back from his face. The acrid smell dissipated, and the rainbow swirls sucked back into the Portal with an angry buzz. The archway haze returned, hiding the ocean of stars from view.

'My, my. What have we here? Who are you precious? What are you? Besides beautiful.' Lust's drawl drew the male's attention and he straightened to watch her sway up the steps towards him. Her greedy gaze soaked in every centimetre of his sculpted form. Merindah's head would barely reach his chest, so Lust adjusted her form, stretching the body's height by twenty centimetres as she ascended. By the time she arrived on the white platform, her head was at his eye level.

'That was clever of you,' his voice was dark honey, accompanied by a knowing smile and a hint of pearly white teeth. Lust felt Merindah's body respond, and a deep warmth kindled low in her belly.

'Just right for you, gorgeous warrior. And all the more of me to ravish you.' She reached to stroke his bicep, and her hand passed through his form. Her eyes flew to his.

A self-satisfied smirk broadened his handsome face. 'I have a few tricks of my own. Though I admit I am easy on the eye, and better than anything you've ever seen.' His voice continued to arouse, stroking her desire. With arms crossed, he leant back negligently on the pillar, his glorious body relaxed.

'And so modest. Mister…?' Lust queried.

He shrugged, confident and accepting of her admiration.

'Call me Yarra,' he responded, and pushed off the pillar.

He stepped closer, his presence radiating heat. Lust's breath caught as the musk of his maleness triggered a flood of her own heat. His voice dropped to a seductive whisper, 'And you are *delicious*.'

Lust laughed, delighted. She shivered with anticipation and twirled with her arms spread. Then her sandal caught the edge of the platform and she teetered. Yarra reached and snapped a very real hand onto her wrist, jerking her towards him.

Without warning, Sister Lust *shimmered* out of Merindah and continued to fall down the stairs, landing with an undignified 'Oomph,' on her butt. Yarra's horrified stare took in the scarlet goddess on the floor then switched to Merindah's small, blue-clad form as she sagged against him. He hoisted the compact bundle of the woman she'd returned to into his arms.

'What in Hell's halls just happened? And who or what are you?' Yarra demanded. His voice had definitely lost its seductive edge.

Lust was speechless. This had never happened before. She was always in control until *she* decided *she* was done. The Voice had promised her temptation and fun for the night when she stepped onto this plane. Lust was sure the events of the last few minutes did not qualify.

Perhaps the possession was a little over the line, just a little though. Then again, I didn't promise not to. She cringed inwardly and climbed to her feet.

Lust was ever the optimist, however. There was still time to save the evening and bring debauchery to the debacle. She was a goddess after all. The cringe forgotten, she tugged on the threads of belief from her multitudes of followers. A dynamo of power gathered, nestling just below the surface. Her pearlescent skin brightened.

'The Assembly forbids possession of sentient beings by lesser daemons,' Yarra declared arrogantly.

'What did you call me?' Lust stomped up the stairs, all sashaying forgotten. No one spoke to her like that, no matter how beautiful they were. She was no daemon – she was a goddess. *Millions* of people worshipped at her feet.

Hands on hips, head thrust forward, fire in her eyes, she spat. 'You listen to me, *Mister* Yarra. Who in Hell's seven realms do you think you are, telling me what to do? I don't know your Assembly, and I don't know you. I'm using that body, so return it and remove yourself from my presence.' She reached for Merindah, and Yarra stepped back, twisting out of her way and shaking his head.

'Not going to happen, daemon. Time for some answers. As the Head of *Heaven's* Seventh Realm Assembly, I command you to kneel for judgement.'

Lust felt a momentary flicker of fright. She didn't realise he meant *that* Assembly. She existed in the First Realm, and had never had contact with anyone from the Seventh Realm before. Yarra's arrogance pushed her buttons, though – and she was *not* kneeling to anyone.

But as she prepared another volley of vitriol and an accompanying power blast to knock Mister Arrogance on his delightful butt, the Voice spoke in her head.

You've completed your task Lust – and then some. The desire is spoken, your gift bestowed. Take your leave for now. Go and find the party, and use your time on this plane wisely. Be back by midnight or risk all.

Lust fumed and took a deep breath as her eyes refocused on the fierce Yarra, then spat internally, *this is way more complex than you promised.*

The Voice was dry as it replied, *I believe it was you who said mere moments ago to take heed of the rules about bargaining with deities. I did not give you leave to possess the subject. It was not a part of our bargain, and you know it. You are well and truly in my debt.*

Lust searched for a loophole, some kind of leverage. *What is this human to you anyway? What are you planning?*

The Voice was silent, and Lust continued, *I want in with whatever you're doing. I haven't felt this alive for centuries. Or perhaps you'd like to find your precious human stalked by all manner of First Realmers? Both Upper and Lower.*

The Voice's tone was reluctant. *Meet me outside the Atrium and we'll discuss it.*

The internal exchange was momentary. The triumphant smile that lit Lust's visage had terrified more than mortal souls. Her posture relaxed, and her glowing skin dimmed as she slipped the power of her followers into abeyance. She planted her hands on her hips and tossed her head at a glaring Yarra.

'Ahem. I will not be kneeling for anyone's judgement. I've no time for arrogant blowhards. I'll find someone else to entertain me. You're on your own warrior boy.' Lust reached across Merindah and ran her fingernails down Yarra's cheek, dusting threads of desire into his skin. Her touch ignited a response, and his mouth tightened.

Lust stepped away, her laugh wicked. 'You'll never know what you missed, Mister Yarra. Perhaps you and I will meet in different circumstances at another time, in another place.'

'See that you heed the Assembly's rules, daemon, or we will indeed meet again.' Lust smirked as Yarra gathered his tattered composure. Without another word she sashayed down the stairs and exited the Atrium.

– – –

Contrary to his boast, Yarra wasn't in any kind of shape to command anything at the moment. Travel through his Mother's Portals always drained his power; and depending on where and when he ended up, it sometimes constrained his magic for hours. Besides, he was more a lover than a fighter, despite his warrior form.

He admired the daemon's self-control though, and her form was a delight. As she left, he couldn't help imagining what it would be like to taste those lips and trace a run of kisses down that neck.

Stars, she pushed my buttons so easily. I'd have been hard-pressed to control her had she knelt. Maybe she wasn't a lesser daemon. It better not have been one of my sisters teasing me. Holy Mother I hope they haven't found out how to use the Gates and get out of the Reverie system without me.

The woman in his arms stirred and he glanced down. She was tiny in comparison: his height topped hers by at least half a metre. But she was a delicious package too, so many beautiful curves. A dusting of freckles across her nose and cheeks added to the perfection of her copper skin. Deep auburn hair lay in soft, tousled waves over his arms.

Yarra took a deep breath to calm his raging hormones.

He hitched the unconscious woman into a more secure grip and glanced around the deserted Atrium. Soaring stormy ceiling, statuary, and silence.

Now what? I have no idea where or when I am, or who this is. So much for harmless exploring and a quick recovery job.

His armful of woman shivered, and her eyelids fluttered. He gazed into a pair of eyes that made *both* his hearts stutter. Deepest ocean blue and brilliant emerald green were startling enough, but it was the ache of timeless wisdom lurking in their depths that snagged his soul. He felt himself respond to her familiar magic. His own magic tickled into awareness, fed by her resonance, and it threaded towards her. It was soundly rebuffed.

Whoa, what have we here? Someone with power to spare.

He breathed in her feminine essence, and again his body responded, desire stirring.

What is it with the women here? I'm like a virgin lad on his first date.

— — —

Merindah blinked a few times, trying to get her thoughts straight, and reached to rub her temple where a familiar ache had begun. Her eyes focused on the face of a man and his amethyst eyes stirred her confusion. She'd seen eyes like this before, but not in this face.

'Hello there. Glad you could join us.' The honeyed timbre of his voice strummed her senses.

Merindah's voice was a croaky whisper. 'Who are you? Where's Sister Lust? What did she do to me? She… She... I couldn't… What happened? What did you do?'

The man's delighted smile was like a burst of sunshine after the rain. His teeth gleamed against his violet dark skin, and her own mouth dried in awe. *Holy Hecate, he's beautiful.*

His smile widened further, his eyes crinkling. She wanted to touch the deep dimples that appeared in his cheeks. *Hell, I hope he's not a mind reader.*

'I believe I've just saved you from possession by a daemon.' His amused response was a little arrogant. Merindah's brow furrowed and she ran her tongue over her lips to moisten them. The man's eyes followed her tongue's progression.

'Daemon? There are no such things as daemons!' she declared. 'They're just made up stories to frighten children, like dragons and bunyips.' Her eyes narrowed as she processed her thoughts aloud. 'Though I *was* just speaking to Sister Lust. And until a few minutes ago, I believed there was no such thing as a manifesting goddess either.'

Something about that isn't right. Of course there are goddesses. No, that's not it.

Her head began to pound, and she pushed ineffectually against the man's chest, only then realising it was bare. His skin was warm and firm; and her hand slowed, trailing over the curve of his pectorals. Her cheeks darkened at his sharp intake of breath. She caught herself and pushed away again, desperately trying to ignore the heat building deep in her belly.

'Let me go.'

He swung her round and set her down.

Her legs wobbled and gave way. She slumped against him, mortified to discover he was totally naked as she braced her arms around his waist to stop from falling. Her face flamed a deep red, and she clamped her eyes shut.

'Sister Chastity blind me.' *Magnificent.* The man swung her back into his arms, and she peered up at his laughing eyes.

'I think you need to lie down somewhere. Where can I take you?'

'But you're naked,' Merindah sputtered. Her mind choked on anything further as his warmth and scent bombarded her again.

He smells so freaking fabulous I could eat him up. Holy Hecate, what's happened to my restraint? He's just a man for Goddess sake. She pushed against his chest.

'Put me down.'

'We tried that. Let's try my way instead. Tell me your name and I'll find the nearest bed.' A grin tugged at the corner of his lips, and she was helpless to suppress the giggle that bubbled up.

Stop that, you foolish woman. Get a grip. You're too old to giggle. You've got no idea who or what he is. Why is a naked man in the Atrium at this time of night, for starters? And don't forget that your stepmother is going to be so cranky that you're late.

'We're both in so much trouble. I was supposed to be somewhere else at least an hour ago, and you're not supposed to be here at all – especially not naked.'

He laughed and perused the Atrium, taking in the marble statues of the fourteen virtues, the mosaic floor, and the long white corridors between shelves of books and artefacts. Wide, padded divans rested before the statues in each niche, placed to allow devotees to adore their deities in comfort. His arms tightened as he strode down the rainbow stairs and headed for the nearest divan, which happened to be Sister Chastity's.

He placed Merindah on the soft cushions and took his arms from around her. She began to shiver, her body struggling to catch up with the bizarre circumstances of the last few minutes. She hugged herself and peered up at the man's eyes. Anything was better than what she had to focus on at eye level.

Seeing her shivering, he sat himself, lifted her onto his lap and wrapped her in his body heat. She wriggled to get comfortable and his face blanched.

'Don't do that unless you want me to forget my manners,' he said, his voice hoarse.

She stilled, her face flaming again and rested her cheek against his broad chest, listening to the strong beat of his heart. *Hearts?* 'You've got two hearts?' She looked up at his face as he nodded. 'Who are you?' she asked.

He hesitated for a moment, searching her inquisitive gaze. 'Yarra. And you?'

'Merindah. Wait. Yarra? Were you named after the Yarran Journal?'

He smiled, 'My turn to ask a question. When are we?'

Merindah frowned. 'What do you mean when? Your accent is a little strange. Do you mean what time is it? It's late. At least some time after nine. And I'm really late for my stepmother's dinner. I am in serious trouble.'

He shook his head, and Merindah's frown disappeared as she watched strands of midnight hair dance around his face. 'Let's start with something simpler. Where are we?' he queried.

Merindah's frown returned, and she gestured around her. 'We're in the Librarium Atrium. And it's pretty obvious you're not supposed to be here if you don't know where this is. Did you sneak in for a look at the Portal? Are you a field hand?'

It was Yarra's turn to frown. 'A field hand?'

'You do know men aren't allowed in the Atrium unaccompanied, don't you? Or in the Librarium for that matter. They only keep a few males around for domestic service. So given your…' she stumbled as her hand traced his sculpted chest. 'Given your physical attributes, I imagine you're a field hand. You know, helping the women in the fields with heavy things, digging things, chopping things down, cutting things up.'

'Why aren't men allowed in the Librarium?' his gaze was sharp, but his tone genuinely curious.

'Well, obviously because they're men. Men aren't very good at intellectual studies, are they? Or at anything much, unless they're told what to do and supervised. But you know this. You're a man.' His mouth quirked and one dimple appeared.

'Thanks for noticing,' he said dryly.

'Well it's hard not to when you're naked and holding me. Wait. Are you from the Temple of Lust? Did Sister Lust send you after she tried to you-know-what me? Are you one of those special acolytes bred and trained to pleasure women?' His responding grunt could have been yes or no, but his jaw had tightened.

Merindah's hand had moved up to his shoulder and stroked down his arm involuntarily. A molten pool in her belly ignited, and she gazed up to see his irises darken to a smouldering violet. Their eyes locked and time stopped. The sky-ceiling seemed to hold its breath.

Merindah's yerlendj quivered. Instinctively she released a single thread, which uncoiled and quested towards Yarra. It touched his belly, searching for his magic, and he groaned and covered her wandering hand, which had moved to his hip.

'If you don't stop now, I can't guarantee your virtue will remain intact.' His voice was a seductive whisper as he nodded vaguely at the statue of Sister Chastity looming disapprovingly above them.

'My virtue is my own affair – as is my choice in consensual partners,' Merindah informed him crossing her arms.

'My pardon lady, I did not wish to presume,' Yarra stilled, his gaze fixed on Merindah's breasts which her folded arms had thrust into greater prominence.

A few moments ticked by and dark clouds gathered on the periphery of the sky-ceiling.

'So do I guess at your permission or will you tell me?' Merindah asked gruffly. She was finding it difficult to remain vexed when she was perched on his naked knee. 'Don't fear retribution. If you're not so inclined, I wouldn't couple with you unwillingly.' Merindah could feel his body's response which he confirmed with his soft-spoken words.

'I am more than willing.'

Merindah followed her desire, consequences be damned. She'd been a partner in half a dozen consensual couplings in the last decade, none of them more than an obligated physical release, a way to loosen the tension. But this... this was different. She wanted to touch every centimetre of his velvet skin, and to be touched by him in return.

'I am also willing. I've never met a male like you. I didn't know your gender could be so, so… magnificent.' She reached with both hands and ran her fingers through his shoulder-length hair, traced his forehead with her thumbs, smoothing the lines away, and moved to his lips, stroking.

His head descended and paused close enough for her to taste his breath. 'Last chance for either of us to back out,' he breathed.

Merindah closed the distance, and their lips connected. It was as though a thousand volts of electricity shot through them both. The lights in the Atrium flared, jagged lightning silently arcing over the ceiling, and the Portal hummed, its ominous mood shifting to expectant.

The two beings on the divan were oblivious to all but each other. As she leant towards him, he reached behind and unfastened her dress, sliding it down to her waist. Merindah smiled as his throat bobbed, his hands trembling as he cupped her face, kissing her lips gently.

Then, with a wicked gleam in his eye, his lips and tongue traced a burning trail over her skin to the curve of her breasts. Her nipples responded as his fingers brushed them and she felt a gush of moisture between her legs.

He pushed her dress lower, then stood and lifted her upright so she could wriggle out of it. The tightness of the dress had precluded any undergarments – which had caused Merindah a fleeting twinge of embarrassment. Bridget had just laughed and told her to be outrageous and think of it when she was listening to a really boring dinner guest.

I'm a long way from bored right now, Bridget.

Yarra's eyes travelled from her feet to her face and she felt the heat build. No male had ever had the temerity to consider her body so brazenly. She gazed up at his face, so far above her and then indicated her sandals.

'If I take these off, I'm going to be even shorter – and even further from your mouth.' He sat and held out his hand. She slipped off her sandals and climbed back into his lap, kneeling astride his hips. They sat for a moment, hands touching, awareness pulsing, sharing a look more complex and profound than either of them had ever experienced.

And then they began. Hands and mouths exploring, magic mingling; they made achingly slow love. Questions disappeared in the heat of physical connection and yerlendj accord. The climax, when it came, stunned them both in its completeness.

Merindah's every molecule vibrated with joy. Sated and panting, they lay side by side, their limbs entangled. When her breath had settled, Merindah traced his lips with a finger.

'How did you come to be here tonight? You're not from around here are you?' He laughed, took her hands, and kissed her palms.

'That's an understatement. No, I'm not from around here. Though I have been. I came to retrieve a journal I left here by accident. What year is this?' he asked.

'Why don't you know?'

'Just tell me,' he coaxed.

'It's 2519.'

He frowned. 'I'm out by more than five hundred years. How could that be? I left it in a temple in 2498. It's probably long gone in this time,' he mused.

'I don't understand.'

He began kissing each of her fingers separately.

'It's not important. I have others.' He moved onto kissing her palms.

Merindah pulled her hands away and addressed him, seeking to unlock the puzzle and learn more about him. 'It's not important – but here you are. What's in the journal? All your lovers' names?' Her teasing held no hint of rebuke, and Yarra wondered at this prize who had literally fallen into his arms.

'It has some of my research notes in it. I've written it in my own personal code. Pictures, symbols and words that will look like gobbledygook to most people, but make perfect sense to anyone who has the cipher,' he explained.

Merindah frowned, searching her memory at his words. It sounded like the contents of the journal she had in her lab. 'What colour is it?'

'Why? There's no way you could have seen it in this time.' He paused his caressing.

'So tell me,' Merindah demanded.

'The deep ochre red of this continent's beating heart,' he smiled. Merindah's mind tried to make the connection. She couldn't imagine what he was describing, and she almost missed what he said next.

'What did you say?' her voice was incredulous.

'I said, I'm researching the gates back there.' He waved a lazy hand in the direction of the Portal. Merindah sat up.

'You? You're researching the Portals? But how can you be? You're a man. Men don't do research. *I'm* doing serious research on them. I'm close, really close to cracking their secret. And why did you call them gates?' His laugh made her smile.

'What? What's so funny?' He shuffled flat on his back and drew her down on top of him.

'Men can do research if they wish. And I'm not strictly a man,' he confessed.

Merindah's eyebrows rose sceptically, and she lifted herself off him enough to glance down at his responsive man parts. 'Looks pretty masculine to me,' she asserted.

He feigned offence. 'So you only want my body, not my mind?'

Merindah blushed, a little ashamed of her gender bias. She shrugged. 'It's your history. Give men the lead, the knowledge, and they can't control themselves. They have to compete, to fight and win regardless of the costs and without listening to anyone else. Those costs almost destroyed Heavens Gate and every soul on it centuries ago. Only by keeping the knowledge out of the hands of men have we been able to rebuild.'

Yarra listened shaking his head. 'I can see where this is leading to. I'm not going to argue a case I don't have the details for. This is not my time or world. I'm a bit distracted anyway. I'd rather be spending my moments with you, researching something of a more biological nature.'

Merindah paused as his smile defused her gathering tirade and rekindled her desire. All questions fled her mind.

After their explorations had brought them to an entirely expected, but none the less entirely satisfactory conclusion, they both slipped into a dreamy half sleep.

On the edge of slumber, Merindah's drowsy mind heard the Voice.

Here is your moment of choice. See what will happen, and choose your way.

She wondered if Yarra heard the Voice too, as she felt joined to him in a way that was more than physical intimacy. Suddenly, the reason that his eyes were so familiar burst into her mind. She *had* seen eyes like that before. The goddess, her Voice, and the visit to her lab all came rushing back. A surge in her magic made her eyes pop open to the swirling sky of the Atrium ceiling above. The Voice spoke again.

This is how you can save the Cosmos, daughter.

I'm a little busy right now. Can this wait?

You did say you would do whatever it takes? Well this is what it will take. The Gatekeeper may birth the key and flame. They will need your strength, love, and protection – and eventually their father's. See.

Merindah's third eye slammed open then and she saw herself standing at a crossroad: one path clear and ordinary, the second path dangerous and extraordinary. She saw all the possibilities in between and the consequences of this moment of choice for every being in the Cosmos. The image shifted to the one she'd seen before of herself in the centre of a vast cobweb of threads, connected to everyone and everything. She understood that no thought, feeling, belief or action was ever created that did not have a consequence. All echoed their energy in the world. Most people barely understood the impact of their actions, let alone the influence of their thoughts, feelings, and beliefs on the rest of creation.

Though whatever choice she made was neither good nor bad – it just was. If she chose safety, this world would continue to slip into dissolution and decay. All the souls would begin their journey through the realms of existence again, as would every other world.

Her mind reeled as countless planets teemed past. Many would descend into chaos and violence, ruled by dark powers. As the Seven Realms of Heaven led to higher consciousness of living, there were also Seven Realms of Hell, catering for those souls living with the baser emotions.

Should she decline, she would be released from her guardianship and ascend Home. But if she chose the painful road, the souls remaining in this Cosmos had another choice – to shift towards and explore the higher emotions, to raise their vibrations and ascend. If she made that choice though, she would spend millennia in the cold and dark – alone.

Merindah felt Yarra stir beside her, a witness to her Seeing.

– – –

Hello, Mother.

Aeon felt a deep flow of love around him. His loneliness and hurt diminished in his mother's energetic embrace. She needed no words – he knew forgiveness and compassion were his.

The shadows in his heart lessened. The way Home had been within him all along.

Aeon smoothed the frown from Merindah's forehead and opened his mind to her, sharing a memory mind-to-mind. He was a small boy, held in his mother's loving arms in the comforting darkness at the centre of the

Cosmos. They shared the same amethyst eyes and midnight black hair, sparkling with silver. An enormous rainbow serpent slumbered behind them guarding a massive tree, the Aether Tree. The memory switched to now. Aeon showed Merindah herself in this moment. Held in the arms of that small boy grown, the man who lay beside her, one hand stroking her face, the other resting on her hip.

His name was not Yarra. He was Aeon: The Firstborn of the Cosmic Mother, Mother of all. Her Voice. He kissed her with such tenderness that her heart ached. She felt a wave of loneliness drift up and away from his soul. Cast out, wandering lost, and now he'd found his way Home, to her.

She reached to touch his lips with her fingers when the choice she faced swelled in her mind. A sob escaped, tears streamed from her eyes, and she turned into his arms. He stroked her back, comforting without words, kissing the top of her head. Merindah soaked up every sensation, every molecule of feeling, watching the threads of their entwined magic as it lay quiescent between and around them. Then she eased back from his embrace and entwined Aeon's awareness with her own.

With a profound knowing, she reached with her yerlendj into her belly. She encouraged an egg's release from her ovary and guided it towards its destiny.

She searched Aeon's eyes and soul and he nodded. Together they encouraged his wriggling sperm to swim through the rich moistness towards the opening of her womb. Merindah closed her eyes.

I am indeed the Gatekeeper. She allowed the sperm through the gate. Mere moments saw the magically accelerated meeting, joining, and creation of an astonishing new being. The explosion of life climaxed in wonder. The sky-ceiling cleared, and sparkling constellations brightened the midnight tapestry. In its dark corner, the resonant hum of the Portal rose and the lapis haze in all seven archways disappeared. The ocean of stars greeted the new child's spirit.

Aeon's hand circled Merindah's belly, feeling the new life, sending it love. His eyes lit up.

'She knows me.' His wondrous smile made Merindah beam. She placed her hand over his on her belly and sent love to her daughter.

'Welcome, little flower, my Bindi.' She felt the tiny being glow and closed her eyes to savour the moment.

Aeon moved his hand to her chin and tipped her face up for another kiss. His eyes swam, and a tear trickled down his cheek. Merindah's eyes moistened as she brushed his tear away.

'You are magnificent,' his voice was ragged. 'In all my years of existence I've never experienced anything close to the ecstasy of making love with you, making life. What a wonder you are.'

Merindah's smile threatened to crack her jaw in half. 'And you're magnificent. Our child is already so loved. Thank you.'

Merindah's curiosity surfaced. 'Why did you tell me your name was Yarra?'

Aeon hitched her closer to his body, and breathed in the lavender fragrance of her hair. 'It's a name I've used in this place before. It means ever-flowing in the language of the one of the original Indigenous tribes. So it's kind of like time anyway. I've found that telling others who I really am tends to alter the way people respond. It's easier to be someone else when I travel.'

'Oh. You're a traveller then, not a field hand,' she teased.

He smiled as he squeezed her gently and kissed both eyelids shut and then her mouth.

'Quiet, woman,' he kissed her forehead and her third eye closed. 'There'll be time for all the questions I can hear buzzing behind these lips. I need you rested. I'm not finished with you yet. I still have to prove that men are good for more than digging and chopping up stuff.'

Merindah smiled and snuggled closer, warm, and content. They succumbed to physical and magical exhaustion, and slept.

– – –

The Cosmic Mother stepped into the physical plane and stared at the son she loved before all others. She smoothed a strand of hair back from his face.

'Thank you, my dearest boy. I'm glad it was you.' She turned to Merindah, touching her flushed cheek. 'And you, child. As Aeon said, you are a wonder, Merindah. Thank you for your courage and compassion. We will not waste your precious gift.' She leant forward and kissed Merindah's brow, urging the cosmic visions to the back of her mind for now.

'Kindness, Chastity, if you would.' The Sisters stepped from their marble likeness and hurried to kneel before the Cosmic Mother. 'Daughters, no need for that.' She drew them to their feet, and looking from one to the other, appealed to them.

'I need to be elsewhere and otherwhen. Asking you to intervene is not like intervening myself. It's not breaking the rules, not really. Perhaps bending them a little out of shape is all.' The Mother's grin brought conspiratorial smiles to their faces, and she flicked a thread at one of the archways.

'Chastity, send my son back through the Gate. It's pre-set to return him to his point of origin. Once he's through, the arches will close. Soften his memory a little if you would, perhaps a beautiful dream.' Chastity's pale blue face blanched at the naked male specimen tangled on the divan, but she stepped forward, lips tight, and began to unwind the bodies.

'Kindness, if you would dress Merindah and take her to her room? I'm off to ensure Lust's small diversion doesn't turn into a full-scale free-for-all. Or perhaps I should allow it. Everyone deserves a little debauchery once in a while.' Kindness hastened to obey then paused, her soft hazel eyes flicked up to the amethyst and her mischievous mouth pursed.

'Remember or forget, what would be kindest for the Gatekeeper?'

The Mother turned back and gazed at the woman curled protectively around the new life in her belly. Rainbow sparkles flew like fireflies around her head, and a deep red light pulsed from her womb. 'Remember, most definitely remember, but *gently*. This moment of light and love must sustain her through the darkest times.'

She stepped back and spun, her arms raised, rainbow threads drifting from the tips of her fingers as she restarted time.

Nightmare

The universe buries strange jewels deep within us all, and then stands back to see if we can find them.

From the writings of Elizabeth Gilbert, Pre-Crack author, poet, and sage – Year of recovery 291 PC, Year of digitisation 295 PC.

Ali's nose twitched with the putrid odour of something rotting. She watched dust motes drift down from the aged corral, eddying in the slants of sunlight, dancing around the flurry of a man's arms and legs.

She jerked in her sleep, and half heard a soft click from above her bed. *What the?*

The dream scene went dark, and for a moment, Ali's disembodied soul drifted in a grey sea. Then she was back with the white-haired birri – the one who'd called herself Dee – but not at the creek where she'd last seen her. Instead, they were somewhere else and something bad was happening. A man was kicking the birri and punctuating the blows with his justifications.

Stop. This is so wrong. Stop it you bastard. Why am I dreaming this? How can I make it stop? How can I make him stop? Ali had no form in the dream and could only witness helplessly as the man persisted, completely unaware of her.

Somehow, Dee was responsible for her own beating – for her stepmother's death, her stepfather's excessive drinking, the poor crops, the diseased stock, the unpredictable weather, and some war the country was fighting somewhere on Reverie, wherever that was. The litany went on, and Ali felt uncomfortably voyeuristic as she sensed Dee drift off into her safe place: her dark place.

How do I know that's her safe place? Ali was not normally this lucid when she dreamed. *Maybe it happened when I got to close to her in the last dream.* Neither was she usually this analytical.

Whatever. This is so not gunna happen in my dream.

Ali reached towards the man, trying to imagine dragging him away. He continued the beating. Ali reached towards the birri, trying to imagine her getting up and protecting herself. She felt herself sliding, falling into Dee, becoming her – but not her. She clung desperately to her sanity.

I'm Ali, this is a dream. A freaking bad dream, but just a dream.

Ali felt Dee's pain become distant as the blessed darkness beckoned.

Dee inhabited Ali's dreams all too often. Until now they'd seemed fairly ordinary fantasies: simple scenes of a rural life, albeit with some magical overtones and a strangely hued heroine. The man was too loose with a slap or a shove to get the birri doing what he wanted, but he'd never been so systematic and lost to anger and violence. This wasn't ordinary by any means. And never had she known the name of the white-haired birri. Her dream earlier today had given her that. This was Dee. He was beating Dee. Somehow knowing her name made it so much worse.

But I'm Ali, and this is just a dream, another example of my gift messing with my life. Either that or it's the damn Feds.

Ali checked her gift and rotated the catalogued, colour-coded layers of her life until the previous dreams lined up. There they were in deep, blood red – every month about this time for the last five months. The vibrant lines connecting the events thickened as Ali watched.

Freaking hell, I'm dreaming of being beaten. That is so sick. What is wrong with me?

It's a freaking nightmare.

It smells so real – that kind of stinky that can only be real. Why didn't the other dreams feel real? What's different about today?

Ali twitched her gift out of focus to concentrate on waking, and felt the birri latch onto her inner dialogue. It interrupted Dee's slide into unconsciousness.

Goddess, it hurts so much. Dee's thought echoed clearly in Ali's mind.

Just a freaking nightmare. I need more meds. Pills will stop this. I'm gonna get some better pills.

Pills? Are they a weapon? Will they help me? Can they get me out of here? Dee asked.

Ali's heart suddenly pounded in parallel with the thud-thud of the beating.

How did she hear me think about pills? She didn't hear me this morning. Apart from the daydream earlier today, Ali usually experienced the birri's thoughts as vague images and sensations, as though she were observing others in a virtual reality training vid.

And why is this beginning to hurt?

The man's blows landed on the birri's arms and legs, and sometimes got through to her belly and chest. He rarely kicked her face: it would show if someone came by, although people rarely did these days.

How do I know that?

With no woman of the house to welcome them, and the shame in Dee's stepfather's eyes, visitors could only tolerate his litany of whining and complaints for so long.

Ali tried to recalibrate. *Where is this place? Is this dream some kind of analogy of what's happening – or not happening – in my life? Am I getting beaten up? Bullied? Am I the victim here?*

Freaking hell don't overthink it, for Fed's sake. You always overthink it. It's a freaking nightmare. Just bloody wake up.

Maybe I need stress classes twice a week. And a holiday.

She felt puzzlement from Dee. *I don't understand what you're saying. Are you my spirit guide?*

Ali snorted. *As if. What kind of spirit guide would I make?*

— — —

This oddly familiar voice had become clearer in Dee's mind over recent times. Peculiar things had begun to happen ever since she'd had her first woman flow five months ago. It was then that she'd felt the energetic itch that was her Grace – her magic – coming alive.

This Brown Lady had never seemed very aware of her before, and usually disappeared if Dee spoke directly to her. Still, she knew the presence was female, and that it came from the Shayde – the space between this world and the next. At least she imagined that's where the Brown Lady came from. Though the lady wasn't like the stories of Shayde Runners that Dee had been told of as a child. Shayde Runners were cruel and dangerous. You hid from them if you could – or ran when you couldn't. The Brown Lady always seemed kind of tired and worried, as though it was difficult to come through the veil that separated Reverie from the Shayde.

Other voices in her head were less elusive, especially Daemon, who was tenacious and could suck her dry of energy if she wasn't careful. Her stepmother had dismissed all the voices as childish nonsense, then hugged her and told her she read too many books. That was certainly not true, although she *did* read everything she could lay her hands on. But just to be sure, her stepmother had bought her an extra iron bracelet for each upper arm. *To keep our secret safe,* she'd said, and hugged her tight again, warning her not to tell her stepfather about the voices.

– – –

Ali experienced the flow of Dee's thoughts while she tried to wake herself up and step out of the nightmare.

Dee's next entreaty was desperate.

Hello. Is someone there? Can you help me? I have no mother to teach me the mysteries of the Grace, of being a woman and of using my magic. Are you a goddess?

A goddess, ha! That'll be the day. Ali's mind searched for a logical explanation. *This is the result of too many stims, or too many bloody meds full stop. It's time for less pills not more. No more pills. Time to quit, or cut down at least. Fed says they're not addictive – that they just help us feel a little better, or a little calmer. Freaking Federation, who the hell knows what they put in them? Bet the Fed Comm don't have to take them.*

You can hear me, Goddess, I know you can. Dee pleaded. *Please help me.*

Ali twitched. *What kind of twisted dream is this?*

It's not a dream! This is happening *to me.* Ali could feel the birri's anger firing up. *This is real! You must help me.*

Ali realised that the thud-thud of the man's feet had stopped. The birri's safe place dissolved with the final kick, and Ali felt Dee's body shudder as the pain slammed back in full force.

Ali struggled to stay apart from the dream. Her mind swirled with agony.

Small whimpers dribbled out of Dee's bruised and bloodied mouth. His boot had found the side of her face, her lip was swelling, her cheek was scraped raw.

The man began to untie his trousers.

Tears trickled from Dee's eyes.

Ali hung on to the last vestiges of herself, pulling back, feeling for the boundaries in her mind. *Is this really happening?*

It is to me.

Who are you?

I'm Dee.

For two ragged breaths there was silence.

I'm Ali.

Oh Ali, thank you for answering. Dee sobbed her relief.

Shit. Are you real? Are you someone? Oh, bloody hell, if this is real, how's this happening? How do I stop it? What the Fed am I doing? Where am I? How do I wake up? Ali began to panic and draw back.

Ali? Where are you, Ali? Why can I hear you? Are you an elemental? Ali pressed pause on her panic. *An elemental? I don't think so. I don't know what that is.*

Are you here? In Dungalup? Or somewhere close on Reverie? Dee's questions held a desperate urgency.

As far as I know, I'm dreaming at home in the North Quad, under the Melba Dome, on Torpid.

I don't know where that is.

It used to be called Earth, Ali said.

I don't understand. Does that mean you're an earth elemental? Are you my spirit guide? Are you here for my awakening? Dee asked.

I doubt it. What's your awakening?

When a woman first becomes able to bear children, that's her awakening. At that time, she also comes into the full power of her Grace, her magical inheritance. She becomes an adult, with adult responsibilities. Her mother chooses a goddess spirit guide to help her, to teach her. She dedicates her life to the goddess who chooses her.

Do those adult responsibilities include being beaten and raped?

Ali's thoughts felt like a censure to Dee. *I must honour my stepfather. It's his right to use my body. He fed me and kept a roof over my head though he suspected I was a daemon child. I owe my life to him.*

You can't let him beat you whenever he feels like it. In no world is that right. Fed, if I'd thought this was real. A daemon child? Ali's mind swarmed with guilt; she'd watched Dee's stepfather bully her for months. *I should have done something earlier. But it was just a dream, I didn't think it was real. I didn't think I could do anything.* She felt horrified at her own apathy and then outraged at Dee's stepfather's casual abuse. *Even if this isn't real*

112

Dee, your life belongs to you birri. You matter. You're just a child, and he's a beast.

Ali paused in her rant and added more gently. *He's been doing this for a long time, hasn't he?*

Dee's thoughts whispered into Ali's mind. *Only the beatings, and only when I got things wrong or was too slow. He was trying to beat the bad spirits out of me. But he got worse after my stepmother died a year ago. Lately he's started saying I had to cater for his all his needs. I've been able to avoid fulfilling them till now.*

His bloody needs. What about yours? You've gotta say no, get away, ask for help.

Dee sobbed. *How can I get away? Are you a powerful spirit or a mage? Can you help me? My magic is hard to control. I don't have anyone to teach me the Gramarye Lore, and I don't understand how to use the Fields and Threads.*

A spirit? Mage? Magic? Whoa, hold on. I'm just Ali – I'm a proji, a nobody, and there's no such thing as magic in the real world. Well, in my world anyway. Remembering her glowing fingers, Ali paused. *Magic? Maybe? Whatever. But I do know that what's happening to you isn't right. I've done my mandatory self-defence classes. I don't seem to have a body in this dream, but maybe I could describe a few moves for you.*

Dee's stepfather, drunk as always at this time of day – yet still able to beat her – finally managed to get his pants around his ankles. He grabbed her by her long white plait and hauled her upright against the wall of the stable. With his other hand he pulled her shirt out and fumbled with the laces of her trousers. Dee tried to stop him, her bruised body struggling to stay erect.

Bastard. Don't let him get away with it. Call for help. Stand up for yourself, birri. Knee him in the nuts, hard, Ali instructed, imagining the deed.

I couldn't do that. What in the Shayde's Shadow are you?

Does it matter? You deserve better. Just do it! Ali insisted.

I don't know what to do. I need help.

– – –

The months of systematic abuse had left Dee's spirit and body bruised and bloodied.

Please help me, Dee wailed. With no hope in sight, she had nothing left. She surrendered, and the spark of her resilience snuffed out. In that moment, a tingle of powerful energy flowed from her Grace, and somehow, Dee knew it was Ali.

She's helping me, and I will let her in. I've got nothing left to lose.

Dee felt strength returning as the lid on her magic cracked open. As her stepfather's leering face got closer, he let go of her hair to prop himself against the wall with one hand and fumbled his droopy manhood to attention.

As he did, Dee slipped into a kind of cloaked drowsiness. She saw herself bring her knee up hard against his exposed genitals. He howled, grabbed himself with both hands and doubled over. She put one hand on each of his shoulders to brace herself, then brought her knee up hard against his chin, snapping his head up. She watched herself head-butting his nose, feeling it squish under her forehead, and saw him falling back into the dirty straw, gasping and moaning. Finally, still in a fog she stomped on one of his hands, feeling the bones crunch under her boot heel.

'Keep your filthy mitts off my friend, you creep – or next time I'll do some permanent damage. She's a bloody child for Fed's sake.' The words came from her mouth, but the voice was not hers – it was Ali's. Dee distantly felt her hands tucking her shirt back in, and grabbing her coat off the hook where she'd hung it to fork the hay. Then she shuffled painfully outside, dabbing at her bleeding mouth, and holding her belly. She found herself regarding the sunset as if it was the first one she'd ever seen.

It's so bloody beautiful. So much colour. Dee felt a sense of awe that wasn't her own as she watched the orange orb setting over the familiar hills that had been her home for the past decade.

I've never seen colours like this. Smelt air this fresh. Our world is so old, so tired, so washed out. This is amazing. It's so alive – my body is buzzing. Hang on, the buzz is healing. I'm hurt but healing. I can actually feel it healing.

Dee was enveloped in a grey pall, unable to answer. She wanted to cry out that it was *her* body hurt, *her* body healing. Ali may have taken over her body with good intentions, but she still felt violated, and voiceless.

— — —

Within Dee's body, Ali hobbled towards the cottage. She stopped to look over the goat fence at a carefully tended vegetable plot. *Jeez, real plants.*

She turned into the garden, examining the small green shoots in neat lines, and a pile of weeds at one side. Her hands hurt where that bloke had kicked her.

Not "that bloke". Dee's stepfather. Dee? Are you there Dee? Huh, I'm totally confused now. Is this a dream or isn't it? Bloody Fed Comm will be behind it somehow, I'm sure.

Ali flexed the aching fingers and shook them a little to move the muscles. As she gave one final firm shake, a flash of green shot from the ends of her fingers and into the earth in front of her. She peered suspiciously at her fingers and then at the dirt where the green flash had landed. The small green shoots around that area were now twice the size of those next to them. She gave her hands a firm shake again, trying to repeat what she'd done. Nothing. She headed towards the cottage.

Huh, magic. No way. This is one freaky dream. My hands haven't glowed green before. They've done the red thing a few times now though. I wonder what that means? I need to stop relying on my dodgy gift and start writing actual notes. Get them down in that dream journal I keep meaning to write.

Ali limped into the front room of the dwelling, gazing around, touching everything, smelling, listening. *This is way better than my squidgy little box.* She smiled and relaxed.

– – –

Finally, Dee found her voice. *This isn't right. This is* my *body, Ali. What have you done to me?*

Dee? Is that you? Bloody hell, I thought I imagined you. Where've you been, birri?

What kind of magic is this? You've possessed my body, and I want it back. You told me no one had a right to my body, now you've taken it.

Ali winced. *I'm so sorry. I didn't mean to. It's just that when I saw him coming at you, I couldn't let it happen, not even in a dream. I felt you letting go and I sort of jumped, and there I was – in you, being you.*

I guess that was kind of permission. Thank you, I think. But how do I get back in control? Dee asked.

Ali's response wasn't reassuring. *I'm not sure. It was like my gift stretched a bunch of the colour thin in the tapestry and shoved me through the gap. You just come back, and I'll jump out.*

Dee felt Ali trying to let go. Nothing.

Dee tried to move her arm towards her face. Nothing.

They heard cursing and crashing from the stable. Her stepfather was coming, and she was helpless again – more than helpless, a mere passenger in her own body. Tears spilt down her cheeks as both souls battled for control of Dee's form.

– – –

It was Ali's turn to entreat Dee. *Come on Dee. You can do it. Open your magic Grace-y thingummyjig. Give him a zap with a green thing.*

That's not how it works, Dee responded irritably. *We are the magic, and the magic is us, or it used to be. If I don't have control, then I'm not the magic. I don't know how to do this. My mother should be teaching me, but I have no mother. I'm an orphan, twice over.*

Ali could hear the frustration in Dee's mental voice. She felt her years of managing cranky clients click into gear, and she realised how she could try to defuse Dee's roiling emotions. Calm congruence would be more likely to help than conflict. Ali was used to finding common ground – used to acquiescing and backing down from her position. It wasn't very satisfying, but it was effective in getting the work done.

Well, I'm an orphan too, and I learn really quick. So teach me, cos he's coming. We can sort out the swap later.

Dee tried to show Ali where the well of her Grace was, and how to open the door. She started to explain, *It's like a puzzle. You open the door and reach, and you* become *the magic. See the rainbow threads all around you? They form the tapestry of the world. You weave them into symbols and pictures with your intent. I'm strongest in Fire and Earth fields, so reach for those – they're mostly red and green, and I seem to be able to manage those without causing too much trouble.*

As Dee spoke, the tears continued to roll down her face, and her body hiccupped a panicked sob. Ali's calm was fast dissolving under the pressure. *I can't see what you mean, Dee. I dunno what you're talking about.*

Suddenly, the cottage door slammed open and Dee's stepfather entered, trousers hastily drawn together. His eyes were red, and his nose still streamed blood. He snarled, lunging to grab his stepdaughter with both hands.

Her vision went scarlet, her Grace exploded.

Time slowed as she *shimmered.*

Her hands glowed, and Ali felt her arms extend into red-scaled claws with long black talons that raked across Dee's stepfather's chest. She roared her outrage, and green flames issued from her throat, engulfing him in a firestorm.

He began to scream, staggering away and slapping at his clothes and skin. He threw himself back out of the cottage, rolling in the dirt in agony, trying to put out the green-tinged fire. Ali followed him out, her horned head towering above the man, her spiked tail lashing furiously.

Dee's stepfather clawed at his face with his mangled hands, until his screams finally stopped. The blaze raged on incandescent; and then there was only a pile of grey man-shaped ash on the dirt. Ali's huge, taloned feet stomped through the ash.

Gotcha sucker. You're toast.

— — —

With Ali's triumphant crow, Dee's spirit shrieked and she snapped back into ascendancy. *Nooo!*

Her stomach threatened to empty, and her glowing talons shook. Ali was gone. Her stepfather was dead. She'd murdered him. Dee *shimmered* back to human and crumpled to her knees.

A shadow swooped towards her and she looked up in horror as a blood red dragon descended on her helpless form – she had nothing left, her Grace and her mind were exhausted. Besides, her life was forfeit, she was a murderer.

When it landed, the dragon *shimmered* and became a large red-skinned human male. Dee sank lower to await her demise at the hand of the deity.

The being bent close, his breath smelt like smoke as he lifted her chin with one finger. His sparkling black eyes bored into her.

'Well, well, well. I hope you enjoyed playing with my fire. Sleene will be jealous my gift was awoken first.' He released her chin and leant back, folding his massive arms across his chest. 'But Meana will be pleased you've begun our task at last.'

'Sleene? Meana? What gift? What task? Who are you?' Dee knew those names, they were powerful elementals, which would make the dragon Wyak, god of Fire. Gifts and tasks from elementals were seldom given – and neither left the receiver unscathed.

'Can you guess?' The being waved a casual hand and a platoon of tiny fire beings emerged from the grey ash of her stepfather. The beings marched over to disappear into Dee's still glowing hands. Tattoos of flame ran up and down her arms. The tattoos vanished into her skin as she shuffled away from the elemental, leaving just her palms patterned in crazed red flames.

'You're Wyak, fire elemental and youngest son of the Cosmic Mother,' Dee's voice was hoarse, her overtaxed heart pounding in her chest. Wyak smiled and nodded. He indicated the pile of ash that had been her stepfather.

'That trick should help set you on the path of destruction, little hellcat. Let's see what else you can be blamed for.' The fire elemental's wild black hair whipped about as he flicked his hands at the house and barn. Red sparks flew from his fingertips and both buildings burst into flames. Within seconds smoke was billowing in thick acrid clouds into the still air. 'That will do it. A little more evidence of your guilt and complicity.' As the flames clawed higher, Wyak raised his arms, exulting in the heat and light of his element. 'Now this is much better.' He pointed his fingers at Dee.

'No, please don't, no more. The animals will burn.' Dee had started to stand; she could hear the goats bleating their distress and the horse neighing frantically in its corral by the burning barn.

Wyak lowered his arms and forced her back to her knees. 'Oh, but we have so much more in store for you. Enjoy the rest of your gifts, daemon child.' He squeezed his hand and Dee fell onto her side, her lungs struggling to take in a breath. As her eyes began to close, she saw Wyak *shimmer* into his dragon form, and with two powerful flaps he disappeared into the clouds of smoke.

— — —

Ali's eyes blasted open back in her cramped flat, her heart hammering. She bolted upright, swinging her legs over the side of the sofa bed. The faint, fiery red glow around her hands faded, but the stink of burning flesh lingered in her nose.

Holy shit, was that bloody real?

She hurried to the bathroom, heart in her throat, and thumbed on the light. Quickly, she checked her hands, turning them over and back, but they were normal. Examining her face in the mirror revealed nothing out of the ordinary apart from pupils dilated with adrenaline for the second time in twenty-four hours.

Just the usual dark rings from lack of freaking sleep and crazy-arsed nightmares. Who the hell celebrates turning into a dragon and killing people with magical fire? Why am I dreaming this shit? Was Dee real? Did I really kill her stepfather? If you murder someone in a dream, is it really a crime? I bet that dragon Jiemba would know.

She surreptitiously checked her shadow behind her for evidence of the dragon and felt her gift surge with red ochre threads.

Loud knocking on her front door interrupted her swirling brain, and she jumped. Her heart leapt back into her throat.

'Ali! Ali, what's happening? Are you okay?' She recognised the voice of her neighbour Andie, and her body sagged with relief. As an IT geek, Andie mostly worked nights from the flat next door. She shared the space with two lads, Nate and Dell, who worked shifts at Fed Man, the manufacturing plant down in South Quad. They'd moved in about eight years ago – not long after Ali.

'Ali, are you there? Are you okay?'

Ali grabbed her dressing gown from the back of the bathroom door and hurried into the other room. 'I'm fine, Andie. I'm fine. I'm coming.' She stumbled over her dillybag strap on the floor, felt for the key and turned the deadlock.

'Hey Andie, what's up?'

In the dimness of the night, Andie's expression was difficult to see with her night-dark skin and chocolate-brown eyes. Her cloud of black curls haloed in the small glow of the few working security lights.

'I heard yelling and it sounded like you were fighting someone. Are you all right? Are you alone?' She tried to peer around Ali and into the flat.

Ali tucked the gown tighter around herself, still shivery from the dregs of the nightmare. 'Yeah, I'm fine. There's no one here. Just a bit of a bad dream.'

Freaking understatement, woman. Ali tried to smile, but it faltered and slid off her face.

'Want me to make you a cuppa? I could sit with you for a bit if you like.' Andie's voice was gentle, and Ali considered the offer for a heartbeat.

Shit, I'd love to talk to someone about all this craziness.

But bloody hell, she's thirty years younger than you. What the hell kind of advice could she give? The young have no common sense and no place advising the old. They haven't lived.

Plus, she'd definitely think I'm nutso and call the Grey Shirts to cart me off in a straight jacket. "Watch Out for Your Neighbour" – they could be a crazy fire-wielding nutbag with a dragon in their head. Would she report me? Am I going nuts?

Ali straightened, running a nervous hand through her curls.

'No thanks, Andie, I'm fine. I've just been working long hours and not getting much quality sleep.'

'I've got some seds that might help. Working nights means sleeping days and sometimes I struggle too. You wanna try one? They're pretty light. Got them from a proper medtech, not on the street. Might just get you a good few hours.'

Ali's thumb flicked her ruby ring and she frowned. 'Bloody hell, why not? I've gotta get some sleep. Thanks.'

Andie's crooked white smile flashed, and she hurried back to her flat. She returned with a small bottle. Ali waved her inside and offered her open palm. Andie tipped two diamond-shaped blue pills out. 'They don't give you the druggy hangover most seds do. You should be good to go in a few hours, and you won't remember a thing. Are you sure you don't want me to come in and sit with you for a while?'

Ali glanced down at her hands, remembering the glowing, the ninja, the dragon, possessing Dee, and Dee's stepfather bursting into flames. She looked up at Andie and shook her head. 'No, no, really I'm fine. I just need to turn off my imagination and get some sleep. The seds'll be great, thanks. I owe you.'

Andie nodded and passed her the bottle. 'Keep the rest. Sleep well. Yell if you need anything else. Just bang on our wall or shout, eh?' Andie's facial scars dragged at her smile. Half her face was disfigured by burns and Ali wondered for the umpteenth time why Andie didn't get them regened.

'I will. Thanks again,' Ali smiled and shut the door. The dividing walls *were* pretty damn thin. She heard Andie walk away and the door to her flat closed. A muffled murmur suggested that at least one of the lads was awake too. Ali flicked on the light and checked the time – just after four. She headed to the fridge for a bottle of water.

Jeez, I've gotta see someone about this. I can't keep pretending it's not happening. I'm gunna start that dream journal. I wonder why I haven't done that before. I love journalling. I'll take these tonight, and then tomorrow I'm making an appointment to see someone about getting some sleep. This old body can't take much more. I so need that holiday.

Ali swallowed the pills and snuggled herself back under the blankets. The events of the night kept her shivering till the seds took effect, and she drifted thankfully into a dreamless slumber.

– – –

A few minutes after she'd settled, Ali's front door opened, and two figures slipped inside. Andie and Nate tiptoed towards the sofa bed. Nate's hazel eyes turned golden in the luminous glow from the handheld scanner he waved over Ali.

'Shit, entropy readings are off the charts. What's she been up to?'

Andie's whispered response was grim, 'Whatever it is, she's gunna get herself realigned or worse, that's what. I'll do the wipe – you go see if she's started another dream journal and grab it.'

She triggered the silver bands around her wrists and as she placed her hands on Ali's temples, a pale mauve glow capped Ali's head. Then Andie closed her eyes, sinking into Ali's subconscious. She grabbed Ali's memory of arriving home last night, fast forwarded a few minutes, then expertly wiped the next few hours.

Andie wove dream memory replacements about the departure of a recent lover named Dean as the reason Ali wasn't sleeping well. She seeded thoughts of an Outside holiday, hoping Ali would take the bait this time. Manipulating minds was a delicate balance. When she removed her hands, she was sweating and shaking. Andie tapped her silver bands and the glowing mauve cap dissolved.

'You okay?' Nate put his arm around her as she stumbled back, grabbing her own temples.

'Yeah, I'm fine. It's just getting harder to wipe her. It's like she's getting stronger, better able to resist. She's a tough old bird. Surprises me how she keeps going with all this shit happening to her. I dunno how much longer the wiping is gunna work. The gaps are getting closer together and bigger. Other people might start noticing her forgetting stuff. It's not an exact process Nate. I can't be too choosy, so lots of basic stuff gets wiped too. I don't think it's affecting her job yet, but it's probably not far off.'

'Let's not get too far ahead of ourselves. We do as the League says. The higher ups know what they're doing. If she's a Chosen One, then we step up the action. We'll keep nudging her towards getting Outside like we've been told. Once she's there, we can control her better.'

Andie shifted, uncomfortable with Nate's word, and his gaze sharpened. He grabbed her arm and swung her to face him. 'Andie, you know better. Don't get emotionally attached to the target. Stay focused on the mission, no matter how long it takes.'

Andie shrugged off his arm. 'Yeah, yeah I know. Find the Chosen, save the Cosmos and all that,' she parroted.

Nate ignored her attitude. 'Let's get outta here. She's right about needing some sleep. You can check in on her tomorrow.' He ran his scanner over Ali one last time.

'Still above acceptable. But it'll have to do.' They let themselves out of the flat and re-locked the door.

Insomniac

To die, to sleep – to sleep, perchance to dream – ay, there's the rub, for in this sleep of death what dreams may come…

From Hamlet, William Shakespeare, Pre-Crack playwright – Year of recovery 257 PC, Year of digitisation 291 PC. (Recovered hard copy on permanent loan to The Federation Chair's personal library.)

Ali pressed save on the report and tilted her head left and right to ease the tension. She'd been chained to the computer screens for hours, the document deadline looming like a reaper's scythe over her neck. The sludgy brown walls of her solitary domain felt more coffin-like than ever today, and her contemplation of the dingy decor left her singularly uninspired. The building's cooling had shut down more than an hour ago when most people had left. Even though Autumn approached, the air was now oppressive and humid.

Federation probably uses the same decorator for all their buildings to keep the people depressed and docile.

She grimaced.

It's worked on me. Losing the will to live as of right now.

Her glance out the grimy window showed an already darkened Friday afternoon with most of the lights out in the building opposite. Domers were hurrying home to families and food, such as it was.

Ali checked the teetering tower of plas folders in her in-tray and sighed. A couple more hours ought to take it down a storey or two. If she could knock this lot on the head, her day would go a hell of a lot better tomorrow.

Who I am kidding? It's a bloody cursed pillar of projects. Every time I work my way to the bottom, it miraculously builds up again. How crazy is that? I could do with some fire magic to burn stuff to a crisp with a flick of my fingers.

Wait, where did that come from? Fire magic? Did I read about that somewhere, or was it one of those crazy daydreams? I can't tell the difference anymore. My memories don't fit together like they're supposed to.

She sighed. *It's not like I can ask anyone about the problem with my gift.*

Gift, yeah right. Curse more likely. It's gunna get me in trouble one day soon. Those Grey Shirts'll be knocking on my door with a little iron bracelet that has my name on it.

She flexed her fingers, half expecting to see the tips glow red. A little part of her was disappointed they didn't. Instead, she flicked her ruby ring around with her thumb, the rhythm of flick, flick, ruby, flick, flick, ruby comforting her.

I've gotta get a life. Nope, on second thoughts, I've gotta have a holiday. Maybe it is time to go Outside and have an adventure.

Idiot. You're surely kidding yourself about being the adventurous type. It doesn't bode well if you're chickening out already and it's still weeks away.

Weeks, who can think about weeks? It must be a whole three minutes since I thought about Dean.

Dean. Ali remembered the months since Dean left being long and lonely. Their relationship had been on rocky ground for a while, but it had still been a shock to go home late one night and find he'd packed his things and moved out. And the very night she needed to feel secure. The night after she'd imagined that ninja attack.

But that was only last night... how can he be months gone? She shook her head, her gift flaring and fading. It didn't fit. And for the life of her she couldn't remember why he'd left so suddenly.

She glared over at the window. Her reflection glared back. The glass held no trace of a rainbow smudge. Her heart skipped at the memory. She reached quickly to thumb on a brighter light, knocking her half-full cuppa all over the files on her desk.

'Dammit, I'm a clumsy klutz!' she yelled, snatching up the cup. 'Sophie, grab a cloth. I've done it again.'

Sophie hurried in, all poise and grace, cloth in hand. She dabbed at the spill, shaking her head, exasperation in her uncommon sky-blue eyes.

Superstitious Domers believed that pale eyes were a sign of thin blood and weak character. People who had them couldn't be trusted, and shouldn't hold senior job rank. Probably *because* of that superstition, it was rare to find anyone with pale eyes and skin holding any kind of leadership in the Dome.

Personally, Ali didn't hold with most of the superstitious nonsense that peppered the suburbs and gave rise to hundreds of twitchy community cliques. The Fed Comm looked the other way for most of them. The Grey Shirts occasionally rounded up one of the groups and posted it on the banned list. Central members disappeared, courtesy of the Fourth Tenet *"Don't Force Your Views on Others"*, and the rest scurried back to their hidey holes. Until the next time.

Anyway, Sophie was an excellent addi, regardless of her eye colour.

'You *are* a clumsy klutz. How did you ever pass the proji assessment?' Sophie admonished her.

Ali shook some of the excess tea off the documents and into the bin. 'Luckily you only need basic physical dexterity, so I managed to scrape through. Like I always do. It'd be nice to do things easy for a change. Slide into the slot with time to spare,' Ali sighed.

Sophie tried to pat at the stain on Ali's trousers as Ali spread the stained plas pages across the desk to dry. 'That's going to need professional cleaning. Do you want me to get it done for you? You could wear your spares home.'

Home. At the thought of her deserted flat, the whole breakup came crashing down on Ali again. *Every trace of Dean is gone.* Ali thought that was a bit odd. He'd never been that tidy when he was there. She figured they'd been good friends, even with the strain, but even though she'd tried to contact him several times, she'd got no reply. His comli number didn't exist. It hurt that he'd changed it since leaving her.

'It's almost as if he'd never really been in my life.' She hadn't realised she'd spoken aloud till Sophie responded. Sophie knew immediately what she was thinking about. She'd been sympathetic but philosophical when Ali had told her about the breakup.

'Plenty more fish in the sea,' she'd encouraged.

That was fine for Sophie. Despite the weak eyes, she was gorgeous, young, and vibrant – and had her whole life ahead of her. Ali felt every *one* of her fifty-two years – single again with no children. And no immediate prospects of ever having them with Dean disappearing from the scene. She tried to recall his face or the way he laughed, but only got vague outlines.

At least she had her job. She was paid well enough for working hard, and she could enjoy some of the finer things in Domer life. That's what Geoff had told her when he'd hired her. That was before she realised she'd sold her soul to the Federation in general, and Geoff in particular.

When I find something finer to enjoy, I will.

Life in the Dome held few real pleasures for her. What she *really* wanted was a partner to share things with, someone to witness the big and the little things in her life. If something wonderful happened now, she didn't have anyone to call. Her last partner was busy with a child, running her hither and thither to various activities or hanging on the arm of her barista husband at some bigwig East Quad function.

After some exhaustive agricultural disasters, a new strain of genetically modified bean meant coffee was the new religion in the Dome this year. Her ex-partner's husband had many worshipping at his altar.

Is that envy?

She thought for a moment. No, that was an unworthy thought. At least that's what her stress class teacher would say.

Ali did love her job. She read all sorts of interesting and fantastical things, and met all sorts of interesting people. Though… she hadn't met anyone very interesting lately. Her head began to ache, the dull clamouring grinding its way through the back of her skull. Her eyes began to water, and rainbow sparkles appeared at the edge of her vision. This was her pre-migraine aura.

It's gunna be a big one.

Sophie raised an eyebrow, waiting as Ali stood pensively.

Then, recovering a little, Ali came to, slipped out of her stained trousers and put on the spare pair Sophie handed her. They were a close enough fit, and both navy, though it was easy to tell they didn't match.

Sophie tsked and marched out.

Ali looked at her desk, then at the stained files, the darkening sky, and found herself remembering the dream of a sunset. Her headache racked up a notch to pounding, and the drums began. She rummaged in her dillybag for some painkillers and swallowed two with the last remaining mouthful of cold tea.

'Ugh.' She sat back at her desk and laid her hands in her lap. Closing her eyes, she breathed deeply to try and stave off the pain. Occasionally she could cut the misery off at this stage if she was focused and still. The distant sound of Sophie rustling around her desk outside drifted in. The ever-present hum of the Dome ramped up as she focused on her hearing, drifting out to muffled beeps of flocars, vendors shouting, and a fire siren wailing.

Fire! Magical fire shooting flames from my talons! No, not my talons, someone else's. Eww, I can smell burning meat, who's barbecuing inside the building? That's gross!

Ali shot to her feet.

'Enough. Time to wag stress class.' *Maybe I should call it by its proper name. Stress release class. Yep, teacher will be happy.*

'Energy flows where the focus goes.'

So if I keep calling it stress class then that's what I'll get, more stress. This is so much hocus pocus. Why did I ever agree to it? Talk about superstitious nonsense.

Ali knew why. Her boss had insisted. It was this or lose her job. A pill would have been quicker. She sighed again. Though she felt guilty about skipping class, she also had to get some sleep if she wanted to keep doing her job.

Her headache had plateaued at a bearable level. Sometimes the migraines benched her for whole days, and they'd been getting worse this past twelve months. Oddly, she'd never missed a day at work: they always downed her on her seventh day – her one day each week off work.

Another bit of me deteriorating. Maybe I do need regen.

'Time to go, Sophie. I've got a class, and if I'm late again, I get a black mark and a second warning.' Ali felt uncomfortable lying to Sophie, but she didn't want to admit she was having a session with a therapist. Some things she preferred to slot under the Sixth Tenet and Mind her Own Business herself.

Sophie came back in shaking her head. 'Only you could be late to a relaxation class. Go on, go. I'll finish cleaning up in here. See you tomorrow.'

– – –

Ali swiped her citzcoded wrist against the flocar scanner, tossing up whether to drive manually. Normally she loved the sensation and control that manual driving gave her, and any chance to ditch the Federation's AI was a bonus. Using the AI meant extra credits deducted from her tally, but a long drive while dodging flocar idiots was *not* what she needed right now. So auto it was.

Her migraine hovered menacingly at the back of her eyes. The flocar engine hummed gently, and she settled back in the sculpted seat for the ride towards South Quad, dialling the air filters to max after the puff of anti-odour. She'd held her breath as long as she could coming out of the building, too lazy to put nose plugs in for the short walk to the flocar queue.

Woo hoo, you're living on the edge, you rebel! No nose plugs for fifty metres. Look at you nudging the status quo. She laughed at herself, shaking her head.

Unbidden, her gift showed her the map of memory holes. She traced the grey lines that outlined the widening gaps and noted that life hadn't been the same since her trip out to the Yarra Ranges almost twelve months ago. Her gift highlighted the day before her fifty-second birthday.

She sobered, realising that that was when the unravelling had accelerated. Her confidence in her own abilities had been the first casualty, Dean the second, and sleep the third. She should've sent one of the juniors on the trip, even though the client had asked for her specifically.

'Why would she do that? How did she come to ask for me by name? I'm not that famous.'

'Sorry. I did not catch that.' The flocar's AI responded.

Ali shuffled back in the autoseat, and the synchro belts adapted, allowing her to lean forward. She slipped off her heels to rub her aching feet. At least this car was clean and relatively odourless. The disadvantage of the sealed air space meant you often got a good dose of the previous passenger's pong. In a Domer summer, that could be ripe, even with the anti-odour each vehicle was fitted with.

'No need for a response. No listening, no recording.'

Damn nosy Feds.

'All passenger citzcodes are recorded for financial transactions and in accordance with the Ten Tenets,' the tinny genderless voice of the AI said.

'Yes, Yes, whatever,' Ali grouched.

The flocar moved into the traffic and headed to the North South Gate. Ali was rarely interactive with AI tech. She was a little old-fashioned in that regard, preferring a human interface whenever possible. But with so many confusing and conflicting bits of information going around in her head; she needed a sounding board to sort through them. AIs were bound to client confidentiality anyway. Or so the Fed Comm assured everyone.

'You can listen and provide empathy? You're programmed for emotion, aren't you?' she asked.

'Yes, I am programmed for basic emotional exchange.' The AI responded.

Ali's desperation increased with every anomalous thought. The dreams and the sleeplessness were one thing; so many missing gaps in her gift another; add to that the physical weirdness of her fingers glowing, but now imagining assassins. She had to stop this slide into chaos.

Is it the lack of knowing how everything fits, or the lack of my being in control that worries me the most?

She'd almost considered confiding in Sophie, but Sophie was too FEN, and it was too awkward with work. Besides, Sophie was wedded to her career, she'd hardly entertain anything outside of those parameters. Ali had briefly thought Andie might listen sympathetically, but what help could she give? It couldn't have anything to do with Andie's area of IT expertise.

What is it that I want from them anyway? Why confide in anyone? They can listen, but then what? They'll probably quote Tenet Five at me: "Control Yourself" – followed by immediately calling the Grey Shirts.

The warning from the dragon's voice telling her to not trust anyone clanged in her mind.

The only one I can trust is myself, but now I can't even do that. If only Dean were still with me.

'Get a grip birri,' she instructed herself, the maudlin feelings tearing her eyes.

'Are you unwell? Do you require a medtech?' The AI asked.
Ali felt her resolve weakening. She stared at the vehicle's dashboard.
The Ten Tenets were plastered right in the centre in all their oppressive conviction.

'No. Silent drive.' Ali sat a little straighter.

I've been in worse. I think. Take a Tenet Nine: "Stick with What You Know". Do what you always do. Write it down, make a list, take some action.

Ali ferreted a fresh notebook and pen from her dillybag and opened the first page. She took a deep breath and began writing about a project brief request she'd received around a year ago from a reclusive woman in the East Quad's Yarra district. The woman was an author and historian who owned an enviable pre-Crack esoteric library. Many of her books were first editions of alchemical, spiritual and allegedly magical tomes. The author wrote her non-fiction under a pen name, but Ali's boss Geoff, hadn't recorded the name in his brief, which was odd.

'Kind of important, don't you think Geoff?' Ali had said.

'I'm sure you'll get all the details we need, Ali. You always do. Haven't let me down yet. I rely on your thoroughness and tact.' He'd steepled his pudgy fingers, and peered down his nose at Ali, endeavouring to seem professional and wise. It hadn't worked. Ali had pegged him years earlier as a manipulative moron.

So she'd waited patiently for the rest of the story. Geoff always loved to spin a yarn, eking out the details so his team had to scurry after him to pick them up like mice chasing ration crumbs. Ali had known from past experience that there was no point hurrying him. It only made the story longer.

'This is a plum project. This East Quad woman is a little loopy by all accounts, but she's prepared to pay well to have her library catalogued and stored. I did find out that she doesn't have an heir and wanted all her things preserved for future generations. Who does that these days?' Geoff hadn't waited for Ali's response before he barrelled on.

'Some strange things in the collection though, so no Fed librarian wanted to touch it in case their reputation was tarnished. Not FEN, you know how it goes. Here's where you come in. The woman is commissioning a new library. She's going to have a derelict warehouse in South Quad restored to house it. And now for the best bit.' He paused dramatically, spinning out the moment.

'It will be a private institute for speculative and spiritual literature and artefacts. Can you believe that?' He leant across the desk, wriggled his fingers and whispered, 'Ooo, magic.'

Ali hadn't known what to object to first. The fact that Geoff was happy for *her* to be besmirched as not-FEN by the assignment, or that some East Quad woman had a tally deep enough to fritter away on this when the West Quad was teeming with people looking for their next ration and a place to sleep.

'Now, whilst you have the best head for organising I've had on my team in a while...'

Ali had rolled her eyes as Geoff tilted his head to prepare his next breadcrumb.

I've got the best head for bloody organising you've ever *had, you freaking idiot.*

'... I seem to remember hearing that you read fantasy to get away from the logical and boring world of project management,' Geoff had smiled benevolently, the effect ruined by his grimace of crooked, stained teeth. They'd always weirded Ali out.

Despite the profligacy of the East Quad toff, Ali had been intrigued. She *did* love reading any kind of fantasy – and the more outlandish and full of magic and wonderful beasts, the better. She'd always felt more at home amongst the fantastical than in the tragically real world under the Dome. Not many fantasy and sci fi works had survived the Crack, and writers of anything weird today didn't survive the Grey Shirts long. But there was still a pretty solid black market in old and second-hand speculative fiction.

Her imagination longed for a real adventure. One that would give her excitement, danger, and the chance to show what she was made of. One where she could be one of those tough but warm hearted heroines she read about. Where she could save the day, save the world – ideally without having to complete a complex Gantt chart first, or have a committee decide which way to fold the plastic sheets. At least that's what she'd thought before she'd begun to have weird dreams night and day and have strange women accost her in the street.

Ali checked the GPS. They were almost half way to her destination. She gripped her pen and continued; the words flowed onto the page in a torrent.

Twelve months ago, her flocar had headed up a winding, hilly road on the outer edge of the East Quad, on route to this reclusive author's home. The Yarra Ranges were protected, the only hills with living trees within the Dome. No new building was allowed, and the tattered pockets of bush were awe-inspiring to someone who'd lived most of their life in the barren, stale environment of the concrete city and suburbs. The trip had taken a couple of hours, and all the winding roads towards the end had left Ali a little nauseous.

When she'd finally arrived, she'd been awestruck at the beautiful, quirky home nestled into the side of a hill. The sign on the iron gates had named it Moonyah, and it had emanated a sense of strength, calm and quiet that was completely at odds with Ali's dingy sterile flat. She'd felt welcomed, safe. The house had even had its own tower, with round walls of deep ochre red stone.

When she'd stepped out of the flocar without her nose plugs, the air had held only the faintest tinge of chemicals. East Quad always got the newest and best filters, although they housed the least amount of people. *Tally talks.*

Ali remembered nodding to the two people who'd looked suspiciously like Grey Shirts, and who'd just happened to be near the front entrance gardening when she arrived. She remembered knocking at the solid wooden door while they'd watched as if she was there to steal something. But for the life of her, Ali struggled to recall the author's face, or any detail about her.

In her mind, the woman was a kind of bluish figure with indiscernible features. She did remember they'd spent an amazing afternoon talking about all things fantasy, talking as though magic really existed. As well as the bewildering array of books, the author had owned a collection of magic-inspired paraphernalia that Ali had itched to get her hands on: talismans, carvings, cauldrons, implements and caskets.

When they'd realised how dark it had grown, the author had insisted that Ali share her rations and stay the night. Ali, for her part, hadn't needed to be asked twice. There'd been nothing waiting for her at home.

So the two of them had conversed undisturbed into the wee small hours before Ali had finally called it quits and fallen into a soft bed in one of the many guest rooms. And that's when the really odd stuff had begun.

Ali paused, taking herself back. This was where her gift had the first big rift. The tapestry was awry, like a bunch of threads had been pulled too tight, leaving an ugly pucker. She was sure this was where she'd dreamed for the first time about a young birri – the one who called herself Dee in yesterday's creek daydream. As Ali wrote Dee's name on the page, odd bits of information crawled from dark spaces of her gift. Reverie, a world where magic was the norm, exotic creatures abounded, and odd beings popped up all over the place, causing mayhem. Just the stuff of your typical fantasy.

She wrote a question in the margin of her notes: *Fantasy or fact?*

Ali stopped writing, slipping into her memories of the dreams. Some dreams had felt light and joyful, some dark and violent, but all had felt so real. She shook herself, and returned to her notes.

When she'd awoken the next day, she'd mentioned her crazy dream to the author, sure that this client would appreciate it.

But, here's another odd thing – I can't remember how the author responded. I just don't recall a single word.

She listed the next thing she did remember: the flocar was driving into the re-charge station in the small suburb at the bottom of the hills. She'd lost a couple of hours and it was almost midday. Weeks later, she still couldn't fill that time gap. She even forgot about the dreams for a few months, but now they were back, worse than ever.

It must *be something about what happened at that house, at that time. It's where it all began, I'm almost certain.*

When Ali had returned to work the next day, Geoff had called her to his office. He hadn't looked pleased, though Ali hadn't had any idea what had happened to make him so cranky. Two Grey Shirts had exited Geoff's office as she'd arrived. Ignoring her, they'd marched off in sync to the beat of some unknown Federation drum, resplendent and intimidating in their ubiquitous grey suits and red ties.

Geoff got right to the point for once. 'Ali, you've stuffed up.' At Ali's surprised look, he'd huffed, 'You knew how important this job was. It could've funded this department for a year or more. We could've been riding a whole different wave of prosperity.'

Ali had suspected he meant *he – Geoff* could have. She'd doubted that she would've received any recognition or reward. After all, why start acknowledging that Ali did most of the best work now?

'What're you talking about?' Geoff hadn't asked her to sit down, so she'd stood uncomfortably in front of his unrealistically tidy desk. It was positioned to impress on his visitors the number of windows in his corner office, and looking into the light always made Ali squint and squirm. That and the view. Ali was not overfond of heights.

Geoff's office was fifteen floors up from hers, and the City was laid out beneath her in all its shambling architectural glory. Every time she saw it, her gift began to populate the view with significant events and dates. As she always did, she'd turned the tapestry down and focused back on Geoff.

He hadn't missed Ali's attention slip though, and his ego sharpened his words. 'Our affluent author has sent word that she's taken your advice and she'll be keeping her library exactly where it is. She thanked us for our assessment, sent a generous recompense for your time and travel with a little for unmet expectations, and that's it. We're not to contact her again. And the message was delivered by two grumpy Grey Shirts. What the hell did you say to her?'

Ali had paled, feeling nonplussed. She'd had no idea what had happened, literally.

'Geoff, I didn't say *anything* that would've made her change her mind. We spent a fabulous day talking about the possibilities for her collection and the institute. I couldn't have been more complimentary. We covered a stack of options for the cataloguing and building. In fact, I ended up staying the night because we'd stayed so late talking.'

Ali had stopped then, and Geoff had glared at her expectantly.

'And…?' His thick fingers had drummed on the desk as his heavy brows drew down. 'Did you make a pass at her? Stuff yourself with her East Quad rations?'

Ali had felt reluctant to mention the dream thing. After all, it wasn't really anything to do with anything. It was just a dream.

'And nothing. I had breakfast and left. On the best of terms, really. I don't remember anything that could've made her change her mind.' That had been the truth – perhaps not the whole truth, but a version of it. She *couldn't* remember, although she'd been determined to work out what was missing in her memory, and why.

Luckily, Geoff had taken her at her word. He rarely understood any kind of individual initiative, so he waved Ali away. 'Ali, I'm disappointed, but I know you would've done the best you could. Today, your best was just not good enough.'

Ali had felt gutted – it was like she'd let the whole department down.

Geoff dismissed her, reaching for his ringing comli. Bad news travelled fast. Everyone in the building knew she'd stuffed up before she left the twentieth floor. Everywhere Ali went, she received sympathetic glances that made her feel worse. That was the evening her over-stressed imagination had conjured the crazy ninja assassin. At least… she *thought* that was the night.

Ali looked at the timeline on her notes. No, that was more recent. With her memory shredding more each day she couldn't be sure.

I have got to get back to regular journaling for work and personal. Why can't I keep this habit going? It's so freaking helpful.

Ali's answer to Geoff's condemnation had been to throw herself into work even harder and longer. She'd arrived at the job before anyone else, and was always the last to turn out the lights after everyone had gone home. Sophie had urged her to take it easier, but she'd felt as if she had to make up for the disappointment by working three times as hard.

Eventually, her efforts had reached the boss's ears. Geoff had berated her and told her to slow down.

'You'll be no good to me if you're dead Ali. Take some time off for Fed sakes. There'll be another pot of gold one day soon. We'll find it. You'll find it, and then you'll bring it to me. Until then, you're messing with my reputation. Head office is noticing the unit's work is suffering a lack of something. I've approved that break you requested.'

As Ali had made to protest, Geoff held up a podgy hand. 'No arguments. Take the time off. Sort yourself out, and don't come back without your head on straight, and your attitude adjusted.'

Ali had felt livid about the attitude adjustment comment. She was the hardest-working, most efficient proji Geoff had.

But Geoff hadn't finished. As Ali had gone to stomp out the door, Geoff called her back. 'Oh, complete that Fisher report before you go too. And allocate someone to take over your other projects. We don't want any more disasters.'

Ali had held her tongue as always, and nodded obligingly.

'Ping. Ping.' The flocar decelerated, her arrival at the destination imminent.

'Drive around the block. I'm not quite finished.' *This is helping me get it straight in my head.*

The hum increased and the flocar accelerated.

Another reason Ali had worked as hard as she had was those dreams. Ever since her visit to the author, each time she slept, she'd dreamed of fantastical worlds full of magic, and sometimes the white haired birri and her prosaic rural life. A couple of times Dee had spoken in the dreams as though she knew Ali was there.

Ali paused with her pen hovering above the page. Something was amiss here.

That totally makes it a dream, doesn't it? What would happen if I start answering back? Have I answered already and forgotten?

Ali added another margin note: *Answer the birri if she speaks to me in the dream.* She erased "the birri" and wrote "Dee". *Her name is Dee. I heard her say that at the creek.*

Occasionally though, Ali felt as if she became Dee in the dream, saw through her eyes, heard, and smelt and tasted through her body. She stepped into her life and experienced what she thought and did first-hand. Oddly, the dreams didn't seem chronological – the timelines were all over the place. Sometimes Dee was a young adventurer who travelled and had amazing, dangerous adventures out in the wild world, building up her awesome fighting skills. Other times, she was a small child doing chores on an isolated farm, surrounded by scrubby vegetation. It felt bizarre to have the body of a five or fifteen-year-old with the mind of a fifty-two year old. Truth be told, she was becoming more and more reluctant to wake up from her dreamlife. And conversely, becoming more and more scared to sleep.

Living in the Dome made it easy to be paranoid. The Fed Comm had cams on every street corner, and wristcodes were required for pretty much any interaction. They always knew where you were, and when you weren't following the Sixth Tenet to *"Mind Your Own Business"*.

Up till recently, her dreams had been her own, but occasionally, she'd felt someone watching her, but only while she'd watched Dee. Unexplainable.

Ali had tried working before going to bed, persisting until she couldn't type a single word or number more. She thought that if she was exhausted, her head filled with her job, perhaps the dreams would stop. They didn't.

Then she'd tried every over-the-counter sed available. But they'd made her unconscious rather than asleep; and dragging her doped-up butt around the office the next day hadn't been an option, so she'd stopped using them. She'd even tried some not-so-legal stuff once, and slept through an entire seventh day off without waking, living the dream the whole time.

So that's why I'm here to see a hypnotherapist. I want to see if she can help me get some restful sleep. It's not because I'm going mad at all. Anyone would see a therapist if all that was going on. Not that I'm going to tell her all of it of course.

Ali leant her head back against the seat and closed her eyes. *Why am I trying to get rid of the only unpredictable and interesting thing in my life?*

Because I always choose the safe route, that's why.

The dreams were scaring her to death. But they were also making her feel alive and excited for the first time in years. So much visceral sensation and emotion. She normally scurried back to her burrow at the first sign of feelings. She wondered if she could get her emotions regened.

Maybe the dreams would make a good story. Ali's life-long habit had been to record every significant event, every interaction in her journal. Her journals were usually where she let her feelings and imagination run riot. She stayed cool, calm, and collected during the day and unleashed all manner of angst onto the pages of her diaries at night. She'd hate anyone to see what she'd written. It would be so embarrassing. She'd be Grey Shirted for sure. But at least it let her function. She used to be so regular with her journaling and it always helped.

Why can't I remember where I've hidden my filled journals, not a single one. She wrote an instruction for herself. *Find old journals! Start journaling again tonight!*

'Ping. Ping.' She'd arrived – again.

Uncovered

The hypnotherapist was a woman of around Ali's own age, with caramel skin and startling purple hair. As Ali stepped inside her house, she felt a wave of cool calm wash over her. A faint vanilla fragrance wafted from a scented candle, completely masking the chemical taint of recycled air. The walls and ceiling colours were muted blues, and large abstract art decorated the walls. The soft hum of a cooler promised a reprieve from the Dome's end of summer mugginess.

'I'm Serena. Welcome to my home and office.'

A young, dark-haired boy raced up the hallway from the living space and hugged the hypnotherapist around the knees. She bent down and kissed his forehead.

'Grandma will be out to play with you soon. Go and find Mummy and you can get the dinner ready with her,' Serena instructed.

The little boy nodded with a happy smile. He turned shyly when he saw Ali, and pointed at her head. 'Look Grandma, she's got angels in her hair! Angels are dancing in her hair! Is she an angel too?'

The hypnotherapist hugged the little boy as Ali put a hand to her hair, smoothing the unruly curls. 'Off you go Raphie, go and find Mummy now.' She turned him and gently ushered him towards the back of the house. 'I'll just be a minute, Ali. Please go in and make yourself comfortable.'

Ali strolled into the office, which broadcasted a professional, welcoming vibe. *Maybe a share house in the South Quad wouldn't be so bad after all.*

Two small shelves of real paper books, which held pride of place on one entire wall, caught her eye. As well as professional tomes, Ali noted, there were two of her favourite fantasy authors. She decided this woman must have connections with the Fed Comm's scavengers.

Once the Dome had been opened and a few people had survived Outside, the Fed Comm had appointed their own explorers to sift through the surrounding countryside for anything of value. Their priorities had started with foodstuffs and machines. Books were usually very low on the list, so they were guaranteed to put a significant dent in your tally if you were keen to acquire one.

Ali stepped closer and sniffed at the distinct smell of the books. Her logical brain knew that the hundreds of organic compounds that composed the paper gradually broke down, releasing various chemicals that smelt like almond, vanilla, and grass. Her emotional brain loved the fragrance for the images of other worlds they evoked.

I wonder if she has any by my mystery author. What was that woman's name again? Ali struggled to remember, her gift roiling in frustration.

Stop torturing yourself. It was one mistake. Not everyone can love you. You couldn't have done anything more; you know you couldn't.

She took a deep breath and sat at one end of the very comfortable, deep-blue couch, and picked up a set of intriguing wooden beads from the white plas coffee table. Each bead was intricately carved with what looked like runes, and embedded with a tiny piece of opal. It was a precious but not particularly unusual stone, though she'd never seen it in this kind of setting. Each piece of opal had the hint of rainbow colour she expected, but it was almost as if they formed a spectrum from red to white with each stone's dominant inclusion colour being different from its mates.

As Ali rubbed her hands on the beads, tracing a red-toned opal, she felt a single image from the day she'd spent with her mystery author pop into her head. The author had been showing her a large sapphire pendant, holding it in front of her face, telling her to look closely at it. Ali had realised that she was sitting at the author's breakfast table, so this must've been after she mentioned her dream. Before she could chase down the memory however, Serena stepped into the room in a swirl of blue, apologising for the delay.

She saw Ali holding the beads and smiled. 'They're beautiful, aren't they? An old mentor of mine gave them to me. Said they'd been in her family for a long time, but that she wanted me to have them after some work we did together.'

The half-remembered image faded from Ali's mind as she let the beads drop onto the table.

'So, let me scan your citzcode, and we can begin.'

Ali drew her sleeve back and swiped her wrist over the portiscan Serena held forward.

'Now, what brings you here, Ali? You mentioned in your message that you had trouble sleeping?' Serena's soft brown eyes were caring, her voice quiet.

'What did your grandson mean about the angels?' Ali diverted the conversation, suddenly reluctant to share any details with this stranger, no matter how professional she might be.

'Angels?' Serena quizzed her.

'He said I had angels in my hair,' Ali prompted.

Serena laughed, her silver earrings tinkling. 'Raphie has a very active imagination. It gets him into all sorts of strife. He probably just saw the light from the front porch around your head. No angels, I'm afraid. Do you believe in angels Ali?'

Ali's smile was a little forced. 'I didn't, until recently,' she admitted.

Serena waited. No judgement, no hint of guile – she was so different from Ali's usual colleagues and clients that Ali felt a little surge of hope.

She clasped her hands together, nervously flicking at her ring. With her gaze focused on her fingers, she almost missed Serena's surreptitious glance above her head. These were dangerous waters for Ali, so this time she heeded the snarky dragon's warning.

'Can I trust that this won't go any further?' Ali asked hesitantly. 'You were recommended by a colleague and I'd hate to think that that colleague may ask you about me later. Or the Federation. Does your patient confidentiality trump *Watching Out for Your Neighbours* and all that?'

Serena relaxed in her chair; hands folded calmly in her lap. 'Ali, everything you say in this room is entirely confidential, just between you and me. I do keep a few written notes to prompt my memory for next time and to record the key points of our discussion. But I have no obligation to report to the Federation. It's one of the reasons people keep coming to see me.' She picked up the digitab from the low table between them. 'And I record the treatment I prescribe and any tasks for you, of course.' She softened the last with a smile. 'Such as sleeping for longer than two hours a night and drinking more aqua.'

'Aqua?'

'Plain water. I'll be prescribing a specific allocation for you which you can purchase at your Quad Store. All the impurities that the water picks up on its journey to the city tanks are filtered out,' Serena explained.

'Oh.' Ali stored that information away. Most Domers flavoured their water to disguise the taste or kill the bacteria. Ali always boiled and made tea with hers. 'Fed Comm don't filter anything back in do they?'

Serena shook her head. 'No. No. Just plain water. I can see from just looking at you that you need better hydration. Have you had a fever recently? You look to be running a little hot.'

'No, just a little busy,' Ali smiled back and calmed her hands, forcing them to stillness and dampening down all thoughts of fire breathing dragons.

Just a dream. She stared at the ruby, which always made her feel a little braver.

'All my files are encrypted,' Serena assured her.

Ali shoved away the images of Grey Shirts banging on her door and dragging her out in the middle of the night.

'Right then. Here we go,' Ali said, taking her courage in hand.

She spent the next ten minutes filling the hypnotherapist in on her current insomnia, keeping the story to the stress of her busy job and the pain of her recent breakup. She figured that would give Serena enough to help her.

Once she'd taken Ali's history, Serena asked her to lie back on the couch and covered her with a pale blue blanket from an antique camphor-wood box in the corner. As she flicked through her digitab, soft music began to play, and the lights dimmed.

Ali's gift kept flicking red ochre fireworks at her, which she ignored.

Then Serena began to speak quietly, asking Ali to close her eyes and to call up various images from her past.

What felt like moments later, Ali opened her eyes and sat up. 'I don't think it's working. Perhaps I'm one of those people who can't be hypnotised?'

Serena's eyes looked enormous; her caramel face a little pale. 'Oh no, you're a very easy subject, very open to suggestion. We've completed our first session,' Serena explained. Ali's gift wobbled in her mind, which usually meant something was not quite right. She watched as Serena took a deep breath to gather herself. 'You've been under for about forty-five minutes, and all the instructions are now in your subconscious.'

'Does it always affect you this much?' Ali asked.

'What? Oh, I'm fine. Everything is fine. I always get very close to my clients and sometimes I can feel what they're feeling. It can make me a little tired that's all.' Serena's explanation made a kind of sense, so Ali eased back on her interrogation. It was too late to back out anyway.

'So what do I need to do now?' Ali felt sceptical that it would work at all.

'I want you to remember to trace an anti-clockwise circle in your left palm once you're in bed and ready for sleep. Then I want you to trace a clockwise circle on your right palm and close your eyes. This will be your ritual to remind your body, mind and spirit that they all need to rest.' She paused, and her expression changed to one of motherly concern.

'If you don't re-charge your battery, you'll eventually cause yourself some permanent damage. Remember: we don't have the technology to regen spirit yet,' Serena reminded her gently, then sat back, more relaxed after slipping into her familiar spiel.

'I'll send the instruction sheets for the ritual to your comli, and you can read them tonight. For now, I've got to finish up our session: your time is over, and I have a young man waiting to take me to dinner.' Serena softened her words with a smile.

'Oh, of course! I'm sorry to have kept him waiting.' Ali stood up, checked the time on her comli and looked at the hypnotherapist. 'You really did hypnotise me?'

'Yes, you were an excellent subject. I don't think you'll be troubled by those vivid dreams again.' Ali felt a great weight lift from her shoulders, though just a hint of regret smouldered in its place – as though she was losing a very dear friend. She made her farewells, then climbed into the flocar for the long ride home to the North Quad.

Ali started the vehicle and tapped in her address with a smile. *I'm back in control. Driving my life and driving this flocar home.* As she stopped at the first set of traffic lights she thought, *Wait, I don't remember telling the hypnotherapist about my dreams.*

She tried to recall the details of the session but couldn't bring a single moment to mind. *Whatever. As long as I get some sleep. I've still got two projects to tidy up before I escape on this adventure thingy.*

A beep from the flocar behind her told her the traffic lights had changed to green and she was dawdling. She accelerated, waved in apology, and drove off towards her flat.

– – –

As soon as the door closed on Ali, Serena retrieved an untraceable comli from a hidden compartment in her desk drawer, and speed-dialled the only number saved on the device.

'What do you have?' a woman's terse voice barked.

'I thought you might be interested to know what turned up in my office today,' Serena said.

'Tell me.'

'A woman named Ali Morrow. She came for help with her insomnia, but while she was under, she shared some very vivid dreams about a world called Reverie. She was having the full experiential interaction.'

A small silence greeted her words before the voice on the other end of the line spoke. 'An Ali Morrow called on me months ago about my personal collection. Morrow was very interested in my work and I allowed her to stay overnight. Somehow, she opened a doorway – Moonya does that sometimes. The cursed thing has a mind of its own, no matter how often we apply the magical dampeners. I thought I'd closed the doorway again, and mindwiped her memory.'

Serena waited; she knew better than to interrupt the Wiyanga – the head of her order, the Daughters of the Dark Goddess. The Wiyanga did *not* tolerate interruption.

'She's not an obvious candidate – much too old and ordinary.' The Wiyanga's voice was dismissive. 'You took a blood sample for DNA?' The last was more a statement than a question.

Serena knew the drill and responded, 'Yes, Wiyanga. I have her screen. It only shows baseline magical DNA though. It's no more than a distant relative of a lower order adept would have.'

The Wiyanga responded with a cryptic, 'Hmm.'

'Is the convergence stirring? Have you seen signs of dark beings straining to come through?' Serena's eager questions referred to the catechism of the Daughters of the Dark Goddess. They believed their deity protected the Earth from daemon beings who existed in a parallel reality. Contact with their goddess was closely controlled by the head of the order and her inner circle, the Trusted Daughters. For centuries before the Crack, all Designated Daughters had watched for signs of the Chosen Ones – humans with odd abilities or connections to other worlds, who would save their world from these malevolent hoards.

'Those things are for the Trusted to know,' the Wiyanga shut down Serena's questioning. 'Though perhaps if you manage this woman discreetly, a place may be found within the Circle.'

'Oh,' was all Serena's excited mind could respond.

'Perhaps this woman is hiding something. She may be a spy from another faction. When are you seeing her again?' The Wiyanga demanded.

'I told her to come back in a week,' Serena replied.

'Good, we can prepare. But there must be no mistakes. Begin the background investigation. Once we've properly tested her, she must be drained and deleted quickly. We cannot afford to have any other faction mine her memory of meeting me or the House.'

'Certainly. I'll let you know when I've completed her testing.' The comli clicked off, and Serena cursed softly. 'Damn, I forgot to mention the angels in her hair.' Her finger poised over the redial.

'Grandma, Grandma. Rations are ready.' Raphie rushed into the room, leaping for a hug. Serena embraced his small body with one arm and slipped the comli into her top drawer with the other hand.

I'll let her know next week after the testing is done.

Neighbours

Tenet Five: Citizens are expected to control themselves and maintain FEN at all times. No strong emotions or Public Displays of Affection (PDA) will be tolerated. All citizens are encouraged to immediately report anomalous behaviour or events to their nearest Cultural Guardian or Federation Representative.
From Federation Expected Norm: The Ten Tenets, Melba Dome, gazetted 14 March 15 PC.

Ali juggled her dillybag, rations and comli so she could get her key into the front door. A creepiness tickled the back of her neck, making her turn hastily and then stumble over the threshold. She crashed to the hardwood floor, rations flying. Her left knee banged against the timber and she bit her tongue as she landed.

'Shit, shit, shit. Bloody hell.' She totally forgot the creepy feeling as she surveyed the damage to her knee and gingerly touched her tongue. Her fingers came away bloody and she fished a hanky from her dillybag to wipe them clean.

'Bloody hell.' She repeated, and swallowed a mouthful of blood-flavoured spit.

'Ugh. Bloody *hell!*' One more time just because she couldn't offend anyone in her own home. The Seventh Tenet insisted you *"Watch Your*

Language", which Ali found really difficult at the end of a long day, but at least she was breaking that one behind closed doors.

She staggered to her feet, almost falling again. Her tumble had broken the heel of one shoe. 'Bloody hell, my favourite pair. Shit, shit, shit.' Her shoe had survived being thrown at the printer, but not tripping over the step. She chucked the broken shoe at the kitchen sink, where it landed with a satisfying clunk.

One advantage of living in an apartment the size of a shoe box. Ali laughed at her own joke. *Ha. I'm hilarious.* Much *funnier than Jiemba.*

She removed the other shoe and prepared to chuck that too. The first fling had felt so good.

'Ah, excuse me,' a deep voice interrupted from behind her. She turned guiltily, hiding the shoe behind her back, her face flaming. She needed to look up, past a well-built body to a face that could have come straight from the vids.

'It could launch a thousand ships,' she muttered to herself.

His white teeth flashed in a fashionably moustachioed face.

'Oh, shit. Did I say that aloud?' Ali squeaked. *Jeez what must he think of me? What would the team think of me? Losing it over a broken heel and a pretty face. So much for the always calm, always measured Ms Morrow. Measured. Right. Get a grip.*

Ali put the shoe on the entry table with her door key, removed her nose plugs, and took a second look.

Yep, gorgeous. Dark eyes, stylishly cut honey-brown hair, moustache and goatee. He's even got transparent nose plugs, so we can still see his perfect nose. Knows he looks good, and knows my heart is beating like a crazy woman 'cause I haven't had sex with a real person in months. Or not since Dean left, which was only days ago? Wasn't it? Oh, who the hell knows.

'Can I help you?' she asked with as much equanimity as she could muster with her cheeks flaming.

'I've got something you need.' He stepped boldly through the door and Ali stepped back. She glimpsed an odd gleam in his eye that defied interpretation.

'Pardon?' One hand fluttered to the base of her throat. She could feel her heart pounding.

'I've got something you need. Or you will need soon. 'No, she wasn't imagining it. This felt weird, more than non-FEN weird. His proximity and size in her tiny room began to feel like an invasion. She took another involuntary step back.

'I do not know what you mean, Mister…?' she queried, raising an eyebrow in her best East Quad voice.

'Jem Stillner. I've got your beans. The can was next to where the flocar dropped you.' He gestured to the mess behind her. 'I thought it might've fallen outta your bag.' Ali looked at the can of bean rations, which he produced with a flourish.

'Beans.' *Obviously, you idiot. Bloody hell, what's wrong with you? You are not your cool, calm, collected self. Lucky your clients can't see you now. It'd be a disaster for your hourly rate.*

'Are they yours?'

'Yes, yes. Sorry, I'm just a little flustered after the spill. Yes, they'll be mine. Making beans tonight. Obviously. Thanks for bringing them up.'

A little paranoia peeked. *And how did he know they were mine? Was he watching me climb the seven flights of stairs because the lift's broken? Another non-priority for the freaking building manager.*

She reached for the can and Jem moved his hand behind his back. Her eyes flashed back to his face and slightly sleazy smirk.

'Don't s'pose there's a reward for a can of beans.' A warning flared in her head and she found herself switching tacks. Her spine straightened.

'No, no reward, except you can keep the can. Finders keepers. It's all yours. Now if you don't mind, it's late and I've got a lot to do.' She picked up the shoe from the entry table and brought her arms up to herd him back out the door. He raised his hands in mock submission, glanced at the shoe in her hand, and stepped back over the threshold.

Ali relaxed at the ease of his retreat and followed it up with a mental command. *You are not welcome to cross my threshold ever again.*

'Didn't mean to overstep. Here's your beans. Have a great night.' He handed her the beans, and as their hands touched, a spark zapped Ali.

'Ouch!' She snatched her hand back, and the can clattered to the ground between them.

They both reached for the beans. Ali picked them up first, and when she looked up, he was close – too close.

'Can't ignore electricity like that,' he murmured huskily. He had the most dazzling white teeth she'd ever seen. Nobody from North Quad could afford that kind of dental treatment, yet his language didn't scream East Quad tally either.

'Hope to see you again soon,' he smirked.

Ali didn't say anything. She just stood there like a robot with her can of beans.

Jem took that as licence to continue. 'I moved in upstairs today, directly above you. I'm planning on making this my centre of operations.'

'Oh.' Ali struggled for something to respond that would discourage further conversation. She grasped the internal door handle.

Where's Andie or one of the lads when you need them? She peered over Jem's shoulder to see if she could spot anyone to help her distract him. But the rest of her building's occupants were uninterested in *Watching Out for Their Neighbour* at this late hour.

'Well, good night. Thanks for bringing the beans,' she repeated, hoping he'd get the hint this time.

'No trouble at all. Glad to do it. It was great to meet you.' He smirked again, then almost jumped back as Ali closed the door firmly in his face.

What the hell was that? I'm all over the place. Weirdo or wonderful? Maybe I'm out of practice. Lost my weirdo radar. Ali leant her forehead on the door, which meant it bounced as two firm knocks shook it.

Biting back another curse, she rubbed her forehead and opened the door a crack. Jem stood there, hands on hips, megawatt smile still on show.

'Did I drop something else?' she asked.

'No, but I didn't catch your name, neighbour.' For a moment, he seemed almost predatory, and she hesitated.

There's power in a name, a little voice whispered into her mind.

Oh, get a grip, woman! He's gunna be your neighbour. "Watch Out for Your Neighbour", remember? It's all about relationships. She must've said that a thousand times this week to clients. Time to listen to her own advice and build a bridge.

'Morrow, Ali Morrow.' She tweaked the corners of her lips, but couldn't quite bring herself to smile. Her nose wrinkled at the more-putrid-than-usual air in the hallway.

Now he even smells off. It's like he's giving out the wrong kind of pheromones. Ali suspected he was using street roids, given his overly buff state.

He gave her another dazzling display of dental wonderment though this time it only made her blanch.

'Listen, Mr Stillson. I'm tired, it's been a crazy day, and it's not over yet. So once again, good night.'

She barely gave him time to reply, 'Stillner. It's Jem Stillner,' before shutting the door firmly in his face, again.

Bloody hell, shit, shit, shit. That's the last *thing I need after today, some creepy guy making weird moves.* She gathered the rations and placed them on the kitchen counter, then rescued her broken shoe from the sink and dropped it with its mate on the floor. She flopped onto the couch, holding her head in her hands.

A few moments later, her comli rang, breaking her out of her gloomy reverie. Ali fished around in her dillybag and checked the caller ID.

'Heya, Sophie.' She put the comli on speaker and took her jangling earrings off, settling back and letting her eyes rove the utilitarian beige walls with its so-called artwork. These were nothing like the beautiful pieces adorning the hypnotherapist's lovely blue wall.

She rubbed her feet on the wooden floor, closing her eyes to feel the sensation. It was one advantage of this building being so old. New buildings were all conplas: recycled concrete and moulded plastic. Her mind wandered around the fact that the floor was one of the only natural features in this whole place, except for herself.

And I'm not totally natural. She gave herself the bird – her erect, regened tech finger ignoring her attitude, looking perfect as always. Distracted by her train of thought, she missed Sophie's opening remark.

'Sorry Soph, what did you say?'

'I said, I wanted to make sure you made it home all right. I hope the class helped. I was really worried about you tonight. I thought you might have had a migraine coming on. You've been working so hard and you just don't look after yourself. Something's got to give,' Sophie said.

Ali squirmed and avoided mentioning the class she'd skipped to go to the hypnotherapist instead. 'I know, I know. I just need to get this report done and then I'm sure things will ease up a bit. We can take a breather before we get stuck into the next project. I may even sneak a day off… or an afternoon at least. Fine, at least a couple of hours. We both live in the real world. Perhaps I'll have a massage or a haircut or get something small regened,' Ali suggested.

Sophie laughed. They both knew that last one was never going to happen.

'I'll make sure to schedule space in your diary, so it doesn't slip by. Anyway you're supposed to be booking a longer break. You need to take it. You're a great boss, and we need you to be at your best. You know we all depend on you. Without you, the unit would be nothing. You're more important than you know, Ali.' Sophie said.

'Soph, you're too kind by far.'

Sophie spoke over her protests, 'Ali, you're the wonder, the one with the wisdom and wit to get the job done. Geoff doesn't know the work, and he doesn't keep us connected like you do. He doesn't really care. You do.'

Ali wondered how much of that sentiment was because she kept Geoff off everyone else's back and regularly pulled all-nighters to save their arses from a zero job rank.

There was a pause, and Ali could sense Sophie building up to something. She rested her head on the back of the couch and closed her eyes. She could guess where Sophie was headed.

'And have you seen anybody else creeping around? Any more strangers in black?' Sophie's question hung in the air.

Ali swung her legs up onto the couch, crossed them at the ankles, and wriggled her toes. 'Well, there was this one guy just now,' she teased.

'What! What did he look like? Did he touch you or give you anything?' Sophie asked anxiously.

Ali laughed, 'No, no, I'm kidding. I dropped a can of beans and my new neighbour returned it. He gave me back my beans, that's all.'

'Oh. What does he look like?' Sophie's voice went down a notch.

'How's that relevant?'

'How old is he? Is he single?'

'Sophie, I'm hanging up now. I still have to eat my rations and I've got a couple of hours on that report to do.'

'Just keeping an eye on you. You need to keep your options open. Your partner radar isn't as tuned in as it could be,' Sophie grouched.

Ali had to agree. It seemed like all her radars were off-kilter. It hadn't crossed her mind to consider a new partner since Dean left months ago. *Or... was it days ago?* Either way, her abandonment was still pretty raw.

'You don't suppose something bad happened to Dean, do you?'

'Who?'

'Dean, my ex. The guy who left without saying goodbye or leaving any trace of himself.' Ali could hear the melancholy in her own voice.

'Ali, I know you mentioned Dean today, but I've never heard you mention him before,' Sophie admitted.

In the quiet pause, Ali's hearing picked out the hum of life under the Dome: the white noise of humanity, living and breathing together.

'I'm sure I must've said something to you. We went out for ages.' She searched her memories, and yep, there they were: little snippets of their life together. Dean and she riding the train to the edge of the Dome to watch the sunrise, eating out at that little cantina in the South quad, exploring each other's skin for hours. Her face flushed, and she felt a warmth begin deep in her belly.

That's too real for my imagination. Maybe I did keep him to myself. 'I must've been too busy to tell you... which is *weird,* 'cause I tell you everything.'

'And that's the way it should be Ali. We're friends, not just proji and addi. You need to tell me everything.' Sophie's tone became more vehement. 'That's the best way for me to help you. No secrets.'

Ali sighed and rubbed her hand across her eyes. 'Why did you ask if he gave me anything?'

'What?'

'When you asked what my neighbour looked like, you asked if he touched me or gave me anything. Why did you ask me that?'

There was an infinitesimal pause that made her think Sophie wasn't replying with the first thing that came into her head. 'I was worried he might have slipped you a sed and been planning to come back when you'd succumbed,' she countered.

'Ew, that is creepy. Anyway, he didn't. And I don't take seds from strange blokes. I *can* look after myself Soph.'

'Okay, then. Okay. See you tomorrow morning.' Sophie's response was a little abrupt, unlike her usual hovering – sometimes haranguing – helpfulness.

Bloody hell, I've offended the only person who bothers to look out for me – even if it is her job.

'Good night. And Sophie...'

'Yes?'

'Thanks for checking up on me. I really appreciate it.'

'Good night.' She heard the dismissal in Sophie's voice. She was definitely going to have to make peace tomorrow.

Ali tossed the comli across the floor, so it skidded next to her dillybag by the door, ready for work the next day. It also meant she'd have to get out of bed to turn off the alarm – always a good thing when she was so tired. She lay back on the couch, stretching muscles that had sat too long at the terminals. Then she eased her skirt zip down her hip, letting her belly loose.

Maybe I'd better do some exercise.

Who are you kidding? You hate exercise.

As her eyes wandered across the familiar moisture stained ceiling, she saw a blown bulb over her work area in the corner. With a sigh, she swung her legs back onto the floor, so tempted to forget the whole meal-and-work thing and collapse into bed. But that meant folding out the sofa bed and gathering the sheets, blankets, and pillows from the linen cupboard. She needed a bigger place with its own permanent bed. Instead, she ate her rations and downed a glass of cold tea from the fridge.

With a replacement bulb in hand, she balanced on one of her ladder back chairs. She'd set herself a time limit to work, and was determined to do some of her relaxation practices and at least read about the rituals Serena had suggested for a good night's sleep.

I dunno why I can never seem to do things just for me. If I had to do the damned exercises for someone else, I'd walk over hot bloody coals to get them done.

The bulb was tight; and as she pulled it out, the glass shattered in her hand, slicing into her thumb. She'd turned the main power off and it was difficult to see clearly in the dark with only the streetlight outside the kitchen window dimly illuminating the room. But Ali could feel her thumb bleeding where she'd gripped the bulb too hard, and it felt like a wire had come down too. She fished around in her pocket for her comli with her other hand until she realised it was on the floor by her dillybag.

Shit. She left the wire and fitting dangling and stepped down off the chair. As she brushed the glass off her hands into the sink, she hoped she hadn't dripped blood everywhere. She could feel the slickness on her hands and smell the metallic tang. She wound the corner of a tea towel around her thumb and padded barefoot across the floor, skirting the area of broken glass. She bent for her comli. With her finger poised on the torch function she heard a soft tap at the door.

It was way past time when any friend would drop in unannounced, and the tap was spookily quiet. If she'd been asleep, she might not have heard it – which might have been the point. In her suburb, you didn't answer a door at this time of night unless you knew who it was – and sometimes not even then.

She was already edgy with exhaustion and spooked by meeting her peculiar neighbour. She endeavoured to rein in her galloping imagination. *Probably just kids messing about.*

At this time of night?

Or mistaken identity? Perhaps they meant to knock on a neighbour's door?

Sometimes Andie got parcels late at night. Thinking about neighbours reminded her of creepy Jem what's-his-name again. She held her breath, tiptoed closer to the door. It was then she realised she hadn't locked it since Jem had returned her beans.

Now that her eyes had adjusted to the reduced lighting, Ali could see the door handle moving. Cold sweat flooded her system and her heart lurched. She reached for her key to stuff it in the lock, feeling along the top of the entry table where she always left it. It wasn't there. Her mouth dried. She had no time to look for it. Panic made her drag the small table across the floor and shove it against the door. The noise of the dragging echoed in the air. Whoever was out there would have heard it for sure.

The handle stopped moving.

There was a pause where she imagined all sorts of beasts and monsters on the other side of the door – human, natural and fictional. In stories, the heroine was always brave enough to open the door, confront the monsters, and kick their arse with crazy ninja skills.

Here in reality, that idea just made her shudder. There was no *way* she was opening that door. She'd seen all the news vids. She knew what happened, and it was never good. Besides, the only ninja skill *she* could claim was throwing her shoes, and she was barefoot now. Her bleeding thumb dripped on the floor. Somewhere in her panic she'd dropped the tea towel. Dark blood red flashed in her gift.

What would Dee do? No, I don't care. Whatever it is, I'm not doing it. None of that shit is real. No one could be that fearless and foolish. She stepped back as quietly as she could, then with enormous effort, shoved the couch against the door as well.

After a pause, a small click, click, click sounded. Someone eased a key into her deadlock. Her heart skipped into her throat for a beat before the ominous feeling eased as she heard soft footsteps retreating. Whoever they were, they were leaving.

Fine, I'm fine. She was about to com the Feddies when she hesitated.

What am I gunna tell them? The other week I imagined a ninja assassin attacked me, then an irritable dragon was chatting in my head, today a creepy guy picked up my beans, and now someone's trying to break into my flat. But they're gone now. Oh, and I saw a hypnotherapist for stress and insomnia on the way home tonight. And the blood is all mine 'cause I'm a clumsy klutz, and I broke a light bulb.

Feeling totally pathetic, she commed Sophie instead. Her guilt surged when a sleepy voice answered. But she *had* to tell someone, and Sophie had insisted she tell her everything. That was real friendship – never mind the dragon's warning against Sophie.

'Ali, what's up? Are you okay?' She could hear the concern in Sophie's voice.

Ali couldn't get her voice to work, and she could hear Sophie on the end of the line calling to her partner Will to get up and call a flocar.

'Ali, breathe. Take one breath at a time. We're on our way. I'll keep the line open. Are you hurt?'

Ali squeaked out, 'No. Well, yes, but it's not that bad.'

'We're only minutes away. Keep talking and tell me what happened,' Sophie instructed.

And so Ali obliged. She sat on her couch against the door and for the second time that night gushed out a filtered version of the crazy last few months. Jiemba's warning held her back from revealing every sordid fantastical detail, but as she talked, her fear gradually began to ease. She wove the tale of Dean, chunks of time – and now her keys – all missing. Something was awry in her life that she couldn't put her finger on, but she had this building sense of paranoia.

She made no mention of her gift, and she left out the glowing hands and dragon too. Nor did she say anything about the strange woman outside the Quad Store.

She'd never really considered her own desire for survival before. In fact, she'd rarely thought about her mortality at all. That was odd, because she lived under the Dome on a half-irradiated continent at the top of the world. She guessed she was like most Domers, who just wanted to be safe, mind their own business and know they'd wake up tomorrow.

At least until the Grey Shirts decided they needed realigning or exiling Outside.

One day at a time.

When she'd stuttered to the end of her story there was a brief silence at the other end. 'Oh Ali. I wish you'd confided in me sooner. I'm so sorry,' Sophie's voice was tinged with annoyance.

'What've you got to be sorry about? Don't be silly. It's all me overreacting, I'm sure. Just talk to me till you get here, tell me anything. Anything that doesn't involve Grey Shirts and being realigned.'

So Sophie talked. Ali didn't hear the words, just the calming tone. Gradually her breathing settled, her eyes closed, and she drifted off.

She heard the loud knocks coincide with Sophie yelling at her on the comli that she and Will were here. She pushed the couch and entry table out of the way, flicked the outside light on and let them in.

Damn, why didn't I think to put the outside light on before?

Because you were hiding like the chickenshit you are.

Sophie hugged Ali as soon as she flung open the door. That meant she must be really worried. Sophie wasn't usually a hugger – she was way too contained for that kind of emotional, non-FEN interaction. Even this late, wearing jeans and a T-shirt, she looked like a perfect advertisement for a South Quad professional in civvies. Neat, svelte, her short blonde hair smooth, her classically beautiful face, clear. She could be a model – except for those pale blue eyes.

Ali was sure she herself looked hideously wrinkled, with tearstains and ruined makeup panda eyes. Despite being Sophie's boss, she envied the woman's poise and confidence. Sophie always seemed to know her worth, who she was and what she was doing.

As for Will, Ali had met him a few times at work events; and in her small flat, he was comfortingly massive. His crisp, blue-black hair was definitely FEN, his jeans and tight white T-shirt neat. The menacing look in his tilted brown eyes belied his calm exterior. Ali felt reassured that he'd be more than a match for creepy Jem or whoever else had been at her door.

'Ali, you left your keys in the door. Anyone could've let themselves in,' Sophie chided, dangling the keys in Ali's face. 'You've got to be more careful. There's a lot of weirdos out there.'

'I'm sure I left them on the entry table. I always do,' Ali told Sophie. She knew she'd left them on the table. Her mind raced to the only possibility: Jem. He must've taken them when they'd both reached for the beans or when she'd been distracted by the dazzle of his white teeth. Her fear bubbled off, replaced by shame.

It was so easy for him to steal them. I'm pathetic. Can't even keep myself safe. Her shoulders slumped.

Sophie shook her head, swiped on the lights, and steered Ali to a kitchen chair. She took charge, boiling water to make tea for everyone and directed Will to install the new light globe and push the furniture back into place. Will used some sort of device to check the other light fittings and power points.

Ali saw a few loaded glances pass between Sophie and Will and knew she was the reason. Sophie placed a hot tea in front of her and planted herself in the only other chair. Will crossed his arms and leant against the kitchen bench.

Here it comes.

'Ali. There are some things about me, about Will and me, that I think it's time to share with you,' Sophie began.

Ali's eyes swivelled from one to the other, and her brow creased. 'What does that have to do with anything? Are you still mad at me from earlier? I don't even know what I did to make you mad.'

'No. No. It's nothing like that.' Sophie gave Ali's arm a brief pat then glanced at her partner. 'Well, I suppose it does have a little something to do with it.'

Will shuffled against the bench and stuck his hand in his back pocket to retrieve something. He placed a thin black cord onto the table. Sophie and Will waited, looking expectantly at Ali.

'What is that?' Ali asked.

Will leant forward, pointing to show Ali the silver tip at one end. 'It's a camera. It was in your light fitting. Someone's been watching you,' he explained.

Ali's mouth opened but no words came out.

Will's calm voice continued. 'It's wireless, so the receiver must be close. And it looks like it's been there a while. That means it's likely someone in this building or close by has been keeping tabs on you, possibly for a very long time. I've checked the rest of the place and I think it's clean. I think this is the only one.'

Ali's gaze rotated from Sophie to Will and back again. 'Why? Why would someone be watching me?'

Will looked to Sophie and nodded.

Sophie took a deep breath. 'Ali, I'm going to tell you a story about cosmic politics and magic,' she said.

'What? Magic? There's no such thing as magic Soph. You know that. We live in the real world. Those fantasy authors make that shit up. It's harmless escapism,' Ali protested. 'What's happening has nothing to do with magic. That cam must be my creepy neighbour. He said he just moved in above me. Maybe he lied. Maybe he's been here for ages, hiding. Or maybe it was from the previous tenant,' Ali began to gabble.

Oh, bloody hell, I hope she doesn't know about the glowing hands or the dragon. Maybe she is going to report me to the Feds.

Sophie reached to capture Ali's fluttering hands. 'Ali, stop. This is not about your creepy neighbour. This is about something that is so much bigger than you and your life. I should have insisted on checking you the other day after your hallucination about the assassin,' Sophie admonished herself.

Ali dragged her hands away from Sophie's tightening grip and into her lap, staring at her addi's pale-blue eyes for answers. Ali tried not to believe the Domer prejudice about pale eyes. But if Sophie reported her, she'd use it – blame the accusations on the instability of her iris colour.

Sophie continued, 'Have you ever wondered why you warranted such a good addi? A proji at your job rank don't usually get one – even if they *are* great cataloguers.'

'I figured it was because I worked hard and was good at my job,' Ali answered. A wave of uncertainly washed through her though, and her voice wavered, 'Anyway, you were there when I got there. I kind of figured you came with the office.'

Sophie shook her head. 'Ali, I'm more than a really good addi. I've had special training as a Guardian. I'm your Guardian, Ali Morrow. I've pledged to give my life for yours. So has Will.'

'Why the bloody hell would you do that for?' Ali blurted.

'Because you may be a Chosen One, a Wyld Magic user, here to save the world from Armageddon.'

Accidental

We are all visitors to this time, this place. We are just passing through. Our purpose here is to observe, to learn, to grow, to love… and then we return home.

Proverb from the First Peoples of Australia,
a Pre-Crack culture that passed on their beliefs and traditions in
stories, song, dance, and art. Regarded as custodial owners of
the country and continent on which Melba Dome was built.
From A History of Melba Dome by Alice Greenway, Federation
Historian, published Winter 185 PC.

Ali treated herself to another flocar and set it to auto. This was becoming an expensive habit, but she just couldn't face a manual commute to Fed Tower this morning. She lay her head back on the contoured seat and closed her eyes. She didn't want to think. She didn't want to feel. She didn't know what to believe after Sophie and Will's revelations from last night.

No, make that this morning.

Sophie had encouraged her to stay home for the day to think about things, but Ali had needed to go to work. It was a source of pride that she'd never taken a sick day. She'd always worked more hours than her contract, and often took work home to finish in her own time. Even before she'd messed up so badly, she'd been a worker: it's what gave her life meaning, or at least a kind of purpose. She was nothing without it. So this morning, when her comli alarm had pinged, she'd got clean, got dressed and got going. Once she reached the office, it would all be fine.

All this nonsense will go away.

And what a crock of nonsense it was. Ali's gift catalogued all the new words and intersections with her current perception of the world. Cosmic intrigue, goddesses and daemons, Domer Factions, Chosen Ones, Wyld Magic, the Shayde, Armageddon... it went on and on.

Ali had listened, dumbfounded, as Sophie and Will had laid out the words of a half-remembered prophecy from the pre-Crack era. Their stories sounded like convoluted myths to explain the creation and destruction of Earth, with a secret organisation – the Guild of Guardians – who were honour bound to find and support the Chosen Ones. These Chosen Ones, of course, would free them from an evil entity and impending doom.

Naturally, they couldn't show her any evidence of either the Chosen Ones *or* the villains; and just assumed she'd take it on faith that they were right. Take it on *faith* that she was one of these Chosen Ones. For no other reason than that they'd been allocated to watch her, so she must be one. *Right?*

Definitely creepy. Ali shuddered. Her real-life weirdness was nothing like a fantasy novel.

Then they'd left with a thinly veiled threat that she needed to believe or else.

Jeez, or else what? What're they gunna do to me?

Stop it. They're not gunna do anything. Sophie's just been digging into the meds too often. They're both a little loopy. It's harmless loopiness. Happens to lots of us left on Torpid.

Wait, maybe I need to report her and Will to the Grey Shirts. Maybe it's them that need realigning.

Ha, as if the Grey Shirts would believe me. No proof, and their word against mine. Bloody hell. "Watch Out for Your Neighbour": it's harder than it looks.

Maybe they're trying to out me to the Grey Shirts? Maybe they ARE Grey Shirts.

Nothing in their story had explained the camera in her light fitting either. Neither Sophie nor Will had had any idea who it belonged to. Nor had it explained why she had the memory gaps, the unshared secrets about her gift, the crazy dreams, the dragon voices, and the glowing hands. Their prophecy didn't mention dragons. Her mind spun as all the broken pieces whirled around in her head. Maybe there *was* something to the whole magic thing? Wyld Magic they'd called it.

Weird more likely.

She'd got scant sleep after she'd hustled them out the door in the wee small hours. So it didn't take long for the resonance of the flocar's propulsion system to lull her into a fitful sleep.

When she felt the vehicle's hum stutter and stop, Ali opened her eyes wide. The view through the side vis was not the lofty brown of Fed Tower – not even close. Outside were the bleak rows of rusty, grey tin barracks that housed the most destitute citizens under the Dome. Somehow, the flocar had slipped undisturbed through the West Quad border. She was back in Dim, back on the dismal streets of her childhood.

Her glance at the shambling humans outside gave her the shudders. Filters over the West Quad were erratic, and the clouds of toxins kept the sunshine far away, leaving most people with sickly grey-brown skin. Ali wanted out of here as fast as she could. She'd escaped four decades ago and stayed away, reinventing herself and creating a back-story that didn't involve being an orphan and growing up in these slums.

'AI, reset destination Fed Tower, City Grid, stat.' She swiped her wristcode against the scanner, which returned one sickly beep and failed.

'AI, acknowledge Morrow, Ali, citizen code 75.313.492.105.' The flocar's internal light dimmed, then the control console gave an ominous hiccup and went blank.

As the situation went from bad to worse, Ali began to giggle. 'Seriously, now my flocar malfunctions and tosses me into the garbage in Dim? After everything that's happened? This is the best these "factions" can do? Get me lost in the West Quad slums?'

In her exhausted state, a little worm of worry added another concern. Shouldn't she be worried? Shouldn't she be on the lookout for assassins and creepy neighbours? Not a chance. Practical and pragmatic, she couldn't take Sophie's revelations seriously – despite all evidence to the contrary – that magic could be real.

Why would I be chosen to have magic? I'm nobody. I'm a proji – at best, a slightly above-average proji – but that's it. My genes weren't even enough to qualify me for reprod program. No great offspring coming from this little possum's DNA.

She knew these streets. She'd lived and worked them for years. And survived. She was tougher than they thought. If Sophie and Will wanted to frighten her, have her run to them for protection, they'd have to try a bit harder than this. She snickered.

Be careful what you wish for. Thanks, Nanna, for another gem.

Her giggles turned to guffaws, and when she'd laughed herself silly and wiped her streaming eyes, she straightened her skirt and jacket, unclipped the safety harness and reached for her dillybag. She scrounged for her comli, found it, and gave it a flick—no coverage.

She sighed. *Typical. That's a pain.*

'Shit, shit, shit.' She attached her nose plugs and thumbed the door, forgetting that the system was offline. Reaching for the backup handle instead, she climbed out. Her plugs scrambled to strain the odours, and she wrinkled her nose in distaste.

Denizens of Dim had begun to gather, and she felt conspicuous in her crisp navy suit and heels. In the time she'd spent laughing, a small crowd had congregated at the front of the flocar. The huddle represented a spectrum of humanity rarely seen around Fed Tower. There were young, old, and very old. Ali felt her stomach twist in revulsion at disfigured faces, missing limbs, and scarred skin. Some of the older bodies were bent and gnarled like the old growth forests she'd seen on the history vids.

No tally for regen here. Barely tally for rations from the looks of the skinny bods on most of them.

Ali's face flushed at her uncharitable thoughts. The guilt of her well-fed figure made her suck in her belly and straighten her spine. Her eyes slid over the tarnished metal shipping containers stacked five high along the edge of the road. She shuddered at memories of hiding in their manky, rusted alleys to avoid the fixers and bullies, or the beatings from Nanna when she got home with less than she'd been sent out to thieve.

These are your people, Alinta Morrow. And you've never been back to offer a hand up to any of them.

I made my own way, and worked hard for what I've got. They could make it if they tried.

Really?

She dismissed the uncomfortable debate in her head. She had to get to work. She didn't want to be late.

Her nose plugs struggled to hold back the olfactory pollutants while her heels clicked on the concrete paved road as she moved to see what they were looking at. Howls of anguish exploded from the front of the car and wrenched at her heart. As she approached, the small murmuring group parted letting her through.

The flocar hadn't malfunctioned at all. It had hit a human and shut down.

Under the right-hand tread was an old man, his wrinkled face a rictus of pain, his few yellowed teeth bared in a grimace. The tread had crushed the right half of his body. An equally ancient woman was the source of the howling. She gripped his only free hand in both of hers as the old man's faded hazel eyes unfocused and his head tipped sideways. The old woman wailed as though the world was ending.

Ali felt pain rip into her. She fell to her knees, losing her breakfast into the chill morning. The people around her moved away, disgust registering on a few grey faces. Ali dry heaved a few more times. The older woman had subsided into soft moans as she rocked herself back and forward, holding the dead man's hand clutched awkwardly to her breast.

Ali retrieved a hanky from her dillybag and wiped her mouth, getting slowly to her feet. Hands trembling, legs shaking, she moved around to face the grieving woman. She'd never been this close to death, never felt pain this raw, this real.

I did this. Guilt hit her then, a physical force that drove her back to her knees beside the couple.

'I'm so sorry. I'm so sorry. I didn't see him. The AI must have failed. I wasn't driving, I had it on auto. I was so tired after yesterday,' Ali stammered.

Tired. You killed a person. Ali's excuses dried up in the shadow of the woman's devastation.

'I'm so sorry,' she repeated.

'Well, that makes it all okay then. Yer sorry.' The voice was young, male, and hostile. Ali looked up to see a thin, tow-haired youth with terrible scars on his face push through the onlookers and reach towards her dillybag.

'Let's see what ya can give the old lady as compo for her old man.' Two other rough youths leered at her over his shoulder. Ali instinctively pulled her dillybag out of his reach, and his pale blue eyes took on an angry gleam as he grabbed her arm, pulling her off balance to get closer to the bag.

She fell awkwardly onto her hands and knees. One of his sidekicks stomped on her right hand and the other grabbed at her hair, yanking her head back. Her stomach tried to heave again, bringing acid and bile into her mouth. Her brain shut down; her eyes fixed on the wispy grey clouds of steamy pollution scudding along the inside of the Dome. All the while, the old woman moaned and sobbed in the background. The small crowd watched. No one moved to help either woman.

'Not so tough without yer flocar, are ya?' The leader kicked her ribs, her attempts to double over the pain defeated by a further yank on her head, forcing it back. Now she faced her tormentor, who ripped out her nose plugs.

The putrid perfume of Dim rushed in. 'Yer breathin' our air now. It'll be good for ya, an Easy Eastie I'll bet. No Feddies down here ta save yer sorry arse either. They won't come 'ere, ya know. We guard our own.'

He yanked the dillybag out of her hand and tipped the contents onto the pavement while his partners pushed her flat on her back and held her down. He rifled through the plas files, a wrinkled fruit ration, pens, lipstick, four stims, some face wipes, more nose plugs, and an assortment of metal file fasteners. The pathetic detritus of her boring life.

'Where's yer credits? Where d'ya keep 'em?' the leader demanded, slapping her hard across the face. He got in close, his sour breath redolent of cheap alcohol and decay.

'Got em on ya, eh?' He started to grope around her body, spending time squeezing her breasts and pinching her nipples. She tried to squirm away from the pain, but his friends held her tight, anchoring her legs and arms.

He gave a final yank on her hair, and she could feel her scalp lifting to match the excruciating pain in her crushed fingers. He thumped her head back on the ground, reached under her skirt and fumbled at her underclothes. Ali's terror swamped her defences, and she tried to jerk out of her human shackles. Their grip tightened, and she began to whimper.

'No, please, no.'

Voicing her fear, begging, seemed to goad him on. A cruel smile cracked his pocked face, one side awry from disease scars.

'Well if ya got no credits, we'll take our compo in other ways. Yer a bit past it, but we'll make do. Won't we, lads?' His mates cheered him on, tightening their hold on Ali. The leader shoved her skirt up around her waist and ripped her underwear and stockings down, exposing her to the cold air and the view of the small crowd.

'Please, someone, help me! Help, please, don't, please don't!'

No one was helping. They didn't care – or they didn't dare. Most drifted apathetically away. Violence and death were as routine as breathing on these streets.

His voice told her she deserved this: Dim's justice. She'd killed a man – one of their own. This was going to happen. She was going to be raped and killed. No one was going to help, no Factions, no Guardians, no Feddies. So much for her being Chosen. She couldn't save the world. She couldn't even save herself.

Ali felt more bile gather in the back of her throat at what was about to happen. She closed her eyes, powerless and despairing.

I can't do it on my own. Someone, anyone. I need help.

Ali screamed as the three attackers laughed and whooped.

I'm here. I've got your back.

Jiemba's presence burst into her mind in an explosion of deep red ochre, her opal eyes dark with rage, her wings spread and her tail lashing. Smoke curled from her flared nostrils. As she opened her mouth to roar, an ember of fire ignited deep in Ali's belly. She felt the heat surge up to her heart and tear down her arms to her hands.

They're gunna burn.

The youths holding her down yelped and let Ali go. Her would-be rapist landed on her all at once, forcing the breath from her lungs. The fire in her belly shut down. Skinny though he was, she could barely inhale. With one hand mangled, she strained to push him off with the other.

Use my fire, birri.

Ali was saved from responding by another voice.

'You two useless twerps take yer trash and get lost. Don't let me see ya around these parts again. Go find another hole to crawl into.' The voice was the old woman's, hoarse from her sorrow. She'd used a broken piece of plas from the flocar to whack Ali's assailant across the back of the head, and he was out cold.

One of the others dragged his unconscious body off Ali, and she struggled onto her side trying to yank her torn skirt down to cover herself. The beating had been delivered in only a few moments, but she hurt everywhere.

'That bitch burnt me, Willa. She's got payback comin'.' One of the youths who'd held her down shoved a raw-looking arm with a blistered handprint in front of Ali. He rounded to swing his boot at Ali who held her rufescent hands in front of her. Their rose glow throbbed faintly in rhythm with her racing heart.

He pulled back, eyes wide.

We'll show you payback.

'What kinda weirdo are ya? Freakin' witch.' The third male sporting burnt palms glared at Ali, threatening a kick too as her hands faded back to normal. She curled up, nursing her smashed right fingers with her left hand, and waited for the next blow.

Witch? That's the best they can come up with after all this time?

'Get outta here or I'll give ya payback ya'll never get up from. Ya know I will.' Willa's authority rang in her words.

Yeah!

Ali's gift showed Jiemba capering about on her hind legs as though she was in a boxing ring, throwing and dodging punches with her front limbs, her massive head zipping left and right. Ali tried to form a single coherent thought.

Something in the old woman's threat must've worked. The blow didn't land. Muttering, the male voices moved away, dragging their unconscious mate. Behind her, Ali heard Willa sob once and whisper, 'Oh Sandy, how can I go on without ya? I can't do it on my own, darlin'.'

The pain in her voice made Ali uncurl. Willa turned to address the few remaining onlookers. She visibly hauled her fragile frame upright. Despite her short, white hair being a mess, her face tear-stained and her clothes covered in blood, her presence was compelling.

'And all of ya gutless wonders just stood and watched. Ya did nothin'. Yer as useless and pathetic as them that did the beatin'. Ya make me sick. Find some backbone, damn ya. Make a choice. Do somethin', anythin'. Learn ta feel. Open ya hearts and feel.' She thumped her thin chest.

The half-dozen people shuffled miserably, but no one challenged her. No one looked her in the eye. As the old woman waved them away, most just hung their heads and left.

I like her. And she has a little magic leaking too. Though… she's got it contained somehow, shielded.

Ali climbed to her knees, whimpering with pain, and ignoring the insensitive dragon in her head.

A small, scruffy birri of six or seven emerged from the alley and raced up to the old woman, throwing her arms around her hips.

'Gran, Grandpa's magic was shoutin' at me. Where is he? Is he okay?' She moved towards the front of the flocar, but Willa stopped her, hugging her young body tightly.

'No, darling Mayra, no. He's gone. He's driftin' again.' Mayra began to cry, her skinny shoulders shaking with sobs

'Bring 'im back, Gran. Bring 'im back!'

Willa's shaking hands smoothed the soft, blonde curls on the birri's head. 'Hush now, it's his time. He knew it was comin' soon, like he told ya.' Though her voice was comforting, her tears streamed unchecked as she whispered, 'Armageddon's comin', an' the Chosen One's here.'

Ali's body and mind howled for help.

No. No. Not the Armageddon madness. I'm not the Chosen One.

You're running out of time. Century's combined already. Get a grip. You ARE Chosen.

Her vision blurred as rainbow sparkles edged her perception. The moment exploded in her gift as a huge fireball. The lines connecting it raced along the timelines like a lit fuse, illuminating a giant spider web of people and events thousands of years apart. Flashes of memories crashed back into her array, tumbling, and churning her order into chaos.

Layer after layer swarmed in. She watched hundreds of lifetimes trying to force their way into the pattern. Her life tapestry bucked and surged, tearing and reforming. She felt her mind being ripped apart, and a primal scream hurtled out of her throat, startling the people still on the street.

Her body convulsed, aggravating her injuries. Her eyes tried to focus on a tall, dark-haired man running towards them. Despite her terror, her gift – still in overtime from the assault – added another layer. Dispassionately, it catalogued him: fortyish and lean, healthier than expected for this location, his skin coffee-brown rather than the sallow grey-brown of most Dim inhabitants.

Even his uniform clothes were brighter. He wore an ochre-red shirt with an emblem on the pocket and gumtree-green trousers, but strangely no nose plugs. He must be used to Dim. There was a sense of restrained power about him. In Ali's tapestry, he registered as a huge pulsing green tree that shot down roots into her future and branches out to the rest of the world. She had no idea what that meant or why her gift ignored her pain but catalogued like crazy. It had never been so reactive. The leash she'd held on it was broken.

She was broken.

It's the magic. Your body's reacting to the magic. The memories are coming back. We need to be joined again. This is going to hurt.

Jiemba sounded excited and only half-apologetic. The pain in her crushed hand pulsed, distracting her. Body-wrenching spasms gripped her muscles, and she clamped her teeth together to stop from crying out and drawing attention to herself again. The memories were still spurting into her head, a coruscating kaleidoscope.

The man stepped around the couple with a small stroke of the birri's head and a touch on the old woman's shoulder. He took in the scene at the front of the car. His shoulders slumped as he squatted silently by the body of the old man. Ali felt like a voyeur, but stiff with the spasms, she couldn't look away. Grief and regret hung like a cloud around his body, and in her delirious state she observed thick threads of silver and blue swarming around his central green core. His brightness faded into Dim's grey.

Ali's spasms eased, and she closed her eyes to stop the vision, hugging her injured hand to her bruised chest. Her body began to shiver, finally surrendering to the shock and pain. Her grunt as her teeth chattered seemed to break the man out of his reverie, and he looked sharply at her.

'Are you the driver? Are you the one that killed him?'

Ali opened her eyes, unable to speak with the tremors that had seized her body. It was all she could do to nod. He walked towards her, menace in every muscle, and vengeance in his brown-eyed stare. He reached with one powerful hand and grabbed a handful of her torn shirt, dragging her to her feet and aggravating the pain of her bruised ribs as he held her close to his face. She could barely stand, sagging as a cloak of blood-red blame erupted from his heart and settled onto her shoulders. His fists shook as he adjusted his hold, trying to restrain himself from doing more.

Paralysed with terror, Ali felt her bladder release. Shame closed her eyes as the warm urine trickled down her quivering legs. She staggered back as the old woman laid her small hands on the man's arm and his hold loosened.

'Tau, Tau, that's not our way. This isn't her fault. It was an accident. Flean and his mates have already assaulted her. Let her go, this isn't our way. Ya know yer Grandad still dreams. He'll drift back if it's meant to be. Or he'll be waitin' at the Gate to go Home.'

'She deserves punishment, Willa. A life for a life.' Tau's eyes glared into Ali's for a moment longer. This close, she could see that his brown irises were ringed with gold. She watched a part of him close up, siphoning off the threads of his grief behind a closed door. Then he shoved her away.

She fell backwards, landing awkwardly on her butt and her injured hand. She cried out with pain, her vision blurring further. Grey fog edged her perception now, the sparkling torrent of memories slowing to sluggish.

We've gotta get your body some healing quick. I can't get to you; the Dome is closing down the channel. It's trying to push me back.

Ali could feel Jiemba's anxiety all mixed up with her own. A part of her watched without feeling and wondered if the threads she was seeing were the same magic threads Dee talked about. Dee – a memory of saving Dee from rape surged to the forefront of her mind. There'd been a dragon, another dragon. She'd burnt Dee's stepfather to a pile of ash. Her mind swerved away from the memory and her logical self noted the symptoms of shock were increasing.

'Hush now, hush, we'll get ya sorted,' Willa frowned reproachfully at Tau, then stooped down and ran her bony fingers over Ali's head.

'Come now, birri. Tell me yer name. We'll getcha sorted and back where ya belong. I've frightened the lads off, but they'll find their way back soon. Ya need to be gone before they bring more than I can handle on me own. Revenge is served quick in these parts.'

Ali shook her head. Her voice scratched from screaming as she whispered, 'How can you be kind to me? I've killed your man.'

'His name was Sandy,' Willa told her.

Ali looked into Willa's dark brown, wrinkled face, and saw that her hazel eyes were rimmed with gold too. Family then. These eyes held a lifetime of wisdom and memories. Willa flashed into Ali's gift as a fierce speckled eagle. Her connections raced into Ali's future as well.

'I didn't mean to. It was my flocar. It must've malfunctioned. I wasn't supposed to be here.' She stuttered to a stop as a flash of pain crossed Willa's face. Ali went on, 'I'm so sorry. I dunno what I can do to help, but I'll do anything I can.' Willa sighed and shook her head, a few wayward tears trickling down her face.

'Gran, Gran.' Mayra was pulling at her grandmother's hip. Willa wiped her eyes and turned to smile at her. She gathered the birri into a hug with one arm.

'What, Mayra?' Mayra was staring at Ali, her gold-rimmed hazel eyes roving all around her head.

'Gran, she's got angels in her hair. Look, they're dancin'.' Willa stared fearfully at Ali, as if seeing her for the first time. The old woman's perusal snagged on her odd eyes, and she peered closer.

Told you she had magic. She's noticed your eyes. She'll pick your magic next.

Jiemba leant into an invisible gale, looking for all the world like a black vacuum was trying to suck her from Ali's mind.

'Are ya sure, Mayra?'

The birri nodded, her blonde curls bobbing up and down.

Ali's gaze moved from Mayra to Willa.

'What does that mean?' she rasped. 'I've got angels in my hair? Someone else told me that. Another child, a yala.' The old woman looked sharply at her but addressed Tau, who was still glowering at Ali.

'We gotta protect this one, get her back where she belongs. They said she burnt 'em with her hands. I should've made the connection sooner.' Tau's head snapped back to Willa. She waved his question to silence and reached for Ali's hands. Ali skittered away.

'Who are ya, birri? What are ya? Who do ya belong to? Who holds yer loyalty?'

Ali just shook her head. She had no idea how to answer.

You don't answer to anyone. Your loyalty is to the All.

'Too many witnesses. We'll deal with it later,' Willa decided. 'The factions'll be scannin' for her with all that's happened. If she used magic, the Grey Shirts'll be comin' too. I dunno how she wasn't picked up before now. Someone must've taught her how to shield. And maybe that someone will know she's not where she should be real soon. We can't have 'em down here, Tau. There's too much at stake. It's taken us too long to gather the ones we got. We gotta get rid of the evidence. Do this first. You'll have ta take yer Grandad Outside later.'

Ali didn't believe in coincidence. She'd fallen foul of yet another crazy cult who were threatening her life, threatening to get rid of the evidence. She *was* the evidence. She wished she believed in the benevolence of the First Tenet *"The Federation Always Takes Care of You"*. Then she'd report the whole damn lot of them to the Grey Shirts.

Tau sneered down at Ali from his two-metre height. The image of a huge menacing tree slammed to the fore in Ali's gift.

'She can't be Chosen. She's got no spine, Willa. She'd cave at the first challenge.'

Willa gave him a sour glance, and Ali's cheeks flamed. Her gift projected the massive eagle staring down the tree, grasping a huge branch in its talons, ready to rip and tear.

'And ya can tell that, moments after seein' her in this shitty tragedy? I've got more to accuse her of, an' I'm not makin' that judgement. Not yet. It's not our place to judge. We care for the land, find and guide. Always have, always will. I'll fix her memories. I can still do that much under the bloody Dome.' Willa turned to Mayra, placing a hand on her shoulder.

She definitely has magic. But don't let her touch you or we're gonna have to do this whole hello all over again.

Ali squeezed her eyes shut and muttered, 'Shut up, you stupid dragon. I can't concentrate.' Ali only realised she'd spoken aloud when she opened her eyes and saw the trio staring at her with their mouths agape.

Willa recovered first. 'Mayra, go and check in the lady's bag and the flocar for some ID. Otherwise we'll have ta get the old scanner and see if we can read her wristcode.'

Mayra wiped her eyes with her sleeve.

'She said dragon, Gran,' the birri smirked and scarpered off. Tau reached down to pick Ali up. She scrambled away from him as best she could. Willa turned to the few remaining onlookers who'd been drawn back by Ali's primal scream.

'Get away. Ya were never here. Ya don't remember anythin', or Tau will come lookin' for ya.' They needed no further encouragement and melted into the dusty alleys.

Ali was in pain, scared, and barely functioning. Her tapestry thrummed, overloaded with the memories, the pattern still bucking and trying to tear loose.

Her survival filters were shredded, and she began gabbling, 'Please! I won't say nothin' about ya being an eagle and havin' magic. I'll do whatever ya want. Please don't hurt me. I don't understand what angels in my hair are. The pink bits are only tints, they're harmless. I'm harmless. I don't have magic, wyld or any other kind. I don't know what all the memories are. I don't understand the pictures, they just come. They're just there. The dragon is just in my imagination.'

Willa's face had blanched at the mention of the eagle, and her body stiffened further with every word tripping from Ali's mouth. When Ali mentioned the dragon, Willa spun to Tau. 'We've gotta hurry Tau. Now. She's a bloody danger to the Stewards and herself.'

Tau had hold of Ali around the waist and she tried to struggle out of his strong arms, whacking his broad chest with her one good hand.

Fire's coming birri. Get ready to burn.

Ali felt the embers in her belly warming. Her hands blooming.

'Let go. Yer hurtin' me, ya big tree.

Willa's face paled further.

'Be still, damn ya,' Tau growled, squeezing her tighter against him. The tightening added to her breathing difficulties and dizziness.

Ali gripped one of his arms with her one good hand, and Tau hissed at the heat.

Willa reached for her, smoothing her hair with shaking hands. Ali looked into her eyes. In her mind, fierce golden eagle orbs pinned her.

'Hush, birri. We won't harm ya. Ease yer fire now. Yer too important to the Dreamin'. This is for yer own good. The Stewards respect what ya gotta do. The Angels mean yer special. Ya got magic, and yer Chosen. The young'uns are better at seeing 'em than adults. Too many years under the Dome wears down the Sight. All those Fed meds kill it stone dead. We'll take good care of ya, Dream Ender.'

She put two glowing mauve fingers on each side of Ali's head as Tau swung her up in his arms. Jiemba's warning shout was lost as the crazy world finally faded out.

Failure

From a shadowed alleyway Lee Wiinj watched as the old woman
and her grandson bundled an unconscious Morrow into a flocar
and took off. Lee leant her slight, black-clad frame against the rusty iron
wall and crossed her arms. There was no hurry: she'd skimmed the abductors
destination from the flocar before they left.

This accident was messy, the target damaged but still living – a citizen
killed in front of a whole lot of witnesses, including Lee herself. She couldn't
see the purpose of it. Unless it had been entirely random. She pursed her
lips. Highly unlikely. *"Mind Your Own Business"* meant everyone had a
finger in everyone else's business. Knowledge was power under the Dome,
and manipulation as natural as breathing for those in the know.

Morrow had been on her way to Fed Tower to work. Even with the
power flickers, flocars wouldn't go *that* far out of their way. When the
power went off, they simply stopped.

Despite Morrow's age and apparent lack of magical prowess, Lee knew more than one group had her in their sights. Gift leakages were becoming all too common in children as the Dome filters weakened, yet they weren't generally seen in older adults. Her attention flicked to the bronze bracelet around her upper arm, hidden now by the long black sleeves of her fitted shirt. A shaving of opal in the band interfered with the Dome's shielding and allowed her limited access to her own gift – her opal dreaming.

Lee considered the possible factions involved and the impact they'd have on her own mission. Someone had reprogrammed the flocar, which bespoke serious tech abilities and possibly political clout. Only Fed Comm connections could get through the Quad borders unchecked. Unfortunately, knowing that didn't help to identify who was pulling the strings at street level. Lee's top suspect for that kind of stratagem was usually the politically connected Daughters of the Dark Goddess. But why would they send Morrow's flocar awry if she had an appointment with one of their therapists in a few days? Lee had purloined a copy of the data on Ali's personal comli. The Daughters could have taken her then.

The Guild of Guardians were notoriously sloppy, but this felt too brazen for them. Besides, Morrow's blonde addi – their undercover agent – was indiscreet and rarely encrypted her Controller reports properly. Lee had noted no hint of urgency in the most recent missive that she'd intercepted. She considered that situation unsurprising, given the addi's pale eyes and entitled East Quad background. It was a bad combination for subtle work.

Lee knew a League of Believers cell occupied the flat next door to Morrow, and had been watching patiently for almost eight years. They might be a contender – but what could have changed their brief so radically to make them do this? Gifts manifested in early childhood and rarely changed in strength after adolescence. She'd never heard of anyone manifesting after fifty. She wondered why the League would still be watching a target with so little evidence of anything out of the ordinary.

A young man shuffled into the other end of the alleyway, interrupting her pondering. Lee pushed off the wall and faced him. His eyes lit up as he saw her step into the thin stream of grubby daylight, her deep green eyes enlarged with dark makeup, her sharp features shadowed. He'd been one of the attackers who'd lined up to rape Morrow earlier. Lee softened her stance with a bent knee and a calculated toss of her black-tipped blonde hair. She knew his eyes would follow the silky, shoulder-length distraction. With a sultry smile she thrust one hip sideways and beckoned him closer. His shuffle became a strut, and he responded with a leer.

When he moved into range, she grabbed his reaching arm and twisted it behind his back. Ignoring his yells, she examined the blistered handprint on his forearm. Even through her gloves, the residual throb of fire magic called.

Her belly tingled. She released the cursing youth with a shove. He fell, moaning, into the rubbish piled against the alley wall. She ignored his anatomically impossible threats and sprinted to her own flocar three blocks away. Her mission parameters had just become a whole lot more urgent.

— — —

The man – his uniform marked him as an Outside Ranger – had gone in and out of Morrow's building in less than three minutes. Rangers weren't an obvious threat, though they had a tenuous connection to the outlawed Stewards of the Living Earth – the so-called Wild Earthers.

Lee waited to see if anyone from the League cell next door would investigate their neighbour's unexpected return. When ten minutes ticked by with no movement, she let herself in through the kitchen window in the back of the building. It was a simple climb up the drainpipes and along the windowsills – the flat had no alarms, and the window lock gave easily.

There could be no misadventure today, Lee sharpened her focus. Her record had been unblemished till now. But… nothing about this target made sense. She seemed innocuous, yet she'd been listed for routine eradication. Then, despite being an unfit older woman, she'd eluded a direct attack in her office. She'd been right there in front of Lee – and then she just wasn't. And now she showed signs of wielding fire magic that left strong residuals.

Lee considered reporting her new findings to the Society before the kill, but this was too good an opportunity to waste. It simplified an investigation by the Feds if the target expired from the injuries sustained earlier in the day. All she need do was choose her mode of transitioning the soul into the next life.

She paused to let her eyes adjust to the dim daylight coming in through the kitchen window. The curtains at the front window were still drawn. The flat was really just a single room with the closet-sized bathroom partitioned off against the shared wall.

In the silence she could hear the target breathing heavily, either asleep or unconscious. Lee crept closer, slipping a knife from one of several sheathed at her waist.

The Ranger had dumped the woman on the couch and dropped her dillybag beside her. He hadn't even bothered to lay her straight. She was twisted awkwardly, half on her belly, one mangled hand dragging on the floor. It offended Lee's sense of order.

She squatted and examined the target's face. Alinta Morrow. That name had been hard to find, she was Ali to most. Lee had seen photos and observed her from a distance, but seeing her this close was different, uncomfortably different. Lee preferred to remain removed from the humanity of her targets.

Ali's face was bruised and marred by tears; her makeup smudged. Dust and dirt smeared her skin and clothes. The sharp odours of urine and blood hung over her. Lee had been tempted to intervene back in Dim before Willa had grabbed the plas to beat off the attackers. Though it was not strictly approved, Lee often found a way to remove children and women from excessive violence even when she'd been sent to an erasure. Not quite the surgical strikes laid out by Society rules, but Lee was finding herself at odds with more than one Boorondaran boundary of late.

Ali's eyes fluttered under her lids, and soft moans dribbled from her mouth with each exhaled breath. Rather than readying her weapons to finish her off, Lee found herself touching Ali's hair, running her fingers through the random curls, and fingering one of fuchsia tips. In her unconscious state, Ali's face was softer than her wary stare in her Fed citz file photo.

Lee traced the spray of lines around the woman's eyes and smoothed the frown on her forehead. She'd observed Ali interact with dozens of people. Her warmth and wisdom shone – she put people at ease and left them smiling. It was no mean feat in a world that punished people who didn't *Mind Their Own Business*. Ali had no political influence, no criminal connections, no family, and – glancing around at her barren flat – no wealth. Her eradication made *no sense*.

Not for the first time in her illustrious career as a Boorondaran eraser, Lee wavered in her blind obedience.

Why did this woman deserve to die?

Ali sighed and turned her head towards Lee's hand, which was brushing dirt from her cheek. Lee's heart beat faster. She felt a warm tingle spread from Ali to her hand, igniting a burning in her belly, and snatched her hand back.

What am I doing? I've been told to erase this woman, Lee scolded herself.

Her mouth dried as she removed one glove and reached forward again. This time, when she cradled Ali's face, her fingers lit with from within with a rosy glow. Her heart pounded as the embers in her belly throbbed into life.

Lee closed her eyes and felt threads of fire magic reaching towards her own burning core. None of her training prepared her for this. Ali's magic was deep and old and complex. It wrapped around Lee's heart and soul, generous and warm. She clenched her teeth to stop a sob escaping. She'd never been touched this deeply, never felt more connected to another person. Her own magic stretched towards Ali and in return was encased in a loving energetic hug. Her senses reeled, and her vision overlaid with an ultraviolet image of Ali's face – but a strangely distorted one, as though the picture flickered between several very different shots.

Lee rocked back on her heels and blinked back tears. *What's wrong with me? I erase people. I don't do tears.*

Her gaze took in Ali's pronounced nose and determined chin, and her eyes traced Ali's soft lips. She licked her own lips and swallowed.

Maybe I do now.

She had no time for these thoughts. The Society of Boorondaran Wise Women was her family, they'd given her all she needed, though she was beginning to realise – not all she wanted. Relationships outside the Society were not tolerated. Nor was failure to complete her mission.

Yet that's what I'm contemplating right now. How can this ordinary, helpless woman make me want to throw away my whole life's purpose? My Society will disown me.

A strange flutter twitched in her heart and a brick loosened in the wall Lee had built around her soul.

She stood and leant to plant a soft kiss on Ali's forehead. Shaking her head, she removed her other glove and set about completely negating her mission, her loyalty, and years of training. That training had given her a reason to go on living, but now it seemed the antithesis of reasonable.

Maybe I can stall the Society with this new knowledge of her magic. They may want to study her.

She rolled Ali onto her back and straightened her limbs, then wrangled the damp and dirty skirt off. Settling a cushion under Ali's head, she found a blanket in the linen closet to cover her with. As she tucked the woman in, Lee's foot kicked Ali's dillybag. She fished out a pair of shoes and placed them beside the couch. She took the torn stockings and underwear into the bathroom. The stockings she tossed into the bin, but the rest was salvageable, so she filled the basin with warm soapy water and dropped the skirt and underwear in to soak.

Lee dried her hands and surveyed herself in the mirror. Her distinctive hair, wavy blonde with the bottom half black was well known in certain

Domer circles. She had a high, smooth forehead; a thin, straight nose; and generous, black-painted lips that rarely smiled. This was the face of a career eraser – but not today. Today, she would report in and face the consequences. Her hands trembled, and she grabbed the basin edge.

Boorondarans obeyed without question. But this wasn't right. This woman didn't deserve to die. In the back of her mind a tiny voice whispered, ***Thank you***.

Her eyes flew up to her mirrored face, paling now from its usual dark gold. Somebody had breached her mental shields. She spun from the bathroom, flicked the light off and was about to exit when she heard a key in the front door. She backed up and pulled the bathroom door close as two people entered. A youngish male announced, 'We'll miss too much if we don't replace the camera. The Guardians won't expect it to be put back straight away, and we need to know what they're up to.'

'Shh, Nate. She's still in bed,' a female hissed. 'I'm sure I saw her go to work. We'll have to do it later. I'll leave her a note to drop in and say hi, then Dell can sneak in when she's with us to replace it.' After a brief scrabbling and scratching near the front door, they exited, shutting the door softly behind them.

With one last look at Ali resting more peacefully on the couch, Lee exited through the kitchen window to face the music.

Diversion

Passion for power above all else is deemed the most desirable of all lust. Seek power with all your might, mind, and magic at every moment.

From Worshippers of Sister Lust Acolyte Manual, Geboor Temple

Sister Lust reached the heavy stone doors to the Atrium's foyer and slammed them open with a flick of her fingers.

The sentry standing to attention outside whirled, obviously expecting Merindah. His mouth dropped open, and Lust smiled. She crooked a finger at him and cast a thread of compulsion. His ceremonial spear slipped from his grasp and clattered to the marble tiles. Lust knew the impact she made on his human mind. His dark brown eyes widened, and the hand he'd poised to draw his firearm fell to his side.

Let's get you in the right mood handsome. Lust saturated his mind and senses with desire, and he shuffled towards the goddess… and was halted by an invisible wall. Panicked, he circled an unseen cage, unable to reach her as he beat his hands against the impenetrable barrier.

Lust's eyes narrowed, suspecting the culprit even before Hecate's voice rang out behind her.

'Enough, Lust. I will not wait while you stupefy the poor man senseless. Leave him be. You're too heavy-handed with your compulsion. It makes them less than they were. You are a beautiful creature with much to offer. Have you ever thought of just being you, rather than trying to live up to every debauched myth of the lascivious Sister Lust?'

A frowning Hecate appeared and glared at Lust.

Lust's lips pursed in annoyance. She could feel the frown marring her perfect features as Hecate waited, one eyebrow raised.

'Fine. Fine. I'll save him for later. When I'm finished with you.' Lust waved in the direction of the sentry, and he froze, eyes staring at nothing.

She strutted to where Hecate stood in a drift of calming mauve light, her robes emitting a subtle scent of lavender. From the corner of her eye, Lust spied a line of blackness that drank in light, a sliver of white sand and azure ocean disappearing as the aetheric doorway snapped shut.

Lust smirked and planted her hands on her hips. *Curiouser and curiouser… and a little bit careless. She's not as clever as she thinks she is.*

Sister Lust craved more than sexual pleasure. Her unquenchable desire was power. Power to indulge her every passionate wish. Power to free her from the strictures of Heaven's First Realm. Over the centuries, she'd exhausted all avenues of indulgence and entertainment in that realm. Now she yearned for something new.

When the Voice had initially approached her, she'd jumped at the opportunity to spend time on the mortal plane. Contrary to what she'd told Merindah, she'd never left the First Realm before. An escape plan had begun to percolate in her devious mind.

Nothing like a little extortion to empower my evening.

'Hecate. Or should I say, Mother?' The being neither confirmed nor denied Lust's guess. Lust's shallow nod bordered on being disrespectful for either deity, and the unnamed goddess's eyebrow rose again.

Lust ignored the warning, her own smile tight. 'I believe I hold an ace in this game you're playing.'

'Is that what you believe?' The goddess matched Lust's stance, hands on hips. Her merciless laugh sent shivers down Lust's spine.

Lust's smile faltered, but she would not be denied. This was her chance to get out of the First Realm, and she *always* got what she wanted. She'd hoped that the Mother would reveal herself, but perhaps it was only Hecate she was dealing with. Even better – Hecate was powerful but not that much more than she. Lust believed she could get the upper hand in any situation by tapping into the being's base emotions.

Be careful what you wish for. A small voice piped up. She slapped the voice away – it sounded like her sister Chastity.

'There are those in the Realms of Heaven – and Hell – who would be most appreciative if I shared your interest in this mortal woman.'

'Would they now?' The goddess's casual disregard of her threat egged Lust on.

'What you had me do might be seen as breaking the rules of your non-interference in this Cosmos, don't you think?'

The goddess's amethyst eyes darkened, and her aura deepened to midnight. Her form *shimmered* and doubled in size.

Lust swallowed. The briefest moment of self-congratulation that she'd correctly guessed who she was dealing with, was lost in her regret that she was attempting to blackmail the Mother, creator of the Cosmos.

Probably not my brightest idea.

Threads of black power leaked from the Mother's hands. 'You dare to threaten me?' The Mother's incredulous voice boomed as her form loomed over Lust, a terrible fury in her dark gaze. Her gossamer gown transformed into slick black armour, and a star-crowned helm framed her furious face. As Lust trembled, the Mother held her arms out to the side and a yellowed wooden staff appeared in one hand, a silver-hilted obsidian sword in the other.

Lust knew that sword, and she feared it. Its name was Justice. Its bite cleaved soul from body, shredding all essence. There was no rebirth, not even the oblivion of the lower Realms of Hell. Nothing was left – just nothing.

Lust's mouth dried, and her magic shrivelled in her belly, terrified. The black threads brought the glacial cold of the Shayde into her bones – the chill sucking the air from her lungs.

Holy Mother, what have I done? How has this gone so bad so fast? Lust's mind frantically sought a shred of leverage. She fell to her knees, prostrated herself, her forehead sinking to the mottled marble tiles of the foyer. She'd made a bad choice. The Compassionate Mother had always seemed so loving and caring – virtues Lust herself sneered at as being soft and weak. She'd only half-believed the ancient myths of the Terrible Mother. They recounted tales of riven realms and shattered worlds when the Mother had searched for her firstborn son after his father had stolen him from the centre of the Cosmos.

Tendrils of night curled out from the Mother's fingers and Lust's bones ached with dread. Black threads licked at her skin, surrounding her as she quivered on the freezing floor.

The Mother's tone dropped, her whisper holding the promise of annihilation. 'I hold the threads of all existence in my hands. Do you doubt I could snuff you and every other being from life if I desired?

Lust trembled. She was so far out of her league. She could not compete with this powerful being, not alone. But deep inside the horror, a kernel of anger simmered. Lust did *not* like to lose.

'Do you?' The Mother repeated her question.

Unable to speak or meet the Mother's gaze, Lust shook her head, hoping that would suffice.

'This Cosmos is one of many I created. What I do with it is my concern, not yours,' the Mother informed her.

Lust quashed her snide thought that the Mother hadn't created it on her own. The Rainbow Serpent had played a big part. Then all thoughts of flippant answers fled as the very air held its breath.

Lust waited for Justice to fall, to cleave her soul from her body. She took one breath, two, then a third. She sensed a minuscule lightening of the air – ruination being reined in. Then she shrieked when a hand touched the back of her head and she fell to her side, curling tightly against the oncoming storm.

'Enough, child. Stand and we'll discuss your penance.'

Daring a peep between her fingers, Lust saw not the black-heeled boots of the Terrible Mother, but the bare copper toes of the nurturer peeking from a floating mauve gown. She unfurled slowly; and with as much dignity as she could manage, got to her feet. A mortified crimson stain coloured her cheeks. If her sisters ever found out about this episode, she'd be the laughing-stock of the Realm. They'd never let her forget it, and her followers would despise her weakness.

Though she still felt shaken, the seed of her anger was growing. No one had the right to terrify her like that. She was the strongest of the fourteen virtuous sisters, courtesy of having the most disciples, and so the one who held the most power. As the goddess of lust, it was her right – her duty – to satisfy her desire. She hadn't held the top position for centuries by backing down from a fight.

Still, she was also an experienced power broker. She understood the value of tactical withdrawal from a poor battle to live to fight another day. And fight she would, playing the long game. Deviously and deceitfully. For now, she smoothed her scarlet gown over her hips and tucked a loose strand of silky black hair back into place.

'Look at me, child.'

Her gaze reluctantly rose, and she tucked her duplicitous thoughts away, planting her best demure smile on her lips.

The Mother laughed. 'Humility does not suit you, daughter.'

As Lust tightened her lips and stuck her hands on her hips, the Mother smiled.

'There you are, dear Lust. Much better. Now enough of that. I have a job for you. One I'm sure you'll enjoy.'

Lust tilted her head, waiting but wisely remaining silent. Her punishment seemed to be forgotten and she didn't want to stretch the Mother's patience again or prolong the chance of being discovered.

'I want you to create a diversion at a dinner party tonight. Nina Nightshayde, the Head of the Occultology Order, is the hostess. I fancy you'll be able to give her a run for her money. And a celebration she and the rest of Geboor won't forget in a hurry.'

Lust struggled to hide her surprise. This was surely way below the notice of the Cosmic Mother. 'May I ask why, Mother?' She paused as the Mother watched her, an unpredictable raptor with its prey clutched tight in its talons.

'It would help me create the right kind of diversion,' Lust added, keeping her voice submissive.

The Mother examined Lust's clear blue gaze. 'It's sufficient for you to know that I'd prefer Nina not realise Merindah failed to attend her soirée. How you help her and all her guests forget the omission is up to you. Short of death and permanent disablement – physical, mental or magical,' she finished sternly. 'Does that sound like something you could manage?'

'Yes, Mother,' Lust's response was restrained. Her hands had come together in front of her waist and she knew the Mother could probably see them itching to reach across and wring her neck.

'Is there something you wanted in return, child? What was it that you were going to blackmail me for? What is *your* deepest desire?' the Mother asked.

Lust took a deep breath, tossing a coin in her mind.

'I want to leave the First Realm of Heaven. I've been there for too long. I know I'm becoming dangerously belligerent. I want to experience life in another Realm. That's why I said yes to your request initially. It was your voice I heard, was it not?'

The Mother's face gave away nothing when she spoke. 'I think your exit from First Realm can be arranged. I don't expect to hear any rumours about the woman you gifted or my oversight.' She tapped her lips with one finger, obviously thinking. 'Once you've completed your diversion, consider yourself permanently excused from First Realm residency.'

Two threads, one white and one red, slipped from her tapping finger and tangled themselves in Lust's belly. A tingle started there and raced to every extremity, leaving her gasping in its wake.

'Thank you, Mother. Thank you. I don't know how I can repay you,' Lust gushed.

The Mother smiled and repeated the warning that had rung in Lust's mind earlier. 'Be careful what you wish for.'

The goddess of desire laughed, sure that she wouldn't regret her request. She couldn't imagine the Mother would play her false. This was exactly what she wanted. She was free to do whatever she pleased on this plane.

Then, as she turned to leave, Lust remembered an earlier curiosity. 'Mother, of all the deities in the First Realm and all the Sisters, why did you ask me to grant the woman's desire?'

The Mother smiled enigmatically and waved her off.

Lust bobbed her head. She would get no more tonight. She waved at the frozen guard and released all bar a single thread of compulsion as he began to move again.

'Sergeant, I believe I may be lost. Could you guide me to the Nightshayde residence? They have a party on tonight. Perhaps you'd like to come as my plus one.' With bewitched adoration in his eyes, the guard presented his arm to Lust. He escorted her from the foyer and the building, abandoning his post without a second thought.

— — —

The Mother shook her head, watching the couple walk away, knowing the man's mind was already lost.

The silver wolf emerged from the shadow at her feet.

'She will betray your trust. Deceit is her lifeblood. Her every word duplicitous.' A low growl rumbled Justice's displeasure.

The Mother absently stroked the wolf's enormous skull.

'Oh I'm counting on it, Justice. I'm counting on it. It's time to shake things up. Chaos breeds change. And this little world is in need of a breath of bedlam.' She laughed then and turned to face the topaz gaze of the wolf directly. She buried her hands in the silver ruff of her neck.

'I think Sister Lust is not the only one practised at duplicity. Do you think we'll hear her scream when she wakes up tomorrow and realises how I enacted my side of the bargain?' The wolf's canine grin bespoke her laughter and agreement.

'Time to stir things up elsewhere, methinks. Are you coming?'

The wolf slipped into her shadow as she opened a doorway into Shayde and stepped inside.

Revelations

*To accomplish great wonders and magic, one must first find
satisfaction in the consistent achievement of mundane tasks and
toils.*

From Devotees of Sister Diligence –
the Acolyte Journals, Geboor Temple

Merindah woke from a beautiful slumber, snuggled in the comfort
of her own chambers, and dressed in a nightgown. She sat up
abruptly. Broad daylight streamed through the crack in her drapes. The heat
of the day already warmed the room.

*How did I get home? Where's Aeon? Don't tell me I dreamt the whole
thing.* She threw her blanket off and planted both hands on her belly. Taking
a deep breath, she prepared to hunt hard to access her inconsistent magic and
draw out a memory. But a deep well was there in a shimmering multitude
of aetheric threads just below the surface – strong, sharp, clear.

Mother's mercy, what the…?

She pushed aside the thought and focused her yerlendj, sending the
tiniest thread of love questing for the newly formed being. A thrill of
recognition at the answering thrum made her laugh out loud.

It was real. It was real! You're there, little Bindi. She carefully
examined the tiny embryo. Its growth seemed incredibly advanced
compared to what Merindah's learning memories said it should be.

Holy Hecate, I'm going to be a mother. I AM a mother. A little nervously, she addressed her daughter. 'My, you're growing fast, little one. Perhaps you've inherited some of your father's temporal magic.' She smoothed her belly in slow circles, caressing the child with her magic.

'Don't hurry, Bindi. There's plenty of time. Speaking of which, where is your father?' There was no dent in the bed beside her. Perhaps he'd slept on the couch in the other room or was in the bathroom? A glance around her bedroom took in the sapphire gown draped over the bedroom chair much more carefully than she would have done.

'How did I get back here and undressed?'

Dread surfaced.

'Flaming Hell Hounds, I missed Nina's party! I'm a goner.' With her head spinning Merindah stood up... then raced for the bathroom, her stomach roiling with nausea.

She made it to the basin just in time to heave up what little stomach contents she had. She splashed her face with cold water and rinsed her mouth. The nausea settled a little, but still seethed in the background like a stormy sea.

Damn, if this is what I think it is, my cast iron constitution is not helping. She placed one hand on her belly. *Perhaps you could hurry just a bit.*

Merindah examined her pale face in the mirror, her skin damp with sweat and her hair a tangle. The smudged make up from last night made a mockery of her earlier elegance. She knew she'd have to face the music from her stepmother, and likely her father as well. She didn't lack courage, but facing Nina looking like something the cat dragged in was not a good idea.

One step at a time. A shower then. That'll give me time to think and remember. A blush raced up her face at her behaviour the previous night. Then a smile tickled the corners of her mouth as she felt her body relive the desire.

I wonder if Aeon has gone back to the fields. Wait, no. He's not a field hand. He's a traveller, remember. Whatever that *means if you're the firstborn son of the Cosmic Mother. Holy Hecate, I slept with a god.*

Another wave of nausea threatened, and Merindah sat on the toilet with her head in her hands till it subsided. When she could stand, she eased herself into the shower and let the water run over her troubled thoughts.

Aeon was so sad when he thought of his mother. But he loved her, and she him. Why did she cast him out?

The water began to work its natural magic. It was the *only* resource Heavens Gate had plenty of. Merindah finally felt human enough to flick off the tap. She wiped her eyes and reached for a towel.

'Here you go.' The unfamiliar voice startled Merindah, and she snatched the proffered towel, wrapping it about her dripping body and staring at the stranger in her bathroom. The woman was about her height, and voluptuous, with soulful hazel eyes that stared back benignly. Her fair hair curled to her waist, and her brows and lashes were a darker shade of blonde. She was dressed for comfort in a soft cream blouse and loose pastel flowered skirt.

The woman closed the lid of the toilet, then sat and crossed her legs, bouncing one rope-sandalled foot up and down. Merindah could smell honeysuckle. As the scent hit her nose, her stomach heaved, and she grabbed the wash basin with both hands, towel and modesty sacrificed to the dry retching.

'Oh dear, things *are* moving rapidly, aren't they?' The woman stood behind Merindah, gathering her damp hair in one hand, and retrieving the towel with the other.

'Who are you, and why are you in my bathroom?' Merindah managed to rinse her mouth and grind out her question.

'Let's get you into some clothes and we can chat. You're in no danger, Merindah.'

Merindah's head snapped up at her name, but she sensed no immediate threat when she searched the guileless gaze. She dared not open her mouth, so she just nodded carefully and indicated with a pointed hand that the woman should wait outside.

'If you prefer. I'll put the kettle on. A cuppa will soothe your tummy,' the stranger smiled. She exited the room and took her overpowering fragrance with her.

Merindah dried herself off gently and checked Bindi with a questing thread. All was well. With her towel wrapped firmly around her this time, she headed for the adjoining bedroom. No sign of the woman, but Merindah could hear the clatter of crockery in her kitchen. She grabbed the first garment she touched in the wardrobe, snatched underclothes from her drawer, and dressed as quickly as she could. Her fitted sea-green frock was tight across her chest and seemed a little snug on her hips, but there were more important matters at hand than ill-fitting clothes. She needed time to think.

With her head a little clearer she remembered her amulet, feeling an aetheric tug to retrieve it. She rifled through the bedside table drawer, undid the concealing spell, and slipped it over her head. Her anxiety eased a notch.

Aeon, you beautiful man, where are you? Note to self: research the god of Time; find out where he can be found – if he can be found.

The nausea throbbed, and Merindah glared at her wardrobe reluctant to lower her head, and wishing she could magically summon her shoes. She lifted fingers to her mouth. Without warning, a pair of soft brown flats whizzed through the air and landed at her feet, summoned by the thread of air that had emerged from her fluttering hand.

Mouth open, she blinked several times. *What in the Seven Realms of Heaven just happened? How do I have such effortless magic all of a sudden? It's like I've been blessed by a goddess.*

Merindah's memory of her meeting with the being in her lab crashed to the forefront of her mind.

I have been blessed by a goddess. She unbound my magic. But... why would anyone bind my magic in the first place? It's cruel. I've tried so hard for so many years, and now I can summon shoes. To her horror, she began to cry in gulping great sobs. She threw herself onto the bed and howled. Soft hands stroked her hair and pulled her into a comforting embrace.

'There, there. Let it all out. Your hormones will be all over the place. Such a lot has happened so quickly.' The stranger peered into Merindah's tear stained face and offered her a crisp cotton handkerchief to wipe her eyes and blow her nose. Her sobs subsided to an occasional hiccup.

'Someone tried to keep me small – to keep me powerless,' Merindah whimpered.

The woman nodded, stroking her back in soft circles. 'I know. Let's get a cuppa and you can tell me all about it.'

As Merindah followed the woman into the kitchen, she noticed that the stranger's feet didn't quite touch the ground. Instead, she kind of floated above it. Merindah stopped, both hands on her mouth, and stared. Not a woman, another goddess. Now that she was paying attention, she could see the rainbow of threads around the woman's hair, and a bundle of honey-coloured threads at the core of her being.

'You're a goddess!' Merindah accused. She looked at the tea things waiting on the table. 'And you've made me a cup of tea?' she stammered. The tears threatened again, and the goddess – whoever she was – enveloped her in a hug, comforting her with a murmured, 'There, there.'

The goddess guided Merindah to a seat at her own messy kitchen table, and poured her a cup.

Merindah took a cautious sip of the peppermint tea, and sighed in relief as her stomach did not protest.

'I'm sorry I didn't mask my aetheric scent earlier. I completely forgot how tender a new mother's tummy can be,' the goddess explained.

Merindah's mouth dropped open again. 'How do you know I'm pregnant? It only happened last night.'

The goddess poured herself a cup of tea and took a long sip. 'Ah, I love peppermint. In fact, I love the taste of anything real.' Then, as Merindah's questioning gaze continued, the goddess replaced her cup in the saucer.

Urging Merindah to take another sip, she began. 'I'm Sister Kindness, one of the Seven Sisters of Contrary Virtue. I was asked to return you to your room after your adventure last evening, and to help you remember.'

'My adventure last evening?' Merindah repeated.

Kindness nodded, her hazel eyes sparkling. 'A lot has happened to you in the last few hours. It's very exciting!' she exclaimed.

Merindah could only nod. *A goddess – another one – is sitting at my kitchen table having a cuppa. I never knew deities dealt with mundane things like tea.*

'Now what do you remember? And how's the tea by the way? I've never made tea before – not real tea anyway. I've only ever magicked it.'

Distracted by the excited smile on the Sister's face, Merindah asked, 'Why haven't you made tea before? And if you magic it why isn't it real?'

Kindness laughed. 'Oh, we're getting way ahead of ourselves. Let's start with yesterday evening in your lab. Do you remember a visitor?' she asked.

Merindah closed her eyes, a small frown between her brows. She remembered standing in her lab gazing out the window.

'I was wishing I could have a bit more attention on my work. I'm trying to solve the riddle of the Portals, you know. To help save Heavens Gaters from extinction.' Merindah cringed at her own words. They sounded very self-aggrandising when she said it aloud.

Sister Kindness merely nodded for her to go on.

'And then I heard the Voice, but it wasn't in my head like it used to be. I've heard that Voice since I was little, but it hasn't been around for a long time. I'd quite decided that all the medicos and mages were right – it had been my imagination, my way of coping with a lonely childhood, with the loss of my mother.'

Merindah stopped. Her lip trembled, and her eyes moistened. She took a calming breath as Kindness leant forward. Then she smiled tremulously, and – voice soft – kept going. 'She was there in the flesh, really there, and she was a goddess too. She never told me her name,' Merindah rubbed her temples and felt the tension ease as her memory sharpened.

'I thought… well, I thought it may have been Sága granting my prayers for wisdom,' she told Kindness. 'I've prayed to Sága for years, but never had any evidence she heard me.

Kindness nodded again.

'Anyway, this goddess told me there was a binding on my power, that someone had nobbled my talents. My *throng* of talents.'

Merindah's head shot up. She stared at Kindness. 'She told me I was special, chosen. That I was the same as her, a divine being born from the womb of the Cosmic Mother.'

Merindah's voice rose as she shot to her feet, her face aghast. 'I'm Armageddon's Gatekeeper,' she announced.

When Kindness stayed seated, Merindah plonked back into her own chair. A hundred questions roared in her mind – her analytical mind that the goddess had told her was brilliant. She didn't feel very brilliant. She felt confused, sick, and angry.

'Someone *nobbled* my magic. Made me feel small and powerless, forever fighting to be seen and heard when all my peers were so much stronger. When my stepmother was so much stronger.' Merindah let herself feel the edges of her yerlendj and sank into its aetheric depths. It was limitless, a plethora of threads that throbbed, waiting for her will to weave them.

She knew she was more powerful than anyone she'd met on Heavens Gate. Even with her small yerlendj, she knew how the magical hierarchy worked. More magical power equalled more everything else power in Heavens Gate.

'Why would they do that?' Kindness prompted, leaning forward again, her face intense.

Merindah took a breath and sorted her thoughts. 'With this kind of power, I'm a threat to anyone who seeks to control me?'

Kindness gestured with her hand for more.

'And with this kind of power, there's no limit to what I could do. What I could discover. What I could teach others. Perhaps even manipulating the latent yerlendj that exists in everyone. Magic would no longer be the remit of the rich and connected.' She stopped as her words sank in.

'Perhaps somebody doesn't want all Heavens Gaters to have stronger magic,' Merindah said. 'Maybe they don't want everyone to access the Portals. Maybe they're trying to stop the beings on this planet from ascending.'

Silence greeted her statement, and Kindness settled back in her chair with a self-satisfied smile.

Merindah felt the ends of her curiosity gather to form a picture, and she ached to pursue it – but a swirl of nausea brought that to a screaming halt.

'This is morning sickness isn't it.'

With a sympathetic smile Kindness nodded at her statement.

'Is the baby's growth accelerated because of who her father is?'

Kindness agreed with another nod.

'Where is her father? Where's Aeon? He needs to be here. Doesn't he? I barely know him. And Sister Lust? Why did she approach me? Why did she offer me a boon and then try to steal my body?' Before Kindness, could reply Merindah got to her feet and began to pace.

Her kitchen and living area were a single, tiny space – only slightly bigger than her workspace. Her chambers were located in one of the more recent outflung additions to the Librarium. Though weathertight, the wooden walls lacked the solidity and sentience of the Tower stone. Just the same as her lab, stacks of dusty books and papers were scattered on every flat surface, including the floor. Tidiness was not one of her strengths. Still, she managed four small steps before she turned and stalked back the other way.

'Why would Lust make me voice my desire, and even grant it? What's in it for her?' Kindness remained silent.

She changed tack. 'He said his name was Yarra, but he was Aeon. Then the Voice spoke to me again, showed me the paths I could choose. Then Aeon showed me a memory.' She stopped pacing and dropped to kneel in front of Sister Kindness. Her voice shook, and tears flowed unchecked down her cheeks.

'It was so beautiful. There was so much love. He's the Cosmic Mother's firstborn son, sheltered in the coils of the Rainbow Serpent beneath the Aether Tree. I made a child with the god of Time.'

She paused again. 'The Voice wasn't Sága was it?' Merindah didn't wait for a response. 'It was the Cosmic Mother who visited my lab and told me I was Armageddon's Gatekeeper. That we were the same. That I'd been born from her womb.'

Kindness held out her hands and Merindah took them. She saw the rightness of what she'd realised in the ageless depths of that hazel gaze. She felt Kindness urging her to follow her thoughts through.

'Together with the Key and the Fire, we will save or damn the Cosmos.'

Kindness nodded again, slid from her chair and wrapped Merindah in a hug, rocking her and stroking her hair as the enormity of the challenge she'd taken on began to resonate.

'Where is Aeon? Will I have to birth and raise this child on my own?' Merindah drew back from the goddess's warm embrace. 'Will Aeon return?' Merindah knew the answer with the shadow that passed over the face of the goddess.

'My dearest child, you are strong and resourceful. Your mind, your soul and your magic are unmatched. You will prevail. And we will abide or ascend as you see fit.' The reminder of the magnitude of her choice rattled Merindah. The fate of Heavens Gate and the Realms of Heaven and Hell were in her hands. She'd got so much more than she'd asked for. It was all jumbled together now: unlimited power, an unearthly lover, and an unexpected pregnancy.

'I just wanted a little fame – a modicum of attention, I think I said,' Her voice bordered on panicked.

Where do I start? Where does it all fit? What's the pattern? Fears and doubts bounced around her mind like butterflies, landing and leaving but never settling so she could sort them out. Her gift for numbers and letters wasn't helping – too many random thoughts barrelled through any order she tried to make. Her mind music clanged and crashed – a cacophony rather than a symphony.

'Start where you always do, where you are. Decide where you want to go. Begin the journey by taking one step at a time,' Kindness instructed.

Merindah took a deep breath.

'You're right. I can do this. First, I need time to think. There will be those who will wish to exploit or endanger both the baby and me. I'll need some allies for when I'm birthing.' She stared at Kindness, whose face was shadowed, knowing some of the truth of her difficult and lonely path.

'You will need to be very careful who you place your trust in,' Kindness advised.

Merindah nodded, accepting that fact and feeling a surge of loneliness. 'How will I hide her? Where? I need a safe place to stay until she's born and then a place for her to live – at least until she's five and they can scan her yerlendj.'

She grasped Kindness's hand, her own heart pounding at everything that had to happen to keep her baby safe. 'Can you teach me how to hide the babe for now and to hide my power from others, the way you've masked yourself? I need time to develop a plan before I get too many questions about how I suddenly became more powerful than anyone on the planet. I don't want whoever bound me in the first place to know I'm free. In case they're still around.'

'Good woman. And yes, I can. Let's begin now before anyone comes sniffing at your door,' Kindness agreed. 'And one more thing before I show you.' Kindness gently squeezed her hands. 'Decide who you want to be on this journey; and be that person.'

Merindah put that advice to the back of her mind. It was too deep for right now when she had more pressing and practical concerns.

Kindness showed Merindah how to weave and invert the aetheric threads of the elements – air, water, fire, and earth – to divert attention from her own yerlendj. Merindah practised until she felt the mask slip into place.

'Will I still be able to use my new magic?'

'You mean your old magic that you've newly found? Try it,' Kindness responded, then added dryly, 'Try tidying up the kitchen.'

Merindah settled onto a chair and closed her eyes. She imagined the kitchen neat, looking and smelling sparkling clean. She drew a small thread of air, wrapped its aether in her own inverted energy and sent it questing. When she opened her eyes, the single thread had become a dozen – dishes, pots, and pans flew, her broom swept, and her cloth wiped.

Kindness peered at the activity. 'Excellent. I can't detect a single thread.' The kitchen settled, the threads bounced back, and Merindah's magic hummed.

'Now for your little one.'

Merindah stopped, horrified. She stared at Sister Kindness and stammered, 'Will… will using magic harm the baby?'

Kindness shook her head. 'Oh no, my dearest Gatekeeper. Using magic will make her strong. Everything you learn, she will learn too. Now let me show you how to cocoon her with energy so she can grow unseen and undisturbed.'

Once Merindah had the colourful energetic cocoon in place, she stroked her belly and sent a questing thread. The baby's energy pulsed.

Merindah smiled down at her. 'Now you're safe little one. I promise to always keep you safe. And I will never bind you against your will.' The baby beamed back her contentment.

Scandal

*Before a request for Reproduction Permission is processed, all
applicants must submit to a full genetic scan. Failure to provide
a current scan report will result in the application being denied.
Bearers of unsuitable genetics need not apply.
Unauthorised births are strictly forbidden, and the full weight of
the law will be wielded against perpetrators.*

From the Instructions for Reproduction Permission Applicants
pamphlet, published by the Global Portal Collaborative
Reproductive Imperative Branch 3107

The sharp knock on the door startled Merindah from her reverie
and she glanced to the chair where Kindness sat. There was no
one there. She stood and checked the rest of the room, and even ducked her
head into the bedroom, but there was no trace of the goddess.

'Are you still here?' Merindah whispered.

No answer.

She was alone.

The knocking became thumping.

'Merindah, I know you're in there. Open up. I want the gossip. Come
on, let me in.' Bridget's strident tones threatened to wake the entire wing.

'I'm coming. I'm coming. Good goddess, woman.' Merindah checked
that the baby's cocoon and her own masking were all in place before she
opened the door.

Bridget bounced in with a flurry of parcels and dumped them on the kitchen counter. She turned to Merindah with a frown. 'When did you have time to clean the kitchen? And why would you? Your messiness is one of your most endearing qualities.'

Before Merindah could respond to any part of the interrogation, Bridget trotted into the kitchen, the torrent of questions continuing unabated. 'How long have you been up? It wasn't tidy last night when we left. And why aren't you at work?' She filled the kettle and put it on to boil, then got out cups and plates. Then she plonked some savoury pastries on a plate, her mouth running the whole time.

'What happened at the party? You must give me details. There are delicious and salacious rumours doing the rounds this morning that it turned into an orgy. A real orgy. I want the goss *straight* from the source. So spill. Oh, and where's your teapot?' Bridget brought the pastries to the table, picked one and took a bite, noticing the teapot and two cups already there. She sniffed and felt the pot with her hand.

'This is still warm.' It sounded like an accusation. 'Who was drinking tea with you? Did you bring someone back from the party to have sex? Who was it? Did I miss them by much? Damn, I knew I should have come sooner. Then I could have caught you in the act. It's just like you to have tea after sex, so prosaic.'

The whirlwind that was Bridget finally noticed Merindah was not responding. Merindah felt the blood leave her face. She planted one hand on her belly, the other covered her mouth.

Bridget took another bite of her pastry, releasing its strong, savoury aroma. Merindah gagged and stumbled past her headed for the bathroom.

Bridget stomped into the bathroom after her. She twisted Merindah's hair back, loosely braiding it out of the way. She dampened a cloth, wiped Merindah's face then lay it against her neck. By this time Merindah had stopped retching and sat trembling on the cold tiles.

'So whose sperm is it? When are you due?' Bridget's tone was terse.

Merindah's eyes flew to her friend's offended face. 'What? What do you mean? I must've eaten something dodgy that's all. I'll be right in a day or so,' she prevaricated.

Bridget stepped back, looking furious – her hands planted on her hips. 'Merindah, I'm your best friend. Possibly your only friend. And I'm a midwife. I know you don't think much of my profession, but could you at least consider that after all these years I might know the difference between the sound of morning sickness and food poisoning?'

Merindah's cheeks darkened bringing a faint rosiness to her pallid skin.

'How could you not tell me you were seeing someone?' Bridget's voice dropped to a whisper. 'You might not love me the way I love you, but you could at least be honest with me. I thought we shared that much.'

Merindah's dismay grew almost overwhelming as she heard the agony behind Bridget's words.

'At least give me that. Honesty.' Bridget slid down the wall and sat facing Merindah, their knees touching in the tiny bathroom.

Merindah clasped Bridget's warm red fingers in her own clammy copper ones. Where did she begin after an admission like that?

'Bridget. I never. I didn't. I couldn't.' She paused as Bridget's eyes filled with tears.

'I know. I have no idea why I love such a dunderhead as you. You are the most stupid smart person I know, Merindah Nightshayde.' Bridget huffed and leant her head against the wall. She closed her eyes, leaving her hands in Merindah's grasp.

Merindah knew Bridget found silence of any form difficult at the best of times and strained silence even more challenging, but she didn't know where to begin. She examined her friend's face.

'Bridget I…' The silence stretched again.

Bridget opened her eyes. 'So what will we deal with first? The exposure of my unrequited love, or your new – and growing – development?'

Merindah's eyes teared up and she sniffed, but didn't speak.

'Let's go with you first,' Bridget began. 'I've been living with my problem for a while now. And I suspect it's not going anywhere anytime soon.' Her attempt at a wry smile missed by a mile. She took her hands from Merindah's and took a deep breath to compose herself.

'Why didn't you tell me you were pregnant?' she asked. Merindah took the cloth from her neck and wiped her face and hands. It was her turn to close her eyes and lean back on the wall.

'I only found out this morning. I've barely had time to comprehend it myself,' she admitted.

'When did it happen? The conception?'

'Last night,' Merindah sighed.

'Last night?' Bridget was incredulous. 'How in the Seven Realms of Hell are you so sick so quickly? There's no way your hormones should have reached that kind of level yet. Are you sure it was last night and not weeks ago?' she asked disbelievingly.

Merindah felt another swirl of nausea and tipped onto her knees to heave over the toilet.

Bridget got to her feet and re-dampened the cloth, placing it on Merindah's neck again.

'This is going to be the longest conversation on record if you're going to be sick after every second sentence. I'm going to boil the kettle again and make you tea. Then I can show you how to ease your belly until things settle and you can get rid of it.'

Merindah's response was muffled in the next heave, and Bridget turned back.

'Did I hear you say you're not getting rid of it? Merindah, you can't imagine that you can take this child to term without anyone noticing. You don't have a licence. You'll be arrested and fired from your job. You don't have a consensual partner to support you both. There's been no foetal scan. The child could have all sorts of things wrong with it. You know how careful we have to be with the world as it is. They'll likely terminate it before you can take it to term. Then even if you do give birth, they'll take it from you forcefully, because you'll be in prison. I could go on and on. What's changed so drastically since yesterday when you assured me you were way past impregnating age?'

Merindah wobbled to her feet, rinsed her mouth, and faced her friend. 'I don't care about any of that. My life completely changed overnight and I'm keeping my child. And you're going to help me hide her from the world.'

Merindah followed Bridget out of the bathroom and stopped before she entered the kitchen. The smell of the pastries lingered.

'Bridget, I'm going to sit in here on the bed. Can you bring the tea in here and eat or toss those pastries? The smell is killing me,' she whispered.

Bridget waved her back. 'Sure, sure. Put your feet up. I'll be there in a minute.'

By the time Bridget returned with two cups of tea, Merindah had opened her bedroom window to let the fresh air disperse the kitchen odours, and then crawled onto her bed. She sat propped up with her head against a stack of pillows.

Bridget handed her a cup, and Merindah's clenched gut eased as she inhaled the peppermint. 'Thank you.'

Her friend hoisted herself onto the other side of the bed and sat cross-legged facing Merindah. 'Spill. Begin with the father,' Bridget ordered.

Merindah contemplated beginning from the visit of the Voice, but Sister Kindness's warning made her hesitate. Bridget was her best friend, but she was certainly not the most circumspect of women. She was terrible at keeping secrets.

Merindah swallowed her guilt at deceiving her friend and wove a story based on just a few of the facts. On her way to the soirée, her hair had fallen down. She'd gone to the Librarium to fix it. Yes, Bridget had told her she needed more pins. While in the Librarium she'd met a man and there'd been an instant and electric attraction. No, she'd never met him before. The attraction had developed to a lovely if hasty conclusion, and she'd left and come back to her chambers. Yes, it was very strange. No, she didn't know about his genetic scan.

Bridget's inquisition then began in earnest. Merindah wasn't prepared for too many details, but she allowed Bridget the basics. He was a field hand who did some travelling; and no, she didn't think he would be around for the birth. Also no, he was not suitable for an introduction to her family. Yes, he was the only possibility unless Bridget believed in miracles. Also yes, he was healthy and seemed fit, no obvious disabilities. Yes, he had some magic. No, she didn't know exactly what kind.

Merindah left out the visits from the three goddesses, the fact that the sperm donor was the god of Time, and the very new but as yet unknown role she was to play in Armageddon. Feeling even more guilt-ridden, she wove a tiny thread of spirit into her story, smoothing over the holes and helping Bridget to imagine and fill in the gaps on her own. It wasn't really compulsion, just a little nudge in the right direction.

As Bridget prepared to launch into another tirade, Merindah held up her hand.

'Enough Bridget, please. Enough for now. I've got to get some sleep, and then I have to face Nina with a solid excuse for why I didn't show at the dinner last night. I don't think *"I was indulging in sex with a random stranger"* is going to cut it. Do you?'

Bridget sighed and eased back from her interrogation. 'I may have good news for you there.' With her smug smile, she looked like a cat who'd just swallowed a canary.

Merindah closed her eyes. 'Bridget, I have no energy for guessing. Any good news from that quarter would be a bonus, so just tell me. Please.'

'Well. I overheard it at the bakery this morning from someone whose brother knows one of the drivers for one of the Librarium's Order Heads. She was telling her friend that she didn't know which Order it was.'

At Merindah's exasperated sigh, Bridget threw up her hands. 'Well, if you must ruin a good story. Fine. I'll get to the point. Rumour has it that some gorgeous woman in a scandalous scarlet dress crashed Nina's exclusive party and not long after, all hell broke loose.'

Sounds like Sister Lust. The image of the scarlet-dressed goddess sashaying towards her with those mesmerising, deep blue eyes made Merindah shudder. She hadn't had time to think of the consequences of bargaining with a goddess, particularly one as devious as Sister Lust appeared to be.

And why did she make the bargain with me in the first place? If she'd wanted my body, surely she was strong enough to just take it. At the mention of magical strength, Merindah made a connection. *Maybe she didn't think she could take me without the bargain. She lulled me into a false sense of obligation and then pounced. But why? From this story, it sounds like she didn't need my body anyway.*

'Merindah are you even listening to me?' Bridget huffed.

'Sorry. Yes, yes. I'm listening. All hell broke loose. But what kind of hell? We do have Seven Realms of possibility after all.'

Bridget ignored the sarcasm, her eyes bright with mischief over the steamy gossip. 'Well, apparently this woman is high up in the Temple of Sister Lust. Can you believe her dress was an exact copy of the statue in the Atrium?' Bridget cupped one breast suggestively. 'Exact. They believe she drugged the entire party, or used some new compulsion spell, even though that's banned of course. The event staff found all the guests having…'

'… sex with random strangers,' both women finished together.

'So you see, there's no need to pretend you were there. No one will remember it anyway. And you can honestly say you had sex with a random stranger too. No one can blame you for getting pregnant then. It was out of your control – all someone else's fault.'

Merindah could see the potential and how this diversion would help. At least Nina would have more to worry about than her not showing up. Perhaps she hadn't even noticed her absence.

'So?' Bridget prompted.

'What?' Merindah responded defensively. She could see in Bridget's narrowed eyes and the determined thrust of her chin that the next round was heading her way.

'Explain to me why a career academic, an archaeological analyst with a well-known aversion to parenthood, suddenly decides to keep a child she created with a random stranger,' Bridget challenged.

'I've created a child.' Merindah paused and placed both hands on her belly. 'A whole new person born from an incredible passion and a joining of magic that was, well… magical.' At Bridget's raised eyebrows Merindah went on.

'You know I'm not child-friendly. But it's not because I don't like them. It's just that I've never really considered having one. My work on the Portals has always come first. I think this may be my last chance to leave a legacy. My work is certainly not going to help me there.'

Bridget looked horrified. 'A child is more than a legacy, Merindah. This is not one of your ancient artefacts or fusty old books. It can't be analysed and catalogued. It's a whole new person. It will have thoughts and feelings, dreams, and desires. It deserves to be here for its own sake, not just a tick box on your ambitious agenda.'

Chastened, Merindah hung her head. 'It's a she.'

'How do you know?' Bridget's question was fair, but without telling her the rest of the revelations, Merindah didn't know how to explain. A loud hammering on her door negated Merindah's need to reveal more.

'Are you expecting anyone?'

Merindah shook her head. 'I wasn't even expecting you.'

Bridget shrugged as the hammering continued. 'I'll go and get rid of them. Probably the wrong chambers. We have to do some more planning before you mess this up and get us both into trouble,' she finished. She got off the bed and headed for the front door. 'And I have to show you how to reduce the effects of the nausea, so you can function. If you don't go to work, people will definitely start to notice.'

Merindah lay her head back against the pillows. She'd barely rested her hands on her belly when she heard an offended squawk from Bridget in the other room.

'You can't come in here. Merindah's not well. She may be contagious.' Bridget's voice was drowned out by much more sultry tones.

'You can tell Merindah that I've come to collect on our bargain. I'm stuck here and it's all her fault.' Merindah remembered that voice. She crawled off the bed and staggered to the doorway to see a brazen Sister Lust saunter into her living area as though she were strutting into a ballroom. She was still clothed in the scandalous scarlet gown that displayed one naked breast. Her hair remained impeccably coiffed on her crown, despite what rumours suggested she'd spent the previous evening doing.

And she wasn't the only guest. As Sister Lust sank languidly into the only armchair Merindah owned, Nina Nightshayde stormed through the doorway. Nina's thin lips curled in distaste at having to enter what must be a hovel to her, and therefore beneath her contempt. Her black eyes blazed, and her angular golden face held a thundercloud ready to rain on Merindah's day.

'This creature says you will explain everything. You will tell me who she is, and why you thought you had the right to invite her to my soirée last night in your stead.' Nina then turned her glowering gaze on Sister Lust who glared back with the same venom. 'And why she saw fit to turn my guests into rutting monsters.' All three women turned and stared at Merindah.

Merindah felt the blood leave her head and she slid bonelessly to the floor.

Discovery

Hold a true soulmate in your heart, not your hands and head.

Mirrabookan Proverb

Merindah closed the door of her lab and rested her forehead and palms against the smooth wood, letting its cool strength soothe her and her churning belly. It had been less than twenty-four hours since her world had turned upside down, and her life had become a waking nightmare. Goddesses, cosmic politics, and her devious stepmother: an unholy trio of trouble. She desperately needed time to think undisturbed, and her lab was her sanctuary – her treasured thinking place.

At least Bridget had helped her to escape her stepmother. Her friend had insisted that Merindah was infectious and too sick to see anyone today. She shoved the thought of the showdown still to come on that front to the back of her mind.

Then, as soon as Nina had stalked out, Bridget had taken Sister Lust off to Bridget's own chambers two floors up. When Lust had resisted, Bridget had simply grabbed her by the arm and marched her out the door. The surprise on Sister Lust's face had been *priceless*. Merindah chuckled when she thought about what the look on Bridget's face would be when she discovered that she had been dragging along *the* Sister Lust, goddess of the First Realm of Heaven. Merindah was very surprised Sister Lust had allowed herself to be led. She wondered why.

Note to self: Borrow acolyte manual for followers of Sister Lust and check for possible motivation.

Merindah tentatively quested an aetheric thread of earth towards her door, seeking a way to keep herself in and everyone *else* out. *Perhaps some kind of solid aetheric shield using my new found powers might work.* She lifted her head, but kept her hands on the door. As her aetheric thread touched the wood, she felt it rebound and slap back. Yet the wood itself felt sleepy, unconscious. Something else was responding.

Excitement bubbled. She'd never received any of these kind of impressions before her unbinding. With her yerlendj contained, it had been all she could do to sense strong magic when she fell into it. Her own skill had barely been sufficient to put together an *I'm busy* ward over the doorway before today. No longer. She had more than enough magic to do whatever she wanted. To *whomever* she wanted.

Not that I would. Cosmic Guardian, Armageddon's Gatekeeper, and all that. She stifled a chuckle. *But it would be so satisfying to see the looks on their faces when I levelled their Tower to dust or blew them onto the next continent. Mmm, I wonder if I could do that?*

She moved to her right, feeling the smooth stone of the tower's external facade under her hand. She quested another earth thread toward the stone, and felt a resonance in the aetheric fabric of the room.

The room *shimmered*. The smooth tower wall rippled and became raised scales, the entire room coated in snakeskin.

Merindah stepped away from the doorway astonished. She pulled her thread back and stuck her hands in her pockets. The wall's altered state remained. Her own state vacillated between feeling smug at the strength of her power and worried about the consequences of what she'd done. She *was* supposed to be keeping her newly released power hidden after all.

Perhaps experimenting with magic in the sentient Tower is NOT such a smart thing to do. When nothing further eventuated, curiosity got the better of her. The previously pristine stone now sparkled with a million motes of subtle rainbow.

It's like the surface of a white fire opal.

Merindah closed her eyes and let her fingers stroke the contours of the pattern. She listened for the music in her mind. A hum tickled her hearing; and a familiar brumal scent brought a wintery shiver.

Not snakeskin, probably not even reptilian – the scales are separate. They're more feather-like, but not quite avian. And it smells like the scent I get from the Portal when I trace the glyphs. She opened her eyes and compared her hand to the pattern. A single scale was at least as big as four of her hands put together. She laid her left hand on the wall, which felt warmer than usual. The aquamarine stone in her mother's ring throbbed with colour, a deeper blue than she'd ever seen.

She closed her eyes again, gently opening her magic and letting it slide through the threads of her recently acquired shield. She drew the aetheric threads of energy down her arms and into both her hands, and enhanced her senses to see, hear, smell, and feel more deeply. The amulet on her breast warmed against her skin.

Hands flat against the scales, she quested with multiple threads of earth, fire, air, and water. And before she'd got further than the surface, the wall seemed to take a deep breath in.

Finally. She stirs my slumber. A deep, sensual voice rumbled its thoughts straight into her mind.

Merindah's mouth dried as she backed into the middle of her room, stumbling against piles of books.

Holy Hecate, the Tower is *alive!* Her first instinct was to run screaming from the room. It was one thing to know there was a somnolent sentience in the tower, but a completely different story to have it manifest and mindspeak you.

I am as alive as you are, little Gatekeeper.

Merindah's body rocked to a stop. Her mind took off in a hundred directions, and her gut ramped up its whirling churn. This powerful entity knew about her cosmic role. Was it here to hinder or help? She could really do with a few allies.

Her second instinct was to find out more. She took a breath. Decided. Her curiosity won, and she circled, examining her room with new eyes. A sense of righteous familiarity tickled her mind.

I know all about you, precious child of the Cosmos.

Merindah gulped to moisten her mouth and willed the nausea to stillness. The nausea ignored her.

'Who are you, and how do you know me?' she demanded.

The walls rumbled with sultry feminine laughter. *I am Iluka. There is no need to speak aloud. I know your every thought, every emotion, and every action taken in this life, and in all those that have gone before.*

Merindah's innate fear and her analytical mind strained in a tug of war. She dug deep. This was what she wanted – this would surely help her achieve her deepest desire as Sister Lust had promised.

This could be what I wished for – my momentous aetheric discovery. I deserve this. I knew I was destined for greatness. Besides, she was safe in the Ivory Tower, the second oldest building in Geboor. She was safer in the Librarium grounds than anywhere else on Heavens Gate.

Her stomach flip-flopped and she rested one hand on her belly and one over her mouth as bile rose in her throat. This child would not be ignored. She was a mother. Though she couldn't see how gestating this creature fit into either the Cosmic Plan or her own plan to be first through the Portal – and, of course, to save the world. The clear visions she'd seen at Bindi's conception were now hazy impressions at best.

What is it you want from me child? Resentment surfaced. *Shouldn't I feel protective and play it safe?* But she had fed her ambition for so long and now this tiny being was spoiling her moment. *Can't you see this is important to me?* The instinct to protect another being – to put someone else first – felt foreign; and she swallowed the bile, ignoring the acid burning in her chest and the heaviness in her heart.

I am SO over being a small player. I want to step into my reputation as Armageddon's Gatekeeper. Nothing is getting in and nothing is getting out unless I say so. My rules. Time to get some straight answers. What's the point of having these powers if I have to hide them?

But what if it puts the baby – my baby – at risk?

She tried calming her swirling gut with a thread of water as Iluka responded.

Are you finished ruminating? It is time to wake. Even I need to stretch after three decades. Patience may be a virtue, but I am tired of waiting. As Merindah opened her mouth to respond, Iluka continued, ***I know, Patience is a Sister Goddess and one of the contrary virtues. I am not complaining – I merely imagined your human version would be much more fun than this. You have played this life way too safe.***

Merindah added a hundred more questions to her list with those statements. She took a deep breath. 'I'm going to speak aloud, because it helps me get organised and reduces the pace of my thoughts. Which is a good thing right now, trust me. And it will distract me from the nausea.'

Right then. Let's start from here and work backwards first, Merindah decided. She heard a throaty chuckle at her thoughts.

'You're Iluka. What does that mean? What human version? Are you the Tower? Are you what keeps the walls warm and the lights glowing when people are around?'

Slow down. Slow down. Iluka means by the sea. You are a human version. I both am – and am not – the tower. And yes, to the warmth and lights.

Merindah's brow drew down. She still wasn't clear on so many things and those answers didn't help. 'You said you know about all of my lives before. What about the future? Can you see where I'm going? Do you know what will happen to me – and the baby?'

Those lives that have yet to be we will experience together. No more separation, no matter how many lessons you say we need to learn. I wish to go Home.

Merindah twisted, head swivelling, trying to work out where to address her questions to. It wasn't helping the residual nausea. She stopped, placing her hands on her belly again, and wishing the child to calmness. 'You know it's hard to converse with you, whoever you all are, if I can't see you. Are you here? Or are you only in my head?'

In answer, the entire wall of the Tower *shimmered* again. An enormous dragon's head emerged from the stone on a sinuous neck. Its crown sported long curled horns that scratched the ceiling, scattering pieces of plaster and dust. Iluka's skull shook, rainbowed scales lifting like a bird ruffling its feathers. Unlike feathers however, each of the spiked scales was a weapon that could do serious damage.

Merindah backed up against the door as the dragon filled her room.

'Dragon. You're a dragon. I thought you were all extinct. Killed aeons ago in a cataclysmic war.' Iluka's huge black eye hovered so close that Merindah could see her reflection in its dark orb. She adjusted her feet on the floor, straightening and grounding herself, then gathering her courage and her magic. *After all, this is not my first interaction with divine and magical beings.*

'Well, I guess you're here, so obviously *not* extinct.' The eye that was as big as her head drew her in. 'Your eye. It's not really black is it? It's like opal too, black opal.' The black vertical pupil of the eye narrowed, exposing more of the flecked iris. Iluka's head moved closer still, peering down at her from half-way to the ceiling. She could see curling eyelashes the thickness of her fingers surrounding the eye.

'They're not rainbows; they're stars. You have stars in your eye, an ocean of stars. Like my amulet.'

The ocean of stars called with a siren song. Merindah felt her baby awaken. She too was being called. The amulet throbbed with heat on her breast.

Home. They're calling us Home. Merindah felt her magic well up like a swollen river pressing for escape against a dam wall. Her baby stirred in its cocoon.

She held a finger up to the dragon, which responded by leaning in closer, scenting her. Merindah quested an aetheric thread down to her womb, calming the child. She was still amazed at the baby's accelerated growth.

Note to self: Check in with Bridget about a possible due date. There were plans to be made after all.

When she opened her eyes, Iluka's head had shrunk to half its original size and the huge eye was almost level with her own. Merindah rotated her neck to loosen it.

'Huh. Thank you, that's a little better.' She wrapped her new aetheric mask tighter and edged around Iluka's head towards her desk and chair. The dragon seemed to flow along the outer wall so that she was still looking directly at Merindah.

She must be powerful to flow through stone so easily.

You are as powerful. More so. I see your magic is unbound at last.

So many questions. Every response brings me so many more.

'I'm just going to make a few notes as we go along if that's okay with you,' Merindah said.

Iluka smiled. At least that's what Merindah thought it was. The dazzling rows of glistening, arm-length teeth felt more ferocious than friendly. Merindah dropped her pen from nerveless fingers, rethinking the whole run-screaming-from-the-room option.

Iluka's laughter rumbled again. Several small books and knickknacks fell off shelves as the room vibrated.

You are in no danger from me, little one. I am the one that should be concerned. You could turn me into a mouse with a thought.

Merindah rubbed her temples. Thoughts of mice chasing dragons raced through her head. There was so much to learn, so much to do. She didn't know where to begin. All her planning and research skills seemed pathetically underwhelming for this situation. A wave of emotion washed over, again bringing tears.

Trembling she dropped into the chair, and buried her head in her hands. 'I don't know what's wrong with me. I never cry, and now all I seem to do is blubber. I miss my Mum.' Her sobs got louder.

The dragon's head shifted closer and huffed a warm smoky breath at her.

Oh, little suli, do not cry. I am here. I will always be here with you. We are in this together. A glistening tear gathered in her huge eye.

'Are you crying too?'

Do not be ridiculous. Dragons do not cry. Iluka snorted a small cloud of smoke.

'What did you call me before?' Merindah asked. She raised a puffy-eyed face to the dragon, and inhaled the burnt coal smoke. Rather than making her cough, it generated the feeling of warm embers stirring in her belly.

Suli. It means star in the language of one of the original indigenous peoples of this planet. You are the Gatekeeper to Armageddon and hold the ocean of stars in your soul. The ocean is your Home. You and it are one.

Merindah's brow creased into a frown again, 'I don't understand any of this. I'm just one person. One very small person. Yesterday I was a nobody – an analyst with the lowest job in the lowest order of the Librarium. And now I'm a somebody. Even though it's what I wanted I don't know what to do first.'

One very important somebody. Take your time and order your thoughts. Get them straight in your head.

'Right, yes, that will help. Order my thoughts.' Merindah scooted her chair closer to the desk and grabbed paper and pen.

'So since yesterday I've been visited by the Cosmic Mother, at least I think that was her.' Merindah tapped the end of her pen on her nose. 'I thought it was Sága at first, then maybe Hecate. Anyway, whoever she was, she told me I need to save the Cosmos, and that I have super-powerful magic that someone bound when I was a child.' She made another note on the paper thinking, *Kindness seems to agree it was the Mother.*

'*Then* Sister Lust appears and offers me a bargain to achieve my greatest desire. Next thing I know I woke up in the arms of a magnificent naked male, and we had amazing sex right there in the Librarium.'

And I never knew lovemaking could be that wonderful, or that males could be that smart and interesting. Merindah shook herself out of her reverie.

'It gets a little hazy after that. I *think* I made a big decision, but now I can't remember exactly what very clearly, which isn't like me – I usually remember everything. It was a third eye anomaly again I think.' She added: *Investigate third eye anomalies* to her paper. 'Are you following so far?'

Iluka huffed, her nod rattling the bookshelves. Merindah lifted her nose to sniff the sudden fragrance, sensing the fiery dust of rocks and earth. Her belly rumbled again and her whole body warmed. The amulet against her breast throbbed. She picked it up in one hand and examined its rainbow stone.

'Huh, opal – like dragon eyes. Where did I get this again?' Another note went onto the paper: *Investigate amulet, origins, and abilities.* This list of unknowns was growing. Merindah blinked, took another breath, and continued, 'Sister Diligence organise me, let's not get sidetracked.'

Her voice sobered, her emotions a confusion of wonder and worry. 'We made a baby. A whole new person. A daughter.' Merindah stared into the distance, not seeing the midday sunshine streaming into her lab. With a little shake she returned pen to paper.

'Add another goddess, Sister Kindness, then Bridget who immediately guesses I'm pregnant. I think she's unreasonably cranky at me and she admits to a chronic case of unrequited love.' Merindah folded her arms and stared crossly at Iluka.

'Why am I telling you the whole story? I've known Bridget my whole life and I didn't tell her.'

Iluka settled her chin onto the floor, Merindah shuffled her chair and reached to stroke her cheek, tracing the warm hard scales.

We are one, beautiful Merindah. I will explain soon. Finish the story. It appears to be calming you to lay all the pieces out. You always did like to see the whole picture. Not as cautious as the matron, but not as impulsive as the maid.

Merindah filed that comment away and continued stroking Iluka's scales, drawing in the most comforting energy with each stroke.

'You are so warm, so beautiful.' Merindah's hands found the soft furred skin behind Iluka's ear and slipped her hands under the scales, stroking, and scratching. Iluka's eyes closed and she began to purr, a low hum that raised the hair on Merindah's arms.

Merindah felt herself falling into somnolence at the resonating sound. She stepped back to give herself some space. She shoved her hands under her armpits, took a deep breath and began to pace in the small space left by the dragon. Three steps left, turn, three steps right, turn.

'Fine, get back on track. Right, I was telling Bridget the polite version when in walked the goddess Sister Lust, in broad daylight, as brazen as they come. Apparently, she'd initiated an orgy at my stepmother's party the previous evening, and everyone except my stepmother was affected.' Merindah stopped and scribbled on the paper. *Find out why Nina was exempted – and whether it was deliberate.* She dropped the pen and resumed pacing.

'Anyway, Lust told me she was there to collect on her bargain. And right behind her marched the evil stepmother herself, who was very unhappy with my new friend and demanded explanations about her ruined party and reputation. Bridget convinced them I had a stomach flu and hustled them both out. So, I got out of there as soon as I could and came here to think.'

She stopped her pacing and addressed Iluka, hands behind her back. 'And now *you* happen. All I wanted was to protect myself and my baby from random passers-by with a simple door ward. Then you started shouting into my head and leapt out of the wall, all giant and draconic, and frightened the life out of me.'

A bit of an exaggeration. I would hardly call manifesting my head leaping out. And I do not shout. When I speak, everyone listens. If a dragon's thoughts could sound affronted, then Iluka had it down pat.

Merindah sat in her chair, wrote DRAGON under the other notes then bounced up again as her belly gave a lurch. She dashed to the door and yanked it open. Before she stepped through, she spun back.

'Before you explain more about your draconic self, I need tea.' Her cheeks reddened. 'And the toilet. Don't go anywhere. I'll be right back.'

Deception

'Ali, Ali? Are you there? Are you okay? Ali?' an insistent voice demanded. Ferocious knocking followed, and the same voice yelled, 'If you don't answer, we're breaking down the door.'

'Jeez, I'm coming! Gimme a minute,' Ali grumbled.

She forced her gluggy eyes open, and tried to focus. Greenish summer daylight seeped through the cracks in the kitchen curtains. *Bloody hell, I've slept in. I should be at work. Why is the light green?*

She tossed off the thin blanket and swung her legs around, feeling stiff and sore. As she leant on her hands to push up, the pain in her right hand forced her to sit back. She sucked in a breath; her eyes squeezed shut.

Jeez, that hurts. What the hell did I do? Ali's mind searched for a reason for the soreness. An internal inventory catalogued other damages too. Bruised wrists, aching ribs, sore knees, and her butt throbbed.

Bloody hell, what was I doing yesterday? Her brain was foggy, and she ran her left hand through her hair, then winced as she added "tender scalp" to the injury map.

Maybe I had a doozy of a migraine and fell over? Must've been a pretty bad fall – I must've hit my head pretty hard if I can't remember. What's the last thing I do remember? She grimaced, recalling Sophie and Will leaving her flat after their peculiar spiel about Guardians, Chosen Ones, and the end of the world as they knew it.

That was so weird.

She cracked her eyelids open again and examined her hands. The knuckles were all scraped raw, the right worse than the left. But it was the vibrant emerald glow from her fingers that had her breaking out in a sweat. SHE was the source of the green illumination, not the dawning day. Dome light was regulated by the UV filters – she should have known that green was something unusual.

Bloody hell! My hands are glowing green. She staggered to her feet, staring at the offending fingers in front of her; then realised with horror as the air hit her skin that she was naked from the waist down.

What the…? On the top half she was still dressed for work, though dirt and watery stains marred the front of her violet shirt.

Wait, I didn't wear this top yesterday.

'Ali, Ali. Open the door. It's Sophie and Will.'

Her brow furrowed at her naked lower half, but the green glowing hands were mesmerising.

Huh, green is new. Pretty. How is it that I'm not fussed that my hands are glowing? Guess it's one more weird thing in my already weird life? She continued to examine them as she limped to the closet, and her heart settled with surprisingly little effort. The glow was strongest at her fingertips, and then the light seemed to follow her blood vessels – throbbing in some, quiescent in others. Her ruby ring beat rosily with the same rhythm. An ochre warning pulsed urgently in her mind, flaring along the threads of her gift.

Does that mean my heart's pumping this green shit around? She unbuttoned her shirt with shaky fingers. A faint emerald glow pulsed over her left breast.

Bloody hell. As she waved her left hand about, it created brilliant emerald curlicues that left an afterburner of light on her retinas. Smiling at her silliness, she wove a green bandage cocoon around her injured hand and watched the threads sink into her skin. The pain eased a notch.

Excellent. I could use a bit more of that… whatever it is. Her thoughts skittered away from the word "magic" that immediately leapt into her mind.

'Ali, what are you doing in there? Let us in.' Sophie demanded yet again.

'Hang on, keep your shirt on.' A sliver of crankiness seeped into her response. She wanted to get rid of Sophie and Will, and investigate her glowing hands undisturbed and awake. There would be a sci-tech explanation for sure. Nothing happened under the Dome that the Fed Comm didn't have a sci-tech explanation for. And surely that explanation would go a long way to filling in the memory blanks and getting her life back to its middle-of-the-road tedium. Exactly where she wanted it to be.

Ali grabbed a clean pair of knickers from her shelf; and as she bent her leg to manoeuvre them on, the raw scabs on her knee split and a trickle of blood rolled down her dirty shin.

Ouch!

She took a breath and chose a different option. The remainder of her clothes came off. She stuffed them in the washing basket and instead grabbed her robe from the back of the bathroom door. As she shrugged it on, she noticed her skirt and knickers soaking in the bathroom basin. A pair of stockings were in the bin. She bent down to fish the stockings out, gasping as her ribs protested. The stockings were in tatters.

Jeez, must've been one hell of a night. I don't remember any of this.

'Ali, I'm going to let Will break the door down if you don't let us in right now.' Sophie was building into a massive snit, and Ali let go of all thoughts of her wrecked and soaking clothes. Her mind refused to process what she'd seen, let alone what she was feeling. Her gift lay dormant, the tapestry grey and silent.

Take one step at a time.

She planted her bare feet on the floor, closed her eyes and positioned both her luminous hands on her belly. She dredged up the grounding practice and took her awareness Home – imagining a globe of deep-red light in her belly. Strong lines connected through her feet to the earth. She imagined her heart as a giant emerald siphon, sucking all the green light back into her body where it faded away.

Three deep breaths. My hands are not green. My hands are not green. My hands are not green.

She peeked through one eye.

Excellent. My hands are not *green.*

An odd thrill at the small win zipped up her spine. *I made the green go.* Standing in her dingy flat, chaos and craziness beckoning, she felt the triumph tilt the scales her way. The moment flared in her gift as a pulsing gold sphere. It illuminated the tangle of connections around it and the tapestry vibrated with colour before fading back to grey.

Ha. Every little bit helps. Come on, birri. You can do this. You're the only one who can. Get rid of Sophie and Will, and then you'll have space to think and follow the threads. Threads. That feels right. Better than lines, I like threads. Healing threads. The tapestry of my life. The ochre watcher in her brain eased into the background.

Guarding her still-tender right hand, she hobbled to the door and cracked it open with her left, squinting at the daytime glare.

'Where have you been? I've been trying to contact you for two days.' Sophie's frantic query almost undid Ali. She felt panic rising in her gut and somehow stomped it down.

'Two days? You only left here a few hours ago. I've been sleeping.'

'Ali, you've been off the grid for more than twenty-four hours. We were here the night before last.'

Ali didn't have an answer for that. She opened the entry wider to let them in. As she shut the door behind Will, she noticed her house key on the small side table. A torn slip of plas was tucked under it and she recognised Andie's chicken scratchings on the edge of a brochure.

Maybe Andie was here and helped me. I hope she knows what the hell kind of bender I went on last night. She slipped the note into her pocket, turning to face an irate Sophie and a glowering Will.

'Did you sleep with those earrings in?' Sophie began her interrogation. Ali reached guiltily for her ears, feeling her favourite purple triangles.

'I just put them in. I was just getting dressed.'

'Why do you put them in before your shower?' Sophie's eyes scanned Ali's matted bed hair and dirty smeared face. Ali stepped back and Sophie moved forward, her hand raised. Ali's threat radar clicked on.

'What's wrong with you, Ali? What happened to you? When I left, you were insisting that you'd come to work in the morning. Then I got an odd text that you decided to stay home. It didn't sound like you, but you didn't respond to any of my messages. Then you didn't turn up for a second day, and I got no text. I had to spin Geoff a mangled story about you being sick. He suspects I'm covering up, because it's not like you not to check in. In fact, it's not like you not to come in even if you're half dead.' Sophie stopped to focus on her, only then seeing Ali's bruised hand.

'What happened to your hand? You've gone all pale. Sit down before you fall down. Will, we need a medtech. You know the one I mean.' Will nodded and moved into the kitchenette, tapping briskly at his tablet.

Sophie motioned for Ali to sit on the couch; and Ali winced as her bruised butt hit the cushion.

Sophie frowned. 'What else hurts? Did you fall? You are such a klutz. Wait. Are you coming down with something? Have you had all your virals this month?' Sophie brushed a hand over Ali's hair and Ali sensed a fragment of memory. A brief image of an old woman with big, gold-ringed hazel eyes and wispy white hair. A speckled eagle, wings spread, golden orbs peering into her deepest secrets.

She closed her eyes, exhaustion slumping her shoulders. *Maybe I am coming down with something. I'm hallucinating again, and I've got no bloody idea if I've had my virals this month or not. I just can't remember.*

The Federation mandated monthly anti-virus inoculations for all citizens. Failure to miss one resulted in a warning. Miss two and the Grey Shirts would be knocking. *"Watch Out for Your Neighbour" and all.*

'Ali, Ali.' Ali opened her eyes wide to see Sophie completing a head-to-toe inspection. 'We're calling someone we trust to come and check you out. Lie back. They'll be here soon.' Sophie swung Ali's legs up, tucked the blanket around her and sat on the edge of the couch. Ali watched the tell-tale single eyebrow lift and knew she was about to be lectured.

'Ali, you are not to worry yourself sick about what I told you the other night. About Will and I, and how we're your Guardians? We've got you covered. The Guild of Guardians is very well resourced, and we can safeguard you and guide you until it's time. You just need to do exactly as we tell you.'

Ali's self-protection filters came off her brain. 'You know how crazy you sound, don't you Sophie? If the Grey Shirts hear about this, you're toast.'

Sophie bristled at her words. 'Ali, you have to take this seriously. What I told you is very important. It's got nothing to do with Grey Shirts. Nothing to do with the Federation. The Guardians are in charge of everything important in the Dome anyway, and you're vital to the Guardian cause. You could be the Chosen One who saves the world. Though you *are* a little older than I thought you'd be.'

Ali's cheeks darkened as she took in Sophie's earnest expression and the hint of fanaticism that had crept into her words. Her survival filter made a last ditch effort to stop her mouth getting her into more trouble.

'You're right. I'll take it seriously. I just need a little sleep. I've got seds in the bathroom. I'll take a couple of those and be right as rain tomorrow. No need for you to stay and no need for a medtech.'

She started to get up, but Sophie pressed her down. 'No. You stay there. I'll get them for you.'

Ali lay back, tense and feeling every ache. The turmoil in her head pounded like a dozen drummers out of sync. Sophie reappeared with a glass of water and two tiny red pills.

'Where did you find those? They don't look right. My seds are blue.'

'It's okay, they're mine. They're very mild, and you'll be good as gold when the medtech comes.' Her smile was the familiar, slightly exasperated one that Ali was used to when Sophie wanted to boss her around.

'Fine.' Ali sat up to swallow the pills and half the glass of water.

As she lay back, she just registered Sophie's hushed comment to Will. 'Those will knock her out till we can work out what to do with her. She's getting messy and annoying.' The response from Will was a distant rumble as she slipped out of consciousness.

— — —

Ali roused with the deep-red ochre presence in her mind pushing against her eyelids. She heard a whispered conversation from the kitchen and smelt a strange, sharp perfume. Her head felt heavy, as though she'd taken too many seds and then woken up too early.

There was a new pain in her upper arm that felt like she'd been jabbed too. Though she couldn't have opened her eyes to save herself, her hearing was on full alert. She didn't recognise the voice. It belonged to an older female – the perfume must be hers – and she was not happy. She had a mean, uppity East Quad cadence to her speech. Ali immediately disliked her and her cloying perfume.

'Your target has had a mindwipe, and very recently – within the last twenty-four hours at most. From what you're telling me, there may have been quite a few. It's hard to estimate with a mobile unit, but I suspect she was first mindwiped at least twelve months ago. You should've reported these anomalies much earlier. There must be another faction interfering with her. You'd better hope we're not too late to save her for interrogation at least.

'This last wipe is odd and seems incomplete,' the woman continued, 'so it's unlikely to hold for long. I suspect it wiped a very traumatic experience and was done in a hurry by an amateur. That can be dangerous if the memories crash back in without warning. Her physical injuries are consistent with being held down and beaten by more than one person. And most likely attempted rape.'

'Are you sure?' Sophie's voice was sceptical. 'She is pretty clumsy. And she gets migraines too.'

'Clumsy doesn't account for the multiple circumferential bruising – from many hands holding her down, nor the scratching on her inner thighs. Not unless she has a *very* rough taste in sexual partners.' The woman's voice was scathing.

Ali's mind reeled as she did a physical inventory. *Attempted rape?*

Will's voice piped in. 'We did find her clothes soaking and torn stockings in the bin. It looks like she tried to clean herself up after whatever happened.'

'Don't assume anything. Do they teach you juniors nothing? She's been mindwiped by another faction. Someone else could have cleaned her up enough to help their implanted memory stick. We'll know more when we interrogate her.' The older woman sounded a little too gleeful at the word "interrogate".

Ali slowed her breathing, trying to get her body to relax. Her mind tried to piece together what she was hearing. Interrogation was not a Grey Shirts word. They always called it an alignment discussion.

Who are these people? Interrogation is totally against the Ten Tenets – unless none of my neighbours are going to be around to watch out for me, anyway. Then I guess it's a bloody free-for-all. Anxiety roiled in Ali's gut.

'She still gets her work done. We had no idea she was missing memories. Although there was that one thing about an ex-boyfriend that I never met. Who could be doing this? We watch her all the time.' Sophie defended their actions, her voice plaintive.

'Someone may be messing with your memory as well, or messing with the whole time continuum, resetting things over and over.' The woman clearly enjoyed flaunting her expertise.

'They can do that?' Will sounded awed.

'What we can do is limited only by our imagination. I shouldn't share this with juniors like you, but it may help you realise what's at stake.' The woman paused to let their awareness of her own privileged position sink in. 'There are legends that the Chosen Ones can slip themselves into little pockets of drift-time to take a break from the rest of the world, or to do things they don't want others finding out about.'

A charged silence greeted that pronouncement and Ali strained to hear the next revelation.

'So what do we do? What if she *is* a Chosen One and not a nice, slightly boring proji?' Sophie asked.

Nice and slightly boring. Thank you very much. Ali bristled, building up a head of steam. *I don't need your help undermining my self-esteem, I've got it covered all on my own.*

'That's what you think of her? Nice and slightly boring? She's your target, Guardian. You watch and report. You're not cleared to make that kind of assessment. We've got no idea when, where or how the Chosen Ones will show up. While I agree that she's not an obvious choice, she still needs watching.'

'Yes, Controller,' Sophie responded, chastised.

'What should we do now?' Will asked meekly.

'Do your job! You know what has to happen. You've been trained for this.'

After a brief silence, the Controller spoke again. 'Don't tell me you've made friends with her. You know you need to keep her at arm's length. If she *is* a Chosen One, there's only one thing to do. And you should never have told her about the Guild and the Prophecy.'

A strained tension settled into the room and Ali began to imagine everything this One Thing could be. They were all bad.

'Take her for Testing. That's what you do. Guild save me from idiots,' the Controller stated impatiently. 'If she's a Chosen One, you know the law. You need to contain and control before she destroys the Cosmos.'

Destroys the Cosmos? I'm a bloody middle-aged proji, for Fed's sake! Ali felt her heartbeat galloping as her mind replayed the crazy story Sophie and Will had spun her. Factions and magic and Armageddon weirdness. It was obviously more than loopiness if the other woman was in on it too. Ali's mind refused to acknowledge any connections with her own crazy dreams and glowing hands. There was clearly only one explanation – this was a bizarre cult.

Bring on the Grey Shirts.

Ali had to get away from these weirdos, and the sense of betrayal that Sophie's words had created. She'd thought Sophie was her friend, but the woman hadn't said a word to defend her. Ali lay still, calming her breathing again until it was slow and even. She fought the effects of the seds, or whatever they'd given her by counting the ways she could make Sophie suffer.

'The injection I gave her will keep her out for hours yet,' the Controller said. She began spitting out orders. 'Make arrangements to cover her absence from work, for a few days at least. Investigate her background. Find out everything you can about family and friends. There must be a connection that you missed. And get her tested today. Her permission is not required. Get it done.'

'She's a Fed ward, so there's no family to worry about.' Sophie's words were hurried. 'She rarely sees the couple of contacts from her orphanage. She spends most of her time working. She doesn't have friends outside of work. I doubt she'll be missed.'

'That history and attitude makes for a pretty easy cover, Guardian. Perhaps she's cleverer than you think, or the other faction is. Make sure she really is an orphan. Family members make the best leverage for persuading people, so unearthing one would be useful.'

Silence greeted her words and the Controller continued, 'Make doubly sure. Get all the birth, education, tally records, everything. And witnesses. You need real witness corroboration, not hearsay. Use the Feds Tenets against them. *"You Have to Take Care of the Federation." "Watch Out for Your Neighbour."* Someone somewhere will tell you the real story. Nobody actually *"Minds Their Own Business"*, and everybody hides dark secrets. Someone will know her business; and once we have those secrets, we use them. For the greater good of course. Now get busy.'

'We'll get it done.' Will sounded grim.

Ali reversed her opinion of him as comfortingly massive. Now he loomed in her mind as an overblown thug. The front door opened and slammed shut as the woman – and her perfume – left.

She could hear the other two shuffling around at the table.

'Best option is to say she's taking that break she was planning,' Sophie suggested, still sounding shaken. 'The one Geoff has been nagging her about for months. They'll believe that 'cause it's true. It'll also buy us a couple of weeks and leave our options open.'

'Agreed,' Will answered, his voice unexpectedly close. Ali's neck prickled as she sensed Will watching her. She commanded her body to mimic peaceful unconsciousness, At last, she heard him move away.

'Come on, Soph. She'll be fine on her own. We both need to leave and get things started. This stuff can't be done by tablet. It's too easy to trace.'

'I kind of hope she isn't a Chosen One, Will. She's dorky, but she's a nice woman. A bit clueless sometimes, but nice.'

'You heard the Controller, Soph. You can't get close to the target. You're a Guardian. You took an oath. You knew the risks.'

'I know. I know. It's just that she always seemed so harmless, such a pushover. I mean she's a great proji, best cataloguer in our unit, and smart about a few things. But she can be so powerless, such a people pleaser. How could she be the dreaded all-powerful Armageddon anything?'

Ali tried not to react as the boring descriptions tripped off Sophie's tongue. *She is totally not getting a bonus this quarter.*

'Not for us to know, Soph. We're only ground troops. We only know what we need to know.'

It sounded like a hug was taking place, then Sophie recovered her poise and Ali heard a whole new vehemence in her next words. 'This is *not* where I want to be. I will not stay a foot soldier. I want into the officer corps. That's where the power and magic is.' Sophie stood at the end of the couch, and Ali could feel her frustration as a squirming, living thing.

'She's made me look really bad to the Guild. I thought she was a simple assignment, literally; and that I had her under control. Now I've got to find something that'll impress the Controller. I need to get back in her good graces.'

'Maybe they'll let you help with the interrogation.'

'Yeah, I'd like that. A little payback for messing with my plans. And best of all, whatever I do to her, she won't remember a thing. She'll still think we're friends.'

Bitch. Ali held her tongue with great difficulty.

Laughing at their own cleverness, Sophie and Will left the flat.

Curiouser

Standing Order 13: The use of combination spells or multiple thread magic is strictly prohibited within the Ivory Tower. All such research must be conducted in the purpose-built Cast Iron Lab located in the sub-basement of the south-east corner of the Esoteric Cosmology Building.

Standing Order 27: All non-Order visitors must request access to private laboratories or teaching areas seven days prior to arrival. Where a request has not been approved, the visitor will not be admitted. Under exigent circumstances, the Head Cosmologist may issue approval on the day.

From Orientation on Standing Orders for Esoteric Cosmology Students, Yaxa Cody, Head Cosmologist, Order of Esoteric Cosmology

As Merindah hurried away from her lab and down the hall, she missed Boris lurking in the storeroom opposite with the door slightly ajar. He'd kept watch on her room as instructed by his Mistress, in case Merindah showed up. When she'd arrived, Boris had dispatched a message informing Nina that Merindah was indeed here.

He smoothed his greasy hair back with both hands, then brushed them down the front of his gown, frowning at the ingrained stains on the dark material. The Occultology Order members eschewed ordinary clothing and dressed solely in hooded black robes as befitted their mysterious and magical birthright.

Boris wiped his hands nervously on his robes again. Nina would likely sneer at his robes. She was forever telling him to sharpen up. Hopefully, he could distract her with the snippet of conversation he'd just overheard.

'Your draconic self,' he repeated. If he could find out more and be the bearer of significant information, Nina might even reward him.

Boris shivered in delighted anticipation; but then hesitated, licking his thin lips. What if he was found out? Merindah would surely report him if he was caught sneaking into her room or even eavesdropping again. She made no secret of her aversion to him being in the Librarium, and his academic position was precarious. He knew his mother was becoming impatient with the steady flow of funds it took to cover his little misdemeanours all over the city. That patience might not cover a Librarium scandal.

But Nina.

Nina Nightshayde was so much more powerful than his mother. And her rewards, the dark sorcerous rewards. His yerlendj throbbed a fiendish frenzy, and his hands trembled to loose the gathering darkness. *Loose the darkness.* He would do this – for his Nina. He checked there was no one else about and hurried across the hall.

Boris skulked at Merindah's door. He laid his ear flat against the old wood, straining for any sound that would give him a clue as to the remaining occupant's identity. Without warning, his ear began to burn – the door heating the instant he touched it.

He leapt back with a yelp, falling on his bony butt and skidding across the shiny wooden floor into the half open doorway of the storeroom where he'd been hiding. He could see the outline of a burnt ear on the previously pristine surface of Merindah's door. It faded as he staggered to his feet.

Tears in his eyes and clutching his injured ear, he raced towards the bathroom at the opposite end of the hall. A sonorous rumble from inside the room followed him.

A sobbing Boris checked his ear in the bathroom mirror. He watched dismayed as blisters filled with yellow fluid and expanded to cover the side of his face. He turned on the taps and splashed cold water on them, which only increased the pain.

Panicking, he felt the binding connecting him to his Dark Goddess thrum. She was coming closer. He needed to get to Nina before she spoke to Merindah. He stuck his whole head under the tap and hurriedly dried himself, looking aghast in the mirror at his drenched robe. Trying to wring it out had only made it worse, and now it was stained, wet, and wrinkled. There was nothing for it. He had to go.

— — —

Merindah returned to her lab and pushed open the heavy door. As she placed her cup of peppermint tea on a stack of papers, she realised that she could see the wooden floor through Iluka.

'Why can I see through you?' she queried.

A precaution, no more.

Merindah fished some crackers from the pocket of her dress. 'Sorry I didn't know what you might like to eat, or even if you get hungry. Being the last of your kind and all.'

Iluka's head solidified, and she chuckled, her ghastly grin looming over Merindah.

Probably not a sensible thing to do. Asking a dragon who's been sleeping for decades what they'd like to eat. Merindah bravely turned her back to place the crackers on the desk where her gaze caught on the red spine of the journal from the far west excavation. The one she'd *neglected* to hand over to Nina with the other, more weighty tomes. She lifted it from the shelf and smoothed the soft cover with her hand, tracing the glyphs.

She remembered something Aeon had mentioned. *He was searching for his journal. A journal that he left in 2498.* She turned to the first page. A single drawing showed a pair of stylised hands bracketing a flattened infinity symbol, though one hand was upright and the other upside down. She turned the book sideways. The infinity symbol became an hourglass held between the hands.

He said his name was Yarra. He was a traveller. And he was looking for his journal. His journal had an ochre cover: "the deep ochre red of this continent's beating heart". And he had others. Wait... Yarra, the Yarran *Journal.* Merindah's thoughts tumbled out as she looked at page after page of tiny pictures, symbols, and words from an unfamiliar language. She'd never seen the original Yarran Journal, only the translated excerpts that had been released to the public.

She stopped at a page that held an image of an archway with pillars on either side covered in glyphs – just like the Portal arches. Her heart began to race. She followed the neat script with her finger, unable to make out any meaning until her eyes snagged on a word.

Suli. Star. Her heart pounding in her chest now, she looked at the grid of alphanumeric figures.

'Iluka, do you know more words from that old language? The one that has suli in it?'

I am fluent in all languages. All species.

Merindah ignored the arrogance and enormity of that statement. She was laser focused. 'Can you tell me what dagun suli means?'

Falling star.

'And luna? Dre luna?'

Moon. Full moon.

Aeon had told her the words in his journal would look like gobbledegook. To an untrained eye perhaps they would. But Merindah was not untrained. This was language, these were real words. Words from that same ancient language that Iluka had spoken of. And if her guess was correct and the translation was legitimate, then the grid on the facing page was an astronomical map.

But why the additional axis of numbers? She flipped back to the first page. An hourglass: time held between two hands. Her gift for attributing colour and sound to numbers began to create a haunting melody that plucked at her soul, strumming her memories. It was as if the key was something she already knew.

He said he wasn't from around here. He was out by more than five hundred years. The god of Time. He is the god of Time and holds infinity in his hands. They aren't just portals to another where – they're gates to another when. They're Timegates.

'They're Timegates!' she repeated out loud.

Of course. It took you long enough. Suli indeed.

Merindah let out a whoop and began to dance on the spot, cavorting like a child who'd eaten too much sugar. She ran to Iluka and hugged the dragon's scaled neck… or tried to. Her arms barely reached a quarter of the way around, even after Iluka had shrunk. The scales scratched Merindah's bare arms, and she stepped back, rubbing at the tender spots.

'Ouch. Sorry. I get a bit exuberant when I'm excited,' Merindah laughed.

Iluka snorted, little puffs of smoke curling from her nostrils.

There is no need for theatrics. You simply used deductive thinking and intuitive leaps of logic. The perfect combination for an extraordinary revelation.

'Do you know what this means?'

I am sure you will tell me.

The dryness of Iluka's comment was lost on an elated Merindah who planted her hands on her hips and smiled triumphantly at the dragon. 'Translating that language is the key to opening and using the Portals. Or I guess I need to call them the gates now, Timegates. Do you hear their beautiful music?'

Iluka nodded, the midday sun that streamed through the window turning the motion into a brilliant array of sparkling rainbows.

Merindah's smile broadened. 'And if they're Timegates, and we consider time as a fourth dimension, then there's every reason to imagine they're inter-dimensional gates too. Though I'd need to check my facts and translate this table fully. Can you believe I worked out the secret of the Portals?'

You have a way to go, though you have certainly made a good start.

Merindah grabbed a thick pen and walked to her research wall. Even though Iluka had transformed the curved wall into scaled skin, her images, papers, and threads had remained more or less in place. Merindah crossed out the word PORTAL on the paper at the centre of the web and wrote TIMEGATE above it.

As she stepped back to view her handiwork, someone rattled at her doorknob. The knob had been loose for years and had to be jiggled a particular way to open and close the door. Distracted by the dragon waiting in her lab, she'd forgotten to put her entry ward back up when she returned from the bathroom. The realisation dropped her mouth open in horror. She spun to Iluka… just as the dragon leapt out of the wall straight towards her.

She had no time to scream. Iluka sprang into Merindah, tearing through her new magical mask and shrinking as she poured her draconic self in. Merindah's body burned, and she fell to her hands and knees, gasping.

The door to her lab finally slammed open and with a powerful thrust of earth magic, her stepmother stalked in.

– – –

Nina sneered at her stepdaughter's semi-conscious form while Merindah moaned from the floor. She'd been incensed when the message arrived from Boris informing her that Merindah had gone to the Ivory Tower. If the girl was well enough to work; she was well enough to explain. The fallout from the disastrous soirée was widening. It was a personal and professional catastrophe.

The sneer, however, was wasted on Merindah, who continued her painful contortions and ignored her.

Even irate, Nina Nightshayde was the epitome of elegance. Her shoulder-length hair was sleek, the colour matching her immaculate black robes, the hood of which draped artfully across her shoulders. A twisted gold belt cinched her waist and accentuated her tall, lithe form in all the right places. But it was her eyes that most people remembered. Jet black and hooded, they dominated her angular face, reflecting a barbed intelligence, and an arrogant disdain for all lesser beings. In a single frigid glance, those stygian orbs sized you up, judged your lack of worth and discarded you. Most people made a warding against evil when she passed by. Nina ignored them.

In her own Occultology Order, Nina generated a fanatically loyal following of worshippers. She accepted their adoration and unswerving service with imperious disdain.

They called her their Dark Goddess, and for good reason. Many of her aetheric practices straddled grey borders. These were borders that the magical world held tightly closed against the Shayde and its creatures who sought to cross into Heavens Gate. Enabling Shayde beings access to the light of day always wrought more harm than good.

'Get up for goddess sake, girl.' Nina gestured, questing a thread of air to lift Merindah. Then she stared, shocked, as the thread slid off when it touched her. Nina's threads never failed. Her aetheric manipulation skills were peerless.

Nina thickened the thread and quested it again, only to see it dissolve again. Her eyes narrowed on the prostrate figure, her mind working furiously as her nose detected an aberrant odour. Had the girl been burning something inside?

Nina's aetheric senses tingled.

Merindah had been the only mage left on Heavens Gate with the potential to challenge Nina's own power. After she'd removed Merindah's mother with an insidious, untraceable wasting disease, that is. So Nina had bound Merindah's yerlendj. Her captive Shayde daemon had required serious convincing to give up the instructions for that little ritual, but Nina could be very convincing.

As promised, Merindah's magical potential had dwindled to a trickle, which her father had put down to grief and anxiety. Then, shortly after Merindah's mother died, Nina had married Merindah's father and moved in. Once she'd moved into the house, she'd found it much easier to dose the foolish male to keep him compliant too – and to gain unfettered access to the family finances.

Up till now, Merindah had been reduced to a gnat – a distant, if annoying, buzz in Nina's life. To ensure she *stayed* out of the way, Nina had sophisticated plans in place to discredit Merindah's every academic foray and eventually get her dispatched to the most distant institution on the planet in disgrace. She tried to check if Merindah's magical binding was still in place, but those questing threads also slid off as soon as they touched her stepdaughter's skin.

She glanced around the small workspace at the stuffed shelves, the messy desk, and the documents stuck haphazardly on the wall. Her gaze caught on the word at the centre of the chaotic web. She knew that Merindah, like most academics on Heavens Gate, was working on a key to the Portals. But she'd dismissed her stepdaughter's mewling theories as rubbish. She had no time for any other Order bar her own.

She stepped closer. *TIMEGATE. Why is PORTAL replaced with TIMEGATE? What has she discovered? Those Portals and their secrets are* mine.

She would have an explanation from Merindah now, no matter how sick the girl was. Nina's determination to be the first and only one to solve the Portal riddle was as inexorable as the planet's oncoming demise. She had already destroyed careers and lives to garner the knowledge and influence she had. There was nothing she wouldn't do to be first. She smugly drew powerful threads of fire, earth and wove in several of the little known spirit threads, ready to slap a compulsion binding on Merindah that would strip the girl's mind from her body entirely.

'Mistress what are you doing?' Boris asked as he hurried into the room.

Nina snatched her hand back at Boris's interruption. Her frown had him trembling, adding a sheen of sweat to his already pungent aroma. But before Nina could berate him, another voice spoke from the doorway.

'Yes, what *are* you doing in Mage Merindah's room – *both* of you?' the imperious voice of Yaxa Cody, Head of the Esoteric Cosmology Order, demanded. The woman had a short, matronly figure, but looks were deceiving. She was formidable – her bark notorious and her bite legendary. Her pale blue robes strained against her fulsome figure, and her white curly hair was a stark contrast to her midnight-dark skin. When there was no reply, she waved them aside, going to Merindah's aid.

She touched her hand to Merindah's forehead. 'She's burning up. What have you done to her?' Yaxa asked in an accusing tone. Her stony gaze demanded Nina and Boris's retreat. Nina stopped herself after one step, lips thinned. Boris scampered behind his patroness.

Yaxa glanced between the two. 'She needs a healer. Summon one immediately,' she ordered Boris, pointing a finger at him.

'I'll look after her, Mistress Cody.' Bridget's firm statement brooked no nonsense from her place at the doorway. She stepped around the robed figures to kneel at her friend's head.

'Good. I'll leave you to it. Find me when she's stabilised. I want a full report. Now, Mistress Nightshayde. I presume you came to the Ivory Tower to see me as the Head of the Order, and dropped in to see your stepdaughter on the way? There would be no other reason you were here without permission. Would there be? I imagined you'd be too busy placating distinguished dignitaries for the next week or three to have time for casual family visiting.'

At Nina's sour glance, Yaxa turned to leave, obviously satisfied she'd won that round. Though the antipathy between them was still fresh, between their Orders it went back generations. 'As I thought,' Yaxa harrumphed. She turned back and beckoned imperiously. 'Come. My office is this way, in case you've forgotten.'

She marched past Boris. 'And you. Get yourself cleaned up immediately. You're a disgrace to the Librarium. Have a healer see to your face after you request one for Mage Merindah. Hop to it.'

She didn't wait for a reply from the flabbergasted Boris, who hung his head and shuffled out behind her. Nina glanced back to the research web on Merindah's wall. She considered the two women on the floor and turned to scan Merindah's desk, looking for clues.

'Mistress Nightshayde. *Unlike* you, I don't have all day to waste. I have important research to conduct. Surely you can organise a family get-together outside of working hours.' Nina wanted to impale her opposite number with a stake.

Instead, she addressed Bridget, her voice frosty. 'You. Tell my stepdaughter she *will* be in my lab by noon tomorrow.' With a final venomous glare for Bridget, she stalked out to follow Mistress Cody, slamming the door behind her.

– – –

Bridget exhaled, her confidence melting. She wiped damp hands on her trousers.

'That was close. I'm sure I'm going to regret standing up for you. Come on, Merindah my love. Let's get you sorted.' She rolled her friend face up;

then threading water into her hands, she began a body delve to diagnose the problem.

Shocked, Bridget realised that all her threads simply stopped at Merindah's skin, burning off into nothing. 'That's not right. What is this baby doing to you?' She fetched a cushion from the single armchair and placed it gently under Merindah's head, feeling the heat of her friend's skin. 'Mother's mercy. First things first. I need to get your temperature down.'

Merindah still whimpered, eyes closed, rolling, and clutching her belly.

Maybe it'd be better if you lost this baby. Bridget smoothed Merindah's damp hair back from her brow.

'I'll be back in a flash. I'm just going to make sure a healer is on the way and grab some iced water.'

Burning

*Most mage-born children manifest a predilection for one type of
aetheric energy, though most can be taught to use all types. The
natural ability to weave fire magic is the rarest form of aetheric
strength found innately. No current theory fully accounts for this
scarcity. However, if the mage is born with strong fire magic, their
questing and spellforms for all aetheric energies can maintain
a complexity and currency not available from those mages born
primarily of earth, air, or water proclivities alone.*

*Spirit magic has not been considered in this paper as the
interaction of fire and spirit threads is considered dangerous
and has not been approved for non-research use at the time of
publication. Though the author notes that this prohibition is
difficult to administer.*

From Notes on Magical Orders and Fire Elements, Yaxa Cody,
Head Cosmologist, Order of Esoteric Cosmology

Merindah ignited. When Iluka plunged uninvited into her body,
molten magma poured through every cell. She tried to scream,
but her lungs were full of ash. She wrapped her arms around herself and
hung on as she fell into a boiling cauldron of flame.

Hush. Hush. It will be over soon. Or at least you will wish it was so.

Merindah was incapable of conscious thought at this point. All her instincts screamed for succour. The dragon had its claws in her soul, and she could not get free.

I am part of your soul, foolish child. Nina Nightshayde's presence forced my hasty and premature union. I wanted time to prepare you, but even now her mind begins to connect the threads.

Merindah's soul was scraped bare, her bones burnt to dust. Incandescent flames seared her from the inside. Coals built a bonfire in her belly. This was not what she wanted, not what she'd asked for. The pain was unbearable. She couldn't do it, couldn't stand the agony another moment. Oblivion beckoned, but Iluka's opal-eyed gaze in her mind was fierce.

No. We will not be separated again. This is what you wanted. Great knowledge comes with a price. You must realise this by now. Your longed for aetheric training begins in this moment. Breathe, breathe in the fire. Fire is our element – your element. The spiritual power of the Cosmos. Feel the molten centre of this planet, birthed in flame. We were born in fire, moulded in flame. Fire destroys, but it also renews. Breathe, my Suli. Breathe.

Breathe? Fire? No, I can't.

Her aetheric body – her soul – detached from her physical self with a soft pop. It stood up and observed the whimpering form on the floor, noting that the body didn't appear to be aflame.

Curious.

The golden thread that joined her aetheric and physical bodies lifted from the base of her belly, the root of her being, and floated up.

I didn't know saving the world would be like this. I don't have what it takes after all. The golden thread thinned, and Merindah's aetheric body prepared to let go. The thread floated through her physical body past a second heart that now pounded next to hers.

Iluka began keening a sorrowful dirge. Blessed release beckoned Merindah.

Someone else will save the world.

She had so wanted it to be her, but indifference filtered through her now, grey and heavy.

Then a tiny white filament issued from the cocoon of her physical womb, pristine and glowing. It reached for her departing soul. Its touch was soft and sad. Merindah felt a new ache begin in her heart space. This was worse than the scorching fire. The flames had scoured, but this threatened to smite her to nothing, to blast her to smithereens.

It was her child, her daughter. *If I die, so does this life that has barely begun.* Since her mother's death, Merindah had learnt to put her own needs ahead of others. It was the way of Heavens Gate. Only the strong survived. There was little room for compassion. The planet was dying and for humanity, no route for their exodus had yet been found. *Is it even fair to bring a new life into this world?*

The conflagration had faded to a distant roar, Iluka's lament dulling behind the mist of grey.

This must be the Shayde that everyone talks about. Where souls drift to when the physical is no more. Waiting for rebirth, ascension, judgement, or nothing. Huh. I thought it was supposed to be full of daemons.

The snowy thread touched her soul again. She gazed into the cocoon and felt its pulse of existence. The choice was not hers to make alone. Her daughter deserved a chance to be what she could not. Perhaps Bindi would be the one who made the difference, the one who saved the Cosmos.

Whatever will be, will be. I surrender to the Cosmic Mother. Her will be done. Merindah's soul let go.

The fire winked out, and Iluka's lament ceased abruptly.

The golden thread shortened, dragging Merindah's aetheric body back to her curled up physical form. Two hearts beat steadily in her chest, the second with a diaphanous sheen. A silver thread joined the gold and lowered to anchor in the root of her being. The tiny white filament withdrew. Her aetheric body sighed and lay down.

We are one.

Who are we?

We are Armageddon's Gatekeeper.

Who are we?

We are Merindah and Iluka.

Merindah's mind – shattered by the events of the last few minutes on top of the craziness of the last day – lay dulled and aimless.

I don't understand.

That is an understatement. Iluka's snark was back, and it goaded Merindah into responding.

Are you supposed to be helping or hindering me?

How could that be a question? Now that our soul heart is restored, we are one.

Merindah began to swim to the surface, surprised to find that the liquid she traversed was flame, though now she felt no burning or pain. Twice now her body had been wrenched from her control. *I didn't enjoy the violation of the goddess taking over my body, and I certainly did not enjoy your appropriation, which was so much worse. You can leave now.* She gave the dragon a shove with her mind.

Iluka's laugh sounded way too delighted for Merindah. **Oh no. Now you have taken me back, we are tethered for good. We have places to go and a baby to grow. Am I a help or a hindrance? Only time will tell. Suffice to say that we are one. I am your soul guide. Look inside. See the space, the yearning. Always there was something missing. Always an incompleteness.** Iluka triggered Merindah's third eye and waited.

Merindah's senses rocked. The Cosmos and its connections flared into being, and she knew. Anger stirred, and she felt heat rising, the coals in her belly flared, threads of fiery red coursed through her arms and sparked at her fingertips.

We are not alone. We have Alinta and Jiemba, Daphne and Kalinda.

Alinta was the brown lady from her Seeing, Daphne was Dee, the blue girl. And they each had a dragon, a twin to Iluka.

Or would that be a triplet? Do they all have two heartbeats? Aeon had two heartbeats. Does Aeon have a dragon? He was a god. Am I a goddess? Are they?

We are so much more. But that is a good place to begin.

Rest now. Iluka closed Merindah's third eye. **I will watch over all.** Merindah slept.

— — —

Bridget rushed back into the room armed with ice and cloths. Her friend had rolled onto her side and lay still. Heart in her mouth, Bridget dropped her supplies and felt for the pulse in Merindah's neck. Her own heart settled when she felt the steady beat but skipped when she felt an echo under her fingers.

She moved her hand to Merindah's forehead, finding it warm – but not the burning she'd felt before. She pressed her lips against Merindah's brow in a gentle caress. Whatever had been happening appeared to have eased.

She rinsed a cloth in the icy water and sponged Merindah's face and neck. At the cold touch of the cloth, her friend's eyelids fluttered open.

'Hello stranger,' Bridget's smile was a little tremulous.

'Oh hey, Bridge. What are you doing here? I was just taking a little nap,' Merindah muttered, pushing up on her elbows.

Bridget knelt back; her eyes narrowed. 'You most certainly were not,' she shot back.

Merindah's cheeks flushed, her eyes searched Bridget's face.

'Don't tell me you don't remember?' Bridget harrumphed. 'I went back to see how you were after dumping that lecherous woman in my chambers. Who knows what I'll find when I get back? Of course, you weren't in your rooms resting as I instructed. So where else would you be but in your lab?'

'I felt much better, and I needed time to think without everyone interrupting me. This is my thinking space Bridge.' Merindah defended herself, struggled to her knees and let Bridget help her to the armchair. She settled in with a sigh and rested her head against the padded back of the chair.

'If you didn't want to be interrupted, why were your stepmother, your Head, and Boris the Bore in here when I arrived?'

'Nina was here?' Merindah asked, rubbing her temples. 'Oh, it must have been her trying to get in when Iluka…' She stopped and glanced at her friend, her copper cheeks darkening. Bridget hadn't missed the slip.

'We'll save that item till later. What did Nina do to you?' she demanded. When Merindah shrugged, Bridget continued. 'You were lying on the floor moaning and burning with fever. That's all I know for sure because my diagnostic delving kept sliding off. Mistress Cody did not look happy. Neither did your stepmother. Cody marched her and Boris off like naughty school children.'

Bridget's voice faltered. 'I thought Nina had spelled you. I've heard rumours about people who don't agree with her disappearing in odd circumstances. I thought… I thought she'd killed you. I couldn't…'

As tears moistened Bridget's eyes, Merindah waved her concerns away. 'Don't be silly. Nina wouldn't dare. Not here in the Tower. You forget lethal magic doesn't work here. It rebounds on the initiator,' Merindah reminded her.

Iluka rumbled in Merindah's mind. ***About that. Now that I am not inhabiting the tower wall, anything goes. And they will have to do something about the lights and warmth too.***

Merindah blanched at the implications of removing Iluka as the source of the Tower's sentience and gifts. That being was now tethered inside her, a part of her, their hearts beating together. Her hands rose to her chest, and her fluttering fingers felt the opal amulet warm. Sighing, she dropped them back to her lap. Another puzzle and another secret to keep from Bridget.

Bridget looked to be struggling with something. She wiped her eyes and shook her head. 'Silly? Don't be silly? I tell you I'm devastated by you almost dying, and you tell me not to be silly. Sister Envy's emerald eyes,

Merindah! I should've known better than to expect emotion from you.' She stomped around the room, gathering her cloths and containers. 'Maybe having this baby will help you learn a little compassion. Who knows, you may even find a little empathy!'

Her dramatic tirade was interrupted by a healer in the pale lavender robes of the Panacea Order hurrying in. 'No need to worry about Mage Nightshayde's health. She can tell Mistress Cody that she's fine on her own. Back to her old self-centred self,' Bridget informed the healer.

'Bridget. I didn't mean to call you silly. I do appreciate your concern,' Merindah said in a placating tone.

'That's the problem. You *don't* appreciate other people's feelings. You don't appreciate my feelings. They don't mean anything to you.' Bridget hustled the startled healer ahead of her and stormed out, slamming the door.

Well, that went well did it not? She is gone and we can begin our work.

Are you trying to alienate my only friend?

She is not much of a friend if she storms off at every small misunderstanding.

I'm not much of a friend if I can't understand what I said wrong, Merindah responded. She sighed and surveyed her room, opening her yerlendj to the aetheric tapestry. She picked up the hints of every being who had left their energy here like vague echoes of themselves. Her eyes lit on the centre of her web. Timegates. She lurched out of the chair and stumbled to her desk, tossing papers and books left and right in her search.

What are we looking for?

The journal. Aeon's journal. I left it here before Nina came. Oh Mother's mercy, please don't tell me she took it.

She did not. It is behind that stack of books near the window. You dropped it when you were writing TIMEGATE.

Merindah reached behind the pile of books and there it was. She clutched it to her breast and inhaled deeply.

Thank you. And I guess another thank you is in order for whatever it is you did back there. Though I'm not sure gratitude is the correct emotion. Why did Nina force your hand… your claw… whatever?

Your stepmother has powerful magic because she has summoned daemons from the lower realms of Hell. Now she has a Shayde daemon from the Seventh Realm in her net, and she uses sorcery far beyond her understanding, or her control. She would have immediately seen through the aetheric mask Sister Kindness taught you. She would have seen that your yerlendj is unbound. It was her who bound you after your human mother's soul moved on.

Merindah plonked herself into the chair, running her hands through the tangled mess of her hair.

Why? Why did she bind me?

The daemon told her you were the only mage who could threaten her plans.

What plans?

Her plans to hold this world to ransom. This world, then the Cosmos.

What? Merindah's head shot up.

Nina is a very dangerous sorcerer. She must be stopped. She is one of those who wish for Armageddon's cleansing fire – a cosmic restart. But there is an alternate view. Others hope the rebirth does not require Armageddon.

But aren't I Armageddon's Gatekeeper? Haven't I changed the game by my awareness of my role?

Yes, you have changed the game. But that does not mean it is over. We have placed you on the board. There are still many players and even more paths to the future.

Merindah processed this cheery announcement and decided it could wait till she was ready to think about it. She gathered her energy to stand and pushed herself off the chair. Her feet left the floor and her arms flailed as she descended again with a thud.

'Holy Hecate, what was *that*?' she gasped.

There are many advantages to having a soul dragon tethered. As well as the wisdom of my centuries, I share my energy and magic. Your human form will be restored to health rapidly, hence the bounce in your step.

There was a small snicker in Iluka's words and Merindah narrowed her eyes, suspecting the dragon's warped sense of humour had deliberately neglected to mention that information. The jouncing had her stomach roiling again and she tiptoed to the window to get some fresh air, placing each footfall carefully.

There is no need to be so tentative.

I didn't want to end up on the ceiling or through the wall.

Merindah grabbed the sill and prepared to shove the sticky window up as she always did. She paused and gently pushed it. It slid up easily, though still with its usual squeal. She grabbed Jensen's Orbital Senses and chocked the window open, breathing in the steamy sea air. Nausea swam through her gut.

I don't suppose you could do something about that? I don't know if I can save the Cosmos with months of this bilious belly. Merindah sensed the complex threads Iluka distributed to her liver, gall bladder and gut.

I may not alter the hormone levels. That is the child's prerogative. But I** **have** **adjusted your metabolism and filtration system. It will help, somewhat.

As Merindah took in another lungful of salty air, she felt her body tingle, and the acid in her gut faded. She rested a hand on her belly, contemplating the occupant. She observed the threads drawing energy from her own, watched blood vessels growing rapidly and pouring nutrition towards a mass on the inside of her uterine wall.

Somewhat parasitic isn't it.

That is one way to consider your situation.

But obviously not the way you would? Merindah queried.

Though we are long-lived, dragons rarely produce offspring. When we do, it is a cause for significant celebration.

I guess I'm just new at parenting – and sharing my body and soul. It's a lot to get used to and very unexpected – not at all the way my life was going this time yesterday. I'll be ready to celebrate when I work out what in the Seven Realms of Hell I've got myself into.

She quested a thread into the cocoon in her womb, closing her eyes to feel the infinitesimal glow of the baby. The response brought a smile to her face. It knew her. *She* knew her, Merindah corrected herself. A warmth ignited in her heart. Green threads sprang forth like a spring planting.

I'm going to be a mother. I am a mother. Thoughts of her own mother flashed into her mind. Then her mother's untimely death. Which brought her back to now. *Why did Nina bind me when my mother died?*

Did you not listen? Your natural power threatened her plans.

Merindah began to puzzle over the pieces she had and her recall of events at the time. Nina had been a mere seven years older than Merindah, a young twenty-two, when she'd partnered Merindah's forty-year old father in a life contract. That had been a few short weeks after her mother had died, which was almost indecent haste.

Her father, who'd become more distant during the years of her mother's illness, became even more aloof with her death. 'And did my mother threaten Nina's plans?' Merindah asked softly.

Iluka's mood sobered, and Merindah could feel her affirmative.

'So Nina killed my mother to get to my father, our fortune, and me.'

Iluka agreed with her analysis.

Merindah's blood heated, and she felt her grip on the window edge harden. The coals that she thought had gone from her belly sparked again into flames. The stone under her hands began to smoulder.

She stepped back, cooling the coals but letting the fire burn. *Nina will pay for her murdering ways,* she promised herself.

'Where do we begin? How can we stop her? What must I do?'

There was none of the earlier scorn in Iluka's tone when she answered. ***To begin you must learn to open the Timegate and navigate the Cosmos. Nina is amassing a mighty army to her cause. Rather than seeking armies you must access the astral places to gather your allies. They are few – but together you are powerful.***

The enormity of her challenge was daunting, and Merindah's fire dampened. She stuck her hands in the pockets of her dress. 'Is that all? I'll get that done before dinner for you.'

Iluka's derisive snort signalled that her short temper was back.

'Seriously, we've had five hundred years of this prophecy, and the best wisdom we've got was so way off the truth of the thing it's not funny.'

Time marches. We have at least until the babe is born.

'Why, do you think I'll get maternity leave? It's more likely I'll be in prison for illegal reproduction, and they'll take her from me.'

Iluka ignored her bleating. ***She will need to go through the Timegate, or she will die.***

Merindah clamped her teeth together. She grounded herself, dampened the fires and took a deep breath. 'Well, I'm not going to let that happen. I promised to protect her and I'm not letting her go through until I know how they work and where – or when – they go.'

Merindah left the window and the scorched sill and sat at her desk. She shuffled a space clear and drew a clean sheet of paper and a pen towards herself. Then she opened the journal at the first page, and copied the first glyph onto her page.

'Let's get started. I've got a lot to learn.'

Marauder

No traffic in the Shayde Arts will be tolerated. Mages found using artefacts, spells, or other practices of a Shayde nature will be bound and dismissed from their Order.
Should the use of Shayde Arts result in significant damage or loss of property, the perpetrating mage will be bound and indentured to the offended party until the sum of the damage is recovered. Should physical harm or death result from the use of Shayde Arts, the perpetrating mage will be summarily executed, and any person associated with the perpetrating mage will be indentured to the family of the victim(s).

From Guidelines for Magical Practice, Global Portal
Collaborative Consensus Gathering, Mirrabooka 2856

Bridget's surprise at being summoned to the Obsidian Tower was rapidly being replaced with dread. She racked her brain for a reason why the Chief Occultologist would summon her personally.

She waved the messenger away; but the young man, his eyes lowered respectfully, shook his head. Her sensitive nose picked up the swing in his energy, an acrid sweat breaking out under his arms.

He stammered a response, 'Your pardon Midwife Bridget. I was told to wait for you. Chief Nightshayde requested I accompany you – immediately.' His eyes flicked up to hers briefly, still drenched with fear, but now with a wisp of sympathy. Her mind leapt from one assumption to the next, attempting to calculate risk and advantage.

'Fine, wait there.' Bridget closed the door and leant back on it, closing her eyes. Her future had just got a whole lot more complicated. She was still smarting about her argument with Merindah earlier in the day.

She snorted. *Argument* implied two people with differing points of view. Bridget suspected Merindah would never be capable of the depth of feeling she herself experienced. It wasn't just about Bridget's feelings for her either. She worried about Merindah becoming a mother. The woman was just as likely to forget to feed the baby because she was chasing down information on a dusty artefact. *If* they let her keep the baby. *If* they found out. No, *when* they found out.

What if that's what Nina's summoning is about? How will I answer? Where will my loyalties lie?

Reproduction was strictly regulated on Heavens Gate. With resources dwindling, a low birth rate kept the population shrinking, reducing the drain on a tired planet. Parents were carefully chosen, their genetics screened and manipulated to strengthen aetheric ability. The children were often removed from their homes by members of their foetally predicted profession as soon as they turned five. There was no time for frivolity when the fate of the world could rest in the hands of the next child born.

Heavens Gate was such a hotchpotch of science and magic, prophecies and policies that it made Bridget's head spin most days. There seemed no end to the regulations and justifications whittling away their autonomy. She doubted she'd live to see the "*Great Exodus*" – as people had begun to call it – anyway.

I'm certainly not likely to be at the head of the line for the first escapees.

'If you have time to stand there staring into space, you have time to take me to Merindah. I want a word with that woman.' Bridget's grey eyes focused on the impatient speaker who'd sauntered in from the bedroom.

'And why would I take you to see Merindah? I told you she was ill. You can see her tomorrow when she's better.'

Bridget had found something slightly more conventional for Lust to wear than the red gown, but the plain green midwife's uniform failed to hide the dark-haired beauty's womanly curves.

'At least both your breasts are covered,' Bridget muttered. She pushed herself off the door and stood in front of a languid Lust, who'd just draped herself over the two-seater couch.

'And what's wrong with my breasts?' Lust smoothed the material over her figure and stood up. She towered over the small woman. At breast height, Bridget found herself comparing Lust's bosom to Merindah's. The one she'd bounced against scarcely a day ago.

'Don't go there,' she muttered to herself and turned to the door, gathering her keys.

'Go where? Where are you going? Wherever it is, I'm coming with you. You are *not* leaving me here. Not when I can't…' Lust cut herself off, her glance in Bridget's direction sharp.

'Never mind, I'm coming with you,' Lust repeated.

Bridget shook her head. 'You can't come. I'm going to see Chief Nightshayde and you've already met. I doubt she'd be pleased to see you again after the trouble you caused at her party. Consider this a lucky escape.'

'I'm not staying here where the sour odour of your unmet sexual frustration has seeped into the very fabric of the room. It's cramping my style,' Lust declared, moving Bridget aside.

Bridget's mouth tightened as Lust flung open the door, surprising the young messenger waiting nervously on the other side. In the face of more female sensuality than he'd ever seen in his life, his copper cheeks flamed red, the stain climbing to the roots of his dark hair. Lust captured his hairless chin between a scarlet-tipped finger and thumb. Her sapphire eyes bored into his.

'What do *you* think of my breasts?' She tilted his head down to view her considerable cleavage. The messenger's look of terror had Sister Lust smiling like a well fed cat. She released his chin, and he scrambled to the stairwell as though the denizens from all Seven Realms of Hell pursued him.

Bridget slammed her door closed, and stood glowering.

'Well, I hope you know the way, child.' Lust smirked. 'It seems we've lost our guide.'

Bridget clenched her teeth and marched past Lust and down the stairs.

— — —

Despite her peremptory summoning, Nina did not admit Bridget as soon as she arrived at the Obsidian Tower. However, a slew of lesser mages, administration flunkies and influence peddlers hurtled back and forth through the echoing foyer of the stone and glass building as Bridget waited.

Occultology was built on the ruins of an earlier structure that had been destroyed by an over-confident student who'd been experimenting with fire and earth magic. Sadly, the young mage had died without leaving the instructions for his explosive spell.

It had taken researchers another seventy-five years to safely replicate his results; and a further seventy-five until they could harness the spell to generate a mobile product for use by non-magical military personnel. On the positive side, the carnage that had been produced in the first conflict using the explosives had occasioned the longest global ceasefire in history. Of course, all of that kind of aggression was now more than a century in the past. These days, the governments of all seven continents poured their resources into unlocking the portals – or stealing the work of portal researchers from other nations.

Lust loomed over the young receptionist, who was visibly trying – and failing – to ignore the magnificent female specimen in front of him. His hands trembled as he wrote, and he'd tidied and shuffled everything on his desk twice. Lust wasn't bothering to hide her smirk as she watched the young male's agitation.

Bridget distanced herself, eased over to the most secluded chair in the waiting area, and examined her surroundings. The soaring glass windows looked out onto the rugged coastline, a stark contrast to the dark stone of the walls. The ever-rising oceans had seeped moisture up past the foundations and stained the bottom rows of stone. There were tales told of the old building having extensive underground spaces, but access past the ground floor was restricted to Nina's inner circle – and they weren't sharing.

Bridget shivered. The dark rock felt imbued with some kind of sinister purpose, as though it breathed with a life of its own. Recent rumours and the evidence before her eyes confirmed that Nina had found a way to match the somnolent sentience and illumination of Esoteric Cosmology's Ivory Tower. But the light these stones emitted was much gloomier than what she'd experienced in Merindah's workplace. Here she felt watched: something lurked at the edge of her mind and hunted for the murky secrets of her heart.

While Lust practiced her intimidation of the staff, Bridget worried at a fingernail. Everyone would wonder why she was here. She'd already seen a dozen surreptitious and calculating looks in her direction. Nina had never once interacted with or threatened her directly, not after that first time almost twenty-five years ago. She hoped that wouldn't change today.

She was so close to being free. She just needed to remain calm and not expect the worst. Luckily for her, Merindah rarely concerned herself with the posturing of politics and power plays. Bridget sighed. *It might actually be nice if she did once in a while. It would make my job a whole lot easier. I could report on that without compromising her.*

As it was, Bridget's objectivity about her role in Merindah's life had been lost early in the first year. *The woman may lack compassion and emotional insight, but she is smart, funny, and generous with her time – when she wants to be.* Not many people gave Bridget their time. Her social connections were flimsy. And Merindah had been such a sad child when her mother had died. Bridget had only been three years older, but fiercely loyal to her dysfunctional family; Nina had leveraged that to her own nefarious advantage.

Lust's shenanigans appeared to have worked, and she beckoned Bridget over. Of course, her hip-thrusting stance and the sultry gleam in her eye made it seem as though she was inviting Bridget for much more than a chat. Bridget's cheeks darkened as every eye in the room watched her trail up the curving stairwell behind Lust.

So much for being incognito, Bridget mused. *Though there was a bit of envy in some of those glances. Must take note of who I need to follow up.*

Thoughts of future leverage were replaced by quivering fear when she knelt, penitent, before Nina Nightshayde moments later. She was driven to her knees, head bowed with a single cursory glance and a thread of fire across the back of her neck. Meanwhile, Sister Lust had draped herself over a chair, crossing one elegant leg over the other and nonchalantly swinging her foot. Her sharp gaze gave lie to the staged indifference, but Nina ignored her.

The Head of Occultology rose from behind the massive stone table that dominated the sombre setting and stalked towards Bridget. The sound of iron-shod heels striking the black tiled floor resonated ominously in Bridget's bones. Nina stopped so close that Bridget could see the toes of her leather boots under the hem of her swirling black robe without raising her head. She held her breath, her heart pounding so loudly that she worried she'd miss any spoken words.

She needn't have worried. Nina leant close to her ear, her venomous tones as clear as crystal. 'When your parents sold you twenty-five years ago, I told you your life was mine. There was one rule for you to stay alive. What was that rule?'

Bridget slowly exhaled and dared to breathe. *I can do this. Things are fine. Nina can't recall the exact date, surely.* Bridget calmed her breathing. 'Be Merindah Nightshayde's confidante and report her every thought, feeling and action to you, Mistress Nightshayde.'

The magical slap to the side of her face knocked Bridget to the floor, blood and spittle dripping from her bruised mouth. She cowered, her courage and yerlendj shrivelling. She added another layer of shielding to her innermost secrets and instead loosed her fear and loathing to Nina's furious glare. Bridget told herself that Merindah would recover from the babe's loss. She could apply for another.

'So why do I have to find out for myself that my stepdaughter is working on a new line of portal research? Why do I find out for myself that she is ill? Why don't I know the depths of her relationship with that old hag who heads her ridiculous Order?' Nina's pointed finger flung Bridget against the wall. Her body connected with the edge of a wooden shelf with a sickening crunch then slid down the stone wall. Bridget gritted her teeth to stop the shrieking pain of her arm and shoulder.

She doesn't know about the baby; Bridget stifled her thought.

'You're only alive because I say you are. I can just as easily say you die – and you will.' When Bridget remained a huddled mess on the floor, Nina hissed, 'Well? Is this not so?'

'Yes, Mistress.' Bridget's swollen jaw and tongue managed the words.

'And what happens if you disobey? What happens if you displease me?' Nina moved closer and grabbed Bridget's curls, yanking them back to expose her bruised face and haunted eyes.

'My family is forfeit, Mistress,' Bridget's voice was strained. 'You will kill my entire clan, every single one.'

Nina's triumphant sneer seared its dark spear into Bridget's heart. 'You choose,' Nina hissed, tightening her hold. 'Keep your lover, or watch your family die.' At Bridget's startled glance, Nina leant down close. 'Oh, I know you have *feelings* for your charge. You didn't think you were my only spy, did you? That I would believe your obedience and the paltry weekly reports you send?'

Bridget closed her eyes, tears slipping through her lids as Nina tossed her away. Bridget had let herself dream, let herself believe. Her twenty-five year indenture was up in a couple of months, and she'd dreamed of escaping to another country, taking Merindah with her. She felt her dream dissolving.

Nina *knew* she'd held back information. Knew she loved Merindah. Now the woman would never release her from the magical contract. Bridget's shoulders sagged, and she curled up on the floor, her family and Merindah on a revolving catwalk to death.

– – –

Hearing a chuckle, Nina spun and saw the dark-haired woman watching her like a hawk.

'Nicely done. A little physically excessive for my tastes, but nicely done nonetheless.' Nina strolled casually towards her. This woman had trashed months of planning and manipulation with her little parlour tricks at the soirée. Nina hurled a complex compulsion thread at her. The thread slid off, dissolving into nothing.

The woman chuckled again. 'You'll have to try a little harder than that, dear. I created the first compulsion weave after all. How else could I grant desires so effortlessly?'

Nina's face hardened. That was the second time in as many days that one of her compulsion spells had unravelled. She needed more power.

'What do you mean, you created the first compulsion weave? That feat is commonly attributed to Sister Lust.'

Sister Lust struck a seductive pose and drawled, 'There's *nothing* common about me dear.'

Nina evaluated the stunning face, shining hair, curvaceous figure, and oozing sensuality. She quested a complex diagnostic, and with a languorous wave from Lust, the delving slid in. Nina was more surprised than she'd been in a very long while.

'Your vibrations are a little flat. But I believe you may be she,' she stated at last.

Lust strode closer to Nina, who stood her ground. The two of them stood eye to eye, close enough to feel each other's breath.

Nina spoke first. 'Why are you here? What do you want?' she demanded.

Lust's villainous grin would have had a lesser woman quaking. 'I believe we can help each other. I'm a little, shall we say, *stuck* at the moment. I made a little bargain with some unintended consequences, which I believe you can help me with.'

Nina began racking up the possibilities in her head. The goddess could be trapped on this plane, which explained the flattened vibrations. Who made a bargain with a goddess and got the better of her? Nina felt a tremor of excitement that another serious player was in the game. She hoped her new opponent would be worthy of her time.

'And what do I get out of this arrangement?'

Lust tossed back her mane of black hair. Her scarlet lips parted in a sultry smile, and she settled her hands on her hips. 'I have a few tricks up my sleeve that I'm willing to share… with the right kind of student,' she offered.

When Nina's eyebrow rose, the goddess went on, 'And I can give you the key to Merindah's deepest desire. A desire I believe you share with her.'

Nina answered by holding her hand out, palm up.

Lust placed hers, palm down over it, and a black flare bathed the two.

Nina edged closer as their hands dropped. 'Bargain sealed. Betray me at your peril. No matter who or what you are.'

Lust's steely glare paired Nina's own. 'Likewise.'

They stepped back simultaneously, assessing.

Nina indicated a heavy iron door in the wall behind her desk. Occult glyphs outlined the archway.

'I have somewhere more private where we can discuss the details,' Nina said. She watched as Lust scanned the carved warnings of painful demise should anyone attempt unauthorised entry. 'Access is by invitation only.'

Lust inclined her head, then preceded Nina through the doorway without hesitation. They understood each other. The damp stairs descended into a musty darkness that reeked of sulphur and blood. The iron door clanged shut behind them.

– – –

Bridget quailed in the corner, forgotten. She counted slowly to one hundred before she decided she could move and possibly escape. She rolled onto her side nursing her injured arm. One eye was swollen shut, reducing her vision, but she still glanced around carefully to make sure Nina hadn't snuck back to snare her.

She took as deep a breath as she could manage, and hauled herself up using the wooden bookshelf that had cracked her arm.

Her contract had less than seven weeks to go. It fell due on her birthday. Bridget had planned what she'd do after her release every single day since she'd been bound as a child. Her only strategy had been to do the minimum required and to remain out of Nina's sight.

Out of sight, out of mind. I should've known it was too easy.

She rested her head against the books, then drew back sharply when a hard spine poked her tender forehead. She glared at the cracked tome, ready to berate it, but her gaze was drawn to its neighbour – a slim red journal, similar to the one Merindah had snatched from her hand yesterday. She wondered if Nina had retrieved it from Merindah's lab when she'd visited earlier.

With a sharp intake of breath, Bridget braced her broken arm against the shelf and eased the journal out with her undamaged hand. The three overlapping circles on the cover confirmed it. She flicked through the pages, many of them with pictures and symbols similar to what she'd seen in Merindah's, though this one felt older somehow. And this one had tidy margin notes that even she could understand. They looked like translations. Bridget's heart stopped when she read one.

The Dogs of Doom come way too soon
When Fate's Foe emerges

She promptly closed the book and listened to reason for two pounding heartbeats until the vicious voice of her owner echoed in her head. 'You're only alive because I say you are. I can just as easily say you die – and you will.'

Bridget tucked the journal into the pocket of her uniform, for once ignoring the consequences of discovery. Her small yerlendj responded as she smoothed the shelf with a wisp of air, removing any trace of her hand. If her servitude was to continue, she was going to start her own one-woman rebellion and undermine Nina and her dastardly plan as often as she could. She'd begin by warning her family to hide and slipping this volume to her best friend. A wave of pain scattered her thoughts. She blinked as the obsidian walls seemed to ripple. Dread began as an itch on the back of her neck as though something had realised she'd stolen the journal, and was about to scream a warning.

Bridget staggered to the door, cracked it open and shuffled through. A final glance at Nina's inner sanctum left her shivering. She closed the door behind her and moved down the stairwell towards the exit with her head lowered, shame and guilt warring for dominance on her damaged face. Nina's acolytes and associated hangers on in the foyer ignored her.

No one offered to help until a woman approached her as she pushed through the heavy main doors with her uninjured shoulder. The woman's clothes, a flowered skirt and soft cream shirt appeared oddly sunny in this dark environment, and Bridget peeped up into a pair of enormous hazel eyes in a face surrounded by a cloud of curling fair hair.

'Hello, dearest child. How brave you are. Let me help you home. I can see you have much work to do.' Her gaze slipped to where the book nestled inside Bridget's pocket. Bridget's one clear eye widened in fear. The woman wrapped a warm arm around her shoulders and shook her head, her laughter bringing light to her words as she guided Bridget away from the Obsidian Tower.

'Oh no, dear. We're on the same side. I'm not able to breach the wards on her door, you see. They're nasty things, Shayde daemons. But you. You, my ferocious little midwife. You faced the dragon in its den. You've helped our cause and your friend more than you could possibly imagine by your courageous deed. And she *so* needs friends right now,' the strange woman finished softly.

Bridget did not relax, but her pain lessened as her resolve hardened. She knew she wouldn't be alone in wishing for Nina's plans to go awry. The woman had stomped on too many on her way to the top. But did she dare to trust a stranger?

'I don't know who you mean!'

Bridget's words brought a delighted smile to the woman's face. 'Oh, cautious child, we both know who's at the centre of all this furore. Merindah needs your help with her pregnancy. No one must know.'

Bridget's gaze darted about, they were still close to the Obsidian Tower and Nina had many spies.

'I have us shielded. No one can listen in,' the woman reassured her.

Bridget remained sceptical, but those hazel eyes pinned her in place. 'This baby will grow at an extraordinary rate, almost a month in every week. Already the child is aware and experimenting with her yerlendj. She's very special, and your friend will need all your skills to stay well. Can you do this? Will you help her, knowing the personal cost?'

Bridget's eyes teared at the question. She knew saying yes would mean certain death if she was discovered. Yet anything was better than betraying her friend with every breath through a life of servitude to Nina. Hadn't that been what had prompted her to take the book?

'What is my life if I can't help the woman I love? How can I say I love her if I don't put her wellbeing before my own?' The stranger's arm sent more warm healing threads into Bridget's body, mending bones and bruises. Bridget barely noticed the pain as they strode off across the campus together.

Translation

Seek not ease, but labour with diligence – your reward shall be order and joy.

From Devotees of Sister Diligence –
the Acolyte Journals, Geboor Temple

A knock on her lab door roused Merindah from her maternal musings. She'd been humming a tune to Bindi and sending threads of magic for the child to feel in her watery cocoon. This pregnancy was quite the distraction – it wasn't like her to procrastinate when there was important work to complete. She really should be progressing the Timegate translations; but instead, she regularly found herself contemplating her burgeoning belly and wondering.

I agree. We should be working on the translations. Time is running out for us and the child. A silly ditty will be no use to her if she cannot get through the Timegate. Iluka had become more impatient and bad-tempered by the hour.

You're very cranky this morning. Didn't you sleep well?

The dragon grumbled in her head, and Merindah chuckled. She already knew the answer. Each time she'd got up to pee during the night – which felt like every hour – Iluka had rumbled awake, huffing and puffing like an ancient crone. Neither of them had got much sleep.

To be fair, yesterday had been pandemonium. Her world had turned upside down and inside out. In the span of a single day, her body had become host to an unexpected pregnancy and her mind host to a centuries-old magical beast. Yet despite the turmoil, Merindah felt oddly content, if still a little nauseous this morning. It felt as though a missing piece of her had returned. The cold hole in her heart had warmed, filled with Iluka and Bindi. Well, partly filled anyway. Now that *they* were there, she realised that other gaps existed. Iluka informed her that those gaps were for Alinta, Jiemba, Dee and Kalinda.

Bindi was her own little flower though. She'd never felt this close to – or this responsible for – another human being. Even caring for her mother had taken more resilience than empathy. Now she had two lives inextricably linked to her own. But rather than feeling the burden of accountability as she had with her mother, this apparent burden lightened her heart.

She didn't doubt the pregnancy. Women *did* get pregnant after unprotected sex with random strangers, even in these days when carefully engineered genetics meant most pregnancies were implanted by non-traditional means. Her memories of the moment of conception still generated a wave of heat.

But oddly, she felt there were points about the whole idea of Iluka that seemed too surreal to be true. She'd considered the possibility of some kind of brain fade or hallucination brought about by the bump in her hormones or an unremembered head injury. Until yesterday she'd believed that dragons didn't exist. That they were extinct or possibly even mythical tales from a simpler time – the only representations of them left were faded carvings and crumbling books. And still there was no evidence to the contrary, apart from this voice in her head.

There was one person she could check with though. Yaxa Cody was the expert in mythological beasts. Merindah had often felt this side interest detracted from Cody's professional credibility. With what was happening to her now however, Merindah revised her opinion. Perhaps the top of the Esoteric Cosmology Order was *exactly* where Yaxa needed to be.

Iluka had rapidly refuted the "dragons don't exist" concept with some impressive displays of magical prowess. Merindah's chambers had never been so clean or decadently decorated, and the exotic food had been delicious – at least until she'd lost it down the toilet minutes later. She looked down at her old but now gleaming knee-high boots.

Dragon shine looks good.

She and Iluka still had much to discuss about the new arrangement of shared mind and body, but Merindah had been exhausted and had eventually called a halt to any more mind-blowing revelations for the evening. She'd managed a few disturbed hours of sleep; and then after a hasty meal of crackers and peppermint tea, had hurried back to her lab.

At a second rat-tat-tat on her door, she checked her aetheric mask was in place and pushed back from the desk.

'Coming, coming! Hold your horses.'

When she dropped the protection and opened the door, a junior blue-robed mage handed her a slim, wrapped package with a smile and a quick bob of her dark head.

'Sorry to disturb you, Mage. A delivery for you.'

'Oh?' Merindah frowned, wondering who would be sending her a parcel.

'It's not dangerous. It's been checked for spells and is safe to open,' the young woman assured her.

'What? Oh,' Merindah smiled distractedly and closed the door, distantly registering the smile fading from the proud junior's face at her lack of acknowledgement. Merindah meandered back to her messy desk, turning the object over and over in her hand. No postmark to indicate its origin. It must have been dropped off downstairs in person.

Well, are you going to open it?

Patience, patience. I thought you'd be better at waiting. Centuries old, and all that. Anyway, a good analyst includes data from all sources, including wrapping. You can't hurry these things.

Lost in curiosity, Merindah ignored Iluka's harrumph. She cleared a space to lay the package on bare wood. It was habit – being grounded with an earth element connection had always strengthened her magic. Although with the magnitude of power now at her disposal, it probably didn't matter. With a wave of her hand, she opened a gap in her mask, prising apart threads to expose the magic within.

There is no need for the theatrical waving. It is more likely to get you killed in combat. The enemy can read your intent through the gestures. You need only to conceive of what you want and then let the energy draw what it needs through you.

Merindah paused. 'Leaving aside the combat and enemy comment,' she frowned, 'Don't I need to control how the aether weaves together? I've heard you can burn yourself out if you use too much. I've got scars to prove that part could be true.' Merindah had recently tried an illegal spell to boost her aetheric thrust with disastrous consequences. She now realised her stepmother's binding must have repelled the spell.

Unfortunately, it had repelled *straight* onto Merindah's belly, which now bore several jagged scars. It had taken weeks to heal, especially because she'd taken several days to admit the injury to Bridget. Her friend had been furious that she'd left it untreated for so long. But she'd healed it as best she could, adding a stern warning to be more careful and let her know before she tried anything like that again.

Merindah absently rubbed her belly which still itched from time to time.

That is not going to happen to us. Trust me. Between us, we have more than enough magic to do whatever it takes.

What about negentropy?

What about it?

Merindah stepped back from the desk and began to pace in the small space, thinking aloud.

'Negentropy keeps the chaos, the entropy, in balance. It uses energy to organise. Though we need the chaos, we need entropy for our bodies, our beings, to work. If we became inert and entered a state of complete equilibrium, we'd die. Wouldn't we?'

So?

'So, how does that work with spirituality? How does our belief in a higher state, raising our vibrations and ascending to the Realms of Heaven work with entropy and negentropy? Or the opposite, descending into the Seven Realms of Hell? And how does all of that work with magic, manipulating aether? How does all of it fit together?'

It is a little early in the day for a philosophical treatise on the fabric of the universe, even for you.

'Work with me for just a bit longer here. I need to get this straight before I unleash myself and these new powers on an unsuspecting world. Before I open – or close – any gates.'

Fine, but be brief. We have a Cosmos to save. And I suggest keeping your true power hidden from everyone.

Merindah waved the last words away. She was already deep into the conceptual thought and "everyone else" was low on her list. 'Now, negentropy makes things more orderly and structured correct?'

Correct. It is anathema to randomness and chaos. A living system exports entropy to keep its own stores low. Those same living systems import negentropy and store it. Negentropy is essential to all beings, and is free energy.

'And our main source of energy is our sun, dying though it may be?'

Correct.

'I have two questions for you then – well, two to begin with at least. Firstly, was our overuse of negentropy – back when we had a very ordered and purely technological culture – responsible for our dying sun, and therefore our dying planet?'

The simple answer is no. There are much bigger drains on energy than the tiny beings who inhabit this sphere of molten rock. But the answer is also yes. Overreliance on technology and negative emotions drain the energetic life force from the planet.

'Hold that thought. It bears more investigation, but leads to my next question.' Merindah took a deep breath and paused to glance out the window. The sea was wild today, reflecting her own tumultuous thoughts.

Second question?

Iluka had watched this view for years while she'd waited for Merindah to be reborn, so it didn't hold quite the same allure for her as it did for her soulmate. She'd far prefer to be soaring through the skies; and her store of patience diminished daily, while the draw to find her distant sisters grew.

'The second question is this: if you and I have an unlimited capacity for negentropy, organising the threads of aether to make magic on a global scale, then is it possible that by using my unbound magic, I will hasten the death of our sun and so the extinction of my people?'

Iluka's laughter was the last thing Merindah expected as an answer.

I forget that your mind and world is so small in this incarnation.

Merindah felt her ire rise, and the coals in her gut flared.

You must think on a cosmic scale, Gatekeeper. You draw your energy and magic not from the fabric of this tiny solar system, as most others on this planet who are bound to this plane do. You are born of the Mother. You draw your energy, both entropy and negentropy, from all systems. Your magic binds and unbinds the Cosmos.

'Holy Hecate.' The coals in Merindah's belly brightened and elevated her body temperature. Her hands glowed faintly red, and sparks flickered at their tips. She grabbed at the cold stone edges of the windowsill and slipped her shoes from her feet. Shuffling her soles on the wooden floor, she drew a deep breath, and then another. The fire receded.

Her voice was hoarse when she spoke. 'Then the prophecy is true. If I am the Chosen one, my yerlendj – my Grace as they call it – could doom our world, and every other world in the Cosmos.' Merindah felt the rightness of her assumption in every single fibre of her being.

Iluka's shrug was disheartening. *It is only one world. There are many more.*

Merindah shoved her window up and held it open above her head as she leant out, dragging in a lungful of salty air. Autumn had brought a chill to the mornings. Her nose wrinkled with the smell of ocean and her senses crackled with the electricity of oncoming storms, the air heavy with expectation.

Feeling her daughter sending a thread of curiosity towards her mind, Merindah calmed. She reminded herself she had a fragile passenger on board, and used a thread of aether to show her daughter the ocean; let her feel the moist, charged air; and let her see and hear the power of the crashing waves. She withdrew the thread and stroked her babe.

Sleep. Grow.

Merindah leant to grab her usual literary window chock… but then paused and instead wrapped a thread of air under one corner. As she let go of the sill, the window stayed open.

Excellent. I couldn't have magicked that before. And the world is still standing. So far, so good. She placed her hands over the scorched stone sill, and smoothed the threads of earth back into their pre-harm matrix.

'Right, now that that's fixed, let's find out how to open that Timegate and do what we need to do.' Merindah turned from the window and gawked at her shadow. It looked wrong. It had a long spiked tail.

What's that about Iluka? She pointed at the grey image that moved independently from her.

Iluka rumbled, and the tail disappeared, Merindah's normal human shadow reappearing and joining her at her feet. She went back to the desk, shaking her head and touching her forehead three times. 'Goddess guide me. Wonder, wisdom and wit is what I need now.'

She rubbed her hands together in expectation, getting ready to dive into her work. But the friction created sparks between her palms. *Note to self: no more random rubbing of hands.* She calmed her fingers and shoved them in her pockets.

'What is it we need to do anyway?' Merindah asked. 'I mean once we can open the gates, where in the Seven Realms of Heavens will we go? Or should I say *when* will we go? I feel like this is bigger than merely putting a spike in Nina's Grand Plan. Or does she have a cranky old dragon on her case too?'

The last comment had been a throwaway, but Merindah felt Iluka's mental start. 'She *does* have a dragon of her own?'

Iluka's reticence was glaring. ***It is unconfirmed. I know she has a captive Shayde daemon. I felt it drawn to this plane two decades ago. The*** *ruins on which the Occultology order erected their building was once a tower like this one, only black.*

'A tower like this one? Exactly like this one?' Iluka nodded in Merindah's head as she remembered the first moment when the wall had become dragon scales and Iluka's head had emerged from the stones.

It was believed the explosion over three centuries ago also destroyed the dragon. But… Iluka paused, her snort showing her discomfort. *Certain signs of late suggest she may still be there. And that she is not happy.* The dragon hesitated, then gathered herself. *The death of her soulmate may have damaged more than the building. It may have damaged her mind.*

Merindah sighed and pinched the bridge of her nose between two fingers, imagining a mentally unstable dragon capable of destroying worlds.

'Tell me something.'

If I can.

Merindah's brow furrowed. The dragon was infuriating, condescending and arrogant. 'Now is not the time to prevaricate. I need answers, information, data. It's how my mind works. I draw it in from everywhere, then it all finds a place in my mind and I make the connections. Lovely, colourful, numeric connections.'

Iluka huffed, and Merindah sat down and folded her arms. 'If you want me to make those connections and open the Timegate, then I need to know more. Who else is privy to this thing we're doing? Who tells you about rumours from Occultology?'

Iluka muttered sub-vocally. Merindah felt the dragon pacing in a cave in her mind, stalking impatiently from one side to the other. It was a strangely familiar habit.

This world really has forgotten all about dragons has it not? Iluka's thoughts held a hint of regret.

Merindah felt the dragon settle and wrap her spiked tail neatly around herself. The weird novelty hadn't worn off, and Merindah paused at the wonder. Iluka looked just like a cat settling down in front of a fire. A very prickly cat.

I do not have time to teach the memories of our full history or tell the stories of the golden times when magical creatures flourished, teeming through every facet of life.

A hint of regret surfaced, and Merindah felt Iluka turning circles in her mind once more before re-settling. *Secret archives in the sub-basement of the Librarium hold a few precious volumes that were saved.*

For now, know this. Dragons do not think of ourselves as just I. Dragons, like everything, are made from the energetic elements of the Cosmos. But, unlike lesser beings, we exist in all planes. We raise or lower our vibrations as we wish. We also remain consciously connected to all things. We see the threads and fields of the cosmic tapestry and ride the weft and weave at will. We can watch through any eyes, hear through any ears, taste, feel, smell, and touch. We can be the stone of the tower, the ocean wave, and the soaring gull. As soulmates you and I are one. You can also do all that.

Holy Hecate, what have I got myself into? Merindah's thoughts churned. Chaos indeed. She plonked into the chair.

'Why me? Why choose me to tether yourself to?'

We chose this. This incarnation you/we chose a separate beginning, to experience existence without the connection to All. To learn of what we ask these beings to do.

Merindah dropped her head on the desk. *This incarnation? Separate beginning? Where do I start?* One deep breath, and the analyst took over – bumping the emotional overwhelm to the side.

She raised her head, clasped her hands in her lap, and asked her next question. 'How many lives have I lived?'

The tense used is incorrect. I find this incarnation's form deeply unsatisfying, the dragon rumbled.

We are living each life as one, so "have lived" does not make sense. Instead, we live simultaneous infinite existences. Connected to all things. Each offers learning. It is too much for this form to take in all at once. I will give you a glimpse.

Merindah could see Iluka's black opal eyes glowing in her mind. A rainbow swirl left each orb, dancing together into a single thread. Then the thread moved out of the dragon's cave in her mind and into the real world. It spun around her head, the breeze of its passing lifting stray hairs like static electricity. Then it gathered in front of her forehead in a single coruscating mass. One breath passed, and a second.

'What's it waiting for?' Merindah whispered.

Permission. We do not force this on you/us.

Unlike when you took residence in my body.

Iluka squirmed briefly, before huffing smoke curls. *That was different. We were in danger.*

'Thanks for asking this time. Fine, go ahead.'

The rainbow globe tapped her forehead once, slamming her third eye open. As with earlier glimpses, the world wobbled before colours, melodies, scents, and tastes all pounded her senses.

This time she observed her other senses coming in for a boost. As she touched the wooden desk to steady herself, she noticed the increased perceptions of pressure and temperature feeding her internal senses, and found herself analysing information that originated from within her body.

Microseconds after she'd reached for the desk, her sense of balance realigned her upright posture. Her sense of proprioception informed her that her form was supported and surrounded by the energy of the world, and she could clearly detect the threads connecting her to everything. She registered that her body was dehydrated and in need of nourishment, and that her hormones were working her endocrine system hard.

She waved her hands in front of her eyes, amazed at the way the energetic threads of air wafted around them. They seemed to swim in a soup of glorious energy. Merindah sensed the vibrations of each item in the room with her enhanced mechanoreceptors. The denser stone felt slower, more distorted than the wooden desk.

Then the rainbow globe tapped her forehead again and her third eye closed, the heightened senses fading. Merindah shivered as they withdrew, leaving her gaping with realisation that her usual world was dull and drear.

Enough for now. Truly, our third eye has so much more to show you/ us. Intuition, time perception, agency, and recognition.

'What's agency?'

It is our sense of choice. The feeling that we have chosen a particular action.

'Well, I don't know if that's working very well of late.' Merindah felt Iluka's mental shrug. 'And recognition? Well, I know what recognition means, but why does my third eye enhance it?'

Recognition is familiarity and recollection. Familiarity can occur without recollection. That includes our sense of déjà vu. Our third eye links this sense to our parallel lives and compounds our soul learning.

The raucous screeching of gulls squabbling drifted through the open window, and the sea breeze sharpened.

I know I asked for attention, for the ability to solve the portal puzzle, and save my world, but this... this is truly amazing. Merindah paused as she contemplated the enormity of her role. *I have so much to learn.*

We are glad you/we are finally realising the significance of the situation.

Can I ask you a favour?

Anything it is in our power to grant.

Can you just use a singular pronoun for now? It'll take me some time to get around the you/we thing.

Iluka huffed.

Certainly. She sounded a little miffed. **Now, can we … you open the package?**

'What? Fine, let's look.' She loosened the knots in the plain brown twine and slipped it from around the rectangular shape. Her name was printed crudely in capital letters on one side, but there was no sender on the reverse. She opened and flattened the brown paper, then leant forward over the now-familiar design it revealed. Her fingers instinctively traced the three interwoven circles and the central eye on the cover of another journal. Her eyes flicked to its twin at the back of her desk. She turned to the new journal and sniffed. Her nose picked up a lingering trace of sulphur.

She retrieved the first journal and lay both volumes side by side. Though her original journal showed less wear, they were a match.

Merindah wiped her damp palms on her thighs and sat abruptly. Her inner sceptic called fake, but her intuition said it was authentic. She opened both covers. The same glyph of Time was inked on the first page. But what she'd decided was a date underneath the glyph was different. On the first journal there was a single date and a dash. On the journal that had arrived today there were two dates, separated by a dash.

She turned the books over and opened their back pages. Her original journal had a number of blank pages. The second volume she'd received was completely filled. *Looks like they're a from and to date then. One precedes the other.* She needed to translate the numerals.

She went back to the beginning and turned a page in each book. The same hand had penned both. But in the recently acquired journal, another scribe had written neat margin notes, and underlined various passages with potential translations. She flicked through the pages. The margin noter had a familiar hand, and with a sinking sensation, Merindah recognised it as she read two red-inked lines.

The Dogs of Doom come way too soon

When Fate's Foe emerges

It was the colour of the writing that triggered her memory. She'd received back an academic paper that she'd submitted for a conference covered in terse scarlet criticisms in that same hand.

The handwriting was Nina's. Nina Nightshayde had been making notes in this journal. The lines of the prophecy confirmed it was one of Aeon's journals. She spotted the other lines from the prophecy on other pages. *Here* was the source of Nina's uncanny influence and rocketing promotion to Head of the Order. Her so-called fragment that she'd found five years ago had come from the pages of this book. But why was the snippet cobbled together from scraps on different pages? Combined in this way, it would be almost impossible to make sense of the lines.

It wasn't a prophecy at all.

Merindah went cold at the thought of how this distraction might have diverted resources and research for the last five years. She was certain Nina's discovery had been a deliberate deception. If this were discovered and reported, it would be the end of Nina's career – and potentially her life – to say nothing of Heavens Gate's languishing future.

Merindah thought it improbable that this was the original Yarran journal unearthed five hundred years ago. She was certain that *that* was in the Librarium at Badangi, nine hundred klicks north. It was on her list of things to visit. She'd applied three times to be given access to the Badangi journal for her research, and had been refused each time.

Where does the Badangi journal fit chronologically with these two?
We could ask Badangi.

'I've already asked. They refused to let me view it.'

Badangi is not the Librarium staff. I speak of Badangi, the dragon who sleeps in their tower.

'What? There's a third dragon? Or is there a flock of you out there somewhere? Is "flock" right? What *is* the correct term for a group of dragons anyway?'

We prefer a grace of dragons if you insist on grouping us together in such an arbitrary manner. Despite being connected to each other and the All, we are separate souls.

'If you're separate souls, why did you tether yourself to me and jump into my body?'

The moment called for it. If you prefer, I can step out.

'What!?' Merindah's indignation surged. 'If I prefer? You didn't give me that option before. I thought I was stuck with you inside me for the rest of my life!' she ended with a shriek.

Iluka's rumble switched from internal to external as a small red dragon appeared on Merindah's desk, huffing a cloud of white smoke. Merindah's anger dissipated as the tiny creature, no bigger than a kitten settled on her haunches next to the journals and peered at the writing.

That is just so cute.

Iluka turned a tiny dark eye her way and drew herself up on all fours, which wasn't very tall in her current form.

I can jump right back in.

Merindah's grin slipped off her face and she shook her head, hands held out in front.

'No. No. Out is better. Out is fine.' The dragon went back to examining the journals with a huff.

'But why are you red now? What happened to your lovely pearly white?'

Our current human incarnation, you if you insist on the singular pronoun, is focused on survival, on physical needs. This is your root chakra and it has the colour red. Iluka, our dragon form, is your soul guide – so currently, I am also red. Though I prefer to think of this deep, blood-red colour as ochre.

Merindah smirked at Iluka's vanity, then leant forward to examine her shiny scales.

'So if I learn emotional balance, to vibrate at the sacral chakra, will you become orange?' She queried.

It is not quite as simple as that, but yes, we take on the dominant vibratory field.

'Huh,' Merindah straightened. 'Thank you for getting out of my body. But why are you still talking directly into my head?'

If I used my voice rather than mindspeaking, it would attract undue attention.

Iluka's tiny head lifted, and she scented the breeze still whispering in from the shore.

Though the aethers are disturbed, and the coming storm may disguise it. Our voices are often confused with thunder.

Iluka's gaze turned back to the journal whose pages appeared to be turning themselves. Merindah's eyes narrowed; and when she opened her aetheric mask a chink, she confirmed that Iluka was turning the pages with threads of air. It was easy to become awed by new wonders when chatting to such a magical beast.

'We'll talk about full disclosure later. But for now, you distracted me and skipped my question. How many of you are there? Wait. I'm asking the wrong question, aren't I? I should be asking how many are on this physical plane right now.'

Iluka continued to read the journals as she responded. ***You are learning. There are seven of us on this plane. Eight if we count the black tower's occupant.***

'One for each Librarium Temple then?' Merindah guessed. The dragon nodded and Merindah went on. 'Right then. I can see there's more to discuss about that later, too. For now, tell me what you've translated,' she instructed.

The dragon sat back on its haunches and turned to face Merindah. She stifled a snort of laughter at the sight of the tiny dragon assuming a teaching pose. ***The words can be translated, but the text still does not make any sense. It appears to be encrypted. And the pictographs complicate the text. Unless we can work out the cipher used, we are no better off than before.***

'Lucky for you, I know someone who eats puzzles for breakfast. They're all just numbers and letters non-randomly rearranged. Numbers usually speak to me, though I've never seen this pictorial language before.'

She sat, drew a sheet of blank paper from a stack on the floor, and took up a pencil. 'The numbers will unlock part of the puzzle, just you wait.'

The ochre sheen on the dragon flared as she lifted and settled her scaled neck ruff.

'You'll need to be quiet while I work on this.'

Iluka huffed and muttered, tiny puffs of smoke issuing from her snout, and Merindah cast a stern eye at her.

Fine. I will contact Badangi and see what we can find out without giving too much in return.

'Not a lot of love lost between your grace of dragons then,' Merindah remarked.

Beings this old have loyalties and quirks that short-lived humans could not possibly understand.

'Fine. You do your thing, and I'll do mine.'

The dragon circled three times before finding the right position, then settled, curled her tail around her and closed her eyes. Merindah felt a shift in the field as Iluka's body became translucent, then faded entirely from view. She passed her hand through the space and felt nothing. Internally, the thread connecting her to Iluka remained, showing her exactly where she'd been.

'Huh. Right then,' Merindah dismissed the disappearing dragon from her thoughts and pulled Nina's journal towards her. She wanted to read as many pages as she could in case it was retrieved. Before she began translating though, she aimed to quest for any trace of her unknown benefactor. A thought in the back of her mind yelled "Trap!" about the whole thing, so she'd make this quick. Nina would surely realise the journal was missing soon, and then Merindah could be in a whole lot of trouble if it was traced to her.

Her plan, such as it was, was to feign ignorance – something she hoped Nina would easily believe.

– – –

'We need help.' Merindah rubbed her temples and admitted defeat.

She pushed back from the desk, 'I'm taking some of the symbols to Yaxa Cody. If anyone can break the code, she can.' The ensuing three hours had seen little progress apart from working out some of the dates. It hadn't helped with the main text nor was there any trace of her benefactor. Merindah rustled under several piles of books till she uncovered her rumpled Order robe.

Fine, but I am coming with you.

How's that going to work? I don't want you back inside me just yet. Merindah grimaced at how dirty the pale blue cloth was as she donned it over her frock.

Iluka huffed her displeasure. *I will sit on your shoulder. I will be as quiet as a mountain.*

Don't you mean mouse? Quiet as a mouse?

With a rumbling huff, Iluka flapped to Merindah's shoulder trimming her size along the way, and fading from view. Merindah felt her tiny weight settle.

No, I meant mountain. Mice are noisy. And you must be more presentable than this.

Fussy, fussy. Merindah's robe flapped briefly and the stains and wrinkles disappeared. She left her lab shaking her head. *No one will recognise me if I'm not a little bit rumpled.*

– – –

The assistant mage showed Merindah into the Esoteric Cosmology Head's room, then closed the door behind her. Merindah's pulse quickened. She was usually here for a telling off and her body responded to the remembered anxiety.

She wiped her hands on her clean robe. Yaxa wasn't a stickler for the forms, but Merindah had thought wearing the order's garment might help. The Head continued scratching out a note in her tidy hand and motioned

Merindah to be seated. Several minutes ticked by, and finally Yaxa closed the book and glanced up. She took in Merindah's flushed cheeks and her eyes strayed to Merindah's shoulder where Iluka perched, supposedly invisible.

With a brief grimace, Yaxa retrieved a sheet of paper from a drawer and laid it on the table between them. It held rows of pictographs followed by rows of words. Merindah peered closely. Yaxa Cody had broken the Yarran code – already. She looked up, her mouth open with a question and watched as Yaxa drew out a slim ochre journal from the pocket of her robe. It was well read, the cover smudged with ink.

Utterly negligent.

How many did he leave here and when?

'I believe this may be important in your research. Yours and Iluka's,' Yaxa announced.

Merindah started guiltily, her cheeks darkening. 'How did you know about Iluka?'

Yaxa's frown faded. 'I've known since I became Head of the Order. It's part of our role as Guardians of the Tower to know. And to know when the one would come who would free the dragon. I had a good feeling about you, Merindah. And my feelings are rarely wrong.'

Merindah sat back in her chair, feeling petulant. 'Good feeling? But you're always telling me off.'

'I was pushing you to work harder. To find a way to release the binding. I always believed in you.' Yaxa's voice softened, 'Your mother and I were friends. We joined the Ivory Tower on the same day, many years ago. She came to me when she first got sick. She was sure someone was stealing her life force and making her ill. But we couldn't stop it.'

Yaxa's eyes moistened before her sharp gaze zipped back to Merindah. 'Why else do you think I'd allow a mage with your apparently puny talent to have one of the best labs in my Tower? Why would I keep defending you against that loose mouth of yours?'

Merindah shook her head, speechless at the revelation.

'You are your mother's daughter,' Yaxa paused, considering. 'We were more than friends. She meant everything to me. I loved her. Still do. Your father was merely a political and anatomical necessity. Your mother's research was necessary for the world. We split for that reason. I was her real love. I promised her I would protect you – and I have.'

Merindah's mind spun like a maelstrom and she plucked out a random thought. 'Nina killed my mother.'

Yaxa shrugged. 'We couldn't prove it, and still can't. So all I can do is keep you away from her.'

'Us. Keep us away from her. I'm pregnant.'

It was Yaxa's turn to sit open mouthed. Merindah lifted an invisible Iluka from her shoulder and placed her on the desk. Yaxa narrowed her eyes, watching.

Merindah began to pace, thinking, analysing. She stopped and turned to Iluka.

We need some allies. Can we trust her?

Iluka grew visible, startling Yaxa, though she'd sensed that Iluka was present. The dragon tromped over scrolls, climbed a small stack of books, and came eye to eye with the woman. The two dominant females stared, sizing each other up. Then Iluka nodded, satisfied.

Yes, we can.

'I need your help,' Merindah began. When a bemused Yaxa nodded, Merindah sat and told the tale of the last few days, leaving nothing out.

Once she'd finished, Yaxa simply got up from the desk and called for tea. They remained silent until her assistant had brought the tea things with a plate of biscuits, which Yaxa accepted without letting the nosey young woman enter the room.

'I guessed you'd need something soon with the baby growing so quickly,' Yaxa laughed, as Merindah inhaled one biscuit and then stuffed a second into her mouth.

Merindah nodded and swallowed, 'Iluka and I have estimated her growth is about a month per week at the moment, though we were going to ask my friend Bridget to check. If we are correct, she'll be born about two months after my birthday.'

At the mention of Merindah's birthday, Yaxa frowned. She grabbed a pen and paper, asking, 'You were thirty-three last birthday, correct? Tell me, how old do you think the young woman from your dream, this Dee, was?'

'Possibly fifteen or so, no older. Though years may be different on a world or in a time where human skin is blue.'

Yaxa waved that detail away. 'One hundred, minus you and Dee leaves fifty-two. Could the older woman be that age?' Merindah closed her eyes to recall Ali. She opened them again, a soft smile on her face.

'She could be. Huh, our ages add up to one hundred. Does that mean anything to you?'

Yaxa turned a page in her well-worn journal, lifted out a loose slip of paper and read.

When a century is combined
Soulbound seeks the mind
Cross cold and space
And time and place
No barrier to her Grace.

When a century is combined
Soulbound seeks the mind
One single year till Convergence comes.
You have until this time is done
To find the others – and join as one.

Merindah's gaze moved from Yaxa to Iluka and back. She stood, placed her hands on hips and took a deep breath.

'I have to become a mother, unlock the portal, discover how to navigate the where and when of the Cosmos, and find two women and their two dragons from two different worlds and times. All in less than a year. Great. I'll get onto it. Right after I go and pee again.'

Duplicity

'A single lie discovered is enough to create doubt in every expressed truth.'

From Guidelines for Cultural Guardians,
13th edition, Year 111 PC.

Ali counted to thirty-three, her favourite number, then forced her eyes open, tipping herself off the couch and cursing as she fell onto her tender knees. At least whatever Sophie and Will had given her had taken the edge off the aches. She still guarded her ribs as she took a couple of deeper breaths to clear her head.

Better.

She stumbled over to her dillybag, which was in its usual spot under the entry table by the front door, and rustled around in it for a stim. Squeezing the liquid under her tongue, she felt the zing hit her blood stream and clear her head. While it lasted, she had things to do, places to go. She did *not* want to be here when they came to take her for testing, interrogation, or the One Thing, whatever that was.

Harmless, powerless, a bloody pushover. We'll just see about that. I'm a survivor. I've got hidden depths and skills that most people would die *for.* Her mind skittered away from the word "die". It was a little too close to this strange new reality. She hobbled to the bathroom, getting steadier with each step. The mirror reflected a dishevelled, bruised chump.

So, Amazing Ali, what're you gunna do? How're you gunna survive this, then? Easy. This lot have got nothing. I survived Dim. Her smile faltered at her childhood memories and the current comparison.

I dunno about that. Sounds like they're pretty well resourced. And Dim was forty years ago. You've gone soft, living in the North Quad and working in the City. It's dulled your reflexes, your terror-honed instincts. You barely listen to that intuition any more.

Thoughts of being at the mercy of these faction people booted her imagination into overdrive, and her hands began to tremble where she held herself upright on the vanity.

Stop. Take one step at a time. What's your *One Thing? Just one.* She knew she had to hurry, but she was dirty and bloody.

First, you're gunna have a shower and wash the crappy feelings away down the drain.

Ali felt sullied by all the things they'd done to her – and worse for not knowing what all of those things were. Sophie's words had undermined her years of hard-wrought confidence in the space of a single conversation. She felt like a gullible idiot – and a sitting duck.

Last time I let myself trust anybody. I'll Watch Out for my Bloody Neighbour. As she slipped out of her robe, the note from Andie fluttered to the floor. She eased her aching body down to retrieve it.

'Ali, come see me about yesterday. A.'

Yesterday. The day that had disappeared. The day she'd got all these injuries.

From what that Controller woman said, it may be one day of many that someone has taken from me. No wonder I have holes in my gift, these bloody factions have been stealing them.

She turned the piece of torn plas over. It was an ad for the Temple Track: a guided walk to some pre-Crack ruins deep in the Bush. No roads, no comlis, no crowds. It took weeks to get there, and they only allowed a few people at a time.

Perfect. I'm gunna walk the bloody Temple Track, and make an offering to some old goddess. Maybe she'll sort this shit out for me.

Ali showered in record time, discovering more bruises and tender spots as she washed and dressed.

Then she dragged a suitcase out from the top shelf of her closet, the tally tag still attached. She'd bought it in anticipation of a holiday in the East Quad years ago that had never eventuated. She stuffed the case with clothes and an assortment of things she thought she'd need – and many that she wouldn't.

She had a hollow feeling that she was never coming back, ever.

Her gift kept trying to reboot the tapestry in her head, trying to show her some connection. It flared into colour, then bleached back to grey.

Probably sluggish with the meds still in my system. She grimaced and paused her packing.

Was Jiemba even real? Maybe they planted that memory too. How many memories have I lost? Maybe I have been Outside before. The Dome's been open almost two decades. Maybe I should go and see that hypnotherapist again. I wonder if she could help me find the lost memories?

She decided that now was not the time; and besides, the idea was completely contrary to her newest resolve not to trust anyone. She had to start thinking and doing things differently. They wouldn't expect the nice, organised Ms. Morrow to be spontaneous and impetuous. She was going to disappear and find another life Outside. The moment blazed briefly in her gift. A tiny golden sun flashed and faded.

Right. Let's go, Amazing Ali. She tipped her case out and began again, this time just packing the few casual clothes she had and leaving the rest strewn on the rumpled bed.

She was *so* not tidying up before she left. *"Passive and harmless." Ha! I can be mean. I can be tough. I can be unexpected. Just watch me.*

Ali glanced around her flat. She'd spent so much time at Fed Tower that she'd never got around to making this place a real home anyway. It was more a place to crash between projects. Grey, bland, ordinary – a mirror of her life under the Dome. Until recently, anyway. These past few weeks, life under the Dome had been anything but ordinary. She straightened her spine as much as she could without wincing.

Green glowy things would be really helpful now. She felt her bare feet on the wooden floorboards, rested her hands on her belly and took a deep breath. She imagined the emerald siphon releasing the threads from her heart.

My hands are green and full of healing threads. She checked her hands, but there was nothing there. If anything, her heart felt empty.

Forget it. Another time when I don't have a body full of meds and so-called-neighbours watching out for me quite so closely.

Hands on hips she took one more deep breath. *So, they reckon I'm their Chosen One, do they? That I need to be contained and controlled? Well, we'll see about that. I've read enough fantasy to know it's up to me to find a way through, and chances are that the more illogical and unexpected I can be the better. I'm gunna channel my bloody warrior woman and show them they can't mess with Alinta Morrow.*

Dillybag over her shoulder and hand on the front door, she stopped.

Who the bloody hell am I kidding? I'm gunna run for my life and hide where no one'll ever find me.

The churn in her gut settled. *Better. No fighting, just hiding and getting the hell out. Yep, much better. That's more like me. I'll work on the toughening up in small steps. Amazing Ali: a work in progress.*

Stepping out with a smile, she dropped her suitcase on the walkway. She locked the front door, turned, and ran smack into Jem whats-his-name. Her dillybag fell from her shoulder, spilling its contents all over the place. She dived to stop her lipsticks and nose plugs rolling over the edge of the walkway and dropping seven storeys to smash on the concrete floor of the foyer.

Jem squatted beside her and began retrieving items too. 'Looks like I've gotta knack for picking up yer stuff.'

His 100-watt smile ignited, and she noticed his tight, black, short-sleeved shirt and too-snug pants. *Does the man have no shame?*

His physicality had no power over her today though. Ali was determined to get away. She gave him a brief quirk of her lips and held out her hand. He put her things behind his back.

'I'll give them back on one condition.' She raised an eyebrow and gave him one of her best withering looks, which he ignored. 'Have dinner with me tonight.'

It obviously never entered his arrogant head that she would refuse. 'No.'

'I'll knock on yer door at eight.'

'No.'

'I know a great little street van a couple of blocks north of here, real private,' Jem finished with a leer.

'I said no. Give me back my things right now or I'll call the Feddies.' She stood firm and held out her hand. This was the new Ali – no more people-pleasing. She may not be a fighter, but she could learn to say no to a jerk like this.

It finally dawned on Jem that she was serious, and his face puckered like he'd sucked on a lemon. 'Ya'll regret turnin' me down. I've gotta long memory, and we'll be seein' each other – a lot.'

The sudden switch from nice to nasty was enough to throw even the new Ali. She backed up till she was flat against the door of her apartment with the handle pressing into her hip. 'Look Jem, it's not personal. I've had a rough couple of days at work and I'm taking some time off. Perhaps when I get back, we can start with a cuppa.'

Why am I backpedalling on this? He's such a creep, and bloody hell, I am a bloody people pleaser. She watched Jem's triumphant smirk emerge and he handed her back the items.

Ali stuffed them in her dillybag. As she grabbed the handle of her suitcase, his arm went around her, his body close. She squeezed herself against the door to escape and he leant in further, pressing the length of his body against her. She could feel his groin swelling against her hip.

'Perhaps a little teaser to get us going? I like the way a real woman tastes.' His hot breath was on her neck and she dropped her luggage to push him away, her sore hands twanging in protest. He caught her bruised and battered fingers in his, crushing them further and bringing traitorous tears to her eyes. He took her ear in his teeth, biting down so that she had to stop wriggling or lose an ear lobe.

Bloody hell, I should've stuck to "No".

'Let go of me. Get off. You're *hurting* me,' Ali pleaded. She desperately tried to think of her self-defence moves. Echoes of Dee sparked in her mind, and Ali head-butted him the moment he eased the pressure on her ear to move to her neck.

Swearing, Jem let her go, and she slammed her knee up into his groin. He howled. She dodged to the side to run but he managed to snatch her arm and jerked her to a halt landing a vicious slap across her face. Head ringing, eyes blurry with tears, she saw her three young neighbours grabbing hold of Jem and hauling him off.

'You okay Ali?'

She nodded at Andie and the two lads. They had Jem stretched back against the walkway rail. Ali wiped her eyes and then held her hand against her aching face.

'Want us to call the Feddies?' Andie asked.

Ali looked at Jem's bloody nose and his snarling face as he struggled with her rescuers. Her gut took a dive, but she nodded again. Andie flicked her comli and made the call. She touched Ali's arm.

'Why don't we wait in our place for the Feddies? I'll get you some ice for that cheek. You two got this covered?' Her two housemates' grim response was to force Jem to the ground with his arms behind his back. One moved to kneel on his neck.

Ali was dazed. Her life had taken on this surreal quality. Every time she made inroads into sorting it out, some new crazy thing happened, and it all went awry in her head again. A series of weird memory lapses, dangerous dreams, mindwipes, strange voices… and now she was starting to attract all the wrong sorts of attention from random oddballs. She felt close to a hysterical meltdown.

I know I put on my professional development goals that I wanted to be seen and heard more, but this is not what I had in mind.

Andie picked up Ali's suitcase and dillybag. Her neighbour's flat was almost a mirror image of Ali's own, only with extra doors for additional bedrooms. In her dazed state, that messed with her head. Something didn't feel quite right, and she hesitated at the threshold.

'It'll be fine. Come on in.' Andie smiled at Ali's apologetic look and ushered her inside, then headed to their kitchenette to make tea.

After a scan of the apartment, Ali realised that their place was not like hers at all. One wall was a sunny yellow, the furniture matched, and there was a plethora of personal items around that made the place seem a whole lot friendlier. And it was messy too. Bits and pieces of electronic equipment covered half the table, as well as a large desk that was already crowded with three comm screens. Clothes were draped over the backs of every chair and piles of plas were stacked on any flat surface. It looked like real people lived here.

Andie brought her a bag of ice wrapped in a tea-towel.

'Here you go. Put that on your cheek.' Ali pressed the cool pack gratefully against her aching face. Andie sat silent and patient while Ali gathered her scattered wits.

'About yesterday?' Ali queried tentatively.

Andie smiled, the burn scars on her face pulling awkwardly at her mouth.

'Plenty of time to chat once the Feddies have been,' Andie responded. Ali kept her gaze steady, trying to register the urgency of her situation.

'That's the problem. I don't think I've got plenty of time. I've gotta go. Now. Before they come back.' The woop woop of sirens broadcast the arrival of the Feddies.

'Jeez, that was quick. They must've been close by for a change.' Andie stood up, her eyes skittering away from Ali's.

Or they already knew something was gunna happen here. They're probably corrupt and paid off by some crazy faction.

Stop it. You're making too much of it. Get a grip. You'll be gone soon. Ali tried to calm herself.

Both women moved to watch from behind the curtain as three Feddies restrained Jem and hauled him down the stairs while a fourth spoke with Nate and Dell. The conversing trio looked towards the window and Nate signalled. Andie opened the door and motioned Ali through, her brown eyes radiating a confidence and compassion way beyond her years.

'Ready? Take a breath. I know you can do this Ali. You're stronger than you think.'

Head high, Ali stepped out to face her latest assailant.

— — —

Ali eased herself onto the couch, conscious of every aching bone and muscle now that the adrenaline rush had passed. Andie plonked onto the other end, shuffling around until she faced Ali. Nate and Dell brought kitchen chairs and sat themselves opposite the women.

Andie spoke first.

'Okay, we heard what you told the Feddies about the creepazoid, but what *really* happened?'

Ali's eyebrows rose. 'That *was* what really happened,' she responded.

Nate and Andie exchanged a long look, and something unspoken passed between them. Nate twisted to Dell. 'Didn't you have a flocar to catch, Dell?'

Dell gave an eyeroll and tossed his head, with a well-practiced flick of his long black fringe. He grabbed his grey factory uniform jacket from the back of the chair and turned a pair of intense green eyes to Ali.

'Hope you're feeling better soon, Ali,' Dell's mellow voice carried a hint of East Quad posh. Ali's response was a tremulous smile. His kindness undid her, and she had no words. His eyes reminded Ali of the emerald green of her glowing hands. She resisted checking, and instead tucked her hands under her arms to hide them just in case the glow decided to make a reappearance.

Dell's smile faltered a little at her movement, and he glanced at Nate. Nate's answering nod had Dell exiting without further ado.

'I'll put the kettle on. You look like you could use a hot cuppa,' Nate offered, getting up from the chair.

'I had the things ready. You'll just need to re-boil the water,' Andie told him.

'How are you feeling now?' she asked, reaching to rest her hand on Ali's arm, before Ali's twitch at her touch had her snatching her hand back.

Andie tried again. 'Sometimes the adrenaline leaving feels worse than the trauma.'

Ali tried to find the words to begin. Her strategy to not trust anyone was leaking like a sieve. The thought of being taken and interrogated sat like a sour ration in her gut. Then Jem's attack had shaken her even more. She'd felt powerless all over again.

She wanted to blurt out the entire pathetic story of the last few months and then hide away from the world, letting someone else take care of it for her. But she knew she didn't have long before Sophie and Will returned and found her gone. There was no time for the unabridged version of her meltdown. She had to get out of the Dome.

Ali searched Andie's eyes. She seemed guileless, and she'd always been friendly – but was she? Did she also have ulterior motives? Ali had thought Sophie was her friend too, and look how that turned out. That betrayal felt just as painful as the slap in the face Jem had given her, maybe more so. Her hand rose to her still burning cheek and her eyes filled with tears.

Ali swallowed hard. *I should've listened to Nanna. Never judge a book by its cover. Nanna was the prime example. Looked like a harmless old granny but ran her army of delinquent Dim kids with an iron fist and an ice-cold heart. Look after yourself first. Another one of Nanna's faves. Right, here goes.*

'Why did you leave me the note about yesterday?' Ali asked.

At the sudden switch, Andie blinked, and her smile slipped. 'What do you remember about yesterday?'

Nate interrupted Ali's response with a cuppa for them both, and Ali sipped gratefully at the warm beverage.

Andie put hers untouched on the small table beside the couch. Nate put his cup on the floor by his chair and sat down. Ali glanced at his easy smile and hazel eyes. She smiled her thanks and focused back on Andie.

'When did you leave the note?'

Andie's gaze flicked to Nate and Ali followed the movement. *Why does everyone look to Nate for direction?*

She took another sip of her tea to settle her nerves. The ochre flare was back in her gift – rainbows sparkled at the edge of her vision, and she blinked a few times to clear her head, hoping it wasn't the precursor for another migraine.

'What's Nate got to do with yesterday?' Ali's question startled Andie. 'And why do you keep looking at him like you need his permission or something? Was he there? Did he see what happened? Did he help you put me to bed?' As her state of undress and the disorder of her clothes and body shot to the top of her mind, Ali's hands trembled, and her cheeks flamed.

'Drink up, Ali. A cuppa will help. Then we can tell you what we saw.' Nate's calm tone reassured her.

Ali took another sip. The whiff of a chemical aftertaste suggested they needed to change their brand of water. 'What kinda tea is this?'

'It's herbal.' Ali's vision blurred and her hands holding the tea suddenly refused to obey her. She had time to see Nate grab for her tipping cup, to feel the splash of hot liquid on her leg and the world tilted. She barely formed a whisper before she floated into darkness, 'Why me?' Her mind screamed betrayal.

— — —

Andie shifted Ali's head into a more natural position and straightened her limbs so that she lay on her back. Nate put Ali's rescued teacup on the floor. He sighed and rested his elbows on his knees.

Andie stood up. 'Things are going to hell in a handbasket. Her body won't take much more of this, let alone her mind. She'll be so overloaded with chems that she'll dissolve!' Andie began to pace.

'Our League is not going to be happy with the latest development. The Guild of Guardians is bold to make such an overt move to take her,' Nate stated, folding his arms and pinning Andie with his gaze.

'Don't you sometimes feel like we're all tarred with the same brush?' Andie asked. At Nate's frown, she went on. 'I mean we're all trying to find the Chosen and keep them under control.' When Nate went to protest, Andie held up her hands. 'Fine, fine, keep them *safe* then, if that makes you sleep better at night.'

Andie moved to stand in front of Nate so that he had to look up to meet her eyes. 'Don't you wonder sometimes if we're doing the right thing? Don't you think the Chosen will know what to do *without* our interference? Who knows what damage we're doing with all this mindwiping stuff.' Andie paused, squatted in front of her team leader, and placed one hand on his knee.

'Nate, we've gotta get Ali outta the Dome. It's not safe for her here anymore. We can't keep wiping her, and it's obvious we can't protect her. Not without giving the game away or starting an inter-faction war.'

Nate shook his head and stood up, gently moving Andie away. He fetched the entropy scanner and ran it over Ali's recumbent form. 'Off the charts again.' He lifted Ali's hands and beckoned Andie closer. He pointed out the faint rosy glow at the tips of all but the third finger of Ali's right hand.

'Fire magic. She has fire magic,' Andie's announcement was reverential.

'For this to manifest despite what we've given her and all the filters the Fed Comm have in this damn Dome, it means she must be a strong wielder. She may even be Chosen,' Nate told her.

'Chosen,' Andie's hushed tone whipped Nate's gaze to her.

'Andie. Get a grip. You're right about one thing. We've gotta get her Outside as soon as we can. She's gotta make the trip to the Temple. If she survives, then we get to guide her.'

Andie nodded, silenced.

Nate continued, 'How long since you saw those Guild Guardians leave?'

Andie ignored the question, moving to sit next to Ali on the couch and picking up one of her glowing hands.

'Andie. I know you like her, but she's a prime target for every faction, not just ours. They'll all want to control her or kill her. And with the way entropy is spinning around her, she'll be attracting every creepazoid with a hint of Shayde in their bloodlines too.'

— — —

The grey mist had held Ali and she floated, desolate, dreaming, and lost. Her soul drifted, drawn to a brighter world where she found Dee, asleep in a warm nest of leaves. Dee recognised her presence in her dream. Ali was hurt. She sensed betrayal and fear.

Ali, what's happened? Who did this? Ali, how can I help?

Ali didn't or couldn't respond, her soul tumbled in a whirl of pain and confusion. Dee sensed her slipping away, and her own soul leapt after her. She followed the thread through the Shayde to Ali's physical body and slipped into it. It ached and wouldn't move. She heard a male voice say something about Shayde.

'Are you Shayde Runners? What have you done to my friend? If you mean her harm, know that I am Dee and I will not allow it. She saved me and now it's my turn to save her.' Dee had learnt some control of her magic since last she'd spent time with Ali. Though it felt sluggish to use her Grace in Ali's body, the glow in Ali's hands brightened as Dee forced the body to sit upright and open its eyes.

A woman dropped Ali's hand as if it had burnt her, and leapt away. The man stumbled back too.

One step at a time. That's what Ali would say.

Dee only had time to note the woman's dark-skinned face looked burnt before the man hissed, 'Andie, do it now.' Dee turned Ali's head to watch as Andie clapped the silver bands on her wrists together. Then she hurried behind the couch and clasped Ali's head between her hands. Dee felt a clumsy weave of magic working its way inside Ali's brain and she pushed back with her own weave though it felt slipperier than usual. Andie began to shake. Dee lifted Ali's hands and pointed them at the man who was lunging forward. Sparks flickered at the end of her fingers as she gathered her flames. His mouth dropped open and he hesitated.

'She's fighting me. The other one. She's blocking the wipe. She's too strong.' The man pushed his sleeves up, revealing matching silver bands. He activated his bands, brushed Ali's hands aside, and put his hands over the woman's. The mauve glow flashed from the bracelets and intensified; amethyst threads streamed into Ali's skull.

Dee grabbed the man's arms with Ali's hands and released her fire, burning his skin and making him hiss. The pair holding Ali's head doubled their efforts, and Dee could feel their panic as they surged into Ali's mind. She drew a protective shield around Ali's trembling soul. Dee touched Andie's small Grace; Andie's heart was troubled, but she meant Ali no harm. This thing they were doing was for Ali's own safety, she was being hunted and these people were trying to help. Ali needed to get Outside to connect to her magic. Dee felt her hold on Ali slipping. She left her shield in place, lessened her hold on Ali's body and fell back into her own – a world away.

– – –

With a final shudder, Ali's body slackened. Andie's trembling slowed and ceased. Together she and Nate delved and tried to wipe the last few minutes from Ali's mind. Andie tried to smooth the trauma as she implanted instructions for Ali's adventure Outside, the helpful neighbours who'd got her organised and booked all the necessary tickets and travel permissions.

The mauve glow faded from both pairs of hands and they dropped to the floor exhausted. Nate stared at the rings of reddened skin around his forearms.

'What the hell happened?' Andie asked. She rubbed her own wrists around her silver bands as though she wanted to rip them off.

'I have no idea, but that young woman's magical potential was vast. We've got to find her before someone else does. If she's able to project into another body within the Dome, then she's dangerous left unconstrained.'

Andie's dark eyes locked onto Nate's. His gut clenched at the shock on her face.

'Nate, couldn't you see? She's not *in* the Dome! She's not even on this *planet*!'

Reunion

Ali existed in a grey nothing. Two lines of people approached, neither seeming aware of the other. Her neighbours Andie and Nate stood at the head of one line. Smiling, they pointed at her and said, 'Forget.' A silver thread emerged from her forehead and flew towards them. As Ali put up her hands to halt the theft, the silver thread spiralled itself into the ruby on her left hand and dissolved into it.

She turned to the line on the right. First was a woman with long, curling fair hair and soulful hazel eyes. Dee peeped out from behind the woman's shoulder. They both smiled and pointed at Ali, chorusing, 'Remember.' The silver thread emerged from Ali's ring and slammed back into her mind.

She jerked awake. The room was dark, the smell of stale sweat and urine the most prominent of the overabundance of odours. And Ali remembered. For the first time she *remembered* what they'd done to her. The mindwipe hadn't taken. Dee had helped her, she'd taken over Ali's body, shielded her mind and fought back.

We were stronger together. Thank you, sister.

Ali gathered her gratitude and felt it pool, soft and warm, in her heart. She imagined sending love towards wherever Dee was. That happy thought done, she took a physical inventory: still a bit sore, but nothing broken. She knew from the recovered memory that Nate and Dell had deposited her in a utilitarian barracks by the North Gate – supposedly still under the impression that she was about to depart on a trek in the wilderness of Outside the next day. For a moment she considered continuing, following their escape plan. Sophie and Will would never find her Outside. It would also reduce the likelihood of dodgy blokes accosting her.

Ugh, that was weird. That Jem whats-his-name was such a loser. How could I ever have thought he was good looking? She shuddered as she recalled their altercation and the ensuing fuss, and seeing him marched off to the Feddie's grey van with his hands in cuffs. The look he'd speared her way was pure hate.

'I'll be back for ya,' he'd yelled.

'That's not gunna help your case, mate.' One of the Feddie's had responded, bundling Jem into their van. *Excellent.* She could tick that problem off her list.

She was on her own now.

Unloading her new supplies took longer than expected. There was a stack of stuff. Her no-longer-favourite-neighbours had provided everything she'd need for going Outside, along with a stack of credits. That worked in her favour – no one could trace her via wristcode purchases.

Until I run out of credits.

Don't think about that right now. One step at a time.

Ali showered and dressed in her own clothes. Sorting her gear for one final time she gathered up all the Outside equipment and tossed it on the bed. She wasn't going to take anything from those neighbours. In her mind everything they touched was tainted.

She packed her own gear back into her suitcase and deposited it into the boot of her flocar. As she got in and switched to manual, she sobered, remembering how helpful her three young neighbours had always seemed. She peevishly hoped they'd regret their aid. Andie. Nate. Dell. She fixed their faces in her mind and repeated their names again.

Eight years pretending to be her helpful neighbours, and all the while drugging and mindwiping her. *They* probably thought she was nice and harmless too. They hadn't mentioned Armageddon or Chosen Ones, but if they wanted her to go to this Temple then it was the last place she was going.

'Enough of that, old birri. Time to plan.' *Mmm, not so much of the old, sister.*

She glanced at her hands on the steering controls – they were steady, covered with a spray of freckles, except for her tech finger, which was a uniform brown. Federation orphans didn't get the full cosmetic replacement.

'So, you've been around the block a few times, but your regen is solid. Not young, not old, just right. And nothing beats experience.'

Except the daring naiveté of youth. An image of Dee flashed into Ali's mind, diving into trouble and strife at every opportunity, and somehow coming out on top.

She's everything I'm not. Young and independent, fearless and adventurous. Ali replayed the memory of head-butting Jem, and took another deep breath. Well, perhaps a little of the young renegade was rubbing off on her after all.

She did a U-turn and headed East, her gift flaring briefly in an explosion of red and orange.

— — —

Ali turned off the main road and parked the flocar off to the side of what looked like a little-used dirt track. Moonya was just over the hill. This house was where her ordinary life had begun to come apart twelve months ago. This house had opened something in her mind, and she was going to find out why.

Okay, Amazing Ali, time to do your stuff.

She donned her black jacket, and lifted the hood to cover her distinctive curls. The late afternoon was cool, the East Quad filters dredging the pervasive humidity away for the privileged few. Ali silenced her comli, stuffed it into a pocket and headed over the rise.

Ten weary minutes later, she was hot, cranky, and her feet hurt. *Maybe I should've kept that pair of hiking boots.* Her slip-on shoes may have been comfy, but they weren't meant for hiking.

She rested against a tree trunk, wheezing. *Jeez, how did my bloody ex-neighbours ever think I was gunna walk for a whole day?* Wishing for some of the green healing magic, she pushed herself off the tree and turned to regard it. Its tattered bark exposed sleek cream and grey skin.

Ali placed her hand on the wood, feeling the bumps and textures. She closed her eyes and breathed in the eucalyptus scent as her gift coloured briefly and then faded back to grey. She rested her cheek on the tree and wrapped her arms around it as far as they would go. Its girth put it at least a few hundred years old. Centring herself, she imagined the green threads from her heart unfolding, feeding into the tree, cleansing, and drawing energy from the earth.

When she opened her eyes again, her fingers were just plain brown.

Worth a try. But now I can call myself a tree-hugger.

She snickered, and headed toward the property, skirting the main gate, and making her way to where the house was closest to the fence.

I wish I had magical powers now. Invisibility would really help. I'm invisible. I'm invisible. I'm invisible.

Repeating the *"I'm invisible"* mantra she approached a back gate that allowed the owners access to a small creek at the foot of the property. The gate was open and when Ali heard whistling, she saw the back of the Grey Shirt sentry further along the fence line taking a leak.

I'm invisible.

Heart in her mouth, new Ali snuck towards the gate before old Ali could chicken out and run away. Just as she went through into the back garden, she heard the Grey Shirt zip his pants. She gave up tiptoeing and ran, disappearing around a corner of the house as the gate clanged shut. She tried to catch her breath quietly and move further away from the sentry at the same time.

Okay, what now Amazing Ali. Where are you going to find the answers? She looked at the house, her gaze drawn to the tower.

Fine, tower it is.

She crept closer, running one hand along the brick wall for support. The bricks changed from cool to warm under her touch. Ali snatched her hand away and looked up. She'd reached the Tower.

Could be just warm from the sun. Maybe I imagined the others were cool to start with.

Ali wiped sweaty palms down her thighs, and flicked her ruby ring around with her thumb, needing its comforting rhythm. Edging nearer to the Tower, she held out her hands, closed her eyes and grounded herself. She ignited her gift, which gave a coloured hiccup and flared into life. She imagined curls of green energy drifting up from the earth and lacing their way around her legs. Then she slowed her breathing and took her attention from a deep red glow in her belly to the ruby ring on her finger.

Remember.

She placed her palms flat against the warm bricks.

Well, it's about bloody time you showed up. Jiemba's voice boomed into her mind.

She snatched her hands off. It was true. Jiemba *was* here in Moonya – the safe place. Ali placed her hands back against the tower wall.

Didn't mean that. I'm really glad you're here. Let's go save the Cosmos.

Not you too.

What do you mean? We are the Chosen after all.

Ali rested her forehead against the warm bricks.

The wall breathed. Jiemba breathed. Ali couldn't understand how she had missed that on her first visit.

You didn't. It was one of the things you told the Wiyanga about.

The Wiyanga?

Woman who owns the house. Thinks she owns me. She's the author you came to visit. She's also the Wiyanga, the head nutbag of the Daughters of the Dark Goddess. One of the crazy factions that've been watching you. And… Jiemba paused for dramatic effect. ***She's the Federation Chair.***

Bloody hell. None of that helps me. Things are going from bad to worse and I've still got so many questions about magic and this damn prophecy people keep spouting at me. My gift is damaged from people stealing my memories. There are gaping holes in the tapestry, and the threads keep unravelling.

No time, we've gotta go.

Go where? And why? I came to find out why my life is a mess. It started here. So why would I trust you? Everyone I thought was my friend has been mindwiping me, drugging me and planning to kill me. And that's just the last few days. What if I don't want *to be Chosen?*

Panic and overwhelm swirled in Ali's gut. *What if I'm not good enough, and I stuff it up?*

Ali, you and I are one. Look deep. You know that yearning you feel? The yearning for the other? I am* the other. *We are the same. Let me in. This is what we wanted. We chose this life. We just got a little side-tracked, that's all.

We?

Fireworks. Sparks and connections created startled chaos in Ali's gift. She searched her soul. The yearning drew her down, deeper into darkness. She held herself still, found the bright kernel at her core.

Remember.

Hurt. Cold. Apart. Fire. Flying. Together. Love. Home.

Ali drew herself closer to the wall, laying her body against the warm surface, her arms spreadeagled. She took one shuddering breath and opened herself.

I don't know why, but I trust you. I choose you. I surrender.

Jiemba drew herself from the fabric of the mudbrick walls and *shimmered* gently into Ali. Her heart settled next to Ali's, their beats synchronous, pounding with the emotion of their reunion.

After what seemed like a lifetime but was probably only a few moments, Ali stepped away from the cooling wall feeling whole. Every cell of her body tingled, and her senses reeled. Through her gift, she could see the threads of energy connecting her to everything around her. Memories swarmed in her head, but she deflected them to focus deep in her belly where glowing red embers warmed her body. A silver thread anchored to the core of her being. She felt Jiemba shiver with anticipation, her soul reflection a miniature dragon in Ali's mind, who began prancing about with wings flapping, snorting fire and smoke.

Now I'm really back. We're tethered. Let's get outta here.

We've got a lot of catching up to do first. And a lot of things to remember. And learn. Like why can I see all these threads here?

The Wiyanga keeps the Dome filters low here because she's a magic practitioner. They'd dampen her power too. It's one of the reasons she's so reclusive in her role as The Chair. Once we get outside the wall of Moonya, it'll be harder for you to see them until we leave the Dome. And harder for you to hear me. But I will always be with you, remember that.

Ali's smile threatened to crack her face in half, and her heart pounded. Escape from the Dome seemed like a doddle with this kind of support.

Right then. First step: get outta here.

Good first step, and easily done. You're invisible so we can sneak back past the guards with a little mind nudge.

I'm invisible? It really works?

Jiemba shushed her with a snort. She had more than invisibility at her fingertips. She felt Jiemba's bubble of joy. ***I have missed you, woman. But it's time to give the guards a mind nudge.***

Ali baulked.

I don't want to mess with anyone's mind. I won't do to them what they did to me.

Jiemba's excitement eased, doused with a strong wave of affection.

Yep, it's really you – in all your glorious and annoying compassion.

Ali felt her mouth stretch wider and her heart soar. It felt so right to have Jiemba and all her snark, right there in her head.

Okay, let's work it out. We'll have to hurry. They'll notice I'm gone soon. I may have given them a little sleepy time, but it won't last long.

Fine. Let's do this.

Ali tiptoed back through the garden and peered around the corner at the Grey Shirt on the back gate. He didn't look sleepy at all.

He was outside the wall, so it didn't work on him. I knew you were coming. I was trying to help.

It's okay. We'll think of something.

Ali intuitively soothed Jiemba's ruffled scales. It felt achingly familiar.

Klaxon sirens went off inside the house. The Grey Shirt at the gate took off towards the noise.

That'll do. I'm invisible. I'm invisible. I'm invisible.

Ali scampered towards the gate and escape. She fast-walked over the hill to her flocar but stopped before racing down the other side. A small woman in dark clothing was peering inside the vehicle. Ali could just make out her blonde hair in the waning afternoon light.

That's the ninja. She tried to kill me. I'm invisible. I'm invisible. I'm invisible.

We're invisible. But she'll smell and hear us if you don't calm down and stop blundering around like an elephant. Sit. Now. Ground yourself against this tree.

Ali did as she was told, dropping to the ground.

So much for being in control of myself.

I am yourself. I'm protecting us. Be calm.

Ali breathed deeply, feeling the strength of the tree against her back, and imagining her panic rolling through her and into the earth.

She's leaving. Let's go before the Wiyanga's Grey Shirts decide to get a brain and look outside the walls.

Ali opened her eyes to see the young woman sprinting away down the road. As she veered to head into the bush she paused, gazing up the hill directly at Ali. The woman raised her hand. Ali held her breath. The ninja lowered her hand and raced off into the night.

I'm not sure how much longer I can hold out. Jiemba's voice faltered.
What? Why?

The Wiyanga has been poisoning me, siphoning off my magic for years. It's hard to stay conscious when the Dome filters are at full strength.

How can I help? I won't lose you again. Ali's resolve was fierce, making Jiemba smile.

Do something they won't expect of you. Get us out of the bloody Dome.

Right. First, we'll get outta the Dome. Then we'll go find Dee. She'll know what to do about the magic.

Factions

*'And some that smile have in their hearts, I fear, millions of
mischiefs.'*

From Julius Caesar, William Shakespeare:
The Complete Works, Pre-Crack playwright –
Year of recovery 257 PC, Year of digitisation 291 PC. (Recovered
hard copy on permanent loan to
The Federation Chair's personal library.)

Nate closed the door. He turned to peer out the privacy hole at the flocar leaving the courtyard with Ali inside.

'She's on her way. Time to move, people. We've got to cover her tracks and protect her back. Humanity needs us to keep her safe, so that she makes the right decision and does her duty.'

He scrutinised each member of his team. 'She'll need time, lots of time. A few hours aren't much of a head start and we don't know if we can trust the Outside Ranger if she begins to manifest more magic or even…' his voice choked on the unfamiliar word, '*shimmer* once she's Outside. There's no way she can hide for long the way she's leaking. She'll need much more guidance to help her disappear off the grid.'

Andie and Dell continued to stare at him, expecting more, so he added an afterthought. 'If that's what she wants to do.'

'Will we be coming back here at all?' Dell asked.

Nate paused, glancing around his base of operations for the past eight years, then shook his head. 'No, we'll set up another base on the Outside, closer to where she's going to return from the Temple. That way, if we miss her going in, we can pick her up on the way out and take her somewhere safe. We'll need the solar comms. Full clean this place. We were never here. Andie dig out the walking gear for us.' He activated his comli and began to type.

'What about Dee?' Andie stopped in front of Nate with an armload of clothes.

'Who's Dee?' Dell paused in his packing.

Andie waited for a signal from Nate to begin. He nodded and kept typing.

She dropped the clothes. 'We'd sedated Ali so we could mindwipe and prepare her for this Outside trip when her hands started to glow red. Her body was taken over by someone named Dee who used fire magic on Nate.'

'Taken over! Fire magic?' Dell's eyes went wide.

Andie indicated the bandages Nate was unwinding from his forearms.

'What the…?' Dell's awe morphed to anxiety.

'She told us she'd defend Ali if we hurt her. It took two of us to do the mindwipe. In the end I think it was only successful because I convinced her this was for Ali's own good, that Ali was hurting. That she was in more danger if she stayed at the mercy of all the other factions trying to find and harm her. I told her if Ali got Outside, her magic would be stronger, more connected to the land. That made sense to her. It took some convincing though, 'cause Dee seemed to think Ali was this amazing strong, wise warrior woman.'

'Really? Our Ali? Strong, wise warrior woman?' Dell struggled to reconcile the words with the woman he'd been watching for eight years.

'And her eyes,' Nate interrupted the exchange, dropping his comli into his pocket.

'Her eyes? What about her eyes?' Dell asked, watching Nate patting cream onto his burnt arms.

'What colour are Ali's eyes?' Nate challenged him.

'Brown, same as most Domers,' Dell responded with a puzzled frown.

Nate shook his head. 'When this Dee took Ali over, Ali's irises changed colour. One was blue, one green.'

'Chimaera,' Dell breathed. 'That's crazy.'

'That's not the craziest part.' Andie's gaze lowered as she gathered herself. With a deep breath, she raised her eyes and stared into Dell's. 'The craziest part is that I believe this young woman, Dee, is on another world. A world where magic is the free and unfettered birthright of all.'

———

Serena was alarmed to see her faction leader at her front door. The hypnotist's usual equanimity fled at the sight of the woman's brooding visage and her hands fluttered to her throat.

'Let me in, you foolish woman,' the Wiyanga ordered, her voice terse.

'Oh, of course, of course. Come in.' Serena apologised.

The Wiyanga strode into the hall, removed her nose plugs, and waited in imperious silence. Serena closed the door and scuttled around to show her superior into the office.

The ancient title of Wiyanga meant mother, but this woman didn't invite a sense of cosy cuddles by the fire. Rather, she was a fierce matriarch, ruling her charges with an iron rod. The Wiyanga was tall and thin, impeccably dressed in a slim black suit, with dark blonde hair twisted into a severe knot behind her head. Rumours of multiple regens made it impossible to guess her age. She walked into the office and took Serena's seat behind the desk.

'Well?' The Wiyanga's striking face settled into a grimace. 'Where is the woman? When is she arriving?' she demanded.

Serena breathed a sigh of relief and answered, 'Oh, I expect her very soon. Her appointment is scheduled for seven. Can I get you some tea in the meantime?'

'Don't be ridiculous.' The Wiyanga peered down her perfectly straight nose. 'Bring me a glass of your best wine.'

Serena settled the wine glass near the Wiyanga's arm a few minutes later and retreated to the other side of the desk. She waited patiently while the expensive, black market vintage was tasted and acknowledged with a brief nod.

After a suitable pause, Serena spoke up. 'If I may ask, Wiyanga, what brings you to this quadrant? Is there something I should know before I meet this woman? Has the plan changed?'

The Wiyanga set the glass down on the smooth, ordered surface of Serena's desk.

'No, the plan remains,' the Wiyanga replied, scrutinising Serena. 'Her testing will decide her fate. The law is the law. The Dark Goddess herself, may She rule forever, tasked her Daughters to watch for the Chosen Ones, and to destroy any pretenders. Under my guiding hand, we've watched well.

In my time, there have been many who have shown promise. They've all failed the final test.' She paused, sipping at her wine.

Serena nodded her understanding. The Daughters had recruited Serena in her early troubled teens. Back then, she'd been open to their heretical teachings, and keen to thumb her nose at the oppressive Federation. It was her way of resisting the monopoly and monotony of life in the Dome. A trickle of unease crossed her mind as she thought about the testing, however. This was real. Up until now it had mostly been secret meetings and lots of talk – perhaps some minor damage to Federation property in other quads. *And if this woman doesn't pass the test?* Serena wondered if she could be a party to what happened next.

'We've culled many an impostor from their arrogant charades over the centuries. The Dark Goddess does not accept frauds,' the Wiyanga stated, settling back in the chair.

Serena's composure began to fray as the silent minutes ticked by. Eventually, the Wiyanga finished her wine and muttered as if she had forgotten Serena's existence. 'A shame about this one. I did enjoy our chat about my collection. Foolish of me to listen to the Fed Comm about cataloguing it. The woman's depth of knowledge far exceeded what I've come to expect in a common Domer. She got through my guard.'

The last quiet comment made Serena blanch. That was a slip in protocol she did not want to know about. The Wiyanga was ruthless when it came to abiding by the decrees of the Dark Goddess. *"Watch Out for Your Neighbour", "Control Yourself",* and *"Mind Your Own Business"* all took on whole new meanings within the secret sect. The Daughters employed physical discipline rather than the mental attitude alignment used by the Grey Shirts to enforce their doctrine. Serena told herself to breathe and forget she'd heard the slip. No good would come of knowing someone had got through the Wiyanga's guard.

Seven o'clock came and went in uncomfortable silence. Serena twitched on the blue couch. Her eyes watched the timepiece tick inexorably on to seven-fifteen.

'Shall I comm her and see why she's held up?'

The Wiyanga tilted her head, her glance thunderous.

Ali didn't respond, so Serena left a message asking her to call. The Wiyanga picked up the opal beads from the corner of the desk and spent the next ten minutes flicking them through her fingers.

Finally, the Wiyanga stood, the beads slipped from her hand and clattered to the desktop. Her anger simmered in every sharp gesture as she pointed at Serena. 'You will bring the woman to me at the City Temple, physically or chemically restrained if necessary. We will know what she knows and from where she heard it. The other societies are infested with unbelievers, half-truths, and pretenders. We will maintain order and purge this Dome of rabble.' She marched to the front door.

As Serena scurried after her, she glanced at a picture of her grandson on the wall and remembered what Raphe had seen. 'I forgot to mention that my grandson said he saw angels in the woman's hair,' she offered.

'What did you say?' The Wiyanga paused in the act of inserting her nose plugs, her voice dangerously soft.

'Angels in her hair. I was going to t-tell you once I'd done the testing,' Serena stammered.

The Wiyanga turned her furious gaze on Serena and slapped her hard. 'You fool. You should have told me this immediately.'

Serena fell against the wall, her eyes wide. She raised her hand to touch the livid imprint on her cheek.

'This changes everything. She must be found and brought to me now. She must be kept away from all other factions. Isolate, control or destroy.' The Wiyanga lifted her comli and thumbed a contact. 'We have a runner. Activate all the assets,' she commanded.

There was a pause as she listened, her eyes blazing. 'You idiots! Get after her now. She can't have gone far. She'll be too weak. Use any means necessary to get her back behind the wall and into the tower. You should have notified me instantly. I'm surrounded by fools.'

Then the strident tone dropped from her voice, and a hint of dread crept in as she ordered, 'Prepare the Water Window. I must inform the Dark Goddess that the Ochre Dragon has escaped.'

———

Sophie and Will let themselves into Ali's apartment a little over two hours after they'd left. Sophie swiped on the light, prepared to bully Ali into doing exactly what she was told. But Ali wasn't lying there unconscious on the couch. Sophie hurried into the bathroom where the empty cabinet yawned.

Back in the main room, Will called out, 'Looks like she's packed for a long break.' Sophie hastened to his side. A frown creased Will's otherwise smooth face. 'Do you think she's gone under her own steam or has one of the other factions picked her up?' he asked.

'She not very brave or adventurous,' Sophie responded. 'If she's gone under her own steam, I suspect it'll be easy to find her. She's probably just booked into a hostel somewhere close. She can't go far in the Dome. Public cams will track her for us. And if it's another faction, we'll deal with that when we know.'

Will nodded and they shifted to sit at the table in the kitchenette. 'What else are you thinking, Sophie? I can hear your mind ticking over. You know I'll admit you're the brains in this partnership,' Will voiced the last part with a shy smile.

Sophie acknowledged his words with a light pat on his massive shoulder. She gazed around the tiny flat, looking for inspiration. The space had no personality. Despite Ali having lived here for almost eight years, there was little to identify it as hers. 'It's as colourless as she is,' Sophie murmured.

'What do you mean?' Will asked.

'Well, she's a nice woman, but there isn't much to her. It's strange. She rarely surprises me. She's so predictable, a kind of easy program to follow. Almost as if she's one dimensional, as if she didn't get the whole personality when she was born.' Sophie paused, the colour draining from her already pale face. 'As if she was only half a person.'

Her eyes found Will's. He made the connection.

'I'll start tracing,' he said.

As Will reached into his pocket for his comli, Sophie began searching the apartment in earnest. Finding nothing that would indicate a destination, she headed to the door, calling over her shoulder. 'I'll check the neighbours, see if they saw anything. And there was that creepy guy she mentioned. Run a check on him too. Jim or Jem something, second name starts with S, I think. You should find him in the building rental log. If we don't get any leads here, we'll have to let the Controller take over.'

She paused to look back at Will. 'And neither of us want that, right? Who knows what she'll do to us if we admit we've misplaced our assignment – again.'

Will nodded, his fingers flying over the screen.

– – –

Jem Stillner lay on his back fuming in the cold dank cell. That *nobody* he'd been sent to secure had got away. What should have been an easy tag and watch had erupted into a monumental disaster – his first mistake in decades. No one got the better of him. No one had resisted his charms, not for years. His client was not going to be happy.

Nagging at the back of his mind was the worry that the Guild would cut him loose, disassociate him. He was not about to let that happen. He'd worked too hard to get in. He sat up and scanned the prison unit again, looking for anything that he could use to escape.

He would chase that woman down and make her regret her refusal. Though he still couldn't fathom how she was a threat and under a watch order that required a high-class operative like himself. She was such a nobody, and kind of old to boot. *She should have been flattered by my attention. We both felt the electricity.*

The cell door window cracked open.

'Stillner. You're out. Your mumma's made bail.' The Feddie's sneer at Jem's surprise made him want to smash the woman's nose all over her face.

'Why anyone would wanna save your sorry skin is beyond me. Quite a record you've got, you pervert. Preying on women, and little girls and boys. You oughtta be castrated.' Jem put his arms through the window grate at her gesture and she tightened plasticuffs around them. After opening the door, she leant close as Jem moved past her and her partner into the corridor.

'If you'd stayed a little longer, we might've done something about that.'

Jem knew better than to take the bait. He could smell freedom. All that mattered was that his Guild was rescuing him. *Anyway, what I do behind closed doors is my own affair.*

As they reached the desk, the Federation officer pushed him against the cold metal surface and uncuffed him. His unspoken question was answered by a flick of the desk sergeant's head. Lounging by the door was a woman with a powerful presence. Her skin-hugging suit was emerald green. Each strand of her chin length black hair remained impeccably in place as she strutted towards him, her hips sashaying with every high-heeled stride. He could feel every pair of eyes in the station locked on that sway, mouths open in awe. She oozed sensuality, and she was *not* from the Guild.

Jem's heart ratcheted up a gear and he felt lust surge into his groin.

The woman advanced, standing too close for a stranger, and cupped the side of his face with cool fingers. Then she slapped his cheek lightly. 'You have been a naughty boy, haven't you?'

Jem opened his mouth to question, to protest, but she moved a finger to his lips and pursed her own. 'Hush now, hush. Time to come home with Mumma Envy. She's got a little hunting job for you. Your precious Guild cut you loose, and now I've picked up your collar and chain. Be a good hound and come along quietly.'

Jem's heart slammed against his chest at the sound of her name and his lust dissolved at the promise of pain in her words. She turned to the officer who had brought him from the cells.

'And thank you, treasure,' Envy purred. She ran an ebony painted fingernail across the guard's full lips. 'Shame I'm in such a hurry. The things we could do with those lips. Such a waste.' She sighed dramatically, her emerald eyes flashing like beacons in her moon-white face.

The officer's pupils dilated; her lips parted. She reached out, but Envy had turned and sauntered away. Jem rebooted his brain. Disassociated he may be, but he was a survivor. He'd find a way to make this work to his advantage. *Then I'll make sure that* nobody *gets what's comin' to her.*

Jem leant towards the officer and breathed in her ear, 'I'll be back to show ya what a real man can do for a slut like you.' He grabbed his crotch and massaged it. The woman recoiled and spat at his feet. Her colleague restrained her from further assaulting him.

'Not worth yer spit, he's delusional,' she stated flatly. With a lascivious smile, Jem sauntered after Envy, faking a confidence he didn't feel. He'd heard rumours about the founder of the notorious criminal gang Cobalt, and he wasn't entirely sure that he wouldn't be better off back in the prison cell.

— — —

Lee slipped into the darkened alley. She waited in the shadows with perfect stillness, ignoring the odours of decay from the overflowing bins. Although she was aware of the scuttling of tiny claws scrabbling in the garbage, she remained motionless. A small shift in the air was her only warning. A second figure in black appeared beside her, a tell-tale glimmer of heat indicating that she'd come from somewhere warmer to this cold, dank place.

Lee's hands were partly raised in attack position, a silver star in each gloved hand. When the other woman greeted her, it was all Lee could do to stop herself falling on her knees in the slime. In that moment, she made peace with her Goddess, begged her forgiveness for failure and lowered her hands, the metal stars tinkling on the cobbles as she let them go.

The other woman's silken voice laughed softly, 'Why do you surrender so easily, daughter? You assume the outcome is dire. Do you not love living? Is not life precious and worth fighting for? Fighting even me?'

Lee kept her head lowered deferentially. 'I failed, Most High Mirnian. The target is not dead. I cannot explain why. Three times I've gone to end her life. Three times she has escaped. Or I've let her live,' she admitted. Lee waited for the blade to fall, and heard the mistress of her Society sigh.

'Dearest child, know this. I myself may have failed to complete this mission. There are forces present in the Dome that I've never sensed before. Armageddon approaches. We are in its Shayde, and all our rules are dust.' Lee looked up, meeting the golden amber eyes of her order's leader.

'Mistress? Is it time? Is she the One?' Lee's mind whirled with possibilities. This is what she had been trained for since birth. This was her purpose. She stilled her racing heart.

'The Convergence has begun its countdown, and the sage sticks fall in patterns foretold centuries ago. The dragon has left the tower,' Mirnian intoned. Her voice dropped to an uncertain whisper. 'That I have seen these signs in my lifetime.'

Lee held her breath.

'Here is your new mission,' Mirnian instructed. 'Locate the woman. Offer her every assistance and any information in your power, or the power of the Society to give. Hold no knowledge from her. Protect her with your life. Make sure she reaches whatever destination she desires, no matter the choice she makes. You must not fail. The Cosmos is watching.'

Her mistress departed, a whisper of jasmine all that remained. Lee picked up her stars, wiped the dirt off them on her thighs. Her single shuddering indrawn breath was the only acknowledgement of this pivotal moment. She tucked the weapons behind her wide belt.

'I will not fail you, dearest Goddess.' She stepped into shadow.

Birth

She journeys with the Cosmos in her heart
A mother
Betrayed
Alone
Apart

Justice she wields
Souls it steals
Compassionate
Terrible
She needs no other

Excerpt from The Lament of the Cosmic Mother

Pain lanced through Merindah's swollen belly, and bloody fluid gushed from between her legs. She fell to the cold tiles in agony. The priceless artefacts she carried as distractions spilt from her arms, clattering messily, and breaking on the hard floor.

'No, no, not now my love! Too early, too early.' The babe was only seven weeks grown. Though her development of a month per week had been remarkable, coming this soon surely held danger.

Merindah's eyes swam with tears. Panic rose as another cramp surged from her belly. She bit her lip to stop a scream and tasted the coppery tang of blood. The wave of pain ebbed, and she dragged herself into one of the alcoves, smearing a bloody trail across the pristine marble.

She rested her back against the cool pillar, and glanced up at the niche's sculpture, then grimaced at the irony. Fourteen deities lined the District Librarium's atrium; and of all the ones she could have chosen to fall beneath, she was *here*. A larger than life statue of Sister Lust stared down provocatively.

It had to be you.

Lust's face smirked at her. Lust encouraged her followers to recklessly pursue their desires. And now, according to Bridget, she was trapped on the physical plane as something less than a goddess – though her apparent lack of divinity didn't seem to restrict the amount of havoc she left in her wake.

Merindah grimaced again. She'd fallen readily enough into Lust's trap. The price of her desire was high, perhaps too high, but it had little to do with the usual pleasures of the flesh. Her pleasure had been so fleeting. And so much had happened since then that she could barely remember her few hours of bliss with the god of Time. She'd seen no sign of him, nor heard any word since Bindi's conception.

A flush of resentment added bitterness to the taste of the blood in her mouth. She'd spent most of the last seven weeks cloistered in the Ivory Tower, decoding Aeon's journals, and becoming more annoyed at his arrogance and cavalier attitude with every page. He exhibited exactly the kind of patriarchal conceit that had driven the citizens of Heavens Gate into their current dire straits. Men had led the centuries of wars, the trashing of their planet, and failed to plan for their sun's demise, and now it was up to the women to find what remained of humanity a new home.

Merindah took a breath to calm herself. She was close, so close to finding the way through the portals. She just needed to avoid Nina for a few more weeks.

As a precaution Yaxa had moved her into a bigger lab higher in the Ivory Tower where she could eat, sleep and wash. She'd ensured that Merindah was always accompanied by a senior mage whenever she spent her allocated research time at the Portal. With Yaxa as her co-conspirator Merindah had managed to stay safe so far. Nina had fumed at her stepdaughter's refusal to attend her in the Obsidian Tower, but could only cite family reasons for wanting it to happen. Luckily, none of those reasons had trumped Yaxa's Head of Order reasons for Merindah staying away.

It had been weeks since Merindah's guardian mages had needed to rebuff the attempts from other Occultology stooges to seize her. Only now

Merindah was ready to try opening the Portal and had snuck away by herself to do just that, coveting her moment of discovery.

So these pains – this birth – could not have come at a more inconvenient time. She hadn't been expecting internal trouble.

A wave of unease from an absent Iluka washed over her, and Merindah tried to calm herself again, sending reassurance to the dragon. Mindspeaking was difficult at this distance. Iluka had a mission to complete in the far north of the continent, and couldn't afford to be distracted.

Merindah's chest began to pound. The pain surged again, and she forgot ambition, desire, and duty as she clutched her taut abdomen. Sweat-soaked and frightened, her mind a chaos of hurt and fear, she blasted her distress across the aether, ripping her mask to shreds.

Her powerful broadcast brought a swift response. Nina appeared in a swirl of magic, her anger palpable.

'Who sent that cry?' Nina demanded. She hissed when she saw Merindah. 'What are you doing here you slack-witted fool?' Then her eyes narrowed as she took in a flushed and panting Merindah and the bloody trail that sullied the sacred mosaic. Merindah watched Nina's nose wrinkle, then she registered her extended abdomen.

Finally, I surprise her.

For a moment Nina looked aghast – then she stormed towards her stepdaughter.

'How did you hide this for so long? A mask? How *dare* you deceive me? Your father will be livid. You'll be banished by the Librarium and the Portal Collaborative.'

'Help me, Nina. Please.' Merindah wished anyone but her stepmother had answered her cry.

Where are all those vaunted goddesses now?

Nina straightened, smoothing her perfect hair back from her brow with one hand. Merindah could almost see the cogs working in Nina's mind, twisting the circumstances to her own advantage.

'You lack the foresight to plan this kind of treachery on your own. Someone must have helped you, taught you how to mask yourself. Who seeks to dishonour me?'

Merindah ignored Nina's inquisition. She was familiar with her stepmother's venomous tongue. Nina's black eyes shone with malevolence.

'Please help me, Nina. For Father's sake,' Merindah begged.

'You got yourself into this mess, you misbegotten whelp. You can get yourself out of it. And if *my* reputation is so much as smudged, I'll make you wish you'd never been born,' Nina seethed. Merindah wrestled with another contraction.

When the swell of the pain had passed and Merindah gulped in air to catch her breath, Nina resumed her cross-examination.

'Where is the father of this illicit coupling? Is he as embarrassed by your condition as I am? Has he abandoned you to your shame, just like your mother?' She leant towards Merindah. 'Is he clawing above his station? Or has he simply delivered his damage, splashing his paltry seed in your wanton womb?'

Writhing on the floor, Merindah reached up and grasped Nina's arm as another wave of pain carried her toward an agonising crescendo. Bright red blood now ebbed from her womb, the puddle widening and creeping across the floor.

'Something's wrong. Too early. Need Midwife Bridget. Please. Help me,' she panted.

Nina tried to loosen Merindah's fingers. 'Let me go. Of course, something is wrong. You got yourself knocked up by some mongrel, and now you're aborting the abomination. It's the best possible outcome. If I hadn't shielded you immediately the Reproduction Registrars would have arrested you for an unauthorised conception. I only did that because I don't want you bringing more shame on our House. Get it out and get rid of it. Then get out of my sight. Your blemish on this family has been tolerated long enough.'

Merindah kept a vice-like grip on Nina with one hand while the other clutched her belly and its squirming occupant. A guttural scream ripped from her throat. Nina hissed again, flicked her free hand in a complex movement, soundproofing them with a magical ward.

'For Hell's sake, Merindah, release me and I'll fetch Bridget,' Nina spat, yanking at her arm.

'Promise?' Merindah knew her manipulative stepmother well.

'Yes, yes. I promise. Let me go. I have questions for Bridget anyway. She *will* clean up this mess without anyone else knowing. I don't want to be here a moment longer than I have to. I've got more important things to do than to watch your life unravel.'

Merindah released her.

Nina paused long enough to sneer at her, then disappeared. Merindah vaguely registered Nina's magical departure as a complex weave of air that she'd never seen before.

She laboured on. The statues of the fourteen Sisters were her only company, Merindah catalogued them in her brief moments of respite. Each Sister stared at her opposite across the vaulted atrium: Kindness and Envy, Humility and Pride, Abstinence and Gluttony, Chastity and Lust, Patience and Anger, Liberality and Greed, Diligence and Sloth. *How many of them spend time wandering among us mere humans? What good or ill do they cause?*

The labour progressed, and in those moments while she gulped in air between her pains, Merindah doubted. Doubted the path she'd chosen, doubted her visions, doubted the Voice, and doubted her role in this world's uncertain future. She wrapped her arms around the child in her womb, trying to connect with and soothe her passenger. She desperately wished she hadn't sent Iluka to Badangi to bargain for the Yarran journal. Though she could feel her dragon in frantic flight, it would take hours for her to return. Hours would be too late.

Beloved Mother, what have I done?

Merindah had been certain of her station in life, and with her research, her purpose. She'd been focused on her future plans as a famous contributor to the global community of Heaven's Gate. This pregnancy that refused to unfold according to any plan was *nowhere* in her list of long desired ambitions.

Cohesive thoughts fled again as she drowned in pain.

– – –

Bridget and Nina re-appeared in the Atrium a few minutes later. Bridget felt dizzy from her first aetheric journey and fearful from the retribution Nina had already threatened. Her gut plummeted further as she took in the situation before her.

'Fix this. Get it done,' Nina said, pushing Bridget towards the labouring woman.

Bridget crouched by Merindah, unfazed at kneeling in the spreading pool of blood and amniotic fluid.

'Here, let me help you Merindah. I'm here now. Everything's going to be fine.' With calm, sure hands, Bridget stripped Merindah's sodden trousers and underclothes off and hiked up her shirt. She gestured to Nina to help, frowning when the woman raised one perfectly arched eyebrow and crossed her arms. She could sense Nina's building ire and knew her inevitable interrogation would be painful.

Ignoring the fact that she likely had only hours to live, Bridget focused on the job at hand. She single-handedly wrestled Merindah into a squat, and grabbed pillows from the nearby divan to brace her friend against the snowy plinth that held a likeness of Sister Lust.

Then she glanced towards Nina again. 'I need some supplies.'

Nina responded with a shrug and remained where she was.

Bridget pursed her lips, removed her dark green tunic, and rolled up the sleeves of her white shirt. Then she settled back between Merindah's legs. Gently, she began to explore inside her friend, assessing with two fingers of one hand. When she withdrew her fingers, they came out covered in bright red blood – too much bright red blood.

She moved the other hand over Merindah's abdomen, feeling the position of the babe. Her brow creased. This child was not shaped like any kind of tiny human. She closed her eyes and delved, hoping Merindah's mask would let her through. It frustrated her that she hadn't been able to examine the child at all, nor would Merindah tell her more than the basics about its father. This time, the delving went deep. But her relief was short lived. In place of an unborn child safely tucked into its cocoon as she'd expected, what she saw could only be a dragon, a creature out of myth.

'Seven Sisters!' Bridget's eyes flew open and her heart leapt into her mouth as she met Merindah's gaze. Her friend was watching her, trusting her, silently pleading for her help.

Nina tapped a foot on the floor, her arms crossed, 'Well?'

Bridget wondered if Merindah knew what kind of being gestated in her womb. *Was it there with her consent?* Whatever the answers were, Merindah needed time, Nina must *not* suspect.

It was only now, that some of the subtle comments from Sister Kindness weeks ago began to make sense to Bridget.

'She's much further along than I would have thought for her first labour,' Bridget said, attempting to downplay her earlier exclamation.

'How long?' Nina asked.

'I'll need to watch her for a little longer before I can make that assessment. I'm sure you'd have time to get some more help or some supplies though.'

Nina sneered. 'No help, no supplies. Do your job, manage with what you've got. No one else will learn about this. And I don't have all night.'

With her own heart pounding in her ears, Bridget delved again. She muted her astonishment at the tiny creature and focused her mind and yerlendj on the job at hand. Merindah's pain and fear were causing the frightened being to *shimmer* between human and dragon form. The dragon's long head now beat against the partially opened cervix as the uterus tightened on its way to the next contraction. A dragon's skull was not designed for a human birth canal.

As Bridget watched, the tiny dragon's sharp talons raked gouges in the rich, bloody uterine wall, and Merindah screamed in pain. Here was the source of the bright red haemorrhage. If the foetus remained in this form, it could rip its mother to shreds, killing both of them in its frenzy to escape. And if the dragon was the only one to survive, what would Nina do to it? What would it do to them? Dragons were supposed to be creatures of unlimited magic. And they were supposed to be extinct.

Bridget swallowed her rising panic and wiped her hands on her trousers as best she could. She began to croon, a low hum that resonated with solace. She sent wave after wave of calm, safety, and love towards the tiny creature. She reassured it that though there would be more pressure, this was the quickest way out. Then she tried to show it that the dragon shape was hurting its mother. *This* made the difference. The dragon *shimmered,* and a human foetus reappeared in its place. Merindah's whole body relaxed. Bridget continued murmuring peace and safety to her charges, feeling their heartbeats steady.

She checked Nina's whereabouts and glimpsed her pacing around the Atrium, staring hard at the statues of the Sisters. Bridget's focus flashed back to Merindah as she heard her gasping breaths change to a low primal moan. Merindah began to push, more bright blood spurted onto the tiles. Bridget continued to whisper, encouraging both mother and unborn child.

Nina came to stand beside Merindah, placed so she could also watch Bridget's face. 'Is it time?' she asked.

'Soon,' Bridget answered.

The time between contractions widened. After each push, a tense silence settled, each woman alone in their thoughts. Three pushes later a round head crowned, covered in blood smeared dark curls. Nina leant forward as Bridget unfolded her tunic and placed it over her own knees to wrap the newborn in when it finally emerged.

'Almost there. Wait now, let it build,' Bridget instructed. With one more moan from Merindah, a puny blue-grey body, all scrawny arms and legs, slid into the world. The child slipped from Bridget's hands onto the tiles, resting in the puddle of bloody fluid.

Merindah drew a deep breath; her eyes refocusing and searching for the small, still form.

Nina reached across, knocking Merindah sideways as Bridget fumbled for her tunic. 'No, it's obviously dead, best thing for all. I'll get rid of it. No one need know.' Nina tried to pick up the slippery, bloodied body, and realised it was still connected via the thick, blue cord.

Bridget pushed Nina's hands away, retrieved the child and wrapped it in her tunic. She placed it on her knees, praying to her goddess that it had died. Then she helped Merindah to sit upright against the pillar, desperately searching for a way to save both Merindah and herself from Nina's wrath and retribution.

'You need to expel the afterbirth,' Bridget told her. She reached over to her friend's lax belly, dug deep with her magic, and began to physically massage the womb with one clenched fist.

– – –

A wave of vicious spasms made Merindah gasp. 'Give me my child,' Merindah grated, pushing Bridget's hand away. 'To help with the afterbirth.'

Bridget's mouth tightened.

Nina's face screwed into a look of distaste and she stepped back, holding her blood smeared hand out in front of her. She gestured and the blood on her hand vanished.

Bridget picked up the child's body and passed her to her mother.

Merindah gathered her baby in her arms, gently unwrapping her. She held her close to her breast, and wiped the blood from her little face with a corner of Bridget's tunic. Tears spilt over as her yerlendj opened and she caressed the blue-grey body with her magic.

'I have a daughter, a tiny flower.' *I am so sorry, little Bindi, that your life is over before it even began. I've failed you. I couldn't keep you safe.* With a sob, she squeezed her child close and felt her heart give out a languorous thump, thump.

'She lives! She lives!'

Merindah rubbed her daughter's flaccid limbs frantically. 'Help her Bridget!'

Bridget didn't hesitate. Ignoring Nina's horrified gasp, she leant forward, put her lips over the tiny nose and mouth and sucked hard, drawing out fluid and clots of blood. She spat to the side, then repeated the motion more gently to clear the baby's airways, finally tipping the child on her side, head lowered. The baby coughed and drew in a deep breath.

Two more breaths and the baby's colour began to change, her lax limbs curled. Then Bridget let Merindah turn her upright as the baby's eyes opened – one jade green, the other sapphire blue. With the next inhale, she began to wail. Both women smiled.

Her mother opened her soaked shirt and turned the babe toward her nipple. The child's angst subsided at the touch of warm skin. She searched for the nipple, latched on, and began to suckle. As she fed, her colour continued to change, warming to a soft shadow-blue, a pale echo of her father's dark purple skin. Merindah's joy exploded. The little girl stopped suckling, looked up and grabbed at her mother's hair. Love and knowing connected them.

Hello, beautiful Bindi.

Merindah touched Bindi's chest over her heart, and the baby's fingers uncurled from her mother's hair to touch her breast in response.

Mumma.

Tiny red sparks ignited at the baby's fingertips, and Merindah quickly covered her daughter's hand with her own. Bindi's odd eyes darkened momentarily to a familiar black opal, and a tiny dark red star appeared on each breast – an aetheric thread of deep ochre connecting mother and child.

Then Merindah winced as her womb contracted and the afterbirth slid out onto the floor, breaking the poignancy of the moment. She closed her eyes, feeling the release and the swell of post-birth endorphins.

And in that moment, her stepmother struck.

Nina ripped the child from Merindah's breast, and clasping Bindi by one fragile arm, turned and marched towards the Timegate Temple, blood dripping from the still connected afterbirth. The baby howled, shocked by her removal.

'No, no! What are you doing? She lives! She lives!' Merindah heaved herself to her knees and began to crawl towards the Temple steps, haemorrhaging a bloody trail while Bridget did her best to hold her back.

'Not for long.' Nina strode up the seven steps and slapped a hand against the first pillar. The blue haze within the arch disappeared, and the Portal opened. Though the Timegate Temple was enclosed under the roof of the Librarium, a million stars twinkled within it – constellations of brilliant swirls painted on a vortex of darkness. The cold black Cosmos beckoned, a powerful thrum seeped into the room, and a swirl of rainbow particles like welcoming arms floated out through the arch.

Nina flung the child and placenta through the Portal.

'Noooooo!!' Merindah screamed.

'What have you done? She lives! She lives!' Merindah sobbed, dragging herself to her knees, fighting cramps and blood loss.

Bridget stood aghast, a horrified witness to the murder.

A flare of red and a flicker of flame snagged three sets of eyes, but it disappeared and there was only the ocean of stars. The Portal began to close, the tendrils of blue mist re-forming.

'Nina, bring her back. Now!' Merindah demanded, infusing a thread of compulsion into her words.

Nina laughed as the threads slid off. 'You will never compel me you fool. My shielding skills are second to none, thanks to our mutual acquaintance,' she said, gesturing to the statue of Sister Lust. Nina watched her stepdaughter stagger to her feet half-naked, stumble across the Librarium floor, and make if halfway up the Temple steps.

'Open the Portal. Open it! Bring her back. Where did you send her? Tell me!'

Nina swooped down the stairs and viciously grabbed Merindah by the hair, shoving her to her knees. 'Don't you mean when? When did I send her? It won't matter. She's dead now anyway.'

In her weakened state, Merindah was no match. In desperation, she dredged up a sliver of her own magic – a cry for succour – and filled it with love. She beseeched Sága, Kindness, Diligence, and the Cosmic Mother to protect her child.

Iluka help me! I need you now. Merindah felt the rainbow particles that spun into seven coloured lights in the hand she held behind her back. With a burst of will, she flung them past Nina at the closing Portal.

Find her. Protect her. Tell her I love her. I will bring her home. Spent, she collapsed. She felt Iluka's presence nearing, screaming retribution at Bindi's loss.

Nina wheeled to follow the lights then slapped her stepdaughter's face so hard she knocked her onto the bottom step of the Temple. She descended to stand over Merindah. 'You'll thank me for this, slut. You'll see. If you were in my position, you'd do the same. Not that I'll ever be in your position. Children are an unnecessary evil. They won't be needed in my new world order,' Nina finished.

Merindah lurched from the step and tackled Nina to the floor. Caught by surprise, Nina took a few moments to wrestle her off.

'Bring her back! You have no soul. Bring my baby back!' Merindah screamed and beat her hands on the shield Nina forced around herself.

Nina's magic pushed Merindah backwards where she landed heavily on the white platform at the top of the stairs.

Sobbing, Merindah got slowly to her feet and turned, beating her fists on the pillar, making bloody marks on the ornate carvings. Exhausted and overwhelmed, she leant against the warmth of the dark stone, hugging it, letting it seep into her forehead, chest, and belly. Blood continued to trickle down her legs, a crimson pool forming at her feet.

Slowly, Merindah's sobs quietened. 'You've murdered my daughter. I'll never forgive you for this, never. Why would you do this?' Her hands began to trace the glyphs on the pillars, feeling with her yerlendj, searching amongst the millions of Portal destinations for the one she needed.

Nina's laugh was mirthless, 'I don't need anyone else between me and your father's attention. And now you've let some other man befoul you. You're disgusting. With you disgraced, I'll inherit your father's Collaborative Seat when he dies. Which may be sooner than you think. You've forfeited your right. I'll tell him you rutted with a common dog like the bitch you are.'

Merindah's fingers stilled as she stared incredulous at Nina. 'You murdered my child for political power? How could you? I would've given you the Seat. I didn't really want it. I never wanted political power. It's knowledge I seek. Knowledge to save our world, our people.'

She paused as a cramp bent her over, her voice a whisper, 'I only wanted to save the world.' Realising she was almost naked, Merindah buttoned the tattered remnants of her shirt together as she shook off the pain. She speared a glance at Nina. 'I'll find a way to make you pay. I'll never forgive you, and I'll never forget. Nor will Bridget.'

Nina's malice surfaced, her eyes like a raptor's hunting glare. 'The Yarran Prophecy is about to ignite a bloody war for power on this complacent and decrepit world. I intend to be the Chosen One, and the power to rule or choose Armageddon will be mine. I created the Prophecy after all,' she smirked. 'I know how it ends. No one will stand in my way. Not your compulsion-dosed father and especially not you.'

Nina ascended the steps to front Merindah, they stood framed by the blue mist of the arch. Whether it was proximity to the portal or because of her raw and sensitive state, Merindah could see the bright lines of aetheric energy build and swirl about them both. She noted a dark thread tighten around Nina's chest, stroking her heart.

'Bridget won't tell, will you Bridget?' Nina flung her arm out, pointing without turning her head. Merindah's head did turn to see Bridget's eyes widen, her body trembling as she mutely shook her head.

'What are you talking about? Bridget is my friend,' Merindah defended the woman who'd only a few weeks back confessed her love for her.

'Bridget and I have a little arrangement,' Nina said. Bridget's eyes filled with tears as Nina continued. 'I own her silence – forever. She has *never* been your friend. I bought her soul to watch you when you were still a precocious brat. Bridget has been, and *always will be*, a slave to my will. A slave *forever*.' Bridget's face turned ashen, and her blood-stained hands rose to cover her mouth.

Bridget's treachery stole the breath from Merindah's lungs and when she turned to Nina, Nina's triumphant glare felt like a physical blow. Her stepmother's fully black eyes sought to drown her in dark power as obsidian threads reached for her. Merindah fell onto all fours, weakened from the birth and betrayal. Her yerlendj was distant, the thread to her soul dragon thinned, and her magic slipped from her grasp.

A kaleidoscope of colour and sound drifted from the Timegate towards her. The ocean of cold, dark stars thrummed through the blue mist of the closed Portal.

'They're calling me home,' Merindah whispered.

'What did you say?' Nina lifted Merindah bodily to her feet, hauling her close.

Merindah's head was fuzzy, her mouth dry. The starsong called her, resonating in every cell. 'They're calling me home…' she said again.

'You're talking nonsense.' Nina held her with one hand and slapped her with the other.

Merindah belatedly raised a palm to her stinging cheek. 'Why Nina, why? You're my stepmother. I welcomed you into my family with open arms.' Tears trickled down her bruised, blood-smeared cheeks.

Nina crowed, 'Finally, you'll hear the truth. I've waited for the perfect moment to tell you this.' She leant close, shaking Merindah and hissed, 'It's not *your* family. You're not your mother's daughter. You're some abandoned mongrel that your mother took in because she felt sorry for you. Your mother couldn't conceive, so they adopted you. I knew when I married your father that your common blood would betray you. You never belonged in the First Families. You are nothing. You'll go out with the trash where you belong. This is my world, mine to rule or ruin as I please without you getting in my way.'

Merindah couldn't think. Too much had happened too quickly. The Voice began whispering, the soft tones finally materialised in her head.

Your destiny awaits child. She shoved the Voice away. Her daughter needed her. She shook her head, trying to make sense of Nina's words rolling around and around in her mind.

I don't belong. Abandoned. I don't belong. My life is a lie. Father and Mother lied to me. My Mother lied to me. None of this is real. Her mind spasmed. How they must've all laughed behind her back. She cringed. How pathetic – an orphan, abandoned and unloved. The enormity of her situation began to dawn on her, consequences stacking on top of each other in impossible towers. In this rigid dying world, where the genetics of your family connections defined your position, livelihood, and life, she simply didn't belong. She was an outsider, a fraud, and now had borne an illegitimate child of her own.

Mother help me.

Your dragon is returning, not long now. Wait for her, the Voice instructed.

Nina gestured at a pillar, seized an unresponsive Merindah and pushed her unresisting towards the opening Portal. As her head crossed the threshold, Merindah felt the rainbow colours wrap around her, so cold on her over-heated body and soul. *This is happening too fast, too fast.* She needed time to think, to prepare, to work out the best way. There must be another journal or an old scroll with instructions on tracing the Timegate trails. Her daughter was the offspring of a *god*. If anyone could survive the Timestream, it would be her.

Primal instinct kicked in and Merindah found the will for a final struggle. Iluka was close – she could feel the silver tether of their connection swelling.

'No, wait, wait! This isn't the way. Don't Nina. Please don't. Help me. Bridget, help!' she screamed, but all she saw was Nina's dark eyes and victorious smile. The struggle was brief. In the quiet aftermath, she heard a strangled sob from Bridget.

You cannot win by strength. She taps her daemon's power, the Voice insisted.

Merindah slumped in Nina's hold and Iluka surged unseen into her body, miraculously here at last. Her soul shifted, joined. Their hearts beat together.

I am back. Let us begin. The child awaits.

Together, they regarded Nina. A thread of the oft-spoken legend echoed in Merindah's mind.

Chosen for her Grace, though driven by her Urges. Merindah alone knew Grace meant wisdom – magical wisdom. It was what Heavens Gaters called yerlendj. She knew the journal entry was about her, about the hours she had spent sating her urges in Aeon's embrace.

Time to go and save the Cosmos, child, the Voice whispered encouragingly.

Merindah's response was clear. *We'll save my daughter first. Then we'll think about saving your Cosmos.*

Shall we start a list? I know you simply adore lists.

Merindah ignored the dragon and the Voice, shaking her head. She gathered her frayed emotions, remembering her daughter's face and the way her tiny fingers had sparked as they'd touched her breast. Iluka's heart pounded next to her own, sharing the memory.

Nina released Merindah, likely considering her sagging form a sign she was cowed.

As soon as she did, Merindah drew deeply from Iluka's strength, feeling her body healing.

'You haven't asked me why I did it. Why would I have a child, knowing the ramifications for myself, my work, my family? My *former* family,' Merindah said.

Nina's lips thinned, and she folded her arms, tapping one foot.

Merindah sighed and lowered her gaze, hiding the blazing power streaming into her body behind a hastily drawn mask.

'Even now you won't listen. Won't hear the truth. Why do you think I didn't tell you? You only see your own path, your own needs. Nobody else is ever relevant. The Cosmic Mother sees all, Nina. Justice will be mine. You can try explaining to Father and the Collaborative what you did. I believe the punishment for murdering a First Family member is execution.'

Merindah stepped back to the archway. With one finger she traced a glyph on the back of the nearest pillar that showed a smear of blood on its own, hopefully her daughter's destination. Power surged into the Portal; rainbow threads swirled.

She closed her eyes briefly, thinking of her daughter – alone in the cold dark of the Timestream – and sent out her intention. *My beautiful Bindi, I'm coming for you. I will find you, even if it takes forever.*

We will find you child. We are coming.

Nina blinked at Merindah's calm acceptance and reached toward her. Merindah raised her head and let the full force of her yerlendj shine. She allowed Iluka control over their shared form and she *shimmered* into an ochre dragon that swung her horned head low and glared at Nina as she staggered back across the temple platform.

'It's a parlour trick, nothing more. Just another glamour,' Nina's uncertain voice belied her dismissive words.

Iluka *shimmered* and Merindah stood in her place.

Nina stepped forward again, 'I'm taking you to the Obsidian Tower, and you will tell me everything you know, or your friend will begin to lose herself, piece by piece.'

Merindah's gaze moved to Bridget who had edged her way to the bottom of the steps. Bridget flinched at the weight of betrayal that Merindah knew must be evident in her eyes. Nina flung out a black thread. It hung visible before Bridget's neck. Bridget blinked once at Merindah, and a world of understanding and forgiveness passed between them. Bridget's stance softened, and she gave her love a small, sad smile.

Merindah turned her gaze back to Nina, uttering a single word. 'No.' As Merindah spoke, Bridget lunged forward into the black thread. Her head toppled from her shoulders, and a sharp sulphurous odour burst into the space. Nina shrieked at Bridget's sacrifice. Thwarted on that front, she spun back to attack her stepdaughter, hands raised with a ball of black energy coalescing between them.

'Nina. I am Armageddon's Gatekeeper,' Merindah declared. 'Born from the Mother to save or damn our world.'

Nina snatched her hands back, the blackness dissipating as Merindah unleashed her yerlendj, dissolving the last of the constraining ward and letting her unimaginable power blaze forth.

'You're nothing,' Nina whispered. 'You're supposed to be nothing.' Merindah smiled, opened her arms wide, and fell back into the ocean of stars.

— — —

The Portal snapped shut.

The pillars shivered and cracked; one lintel rocked then tumbled to the floor.

The Timegate Temple went dark.

And Nina began to scream.

Soul Staff

The Opal Dreaming Chronicles
Book 2

...coming soon

Honing

For comes among us
Unseen by all
The Spirit Child
Held in its thrall
Fire and Earth
Wind and Water

No place is safe
From the Daemon's Daughter

Excerpt from The Spirit Child Omens

The hunger gnawing at Dee's belly was an old friend, a familiar enough companion that it could be ignored for a while longer. But thirst – thirst could not be put off so easily. The hallucinations of dehydration brought strange voices, and she already had so many of them in her head.

She needed water.

A whisper of breeze tickled her face and Dee touched two fingers to her lips, flicking a breath away with a prayer of thanks to Jindi, goddess of Air. Dee's thick coat of red desert dust was courtesy of Jindi's never ceasing attention. At least the dust kept her from frying under the sun's burning eye, though her shadow blue skin had darkened from her months of travel through the parched landscape.

She trudged across another crumbling ridge, its patchwork grey and brown stone broken by a scattering of straggly bushes. This was her world now. Her sheltered village existence had been expunged by fire. Fire that had purged her life of stricture and punishment, though it hadn't burnt away her guilt and shame. They smouldered like a half-lit fuse in her belly, and her barely constrained Grace - her storehouse of magic - throbbed with flame; a tainted gift from Wyak, god of Fire.

Dee could hear a myriad of voices in her head urging her to use her power. Tiny prickles of heat tumbled through her veins, crooning their destructive seduction. The wyldfire was poised to ignite.

Falling to her knees in the thrall of her magic, she missed the stony ground's sharp welcome and the new grazes they gave to her skin. Dee opened her pale blue palms and a green-tipped flame danced on each. Then a dozen appeared, then a multitude. All of them traipsed down her fingers and leapt onto the dry scrub.

She watched mesmerised as leaves shrivelled, curling from dark green to black. Branches reddened, became white hot, then crumbled to ash. Still more flames emerged on her palms. This time a legion of fiery troops raced up her arms, and launched from her shoulders. White smoke curled around her in sensual waves, her nose filled with the smell of char, though her breathing was not troubled, nor did she burn. But precious moisture trickled down her dusty cheeks.

Fire cleanses, but it can destroy too. It can destroy you. "Reason", she'd named that voice.

She clenched her hands at the words and the flames snuffed out. She felt their withdrawal like a pain. An eerie emptiness filled her belly. That void had its origins long before her stepfather's murder had forced her from her home. Now two months later, the ruins of her former life were little more than a bitter taste on the back of her tongue, her time in the wilderness had scraped body and soul bare.

The fire cajoled, screamed, and demanded life.

Reason spoke again in her head. *Use fire to destroy or to create. You always have a choice.* You *are the magic,* you *control the magic, don't let the magic control you.* Other voices began clamouring for a hearing. She shook her head, and covered her ears.

'Stop! All of you! Leave me alone!' she screamed.

Her internal crowd fell blessedly silent.

She leant over and rested her forehead on the stony soil, placed her palms flat, craving grounding. With a sob she scrabbled in the earth, searching for cooling respite from the molten energy in her body.

I matter. I matter. I matter. Ali had told her that. Told her that what she believed, thought, felt and did mattered, and that's all that counted. *I matter. I matter. I matter.*

— — —

Garule, goddess of Earth was not without sympathy for this creature that the cast out children of the Cosmic Mother had burdened with the fate of the world. The sacrifice of the one for the many was an uncomfortable reality when you watched the one suffer. Her older sister Meana could rail at her all she liked, Garule could not let this child lead the planet and its creatures into oblivion. There must be less destructive ways to get them Home.

She sensed her younger sister was near, Jindi's cool caress soothing the fire child. Garule added a guiding thread of earth into Jindi's breeze, a hint of moist, dark soil teeming with life. Mutual disregard meant neither sister acknowledged the other, nor admitted this aid was treachery against Meana's Grand Plan.

— — —

With the freshened breeze, Dee's senses stilled, her skin cooled. The fire in her belly became quiescent, though the hunger still clawed for attention. A two fingered kiss and thanks went to Jindi and another to Garule as she bowed to the dirt again. She blinked tangled white hair from her eyes, putting the faint image of a woman's face outlined in the dirt down to more hallucinations, especially when it disappeared after she tried to focus on it. Yet the thought of Garule and Jindi weaving their way through her world calmed her.

Perhaps they're here to balance Wyak's curse.

But I don't want to be a plaything of the gods. Dee wiped her dusty palms on her thighs then rubbed her tears from grubby cheeks.

I can do this. I can find a way. I just need to find Ali. Find the domed city. But first water and food. She breathed in the moisture laden air and caught a whiff of green growing things. Dragging herself to her feet she took her trail east, clicking her fingers to encourage her four-legged companion. Nellie still quivered at the latest fire show but shook herself and clopped after her friend. Dee's self-protection sensory sweep located her avian guardians at the edge of her seeking. With the lack of vegetation and camouflage available, the two birds who had been a part of her life ever since she could remember had preferred to stay out of the line of her hunger and slingshot. It seemed as though the magpie and owl – Maggie and Boo – had both decided discretion was the better part of valour. Perhaps they were right. She was very hungry.

By late afternoon she'd hit steeper, rockier hills and valleys where black faced wallabies grazed. Unused to humans, there'd been lots of ear flicking between the mob, the buck standing tall to out scare her then giving the alarm which had sent his family bounding away. She left them alone. She didn't have the energy to waste chasing them. She needed water first.

A few minutes later, Dee stumbled around a huge boulder and into glorious shade. She trailed her fingers along the scaly bark of centuries old trees, inhaling their ancient fragrance, and threading her fingers through their breeze tossed leaves. Dizzy with relief, she squatted in the glorious shade on shaky legs, rubbing her fingers across cool stones, holding them to her nose, eyes closed, connecting to the weight of earth, feeling their permanence.

She felt so small, so alone. *I'm better on my own, away from others. At least that way I can't hurt anyone.* In fact, she didn't miss other people. She had all the company she needed in her head. Real people wouldn't understand her.

Now that I'm more of a freak than ever. Tears threatened to tear open scars long held closed. She brought her anger to a simmer and soldered them shut again.

As the warmth bled from the day, she found a damp animal trail at the bottom of one valley and followed it to a small billabong tucked into a narrow gorge. By the look of the tracks crisscrossing the sandy clay this place was well loved by the local fauna. Dee took off her tattered shoes and waded in, feeling the mud ooze up between her toes, and the blessed cool seep up her legs. She ignored the sting of her scraped knees and the threat of leeches or worse as the moisture soaked into her ragged clothes. Dee's slight form had hardened of necessity and living rough had changed her. Her nails were black, her shadow blue hands stained and scratched.

Nellie bleated at her from the shore. The white flag of the goat's wagging tail, a sharp contrast to her all black coat.

Before she churned it up too much Dee cupped her hand and took sips of the cool water, careful not to drink too much too quickly. When she'd had enough, she filled both her water bottles, waded out and waved Nellie in. The goat stood belly deep and drank, her tail a blur of delight.

Dee rested in the shade of a manna gum, taking sips of delicious water and deciding whether she could walk any further today.

Tired, famished, but at least not thirsty. She sighed and put her shoes back on her damp feet.

A rustle drew her eyes to Nellie munching on blackberries tucked behind a slab of granite. She staggered up and shoved the goat away. Nellie bleated her affront.

'You can eat grass, Nellie. It doesn't work for me.' Ignoring the many thorns, Dee picked and devoured every last berry, the taste of fruit mixed with a hint of blood from the pricks and scratches. As she searched for more, Dee noticed the vines had hidden an opening in the jumbled cliff face. She edged in, her pack catching on the jagged sides. She backed out again, and dragged Nellie forward.

'You go first.' The goat was happy enough to get pushed into the dark passage which reassured Dee that it was safe from major predators. She'd seen traces of dingo in the crowded tracks around the billabong.

At least a cave would be warmer. The nights had cooled as she'd gradually climbed into the Yoorong Divides, the mountain range that lay its meandering spine close to the eastern coast of the continent.

Shuffling sideways into the opening behind Nellie, Dee felt the rock wall beside her drop away. A musty scent tickled her nose. After her eyes adjusted to the dimness, she made out a large stone basin set on a wide pedestal, the whole thing moist and green with moss. The floor was strewn with broken hand-hewed stones.

As she neared the basin it began to glow with a soft yellow light. The illumination increased till she could see the outline of some kind of temple deeper in the cave. Tall dark pillars supported arches around a small domed roof. The temple stood on a platform above seven steps that had once been painted different colours, just visible through the layers of dust. Now she could see several of the pillars were broken, leaning drunkenly against each other, the roof barely held in place. The air held an unfamiliar fragrance, wintry cold mixed with the dust of centuries, and oddly, a hint of lavender. Dee shivered and Nellie trotted to her side, leaning against her knee.

'You too huh.' Dee patted Nellie's head.

The round basin was as wide as her outstretched arms. The pedestal placed it at shoulder height. Despite a bleated warning from Nellie, Dee stepped closer. Noticing glyphs around the base, she dusted them off and tried to decipher the symbols. It was in no language she recognised. She could read Common well enough; her stepmother had made sure of that. She'd learnt a smattering of the Old Tongue for ritual days, but that was the extent of her reading skills.

Dee dropped her pack onto the ground and stepped onto the pedestal. She peered into the basin, hoping none of the words had been warnings for the uninitiated to not look.

The basin was filled with dark viscous liquid. Though every other surface held years of dust, the surface of this liquid was pristine. As she leant over, she saw her reflection clearly lit by the glow of the basin's internal rim. Her face was thin, her eyes huge, one emerald green, one sapphire blue, wisps of dirty white hair stuck out like a nimbus around her head. She'd lost her comb weeks ago and with only her fingers to keep it tidy, her long white plait had soon become a tangled mess and too hard to manage. She'd hacked her plait off and now if any hair got in her eyes, she hacked that off too.

She ruffled the water with her blood and berry stained hand, smudging the confronting reflection. The liquid felt thick and oily and she wiped her fingers on her trousers, adding more stains. Disturbing the surface had released a sulphurous smell and Dee wrinkled her nose. Turning from the basin she stepped back down the plinth and gave Nellie a scratch behind her ears.

'Nothing to drink there Nellie. Just some stinky old oil.'

Nellie bleated her unease, her bright yellow eyes wide.

'I agree. Let's sleep somewhere else. This doesn't feel right.'

Dee bent to grab Nellie's short lead rope and noticed a pale yellow mist curling over her feet. She spun around, stumbling over the uneven stones. Liquid light poured over the edge of the basin. Dee and Nellie retreated as the light began to intensify. It brightened till Dee had to shield her eyes. The goat dragged on her lead trying to get out of the cave. The glare softened and they looked up to find a beautiful golden woman with shoulder length dark hair looking out of the mist.

'Oh Lady.' Dee stepped back.

The woman smiled, though her face was stiff, and the eyes were all wrong.

'Voice your petition,' the golden woman said.

'What petition?'

'Voice your petition,' she repeated.

'Who are you?' Dee asked.

'I am a mage of the Cosmic Logos, called into being at your request.'

'Oh.'

'Voice your petition.'

'What's the Cosmic Logos? I only know about the Cosmic Mother, the Lady of the Rainbow Threads.'

'Your petition has triggered the need for a biological response.'

'I don't understand.' The mage seemed to freeze in place, her body now insubstantial. Dee and Nellie moved in for a closer inspection.

'How did you appear in the basin? What kind of Lore is that?' The mage didn't answer.

As Dee watched, the mage flickered, solidified and then glanced around. Her black eyes noticed the ruins of the temple, the dust covered rubble strewn across the ground. Dee followed the direction of the mage's gaze and saw large scorch marks across many of the stones. When she looked back the mist had dissipated but the mage still floated above the basin. Rather than the long white robe she'd first appeared in, now her robe was black, and belted with gold.

The sharp gaze found Dee and she felt Nellie tremble at her side.

'Who are you? What's happened here? When is this?' The mage's tone was peremptory.

'When? I don't know what you mean.' Dee replied.

'What day? What year?' The mage's gaze intensified; her black hooded eyes narrowed at Dee's silence. Dee had seen enough mean looks in her time to know this woman or whatever she was, was prepared to get what she wanted at any cost. Dee felt around her feet for her pack and eased it onto one shoulder, nudging the goat to get her moving.

'I'm not sure of the day or year. The king of Millanthrone just celebrated his sixtieth birthday if that helps. At least we heard a little while ago that he had a big celebration last year, so by now he's likely sixty-one or two. It takes a while to get the news out here.'

'Millanthrone?'

'You know, from the coast to the foothills, north to the Wilds, south to the sea, west to the Red Desert, Millanthrone,' Dee said.

'And who is this King?'

'King William.'

'King William. Does he have any number to go with that?'

'I don't understand. He's just King William.'

Anger built in the mage's voice; her hands planted firmly on her hips. 'How can he have let the Temple fall into such disrepair?'

'I didn't know it was a temple, really, I didn't. I wouldn't have touched anything. I was only looking for somewhere out of the cold for the night.'

'Well it's obvious you did touch something, didn't you, something you should not have. Or I wouldn't be here.' The mage paused and peered around again. Dee backed up another few steps.

'Does this William have any children?' the mage asked.

'Yes, King William has one son, Prince Heathcliffe. His great grandfather, another William, he had lots of children, but they all died from the curse and there was only one daughter left. She married someone from Red Desert, and they had one son. And then he had one son who was another William, and then he had one son, so I guess this one's the third William. And this William married someone from the coast, Queen Beatrice.' Dee realised she was yabbering and stopped, biting her lip. She put one hand on Nellie's head, reassured by her friend's solid presence.

'Generations. Where are the Gate Guardians? Who watches the Timegates?'

'I'm sorry I don't know what you mean. I've never heard of the Gate Guardians or the Timegates. Perhaps they're in Raya City.'

The mage was not appeased. If anything, her frustration and anger grew with every answer.

'Never heard of it. So much time to play with. Where did you go, Gatekeeper?' She seemed to shake herself a little, smoothing her hair back with one hand. While she was distracted Dee backed away a few steps further. Nellie turned to trot out.

The mage looked up, pinning Dee in place with fierce dark eyes.

'How did you activate the water window? It requires magic to open.'

'It wasn't me.' Dee felt the lie squirm in her gut. The mage's eyes narrowed.

'You activated the window. Did you touch the water?'

'Everyone has magic here. Anyone could have opened it.' Dee said.

'Everyone has magic? Well, come here child, I want a closer look at you.' Her voice sharpened when Dee didn't move. 'Come here now.'

Dee's hands began to tremble. She felt the fire in her belly stir.

'Actually, no, thank you, we'd better get going. We'll find somewhere else to sleep.' Dee pushed Nellie behind her and started to edge towards the opening.

'There's a team of men waiting outside, and we've been gone longer than we thought. We were scouting the cave for the army, we have to go now, or they'll come in, and disturb you.' The mage laughed, her eyes darkening.

'We both know that's not true. The truth is you're on your own and nobody will miss you. And I haven't had anything new to play with for months.' The pale glow of the light began to darken. The mage's hair began to stream out behind her as if a great wind was blowing, though the air of the cave remained still.

Hell hounds we're in trouble now!

The mage raised her hands, black sparkling lightening shot from her fingers, and twisted towards Dee. Dee screamed as the coils snatched her body, twirling and tightening around her, dragging her towards the basin.

'Help me, Nellie, help.'

Nellie dug her hooves in and tried to drag on Dee's shirt pulling her back towards the entry. A new black coil leapt out, grabbed Nellie and flung her against the far wall with a sickening thud.

'No, stop. Stop!' Dee screamed, panic rising. Her physical reserves were empty, the wyldfire a constant drain. Her Grace was locked out of reach behind her fear. She thrashed and kicked and managed to wedge her feet under a large chunk of broken stone. The coils pulled.

'Come closer little one.' The mage beckoned and with a tug, the coils pulled Dee free and dragged her towards the basin. She grasped for anything to slow her, her hands grabbed a piece of mosaic and she hurled it at the mage. It went straight through her as if she were mist.

'You'll have to try a little harder than that child. Perhaps you don't have much magic after all. No matter, I'll suck you dry of the spark and then you'll have none.' The mage gestured more forcefully now, impatient. Dee kept struggling, terrified, certain these were her last few moments of life. The coils tightened painfully. She prayed for help, calling on every deity she knew. As she was drawn almost within the reach of the woman she called aloud, 'Cosmic Mother I beg you, I want to live, help me.'

Somewhere in her head she heard an audible click as though a gate had opened. She reached through the gate into an ocean of stars. She remembered falling, and fear and then pain, so much pain. But before the pain she remembered something else, warm and strong, holding her close.

Mumma.

Dee felt little red sparks race from her belly up through her heart and down her arms towards her fingers. Her body twitched and was still. The coils tightened one more time, sensing acquiescence. As they were about to deliver her to the basin, Dee *shimmered*. The wyldfire in her belly roared.

Her skin turned red, black talons grew from her fingertips, scales rippled from her talons and up her arms which thickened and lengthened. Her jaw cracked and stretched, dagger-like teeth emerged, her body creaked, and her bones grew and warped, easily snapping the coils from around her middle. From her back large segmented wings sprouted and flapped, washing the stone debris across the cavern floor with each thrust.

No more.

The mage watched, stunned as the enormous red dragon leant down to peer at her with a large black eye. The dragon could see the mage's emotions roiling across her face.

'Your eye has stars, galaxies of stars. It's as if you've captured the Cosmos.' She recovered her poise as the dragon's vertical pupil narrowed on her.

'Dragon. Your magic *must* be mine. I *will* have it.'

The dragon drew her head back and roared, fire streamed from her jaws to singe the roof of the cavern, and she trumpeted again and again, feeling the power in her form. She was free.

I am Kalinda and you will never have the magic.

The mage flinched as the dragon's voice shouted into her mind. Kalinda stomped her foot, three more Temple pillars tilted and took the remaining roof with them as they crashed to the ground in ruins.

'Stop. You're ruining the Timegate.' Raising her hands, the mage sent out the black coils again, thicker this time and many more. With a snort Kalinda burnt the coils to ash, stepped towards the basin, and with one front claw, tore the pedestal apart. She advanced towards the mage, crushing the rock with each massive foot. Fear replaced cunning on the mage's face.

With a final tromp the dragon lifted her foot and smashed the basin. The mage disappeared, and the dark liquid sprayed out in a million sparkling droplets – much of it over Kalinda. She tramped and stomped until the basin and the plinth were dust.

'I think she's gone dear,' a new voice said dryly from behind her, 'for now.'

Thank you

Thank you for reading *Ochre Dragon*.

If you enjoyed the story, please consider taking a moment to write a short review on your favourite platform. As an independent author, I rely on reviews and word of mouth to share my stories. Even a couple of sentences will help. Your support and feedback are greatly appreciated and can really make a difference.

To find out what happens next to Dee, Ali and Merindah, and to get early notification of the release of *Soul Staff: The Opal Dreaming Chronicles Book 2*, you can visit V. E. Patton's alter ego – Veronica Strachan – and sign up for an occasional newsletter at www.veronicastrachan.com. Or follow me on Twitter (@truedialogue) and on Goodreads.

About the Author

V. E. Patton spent as much of her childhood as she could lost in a good book. She spent most of her adult life lost in a good job as a nurse, midwife, CEO, coach, and facilitator (amongst other things). After years of encouraging her children and clients to follow their dreams, she finally got around to remembering what she wanted to be when she grew up – so she began writing fiction.

Ochre Dragon: The Opal Dreaming Chronicles Book 1 is her first fantasy (in a book). She hopes you get lost in it.

V. E. is currently completing *Soul Staff: The Opal Dreaming Chronicles Book 2,* which is due for release in late 2020.

Her novelette, *Peace on Earth,* was published in *Christmas Australis: A Frighteningly Festive Anthology of Spine Jingling Tales,* along with stories by seven other Australian authors.

V. E. (writing as Veronica Strachan) and her daughter Cassi teamed up for a new children's picture book series, *The Adventures of Chickabella.* Book 1 is *Chickabella and the Rainbow Magic,* and book 2 is *Chickabella Counts to Ten.* Book 3: *Chickabella Shapes Up* is coming late 2020.

Also as Veronica Strachan, you will find her memoir, *Breathing While Drowning: One Woman's Quest for Wholeness,* as well as a guided journal *The Wholeness Quest Workbook & Journal.*

V. E. lives in a mudbrick home in north-central Victoria, Australia, with her ever-patient husband, one of her three adult children, and a menagerie of animals.